Extraordinary Praise for
CLINTON McKINZIE's Novels

CROSSING THE LINE

"Antonio Burns is back . . . and that will make climbers and mystery-adventure lovers happy. . . . [McKinzie's] work contains what may be the most authentic climbing scenes and descriptions found in the fiction world."
—*Los Angeles Times*

"Action-packed, compelling . . ."—*Denver Post*

"Breathtaking scenes . . . an adrenaline rush . . . *Crossing the Line* is a high point in a highly entertaining new series."
—*Fort Lauderdale Sun-Sentinel*

"A gripping thriller that is truly impossible to put down . . . Thrillers do not come any better than this. . . . This is undoubtedly the best of the series so far."
—*Wichita Falls (TX) Times Record News*

"Fast-paced thriller delivers . . . will keep the adrenaline junkie turning pages."—*Winston-Salem Journal*

"Gripping . . . a daring adventure that cuts like a knife and has all the adrenaline its author finds climbing rock walls like his fictional alter ego."—*Windsor (Ontario) Star*

"A very good thriller: the series best by far."
—*Kirkus Reviews*

"The author . . . cleverly builds his story. The novel unfolds like an elegant juggling act, and McKinzie's literary gymnastics pay off splendidly."—*Booklist*

POINT OF LAW

"Its fast-paced plot is rife with legal references, law-enforcement lingo, smart dialogue, and vivid characters. . . . This highly readable thriller is guaranteed to set readers' hearts racing and establish McKinzie as a rising voice in the genre."—*Publishers Weekly*

"Plenty of page-turning excitement."—*Winnipeg Free Press*

THE EDGE OF JUSTICE

"One of the strongest debuts of the year."
—*Chicago Tribune*

"A fast-paced and promising debut."—*Washington Post*

"This book signals the start of a great new career. Clinton McKinzie delivers a story pulsing with intrigue and character that is as poetic as it is harrowing. This one's a true winner."
—Michael Connelly

"Action-packed . . . [a] page-turner."
—*USA Today*

"An adrenaline-pumping, heart-pounding thrill ride with a terrifying climax that left me clenching for a handhold. Clinton McKinzie writes with the voice of a true adventurer." —Tess Gerritsen

Also by Clinton McKinzie

CROSSING
THE LINE

CLINTON McKINZIE

DELL BOOKS

CROSSING THE LINE
A Dell Book

PUBLISHING HISTORY
Delacorte hardcover edition published May 2004
Dell mass market edition / March 2005

Published by
Bantam Dell
A Division of Random House, Inc.
New York, New York

Library of Congress Catalog Card Number: 2003064602

ISBN 0-440-24081-6

Printed in the United States of America
Published simultaneously in Canada

www.bantamdell.com

OPM   10 9 8 7 6 5 4 3 2 1

For Dempsey, My Manassa Mauler.
You were the best friend I've ever had.

ACKNOWLEDGMENTS

Two of my passions, climbing and crime, have something in common other than just providing a thrill. Both passions require you to rely on others—a need that for me, with my soloist tendencies, is absolutely necessary to keep me out of trouble. Climbers call it the Brotherhood of the Rope when you put everything into the hands of your belayers. And it's just as important in the courtroom, when you're dealing with other people's lives, as it is on the rock, when you're only risking your own. As a prosecutor I learned to rely on the advice of my colleagues, the skills of investigating officers, and the assistance of the staff, before ever heading out before a judge or a jury.

My other great passion, storytelling, shares this trait. The Brotherhood of the Rope definitely applies when venturing into unknown terrain with a new book. Several people have worked very hard to keep me safe and on route and I want to thank them here. John Talbot, my literary agent, made this new career possible. Danielle Perez, my editor at Bantam Dell, once again provided truly expert guidance. Robin Foster made my prose readable and kept me honest with people, places, facts, and dates. Bantam Dell Deputy Publisher Nita Taublib and Publisher Irwyn Applebaum had faith in my story. My parents and my wife had faith in me. Thank you one and all for holding the rope.

CROSSING THE LINE

1

Beware the Jabberwock, my son!
The jaws that bite, the claws that catch!

— *"Jabberwocky"*
Lewis Carroll

ONE

My rust-shot Land Cruiser, the Iron Pig, swayed within its lane on Highway 191. It was rocked side to side by gusts of wind barreling down off the high plateau of the Red Desert. Balls of uprooted sage the size of beer kegs rolled across the asphalt amid slithering snakes of sand. Out of respect for the wind and the tumbleweeds and the writhing grit, I held the needle at just below the seventy-five-mile-per-hour speed limit. But even though the highway was clear of all other traffic, the massive grille of a Chevy Suburban rode hard on my old truck's bumper. Its windows were darkly tinted and antennae bristled from its roof.

I glanced in the rearview mirror and my knuckles whitened where they gripped the wheel. Another gust hit and for the hundredth time I considered stomping on the brake.

No, Ant. You've got to play nice. For Roberto's sake.

But I needed to vent.

"You guys are real sly, real inconspicuous, using a truck like that. Nobody would ever suspect it belongs to the FBI."

I said it loud enough to be heard over the howl blasting through the wide-open windows.

A moment passed, then a voice called out from the seat behind me.

"You sound jealous, Burns. You need to understand that the taxpayers wouldn't approve of us spending too much time waiting for tow trucks, which is something I expect you do quite often in this piece of shit."

Her voice was clipped and sharp, and the curse word she uttered had come out strange. I'd only met her five hours earlier, in a hotel suite in Salt Lake City, but I suspected that Mary Chang didn't use even the mildest profanity lightly. She'd seemed nice enough then, but a little rigid. Tense, formal, and maybe nervous. The long, mostly mute drive hadn't loosened her up much. It hadn't exactly relaxed me either.

I looked at her in the rearview mirror. She was huddled against the side door directly behind me. Her small hands clasped her ears, trying to either cut the noise of the wind and the tires or hold back her jet-black hair. Her eyes, which even in the still air of the hotel suite had been narrow and hooded, were now nothing but slits.

Hearing our voices, my wolf-dog jerked her head back into the truck. She twisted around to stare curiously at the woman seated beside her. One of Mungo's lips had been curled inward by the wind, exposing a row of long teeth. The effect was goofy rather than menacing. She canted her head as if trying to understand our exchange. A ribbon of drool fluttered out of her mouth and pasted itself across the FBI agent's white silk blouse. In the mirror I watched Mary grimace, wrinkling her nose as she looked down at her shirt. I had to hold back a smile.

Good dog.

After a moment the beast turned again, dusted the agent with her tail, and swung her head back out the window.

I didn't like federal agents. Not even young, pretty ones. They tended to treat local cops with either condescension or disdain. Mary's silence and aloof, serious expression for most of the ride reinforced this belief. They also stole our best cases and never shared the credit. Bigfooting, it was called. I knew generalizations were small-minded, but it was a prejudice that right then—after five hours of being tailgated by her jerk of a partner in that black behemoth—I was having trouble conquering.

I couldn't see him through the tinted windshield just yards off my bumper, but I carried a vivid image of him from that morning. Tom Cochran was a red-faced man with red hair that was carefully styled into a sort of pompadour. When we'd been introduced in Salt Lake, he'd let my hand hang empty in the air between us for a three-count before shaking it.

"You're the guy they call QuickDraw, right?" he'd asked, using the nickname the way it was intended—as an insult. The scowl he gave me was one I suspected he practiced each morning in the mirror while he moussed his hair. But I knew he'd come around once I got myself into a better mood. Being likable is a part of my job, even though it takes more and more effort as the years go by.

"Can't we turn on the AC?"

It was almost a plea, but I wasn't yet ready to be nice.

"Nope. Roberto hates air-conditioning."

I nodded my head at the man riding shotgun next to me. Roberto was slumped in the reclined passenger seat, apparently asleep. Flaps of dark hair whipped across his face and obscured his features. His arms were folded loosely on his chest. Around his throat was a braided leather cord with a turquoise stone set in its center.

"He *is* in custody," Mary pointed out.

Which was technically true, even though she'd taken off his handcuffs in Salt Lake as a kind of good-faith gesture. But I didn't care. I found her eyes in the mirror.

"He's also my brother. And he's doing you guys one hell of a favor."

A movement at the periphery of my vision caused me to look his way again. Roberto wasn't asleep after all; his thumb twitched erect for a second before lying back onto his fist.

"Don't forget we're doing him one, too," the FBI agent said.

Outside was a desert landscape of red earth and sagebrush, corduroyed with dry gullies. The sun was baking the ground. Waves of heat drifted upward like clear smoke on the blacktop ahead. I reached for the CD player—the only obvious modification to the old truck other than the oversized tires and the front-mounted electric winch—and cranked up the disk Roberto had given me.

It wasn't at all what I'd expected. The music was weird and disturbing. As a kid he'd liked hard rock and punk. The Dead Kennedys. Suicidal Tendencies. Even, in milder moods, The Clash, and, later, Red Hot Chili Peppers. But this was some sort of opera. The plastic case said *José Cura. Puccini Arias.* A man sang in a tenor that sounded dark and thick, his voice carrying what seemed to me like an undercurrent of suppressed rage. It made me wonder what my brother was on these days.

The music began to match the landscape as the miles passed. It concentrated the intensity of the heat and the sun and the wind, and gave it an almost liquid sensation. As if the world had melted into mercury and the colors of the sky and the red desert were reflections on its surface.

What is he on these days?

At first it was only adrenaline, an addiction we both inherited from a father who spent every moment of his generous military leave dragging his sons up mountains. Then, as a young teenager, Roberto began to experiment with pot and hash and soloing—rock climbing without a rope. Psychedelics

and ever higher ropeless ascents followed. And then it was cocaine, at about the time the climbing magazines made his big-
wall solos famous. He dabbled with everything, and perfected
what he claimed was the ultimate way to take the amp of
adrenaline and push it through the roof: speedballs, an injected combination of cocaine and heroin. Judging from the
music, I guessed that these days he'd backed down to just the
horse.

Roberto suddenly lunged forward in his seat.

"Ant! Check it out! That Sentinel Rocks over there?"

He pointed out the window to where some jumbled granite boulders wavered on a distant ridge. I turned down the
music and tried to bring the shimmering escarpment into focus.

"Yeah, 'Berto. I'm pretty sure. Dad took us there a couple
of times when we were kids."

"Pull over, che. I need to get some air under my feet."
Roberto twisted around to look at the federal agent. "You
mind?"

In the mirror I saw Mary jump, alarmed at the speed with
which he moved. Maybe that was why she seemed so nervous.
She was scared of him. I was a little bit, too. .

"Sorry. No stopping. We're on a tight schedule."

Roberto pushed his sunglasses up onto his forehead and
showed her his strange blue eyes. They matched the
turquoise, but were totally out of place against his brown skin
and black hair. He smiled at her.

"C'mon, now. I'd be a much happier rat if you'd cut me a
little slack."

She wasn't able to hold his gaze.

Looking away, out the window, she said, "Mr. Burns, we
have a job to do. This isn't a rock-climbing vacation."

A blast of wind punched through the truck, and I had to
wrestle with the manual steering. Roberto remained twisted

around in his seat, the half-mocking smile still on his mouth. His voice, slightly slurred with a Spanish accent, was soft and soothing.

"Listen. Your job's to nail Jesús Hidalgo, and it requires me risking my neck, not you guys. I'm the one he's going to come after when he finds out someone's been talking about him. And you people have kept me in a box for like two weeks. So c'mon, I need a break. Just one hour. A little climb. Please? Pretty, pretty please?"

Mary Chang continued to squint out into the wind. She shook her head again with her hands still clasped around it. Not in negation this time, but slower, as if in pain. Then she dropped one hand to look at her watch. Letting out a sigh, and maybe another curse, she dropped the other hand and reached for the purse at her feet. She came up with a cell phone.

"We're going to turn off and stop for a bit," she shouted into the phone. She listened for a minute, frowning, before saying, "No. We're stopping for one hour. Just do it. No, Tom, you listen. I'm in charge here. We're stopping."

She didn't look at Roberto when he grinned even broader and said, *"Gracias, guapa."* He turned back to the sight of the distant rocks through the windshield.

"Thanks," I added, feeling guilty for having vented on her earlier.

The Suburban flashed its lights and honked its horn when I wheeled the Pig off the highway even though it was obvious I wasn't going to stop. A wave of red dust billowed out from my undercarriage and swept over the truck behind me. No more gleaming wax job for the Feds—there wasn't a car wash within a hundred miles. The Suburban fell back. We bounced and switchbacked for a mile and a half up a dirt double-track toward the base of a leaning sandstone tower, which stood on the ridge like a drunken sentry guarding a mighty herd of chaparral.

Parking in the shade of the rock's overhanging wall, suddenly the heat and the wind and the noise were all but gone. The air here was almost cool in the deep shadow. The ground was littered with crumpled cans and broken glass. Black smoke from old campfires stained the stone rising up over us.

Cheyenne had probably once huddled here in the fall, waiting for the buffalo to come south. Basque sheepherders would have taken advantage of this sheltered spot once the buffalo and Indians had all been conveniently slaughtered. Now, judging from the litter of green glass, beer cans modified into crank pipes, condom wrappers, and cigarette butts, it was only used by teenagers from the ranches north of Rock Springs who came here to party. I knew a lot about such parties—I'd often joined them, undercover, as a special agent with Wyoming's Division of Criminal Investigation. Back in the days before my face was front-page news.

Roberto hopped out of the truck and began rooting through the crates of climbing gear I kept in the back. He dragged out harnesses, carabiners, and a rope while I let the wolf-dog out of the backseat. Mungo gratefully crouched and watered the dry earth, then danced over to my brother's side. She was fascinated by him. She pranced around him like he was a strange, handsome dog or a wolf himself.

"That's the ugliest mutt I've ever seen," Roberto said, not unkindly, as the now very dusty Suburban skidded to a halt behind us. When Mungo leapt away from it, he added, "Skittish, too, not like that monster Oso. *That* fucker would have charged, then torn off the bumper."

Mungo wasn't pretty. She was bony-spined and her heavy gray coat hung from her frame like secondhand clothes. Her usual attitude was cringing; tail tucked between her legs and head held low whenever anyone paid any attention to her.

Lately, though, she'd been showing a little more backbone. It was something that had started after she nipped a man she thought was threatening me, and tasted blood for the first time. But she still wasn't anything like Oso. He'd been a hulking brute with a surprisingly soft, squishy heart until a suspect in a murder investigation blew apart his muzzle with a hollowpoint bullet. My fiancée rescued Mungo from a wildlife refuge that was about to be shut down and have its animals destroyed. Rebecca had thought this craven creature could replace the beast I'd lost last fall.

"What do you think you're doing?" Tom Cochran yelled at us through a rapidly descending window.

Mungo jumped again, backing away from the truck and the voice.

"Well? What do you think you're doing? We don't have time for this!" he yelled again.

I decided that I definitely wasn't in the mood to start being nice. But I was pleased to see that, even backing away, Mungo had squinted her yellow eyes and raised her lips. It wasn't much of a snarl, though—it was more like a nervous grin.

"Taking a break, asshole," Roberto answered for us all. Then to Mungo, in a lower voice and while bending to stroke her bristling fur, "Hey, it's okay, girl. Ignore him. Dry air up here's messing with his hairdo."

"What did you call me?"

Tom threw the door open and leapt out of the Suburban. He was wearing new jeans and pointy boots with riding heels. Going cowboy, like so many did when they visited my state. He'd taken off the dress shirt and sport coat he had been wearing in Salt Lake and was now clad in a white T-shirt that was a couple of sizes too small. The taut material allowed him to display his pale, puffy biceps. He held his arms out from his sides a little farther than he needed to, even though he was wearing one of the Bureau's new 10 mm guns and a pair of handcuffs on his hip.

Mungo's eyes twitched toward me. Her clenched teeth were exposed now. I was tempted to nod, just to see what she'd do, but shook my head and showed her my palm. Then I flicked my fingers at her. Quick as a rabbit, she spun and leapt into the brush.

Roberto straightened up and looked right at Tom.

"A-S-S-H-O-L-E, if you can spell better than you listen. I called you an asshole, asshole."

Tom stared back, his face growing redder beneath his mirrored aviator's shades. The color of blood in his face merged with all the freckles. He hesitated before stepping forward, long enough to give Mary time to get out of the Pig and come between them. She held up a hand in each direction.

"Cut it out, both of you."

"I've had enough of this," Tom said, looking at my brother but talking to her. "Two weeks of this guy bullshitting and giving us nothing but lip. Let's haul his junkie ass over to Colorado and see how he likes those escape charges they have waiting for him."

I wondered if they were playing good cop/bad cop. With me, a cop, and Roberto, who had been dealing with cops all his life, it would be a silly game. Roberto apparently decided to bring this fact to their attention.

"Guess that means you don't want to catch the guy who sliced and diced your buddy down in Mexicali."

And that jacked up the tension, as my brother knew it would. He'd told me earlier that both the Feds in our little caravan had worked with the narcotics agent whose death in Baja California two months ago had been in all the papers.

The blood drained out of Tom's face as fast as it rose in Mary's.

"You scumbag," Tom said in a lower, harsher voice. His

fists were balled and beginning to rise. "Don't you ever mention that again."

He stepped so close to Mary that he was looming over her. But I noticed that he didn't try to step around her. Still, he was playing with fire. They both were.

Roberto was smiling. Mocking.

"What, Mexicali? Or your dumb buddy who got himself cut up?"

"Stop it, 'Berto. Shut up," I said.

I'd been taking a perverse delight in the confrontation, but I didn't want to hear a dead narcotics agent derided. Not even a federal agent. Nor did I want my brother to blow his one chance at amnesty.

Mary seemed to be thinking, as if considering just how much they really needed Roberto and his information to do whatever they were intending to do. I took one of my brother's arms and pulled him back before he could do anything to hurt Mary's decision or further squeeze Tom's trigger.

I was surprised that Roberto didn't resist. He let me lead him a couple of feet closer to my truck.

Belatedly, Mary made her decision. She faced my brother and pointed a finger at him.

"That's enough, Mr. Burns. We need you, but not enough to put up with any abuse or provocation. If you don't want to cooperate, then you'll be turned over to authorities in Colorado tonight."

She waited for my brother to say something. He didn't. She glanced at her watch.

"All right then. You have one hour."

They must need him very badly, I thought.

Roberto maybe sensed it too, because he jerked his arm out of my hand. *Oh shit.* He stepped forward, back up into Tom's face. My brother wasn't as big as the FBI agent—the top of his head came even with Tom's freckled nose—but there was an obvious menace in Roberto that dwarfed the other man.

I tensed, readying myself to tackle him from behind. Things were on the verge of really getting out of control. Roberto, when he fought, battled like a Norse berserker.

"You're right," my brother said quietly. "I shouldn't have mentioned that. Sorry, man."

Then he turned away and went back to sorting through the crates of gear.

I stared at my brother's back. *What's going on with him?* I'd never seen him back down. Not from anything. Not in his entire life. He'd never cared about the consequences. *Destraillado,* Mom called it. Unleashed. I looked at Tom and saw that his fists were still clenched.

"He should be in handcuffs," he told his partner. "Hell, they both should be in handcuffs. A lunatic and a renegade cop. I can't fucking believe we have to deal with these people."

Noticing me watching him, he spat in the dirt.

"Bite me, Tom," I said.

"Cool it, all of you. That's enough."

Mary swatted at herself, attempting to dust Mungo's hair from her skirt and blouse, and plucked at where the clothes were pasted by sweat to her skin. Tom couldn't help but watch her, and I saw that my brother, smiling again with his eyebrows raised slightly behind his sunglasses, was doing the same. The disheveled hair and clothes were undeniably sexy on her. They were such a contrast to her rigid personality. Especially in this testosterone-charged environment.

She must have felt the eyes, because she stopped touching herself and walked stiffly in her heels to the rear of the Suburban. From a cooler she took out three bottles of water and passed them around. It was a peacemaking gesture.

I joined my brother in examining the rock that was

leaning over us. There was a single crack splitting the overhanging wall of the eighty-foot tower. It started out three
inches wide at the bottom then contracted to just an inch or so
before it reached a cavelike alcove near the top. Above that,
the final few moves to the summit were invisible as the sun was
right behind it and the indirect radiance made close scrutiny
impossible.

"Which end you want?" Roberto asked, swinging the
coiled rope in one hand.

"The sharp end."

"Okay, little bro. You lead."

The rope hit my chest. I unwrapped it from where it was
tied around itself and began carefully flaking it out on the
ground, working out the kinks. Roberto shimmied a harness
over his brown canvas pants and dragged off his shirt. The
two federal agents watched us as if we were performing some
voodoo ritual.

I was pleased to notice that there weren't any scabby pin-
prick tracks on the insides of Roberto's arms. It didn't mean
much—I had known junkies who injected their thighs, scro-
tums, and even between their toes to escape being marked—
but it was a positive sign because my brother had never cared
about detection.

He looked good, too. Fit and almost ridiculously strong,
although his normally dark skin seemed a little translucent
from two weeks confined indoors. He'd even cut his hair,
which used to reach halfway down his back. It was still tangled and dirty, but now it only hung far enough to touch the
slanting ridges of his trapezius.

After shimmying into my own harness then tying in to one
end of the rope, I clipped a handful of cams and hexes onto a
sling and put it over my head and one shoulder. My climbing
slippers were warm from the sunlight that had been beating

down on the truck. They were tight enough to curl my toes but familiar as I squeezed my feet into them and laced up.

I was aware of the Feds watching us, wondering how we were going to climb a wall that overhung more than fifteen degrees and was marred by only that single parallel-sided fissure. Reaching up, I placed my right hand high into the cool crack and made a fist—my folded thumb against one side and the heel of my palm pressed against the other. I placed my left hand just below it in the same way. By clenching my fists and flexing the muscles in my hands, I was able to lock them in. A jam, it's called. Weird, but it works. I pulled up on the clenched fists and got a foot wedged in a couple of feet farther down by turning it sideways then twisting it in with my knee raised high.

I wriggled up this way, replacing fists and feet always higher, as sweat ran over my skin and my breath grew ragged. The crack narrowed until I was able to hang securely off a single jammed fist. Then a cupped hand, and finally just my torqued fingertips and toes.

"Wow," I heard Mary say from below me. "Look at that."

It was the first real sign of life I'd heard from her. And I took an embarrassed pleasure in bringing it out.

"It's not that hard," Tom said dismissively. "Takes practice, is all. There's a trick to it."

"Then maybe you ought to go next, Tom."

I smiled to myself but didn't look down. I didn't hear if Tom made any response.

Blood began to stain the yellowish stone because I hadn't bothered to tape up. I was setting my jams far too quickly, showing off a little for my brother and the Feds. Every ten feet or so I slotted a mechanical camming device into the crack and clipped to it the rope trailing from my harness. I could feel the slight weight on the rope from Roberto's belay.

After ten minutes of grunting and panting I hauled myself

over a small ledge and into the hole eighty feet off the ground.
In this small alcove were two old bolts someone had long ago
drilled into the rock. They felt secure when I tried to shake
them, so I clipped a bight from my end of the rope into them.

"I'm off," I yelled down.

Roberto started climbing before I even had him on belay.
I reeled in the rope as fast as I could, my bloodied hands shoving the rope through the belay tube and getting warm from
the friction. I couldn't see him when I craned my neck out
over the edge, but I could see the two federal agents in the
shade below. They were gaping upward with open mouths.
Even Tom wasn't able to look away. Mungo, too, was watching. Her long snout poked out of a spiny bush behind the
agents.

I couldn't see Roberto, but I was long familiar with the
way he climbed. Fast and smooth. My brother was elemental
in a way, one with the stone yet untouched by the forces of
gravity. He sort of graced his way up the rock without any of
my less elegant grunting and gasping and bleeding.

When he planted a palm on the ledge and mantled up on
it, I saw that he hadn't bothered to lace up his rock shoes. I
clipped a bight from his end of the rope into the bolts and
said, "You're off."

"You're looking strong," he told me, punching my chest.
"Still a wiry little guy, but strong."

I felt the flush of a little brother's pride at the words.

"You're getting slow, 'Berto. Thought you would have
been up here a long time ago."

I don't think he heard me. He stood on the edge—toes in
space—and stared out at the desert landscape without expression. You can see a long way in this state. A lot farther than
you can from a prison cell. I hoped he was realizing that.

We don't look that much alike. His face shows more of
our mother's mestizo heritage than mine. His cheekbones are

higher, his nose slightly hooked. But like me, he has our father's square Scots jaw. Our eyes are the greatest difference between us. Mine are coffee brown; his are a brilliant blue, the color you see looking down into the deepest part of a crevasse. I also carry a long white scar on my left cheek from a rockfall—a reminder of my own mortality. Roberto has no such scar.

His chest, shoulders, and back still held the taut slabs of prison muscle from the time before his escape ten months earlier. Since then he'd been on high peaks in South America, and the exertion and deprivation had carved distinct lines through the bulk. *Honed* was the word that best described him. He looked like he'd been carved out of stone.

"How is it that you know this narco Hidalgo?" I asked him when he slumped down beside me. It was the first time all day that we'd been alone.

"Dude used to think he was a mountaineer. I saved his shit on Aconcagua 'bout ten years back." Then he shrugged. "After that, I did some muling for him and his buddies. They call themselves the Mexicali Mafia."

I remembered the story, but I hadn't realized that the man Roberto rescued was the notorious drug lord. Roberto had come across three men dressed in designer mountain wear—the kind of clothes made for anything but mountain climbing. Puffy jackets by Ralph Lauren and leather boots that had never been treated to repel snow and water because it might ruin the finish. The three were in bad shape, weak and suffering from cold, altitude, and hunger, near the summit of the twenty-three-thousand-foot peak. Roberto tied them all into a rope and more or less dragged them down. When I'd first heard about it, he only described them as a trio of rich guys from Mexico City.

"You've met him, too," he added now, turning and grinning at me.

"Bullshit."

"Well, almost. Remember that time we were down in Baja . . ."

He reminded me of a trip we'd taken eight years ago, when I was in grad school at Boulder. Dad and Mom were in Saudi Arabia, leaving the two of us on our own for Christmas break. It had been a cold early winter, so we headed south when I picked him up from where he was living in Durango. We drove the Pig all the way down to the Sea of Cortés. For one week we kayaked and dove, sleeping on deserted beaches, spearing fish to cook on yucca fires, mellowing at night on Tecate and lime (me) and tequila and hashish (him). The next week we climbed pristine desert walls in the Sierra Juárez.

Roberto had heard about a particular one—supposedly virgin, unclimbed—but never seen it. He knew how to get there, though, and we cut through then retied a barbed-wire fence on the way. On this particular wall—a twelve-hundred-footer—we'd been caught by a freak rainstorm then darkness when we were high up on it. The water sluicing down the wall made it impossible to finish the climb and hike off, and we hadn't brought enough gear to rig all the rappels necessary to bail. So we spent a long, wet night on an edge not much wider than a bookshelf.

Waking up hadn't been pleasant—it was a bullet striking the rock near my head that brought me out of my shivering stupor. Splinters of quartz had cut into one of my ears.

Two men and a battered Jeep were parked near my truck at the base of the wall. One of the men was aiming up through a rifle's sight for a second shot while the other was bent over like he might be laughing.

Roberto shouted down at them in Spanish—words I didn't think at the time would help our situation: "Mother-fuckers! You shoot again and I'll cut your throats!"

The one with the gun yelled, "You're trespassing. Our

boss doesn't like trespassers. Put them back on the ground, he told us."

"I'm invited, you dumb animals. Go tell him it's Roberto Burns. Before I come down there and stick that rifle up your ass."

The men laughed some more and the one with the gun pointed it. But there was an uncertainty in both their gestures. The rifle didn't fire a second time.

"You really know the guy who owns this place?" I'd asked him as I frantically readied the soggy ropes for a sprint to the summit.

The men got into the Jeep and drove away to check with their boss.

"Sort of. You wouldn't like him." He laughed. "Trust me. We need to get out of here, *che*. Fast."

And we did. Driving out a different way and over another barbed-wire fence before the men returned.

"That was Hidalgo's land," Roberto said now. "His inland *estancia*. He told me about that wall after I pulled him off Aconcagua. Said I ought to come down sometime and give it a shot."

"If you really knew him, then why were we in such a hurry to get out of there? Why'd we drive over all those fences instead of just going by the house?"

"I didn't want you to meet him, bro."

Now it gave me a small thrill, learning that eight years earlier I'd come close to meeting one of the continent's most brutal drug lords. A man believed responsible for hundreds of torture killings—his way of silencing those whom he suspected of disloyalty. His method was not only to kill the suspected individual, but to also kill every member of his family. Even close friends sometimes. It was a method that assured no one would ever testify against him. Simple and very effective. No one would sentence their entire family to death no matter what kind of protection or reward they were offered. And I felt a different sort of thrill, too, because my brother had been protecting me from him even way back then.

Roberto sat forward, leaning over far enough so that between his legs he could gaze down on the Feds, the wolf, and the two trucks parked below.

"I'm surprised they let us do this," I told him.

"Didn't have no choice, *che*. Those two want Hidalgo bad. They'll do whatever I want."

If they were dealing with my brother in the first place, it had to be true. What I didn't understand was why he was dealing with them. Putting himself in danger of more time in prison if things didn't work out, and risking a bad, bad death if they did. And maybe for not just him, although I didn't want to think about that. Not yet.

"I still don't get why you're doing this, 'Berto."

He shrugged. "Things are changing. I can't explain it right now."

I didn't push him. I'd save it for later.

He glanced over his shoulder at me and then down again. "Now watch this. I'm gonna freak 'em out."

He stood and reeled about thirty feet of slack from his harness. Next he made an overhand knot. I didn't realize right away what he was doing because I was thinking about what he'd said, and trying to guess the reason or reasons he was here.

What was going on with him? Why didn't he just stay in South America, where Grandpa's compadres from the bad old days during Argentina's Dirty War could protect him from extradition? Why hadn't he knocked Tom Cochran's teeth down his throat? And why had he apologized?

I didn't think I'd ever heard him apologize before. Not in thirty-two years of knowing him.

The click of a carabiner's gate snapping shut startled me

out of my thoughts. He had clipped the knot to the bolts. He'd also unclipped his own anchoring knot. He dropped the coil of slack rope next to me on the ledge.

Finally I realized what he was about to do.

"Don't do it, 'Berto. You'll ruin my rope."

"You don't need a rope, Ant. You've got to learn to let go."

Then, with a scream of utter terror, he spread his bare arms and jumped off the ledge.

Long seconds later the carabiners and knots slammed together with a sound like a whipcrack as his weight hit the end of the rope. I rechecked the bolts then leaned over to see the mouths below gaping even wider. It was as if a flash-bang grenade had exploded over their heads. Mary Chang was frozen in place and seemed to be gasping for air. Tom was swearing loudly.

Swinging free above them, laughing silently, was my brother.

And he was just getting warmed up for really scaring the hell out of all of us.

TWO

It was nine o'clock at night when we finally rolled through the town of Potash and neared our destination. Like the epithet QuickDraw, which had been slapped on me, the town's name was supposed to be sardonic and dismissive.

A couple of decades ago this dry, dusty region had been stampeded by surveyors, roughnecks, and the entrepreneurial leeches who followed them. All were looking to make a fast buck and then get out. Nearly all of them got out, but without the buck. Instead of oil and gas under the rocky soil, what they found was a mineral valuable only as a base component of fertilizer. *Potash*—said like you're spitting out a mouthful of the area's alkaline water—was what the town was designated by the few unfortunate souls who stayed—or were left—behind.

There were a couple of boarded-up fast-food joints near where the state highway veered off, and then a mostly deserted main street. The buildings were all made of tan brick. Their sturdy construction signified that, at one time at least, someone had had hopes for this place. That hope appeared to be long dead. Many of the store windows yawned wide and dark, like toothless old ghosts, and the interiors were stocked with only trash and tumbleweeds. Thoroughly graffitied boards covered others. Only a few retailers remained intact and, perhaps, occasionally open for business—three pawn-shops, a feed store, and a hardware merchant.

Both ends of the main street were bookended by a pair of bars. It was Friday night, and a lot of pickup trucks were crowded around them. Outside of one bar on the south end of the street two vaqueros were pissing on the hood of an old patrol car emblazoned with the seal of the Potash Town Marshall. They barked and howled at Mungo, whose head was in its usual position, hanging out the window.

"My kind of town," Roberto said.

"That doesn't surprise me," Mary Chang responded, in an almost teasing tone that did surprise me. The fact that we would soon be reaching the end of the road, along with the cooling effect of the night, might finally draw her out of her shell.

She'd refused to join our conversations on the long drive north. Refused, pretty much, to speak at all. Not that it was likely she could've added much, since we mostly talked about Mom and Dad and mountains. But I'd repeatedly tried to get her to tell me what the plan was, what they wanted my brother for, other than to pick his brain about Jesús Hidalgo. She'd kept saying later, later. So I stopped asking and had gone mute myself.

I thought I was going to hate working for the Feds. Little did I know just how much.

On the other side of Potash were sagging trailers on jacks with tattered flags of laundry fluttering in the wind. Blue TV lights flashed from behind the windows. Most every trailer—despite the apparent poverty—was equipped with a satellite dish. We passed the frames of cannibalized cars and appliances and then passed what was officially marked as the town dump, the sign being the only thing that distinguished it from the surrounding landscape. Finally we were beyond civilization, such as it was in this part of the state, and beginning to crunch and bump along a dirt road.

Like most nights in the state, the sky was crystal clear. The ever-present wind off the plains swept it clean.

"Turn off your headlights, please, Agent Burns," Mary instructed me.

I flipped them off. The stars provided more than enough light for driving at the crawling speed the condition of the road demanded. Behind us, the Suburban's lights went out, too. Mary used a penlight to study a map on her lap. She somehow managed to navigate us through the maze of dirt roads that wound among rocky desert knolls.

Whenever we reached the top of a ridge, I would study the eastern horizon for the starless voids that were made by the peaks of the Wind River Range. The foothills to the peaks began only a few miles from us, on the other side of the Roan River. The peaks themselves, rising to just shy of thirteen thousand feet, jutted up six thousand feet off the plain. Their shapes were familiar to me. In the past I'd climbed most of the more vertical edges of shadow. Maybe there would be a chance to get up there again, I thought. Maybe with my brother.

I braked to a stop before a barbed-wire fence that was strung across the road. Sandstone outcroppings stood on either side, preventing me from driving around it.

"This is it, gentlemen. Our headquarters for the next couple of weeks."

Roberto turned and looked back at her. "I guess the Four Seasons back there in Potash was all booked up."

I didn't say anything, but I was thinking that it looked like the back entrance to a prison. Roberto was probably thinking it, too.

Mary got out of the backseat and tried to unhook one side of the fence from where some iron spikes had been driven into the rock. She struggled with it, trying to peel it back in order to clear the road. I watched from behind the steering wheel as she put her shoulder between the barbs on a vertical line of wire.

"Where are your manners, Ant? Girl's going to ruin her clothes," Roberto said, opening his door and stepping out. As if eight hours of desert heat, blowing grit, and wolf hair hadn't ruined the expensive-looking skirt and blouse already.

It was like Roberto to see the girl in her, a person Mary Chang seemed to take pains to hide with her formal clothes and stilted speech. And it was also like Roberto to open a fence for a female federal agent who planned on putting him at great risk by acting on whatever information he provided, and would probably like nothing better than to drop him back in the cell she'd only temporarily sprung him from.

Once they'd scraped the fence back, I pulled forward far enough so that the Suburban could fit through, too. Roberto and Mary closed the fence, reattaching it to the spikes, and climbed back in. After another hundred feet, the dirt track entered into what resembled a great pit or a crater.

It was surrounded on three and a half sides by steep slopes of rock, sage, and chaparral. Stars low overhead threw dim shadows from ribs of sandstone that poked out of the canted earth like the bones of some fossilized monster. Against the crater's back wall were some dark buildings. I realized then that Mary had planned it this way—that was why she'd allowed my brother the time to "get a little air beneath his heels." Our arrival was meant to be veiled by the night.

It was once a hunting camp but it had gone bankrupt a few years earlier, Mary explained, elaborating on anything for the first time. The bank that now owned it was unable to sell it so they were willing to lease.

I knew that several years of drought in the region had

driven the elk into the mountains, and the only things left to shoot on the alkaline hills were rattlesnakes and a few skinny antelope. Anyone with money and sense would buy a place higher up in the pine forests below the peaks.

"I arranged, through a dummy corporation, and then through a law firm in Denver, to lease it for the fall," Mary went on. "The bank thinks we're a B-movie company that's going to use it for a Western set. Behind that hill"—she indicated the sharp, spiny-looking ridge behind the buildings— "the land drops three hundred feet to the Roan River. Jesús Hidalgo has been staying at a property on the other side, only a half-mile upstream."

It was bizarre to think of him being so close. Of this legendary bad guy, head of the Mexicali Mafia, being in my state at all. I'd become a Wyoming cop to take down drug dealers, but never imagined I'd get the chance to participate in taking down *the* drug dealer. I didn't even mind that the Feds would surely take all the credit. If everyone would just loosen up a little, this might even be fun.

Mary added, "According to our intelligence, he's there right now and intends to stay for a while."

Her words gave me a charge of anticipation, not unlike what I felt when staring up at a virgin wall. But Mary again refused to give any further information on how we might climb it.

In the starlight I could make out a large cabin that probably served as the camp's dining room, kitchen, and lounge. Three smaller cabins stood nearby. Off a little ways, against the edge of the crater, there was the black shape of a barn that appeared to be tilted a little to one side. The only trees were some stunted junipers along the slopes and ridge and a few dehydrated cottonwoods near the main cabin.

I started to park the Pig in front of the main cabin, when Mary ordered me to drive to the barn.

"He has a plane," she said by way of explanation. "It flies up from Mexico City or Mexicali every couple of weeks. We don't want to take any chances."

I thought they were being overly cautious. But then I didn't yet know their plan.

The two swinging doors leading into the partially collapsed barn were open. The darkness beyond them resembled a black hole. Mary got out again and shone her little flashlight's beam around the interior. The narrow cone of light revealed a cracked and heaving concrete floor, piles of rotting timber, and some corroded farm implements.

I pulled to one side, letting the Suburban drive in first. When I wanted to leave I didn't want to have to ask Tom to move his car.

Without being told, we were quiet as we got out of the trucks. Doors were bumped shut with hips rather than slammed. Mungo stayed so close to my side that she was leaning against my thigh. Overhead, the barn's roof creaked and groaned in the wind. I doubted that if the inevitable occurred it would do much damage to my rusty iron truck. But it would sure play hell with the fancy paint on the Suburban. The taxpayers, of course, would foot the bill to keep the Feds looking sharp.

We walked as a group over packed dirt and through weeds to get to the main cabin. Tom walked behind Roberto, staring hard at my brother's back. Just three hours earlier he'd seen him come screaming out of the sky. Now Tom acted as if he expected him to be jerked back up into the air.

Mary knelt on the porch before the door and again used her flashlight to work the combination on the padlock. The door stuttered open. She shone the light inside.

"Welcome to our new home, gentlemen."

Sand was sprinkled liberally over the plank floor from where it had blown in through chinks in the log walls. Spirals of dust floated in the flashlight's beam. Mouse turds lay among the sand and dirt. There was a kitchen area along one wall, with a stove and sink, and two wooden picnic tables with benches that were the only furniture in the large room. The interior doorway to an added-on bathroom was open but a brief glimpse of what was beyond wasn't welcoming even after hours on the road.

Following Mary and Tom inside, I swept my hand through cobwebs next to the doorjamb, and felt a light switch.

"Don't," Mary said, turning suddenly and pointing the beam at my hand. "The electricity's supposed to be on, but first I want to cover the windows."

There was a retching sound from the kitchen wall. Tom had turned on the tap and brown water was beginning to cough out of it.

"Water works," he reported. "At least I think it's water. Good thing we brought our own to drink, but I'm not looking forward to showering with this mud."

Roberto alone remained outside. After two weeks locked indoors I understood that he had no desire for walls. Not that he ever really did. I was like him in that way, more comfortable in a tent than in a house. It probably had something to do with growing up as a military brat, with a different house on a different base each year. For him it was worse, the result of too many additional years in prison. The closest thing to a permanent home either of us had known was our grandfather's ranch on the Argentine altiplano.

After examining the lodge, I walked back out onto the porch and found him sitting on a step. He was putting the finishing touches on a hand-rolled cigarette, licking an edge of the paper. At least I hoped it was a cigarette. He struck a match against the sole of a motorcycle boot, and I was relieved a moment later when I smelled some kind of scented tobacco.

But I wasn't at all relieved by the way his hands seemed to be shaking.

"You okay?" I asked him, not really sure what, if anything, was the matter.

He smirked at me and blew smoke out of his nose.

After a minute, he asked, "Your girlfriend, that Rebecca, she still packin'?" Meaning, I assumed, had she gotten the abortion that had been an unspoken possibility for a while.

"Yeah. She's due in February, Tío 'Berto."

The smirk was now a genuine grin and I returned it. I knew he didn't like Rebecca, or at least he knew she didn't like him, but he seemed pleased. He looked down at his boots but didn't say anything else.

A little later Mary removed the padlocks from the doors of the three smaller cabins. They were identical, empty but for metal cots and bare, dusty mattresses. Roberto and I were told to share one, which fit with my understanding of my role here—to serve as my brother's babysitter. Mary and Tom would each have their own.

I assisted the two federal agents in humping duffel bags, metal suitcases, ice chests, and heavy rolls of black construction paper from the Suburban into the main cabin. It wasn't because I was all that eager to help, but because I was anxious to know just how their task force planned to use my brother's information to take down Jesús Hidalgo.

Mary armed herself with a bucket of bleach, took a deep breath, and headed for the bathroom. Using rubber mallets, Tom and I hammered sheets of tar paper over the windows and the places where we could feel the wind blowing through the log walls. We worked in silence, the two of us wordlessly agreeing that silence was probably the only way not to antagonize each other. When we were done Mary turned on the lights—three bare bulbs hung from rafters—and revealed a room that looked a little cozier, if dirtier, than it had in the

dark. We swept the room and wiped the surfaces. As a final
touch a heavy blanket was hung over the front door.

Now, even at night, there would be no sign that anybody
was using the old hunting camp. We were going to be like
ghosts.

THREE

"These are our operational rules, gentlemen," Mary announced.

She'd asked my brother to come in from the porch and then assembled us around one of the picnic tables. The table's rough surface was already cluttered with expanding files and a pair of laptop computers. She was standing at the end as if to deliver a lecture.

"We aren't going to take any unnecessary chances here. Stay off the ridges around the camp, and out of sight during the day if you hear a plane overhead. We'll use only our encrypted satellite phone, and you'll use it only with Tom or me monitoring. We don't want to risk being overheard—the bad guys have started using some pretty advanced technology. They have radio scanners and some equipment that can intercept both hard-line and cellular calls. The same goes for e-mail once we get the computers set up. No one will leave the property without checking with me first. Please don't use any lights at night other than in this cabin. We're to be invisible here. No one's to know this camp is occupied, especially not by us."

Her white blouse was streaked with dirt and her hair was

half in her face. I liked her better this way, dirty rather than
clean. I noticed that she didn't wear a wedding ring or jewelry
of any kind. She looked too young, too small, to be giving orders to the three of us—she couldn't be more than thirty years
old and she couldn't weigh much more than a hundred
pounds. Yet her voice was confident, and she was acting as if
she were speaking to a packed room of eager agents rather
than just her resentful partner, a semi-disgraced state cop, and
a drug-addicted felon.

"Am I forgetting anything, gentlemen?"

"Keep your badges shined up and the toilet seat down?"
Roberto suggested.

Mary's lips twitched into a tolerant smile. Tom remained
stone-faced.

"Where's the rest of your team?" I asked.

She looked at Tom, then at me.

"This is it, Agent Burns. The four of us. If we had any
more people here, we would be too conspicuous. That's where
we've failed in the past."

I knew something about the failures, despite not knowing
much more than the legends about Jesús Hidalgo. For ten
years he'd been responsible for a good portion of the almost
thirty billion dollars in narcotics coming into the States across
the Mexican border each year. For ten years the Feds had
failed to get an indictment against him, much less an arrest or
conviction. There were Mexican folk songs about Hidalgo,
narcocorridos of polkas or waltzes, that lionized his ability to
make fools of the American authorities.

"So exactly what is it we're doing here that would be too
conspicuous with more people?"

I'd assumed, ever since the FBI requested my assistance a
week earlier, that my brother would simply be giving up information about Hidalgo in return for the dismissal of the escape
charges in Colorado. And some time in a locked rehab facility,

of course. My job would be to help pull the information out of him and keep him under control. My office and I hadn't known that Jesús Hidalgo was even in my state, much less that the Feds would be taking my brother and me to the vicinity. And I was surprised by the equipment I'd helped lug into the main cabin—it was surveillance stuff, not just tape recorders and video cameras. Some weapons, too, I guessed, were in those locked steel suitcases.

"I'll get to that. But in short, we're going to arrest Hidalgo. Right here in Wyoming."

"Well, you'd better have some more guys when it comes to that," I laughed, not thinking she was serious. But she looked serious. "He's bound to have bodyguards, right? A lot of them, I bet."

Sicarios, they were called. A respectable drug lord never went anywhere without at least a handful.

Mary nodded. "He does. And we will. But first let's get some things out of the way."

She had planned this lecture out carefully, I realized, and knew exactly how she wanted it done. She might as well have had cheat notes in her hand.

"First, because for the next few weeks we'll be living in close proximity, I want to tell you a little bit about me and Tom and what our roles are here."

She told us that she had a law degree from American University and a master's in criminal justice from John Jay. She went on to say that she'd been with the Bureau for five years, and I figured that they must have been prodigious ones, because she was really young to be in charge of a case like this. Two years ago she had been assigned to the Bureau's San Diego office for the purpose of investigating the Baja cartels in conjunction with the DEA and the Mexican Attorney General's Office. Her job now, she said, would be to supervise our investigation as well as liaison with the prosecutors in the U.S. Attorney's Office.

All this, I thought as she spoke, was *not* to tell us anything about her, but instead to formalize her. To let us know that she didn't want Roberto or me to know anything about her other than her professional résumé. A wall was being very deliberately erected.

She indicated Tom, her partner, with a nod of her head. He was listening to her with his arms folded across his chest.

"Tom has been with that same task force for five years. Prior to that, he worked in El Paso and Juárez. There he worked to secure indictments against Amado Carrillo-Fuentes, the head of the Juárez cartel, who you may have heard of, and the men and women he employed. Carrillo was known as the Lord of the Skies because of the fleet of passenger jets he used to bring cocaine into our country. Tom was also able to get indictments against several of his lieutenants, two of whom were brought in the backseat of his personal vehicle into the United States, where they were arrested."

I'd heard about that. It had caused an international stink several years ago when the two Mexican nationals were more or less kidnapped from the streets of Juárez then driven across the bridge to El Paso, where they were arrested, tried, convicted, and jailed. The Mexican government had been furious. So had been many American legislators. While Tom was completely lacking in social graces, I had to admit that he had balls.

Mary continued: "Tom went to school at Rutgers in New Jersey and spent two years with the New Jersey State Police, and another two with the DEA, before joining the Bureau. Tom is going to be in charge of the operational end of things."

No advanced educational degrees for Tom. He must not have any, which didn't really mean anything anyway for a cop. Not when it came to ability. But I guessed it was why Mary had been able to countermand him and give Roberto and me time to stop and do a little climbing. It also explained his slightly hostile attitude toward Mary giving him orders. A law degree would go a long way in a place like the Bureau. And it could create a lot of resentment.

I was suitably impressed, though, with his accomplishments in El Paso and Juárez, which were almost as bad and dangerous a posting as Tijuana or Mexicali. Clearly the guy was experienced. And Carrillo had been a bad guy on nearly the same level as Hidalgo before he had died: I'd read about him in *The New York Times*. The two had been rivals for a couple of years, Carrillo heading the Juárez cartel and Hidalgo the Mexicali Mafia. The narco from Juárez—worth billions of dollars, and made nervous by the kidnapping and arrest of the two lieutenants—had accidently died while undergoing plastic surgery and liposuction in Mexico City. But his face was a mass of ham-handed stitches—it seemed unlikely real doctors would have committed such butchery. It was rumored that his enemy, Hidalgo, had been one of the masked "surgeons." If Tom ever dropped his tough-guy act, I intended to ask him about it.

Now Mary looked at my brother. I realized she was going to introduce him, too. As if she and Tom hadn't already read everything in his files, as if I weren't his brother. I wondered if she had a file on Mungo.

"You never attended college, did you, Roberto?"

"Nope. I'm a little dumb," he answered, his slightly slurred voice registering amusement at what was obviously a setup.

Mary delivered it. "But a graduate of the Colorado Bureau of Prisons and the federal penitentiary all the same."

Roberto smiled for her and exhaled a polite laugh while I tried not to roll my eyes.

She went on. "One conviction for manslaughter, three for felony assault, two for disorderly conduct, one for assault on a peace officer, and one federal conviction for the destruction of communications equipment. Is that right?"

"Bastards shouldn't have taken so long to put in my phone."

Mary actually smiled at this. It was the first real smile I'd seen break across her face. She had his file in her hand—she picked it up off the table while she was talking—so she had to know that it wasn't a joke. It really was the reason he'd taken a chain saw to six miles of telephone poles.

Tom, of course, only snorted with contempt.

Then Mary made clear her reason for reciting Roberto's criminal history.

"Currently wanted for escape in Colorado, with nationwide warrants out and extradition to be sought from all treaty nations. And a Justice Department authorization to remove him from noncooperating nations by whatever means necessary."

In other words, they owned him as long as he cared about not having to watch his back for the rest of his life.

Mary now looked at me, saying, "Over the last two weeks your brother has been kind enough to provide us with some very useful background on Hidalgo. He knows more about our target's methods of operation than anyone we've yet been able to, uh, interview."

I wanted to say something, to object, but I didn't yet know what I should be objecting to. I just had the feeling that she was trying to sell me something with all this. Everything she said felt so carefully scripted.

She started in on me before I could get anything out. Introducing me to Roberto and Tom now, like we'd never met.

"Special Agent Antonio Burns of the Wyoming Bureau of Investigation—you prefer Anton, right?"

"Yeah."

She had a file on me, too. It was a manila folder expanded to nearly three inches wide from the morass of well-thumbed documents within. Newspaper clippings as well, I could see. A fat rubber band kept it from exploding in her hands. As she had with Roberto, she now talked about me without referring to it other than to simply hold it. Like she was holding my soul or something.

"Anton also has a master's in criminal justice, from the University of Colorado. He has been a narcotics officer with the Wyoming Division of Criminal Investigation for eight years, primarily working undercover. He has been involved in some very colorful cases."

"Colorful," Tom said, speaking slowly and deliberately. "If your favorite color is red. I know all I want to know about *you*. I had to work with assholes like you in Mexico."

Time seemed to stall. A silence that lasted several seconds dropped over us. I could feel my brother's blue eyes on me, asking, *What you gonna do, Ant?*

I leaned across the table. "What have you heard about me, Tom?"

And I immediately wished I hadn't.

Tom leaned across, too, as if to meet my aggressive posture head-on. He didn't hesitate this time, the way he had earlier when he'd tried to put Roberto in his place. I had the feeling I didn't make him nearly as nervous as my brother did.

"That two and a half years ago you killed three men in cold blood. That they call you QuickDraw around here because you'd rather pull a trigger than make arrests. That you've been investigated for—"

"Tom!" Mary said sharply. "We've been over this. The shooting was ruled justifiable. Anton was exonerated—"

"By his own office. A bunch of hick cowboys. No one with any real investigative experience. We looked at their reports—and they were a total whitewash. Complete bullshit. They just took his word for it."

I wondered how many times that night in Cheyenne was going to come back to haunt me. At one point in my life I'd been ready to beat the crap out of anyone who repeated the scornful nickname. It had been invented by a newspaper columnist whose son I'd once arrested for selling ecstasy. But now I felt very little. Not even the righteous indignation I tried to put in my posture and gaze. Just weariness. And the growing suspicion that for some reason the two federal agents were putting on a show.

"Tom, we've been over it. Our superiors have been over it. The U.S. Attorney's been over it. It was decided that we could work with Agent Burns and his brother. Now, if you don't want to be a part of this, just say so right now and we'll get someone else in here to take your place."

Tom glared at her briefly then snorted.

"Not likely," he said. He didn't elaborate.

Instead he lit a Marlboro with a hard snap of a silver lighter and blew the smoke in her direction. I'd been watching him smoke them all day in the rearview mirror as he tailgated me, then watched him flick them out into the desert.

I thought it was interesting that Mary didn't contradict his statement. Surely there were hundreds, if not thousands, of agents who would love to be in on taking down a guy the size of Jesús Hidalgo. Who would love to avenge their murdered colleague. As much as I disliked the uptight Feds, no one could accuse the individual agents of ever being cowardly.

But Mary just fanned the smoke away. Her expression was neutral, sphinxlike, but as she stared at Tom, I thought I could see a dark spot of anger on each of her cheeks. Maybe he had stepped beyond their script, if they had one, or taken it a little too far. I wondered what was between them. What were they really up to, playing this game.

"All right, then," Mary said, her coffee-brown eyes barely visible between her heavy lids. "Tonight we'll finish unpacking the gear and setting up a surveillance point on the ridge. Tomorrow we'll start the surveillance. Tom, why don't you give us a briefing on our location here."

With sharp, curt gestures intended to display his annoyance, he unzipped a nylon briefcase and took out a large piece of paper. Unfolded on the table, it proved to be a color photograph of the area in the daylight. He spoke through the cigarette clenched in his teeth.

"All right. Listen up. We had a satellite company out of Colorado take a digital picture for us from four hundred and twenty-three miles up. Here's where we're at, and here's Hidalgo's place. That so-called town we drove through, Potash, is eight miles to the southeast."

Our little crater with its five buildings stood just to the west of a wide red river. The buildings were little more than square-shaped pinpricks. Roan River was shown as being maybe a quarter-inch wide, which translated on the map to almost a hundred yards, just on the other side of the hogback ridge behind us. On the other bank, a little to the north, was a U-shaped building and two long rectangles.

The U-shaped building, we were told through a haze of smoke, was Hidalgo's residential compound on the bank of the river. It consisted of a single sprawling house set around a turquoise swimming pool—an unusual luxury in Wyoming and something that must be enormously expensive to heat and clean. The house and the pool overlooked the river. The two long rectangles, farther away from the reddish stripe of water and maybe a half-mile from the house, were two trailers. These had once housed miners, but were now inhabited by Hidalgo's bodyguards. The mine was nearby, evidenced by an acre or more of broken stone that had been dragged out of the earth.

Tom pointed out the silver roof of another trailer—this one far smaller—that was nestled in some trees south of the whole complex and alongside the only road that led into it. We were told men with automatic weapons were almost certainly watching the road twenty-four hours a day.

"What's he doing operating a mine here?" I asked.

"Laundering money, we think," Mary said. "Or setting it up so that he can launder money. The mine has been abandoned for years, but we have some satellite pictures that show him moving trucks and machines into the mine. Things have been getting a little hot for him in Mexico, too. There have been a lot of killings lately, and the new government under Vicente Fox has once again sworn to eradicate the past decades of corruption that have allowed the cartels to flourish. They have even been making some noise about shutting down the tourist hotels and pharmacies Hidalgo's been using to legitimize his illicit proceeds."

That brought me to one of the questions that had been bugging me all along.

"What the hell's he doing in Wyoming?"

"His old buddies down in Baja have been trying to knock him off," Tom said, looking at the map, not me. "The survivors of his wars with Carrillo in Juárez and the Arellano-Felix brothers in Tijuana have gotten sick of Hidalgo's thugs pushing them around and taxing them. Plus the boys operating out of Sonora and Tamaulipas think he's too greedy and too ambitious. Everyone's gunning for each other. A couple of hundred have died this year already. Mostly soldiers, but a few big boys and even some of Hidalgo's hired judges and politicians. It's a war zone. So Hidalgo, no fool, has come north to sit it out for a while. Until his hired guns can find and finish taking out the last of the Arellanos and their politicos in Baja. Then he'll finally have a secure hold there."

I'd read about the drug war in Baja, but thought it was pretty much over. Hidalgo and his Mexicali Mafia had won against the Arellano-Felixes, just as they'd partially dismantled the Juárez cartel by taking out Amado Carrillo. Of the several Arellano-Felix brothers who had operated out of Tijuana, one was believed to be dead and one was in Mexican custody. They'd been put in their respective places by Hidalgo and his legion of *sicarios* and bribed Mexican justice officials.

The news of government corruption in Mexico was something that didn't surprise me. Past presidents had been proven corrupt, as had army generals and, recently, a former Attorney General himself. A few years ago a top law-enforcement official testified to the Mexican Congress that up to eighty percent of police officers, prosecutors, and judges were in the employ of the cartels. The DEA put the number at closer to ninety percent. Presidente Fox admitted that the pervasive influence of dirty money had infected law-enforcement organizations throughout the country. It was a country where every time a new drug-fighting agency was created, it was shut down within a year or two for rampant corruption. Mexico's unofficial motto was *Plata o plomo*—"Silver or lead"—as in *You can take my money or you can eat a bullet.*

I'd spent much of my childhood on Grandfather's *estancia* in Argentina and knew that Latin "government" was often merely a commodity, something that was bought and sold. Politicos like my notorious grandfather left office either rich or dead.

"But why here? Why Wyoming?"

Tom allowed himself a bitter chuckle and looked across at me.

"To enjoy our nation's constitutional protections, Quick-Draw. Its police and its laws. Formal procedures like arrest warrants and Miranda rights, and cops who are straight, who execute warrants and not their suspects. Most of the time, anyway," he said, giving me a significant and nasty look. "Plus, this lovely state of yours has no income tax. Maybe Hidalgo's thinking about applying for residency. He should fit right in."

"Maybe we should tell Agent Burns a little bit more about him," Mary said.

"I'd appreciate that," I snapped at Tom. God, the guy was a prick.

Until a few weeks ago, when I'd learned from Roberto about his deal with the Feds, I hadn't been entirely sure that Hidalgo wasn't just another myth. Like the *chupacabra,* the goat-sucking demon that had much of Latin America terrified a few years back.

Tom produced a single piece of white cardboard from his briefcase. He slapped it down on the table in front of me, over the map. It was an enlargement of a passport photo. I could tell because of the dark ridges where the stamp had been.

"This is the best one we have," Mary said. "With a little luck, in the next couple of days we'll get something a lot better."

The photograph, grainy from the enlargement, portrayed a chubby, dapper-looking man in a suit and tie. He was smiling easily at the camera from beneath a Saddam Hussein–style mustache. His longish hair was slicked back but not so much as to make him appear a greaser. He was handsome, but plain. Nothing like what I expected, not some red-eyed and dripping-fanged devil. But on closer examination, I saw that his eyes were bright and hard. They stared straight at the camera—straight through it. The eyes gave me the creeps. Although I'd done a hundred undercover investigations against suspects whose photos I'd studied, I already felt more than a little exposed.

"He's gotten fat," Roberto commented, glancing at the picture. "Serves him right. Guy always ate like a pig. Eats those Twinkie things—*Gansitos*—all day long."

"Tell me what you know about him," I said to Mary.

Mary closed her eyes for a moment, as if preparing for a recitation. When she opened them she spoke quickly.

"From what our task force has pieced together over the years, and from what, in the last two weeks, we've learned from your brother—"

"Which is suspect," Tom interjected. "To say the least."

Roberto only raised his eyebrows as he fingered the leather cord around his neck.

Mary continued, "Jesús Ruiz Hidalgo-Paez, also known as El Doctor because of the chain of pharmacies he owns, was born in 1965 in Culiacán, the capital of the western state of Sinaloa. It was and still is something of a bandit state, where many of the citizens worship a thief who was hung there by the Mexican army in 1909."

I'd seen the medallions hanging from the necks of the transporters we occasionally arrested as they drove through Wyoming on I-80. The highway was the principal way Mexican narcotics were moved across the border from the Southwest to the East Coast. Malverde, I remembered, was the name of the mustachioed saint I'd seen depicted in swinging gold. Supposedly he was some kind of Robin Hood, and in recent years he'd been adopted as saint by the narcos.

"His family was what passes in Mexico for middle class, his father being some kind of minor government functionary. When he was seventeen, Hidalgo began working for a man named Rafael Caro-Quintero, one of the country's earliest large-scale traffickers. He's now in prison, by the way, in part for the murder of a DEA agent, one of only two American cops the cartels have dared touch."

I nodded. I'd heard about that. And I knew the second cop had been their colleague, but I wasn't ready to talk about him yet. "About fifteen years ago, right?"

Tom spoke before she could confirm my recollection.

"Quintero *runs* the prison. At least when he's not partying back in Sinaloa, on parole. He keeps African lions there. He likes to entertain his party guests by throwing suspected informants into the pen with them."

Mary continued her recitation as if neither one of us had spoken.

"Hidalgo started out as a sort of minor bagman for

Quintero. He paid out the bribes to the local politicians and law enforcement. He was apparently good at this, because soon Quintero was flying him to Mexico City to make the pay-offs there, too. After a while Quintero discovered an additional job for his protégé; he made Hidalgo his chief enforcer. Even when he was only twenty years old, Hidalgo understood better than anyone the power of fear and brutality. He capitalized on it, taking it to a level far beyond anything Mexico had yet seen. He earned a very serious reputation. And this made him even more popular and more effective as a bagman in Mexico City."

Mary went on to explain how at the age of twenty-six, Hidalgo was permitted to start his own trafficking operation provided he pay a tax to Quintero's successor, his brother Miguel. This was at a time when American law enforcement was finally shutting down the air trafficking from Colombia via the Caribbean and had put a stop to the Juárez cartel's fleet of 727s that flew as far north as Manhattan. The method Hidalgo used was simpler. Young illegal immigrants—mostly just kids in their teens and early twenties—entering the U.S. anyway were paid anywhere from a hundred to a thousand dollars to carry fifty-pound packs of cocaine with them. With thousands of people crossing daily, all of them desperate for a few dollars, he had no trouble finding eager recruits. And if some were caught by La Migra—the INS—it was no problem for Hidalgo. Profits were so enormous that he could afford to lose ten loads for every one that got through. Later he upped the quantity by loading trucks with cocaine and heroin, then bribing American border guards to wave them through. The low-paid officers had a hard time resisting a twenty-thousand-dollar payment for simply waving a certain truck through. Especially when the alternative—for refusing the offer—might be death.

Hidalgo was innovative in another way, too. Instead of working for the Colombians, where nearly all cocaine comes from, Hidalgo bought it from them directly. He had it transferred onto fishing vessels and speedboats out near the Galápagos Islands then brought north thirty-seven hundred miles into the Sea of Cortés. It was trucked in to the border town of Mexicali, where it was cut and processed and then smuggled through the desert.

His success angered the Tijuana cartel being run by the Arellano-Felix brothers. They claimed all of Baja, and believed that Hidalgo needed to pay them a tax, too. Hidalgo refused. Soon he was also refusing to pay Quintero, his former mentor.

"Starting about ten years ago, the other cartels began using all their pull with the government to get Hidalgo arrested," she said. "There have been several attempts, but each time the judge who signed the indictment was murdered within twenty-four hours. So the established cartels began kidnapping Hidalgo's men in the hopes of hijacking his operations. They tortured his lieutenants and other flunkies but discovered only a single amazing fact: Hidalgo's men wouldn't talk. Their loyalty to Hidalgo was fanatical. The reason soon became apparent. If anyone was even suspected of talking, his entire family would be killed. Everyone, from grandparents to grandchildren to distant cousins. A whole extended family, wiped out."

I looked at my brother, wondering if he'd known about this when he knew Hidalgo. Wondering, also, if it was such a good idea for him to be talking about the narco.

"This true, 'Berto?"

"Yeah. Probably." He shrugged. "I heard the rumors, but never saw anything like that. Jesús denied it when I asked him about it. When I started to think maybe it might be true, I split."

Tom snorted again derisively. Disbelieving.

But I believed my brother. Roberto had always been passionately intolerant of abuses against women, children, and dogs. It's what had caused him to kill a man in a bar in Colorado, and thus earn a manslaughter conviction. The man had stuck his hand up the dress of a young woman Roberto was with. Once, with me at a sidewalk café in Boulder many years ago, he'd broken the nose of a Denver news anchor who'd slapped a woman. He'd only gotten a misdemeanor assault charge out of that one.

"All I did was some guiding for him," Roberto continued. "You know, taking mules—the kids with backpacks—through the desert in Arizona and California. They were dying like flies from the heat and lack of water. Plus they were getting ambushed by guys from other cartels, and those gringo vigilante ranchers."

I could picture it: Roberto showing a bunch of hardscrabble kids how to live off the land while avoiding all the desert's dangers, not to mention the authorities. Leading them through the wilderness like a manic messiah. He would have thought it was fun. For a while, anyway. Until he learned just how vicious his employer could be.

"Hidalgo's signature, by the way," Mary said, getting us back on track, "is a little something he borrowed from his colleagues in Bogotá. There it's called the Colombian Necktie. The narcos slit an informant's throat and pull the tongue out through the wound. Only in Mexico it's called *la corbata de Jesús,* after Hidalgo. The Colombians generally shoot their victims first. Hidalgo likes for them to drown on their own blood."

She resumed her lecturing tone.

"Over the last ten years Jesús Hidalgo has become the leading importer of Colombian cocaine into the United States. We, along with the DEA, estimate that Hidalgo is responsible for something like a quarter of what enters our country from the Southwest border region. After more than twelve assassination attempts that we know about, Hidalgo bought this property in Wyoming as a sort of safe house." She pointed at a window freshly covered by tar paper at the rear of the room. "Not in his own name, of course, but in the name of one of his attorneys. As Tom said, he's protected here by all the liberties and rules of our laws. Because of the layers and layers of lieutenants he uses, their absolute loyalty, and the simple genius with which he covers his tracks, we don't have enough evidence to even get a search warrant, much less an indictment."

It was hard to believe that such a man could be living free and safe here in Wyoming. In *my* state. A state where I was a drug-enforcement officer.

"You haven't been able to turn any of his employees, or get an informant in there?" I asked.

"We had one who did get close," Mary said quietly. "A rookie agent. Tom and I were very involved in supporting him. Hidalgo somehow came to suspect him and had him killed. Two months ago in Mexicali."

"La corbata?" I asked.

She nodded.

This, I realized, was the dead FBI agent my brother had alluded to on the road. The one I'd read about in the papers, but hadn't really thought much about. The necktied agent had probably been their friend. Now he had a proximity to me, too. Now he was real. The second American cop the cartels had dared to touch. It struck me not just as murder, but as a war crime in the so-called War on Drugs. It made me feel both sick and enraged to think of that being done to anyone, especially a cop. And I realized why the FBI wanted Hidalgo so badly that they were willing to put up with my brother.

But I still didn't know why Roberto was putting up with them.

In a low voice, and for once without rancor, Tom added, "His mother and stepfather were both killed in Newark six weeks ago. A home invasion gone bad, the local police say. A sibling in Los Angeles was found with his tongue on his chest last week. The two sisters are with federal marshals right now, and they didn't even know their brother was working drugs for us."

"As for traditional confidential informants, none of the smugglers or dealers we've arrested has been willing to talk," Mary said. "No matter what sort of concessions we offer. We've even tried offering dismissal of all charges, a hefty reward, and a place in the Witness Protection Program for them and their entire extended families. Not a single one of them has been willing to take that kind of a gamble."

This explained all the surveillance equipment I'd helped carry into the lodge. They were going to try another way in.

"I know I'm just supposed to be your local connection," I said, not mentioning the obvious other job of bird-dogging Roberto while they pump him for information. "But what else can I do? What's the plan here?"

"Your primary duty will be to set up and monitor various clandestine drops in town," Mary said. "We understand that some of Hidalgo's men go in almost every night, and you'll be better suited for checking the drops than any of us will."

That was certainly true. Neither Mary, a young Chinese woman, nor a New Jersey asshole/wannabe cowboy like Tom would be likely to pass unnoticed in Potash. The town did have, though, a large and itinerant Hispanic population. Because of my mixed blood and languages, and because I'd spent most of my career working in Wyoming under various covers, I was the logical choice.

"So you *do* have an informant?" I asked, surprised.

Mary looked at me and then away, the way someone does when they're ashamed of something. She looked to where Roberto was bent over on the bench, his back to us, as he massaged Mungo's lanky hips.

"We will soon," she said.

FOUR

It was almost four in the morning when Roberto slipped out of the cabin we were sharing. If he hadn't been betrayed by the rusty hinges on the door, I wouldn't have heard anything at all. I slept lightly, but I'd somehow missed the hiss of skin writhing out of a sleeping bag and the sound of bare feet padding across the plank floor. My brother moved like a phantom when he wanted to. It was strange, though, that Mungo hadn't made a sound.

I pushed a button on my watch so that I could read the oversized display.

Three-fifty-eight.

The watch was a Suunto altimeter, and it was nearly twice the size of an ordinary wristwatch. I wore it even though it was big and clunky and couldn't be worn with a suit when I had to appear in court. It had been a Christmas gift from Mom and Dad nine months ago. Roberto wore one just like it, also scarred with gouges and scratches. That was why I wore mine—a little bit of big-brother worship.

Not for the first time I wondered if my regard for my brother was misplaced. Roberto and the FBI were putting not just him but our whole family in a lot of danger. If Jesús

Hidalgo figured out that Roberto was an informant before he could be arrested, we'd all be wearing bull's-eyes on our backs. Or, more specifically, around our throats. It wouldn't matter that Mom and Dad were a continent away, retired and living in self-imposed exile in Argentina. Hidalgo's reach into South America was probably even stronger than it was in the States.

But along with trepidation and fear, what I mainly felt was a thrill. Like when I was high on the rock, running out of gear, and knowing that every move up into the sky would increase the risk of a major fall. I knew too well I wasn't invincible, and that knowledge usually only increased the sweet rush of adrenaline. But I realized I had to make very sure that this operation didn't fail like all our government's previous attempts to indict and arrest the Mexican narco king.

I held the watch low to the floor and pushed the button again. The blue glow was reflected in Mungo's eyes.

She was awake, had heard my brother getting up, but instead of standing and snuffling a warning, she'd remained immobile, as if conspiring to give Roberto a clean getaway. I brushed the top of her bony skull with my knuckles.

"You little bitch," I murmured to her. "Who feeds you? Who takes care of your every need?"

Her tail guiltily swept the floor.

I sat up in my bag and looked out the dirty window. The camp was lit by starlight so bright that it cast faint shadows from the buildings and the trees.

He wasn't out smoking on the porch. He wasn't anywhere I could see. The wind had died and the crater was as still as a painting. I watched for a while, shivering, thinking maybe a ghost would come gliding out from behind one of the buildings. But nothing moved.

I knew that Tom Cochran was out there somewhere, too. Huddled in camouflage clothing up on the ridge above us and peering through the telescopic lens of the camera he'd lugged up that way. Maybe even listening to the directional microphone I'd watched him unpack in the main cabin.

I didn't get up to raise an alarm. Where would he go? Back to exile in South America? Back to being hunted? The Feds hadn't bothered to handcuff him because there was no point in restraints. If he wasn't going to cooperate fully then he wasn't any use to them at all. The operation would be over. And these were Feds, after all—they couldn't care less about the Colorado state escape charges.

I hoped he'd run. But I knew it wasn't likely. He'd already made up his mind.

For a moment I worried that my brother was out there stalking Tom, up on the ridge. A physical confrontation between one of the Burns brothers and the surly Fed was probably inevitable. But I dismissed that concern, too, since Roberto, for whatever reason, seemed to have taken a pass on earlier opportunities to beat the shit out of Tom. I knew that he wouldn't seek some kind of payback in the dark. It wasn't his way. I guessed the chore of straightening out Tom— through charm or violence—would be up to me.

But I needed to be smart about it. I couldn't blow this operation. For my brother and his deal, for the family's safety, and also because it was likely to be the biggest case I'd ever work on. It was my chance to use the law to do some real good by ridding the world of Jesús Hidalgo.

And that was my way. That was why I'd become a cop. To enforce the rule of law. Not only the written law, but the laws of any civilized society, too. The laws that allowed people to live together and interact peacefully. Deliberate rudeness was almost as intolerable to me as selling meth to schoolkids. Even the sight of someone intentionally running a red light or cutting off another car had the potential to make the blood roar in my ears. What made them think they were so superior? What made them think they could get away with it?

Yet I could be as bad as any of them.

I'd already broken one rule that night. A breach of security that I'd be furious about if it had been committed by Tom or anyone else.

My transgression was to make a telephone call. Without a monitor, and without Mary's permission, although I took the precaution of borrowing the encrypted satellite phone from the pile of gear before walking out into the night. Tom and Mary were busy going through papers and studying maps. They didn't notice me take it and head outside. I wandered up the dirt road toward the gate.

The call had been to Rebecca Hersh, my sometimes fiancée and the mother of my unborn child.

"Anton! How's the new gig?" Rebecca had asked in a light tone. "This thing with your crazy brother?"

I measured her voice for clues, knowing that she hated my job. And that she felt threatened by my brother. The two combined had not made for the greatest of good-byes when I'd left her loft in Denver two days earlier.

I considered lying, but that was a route I was incapable of taking with her, both practically and morally. She was a reporter and could scent untruths better than most cops. And although I could lie my ass off all day and night when working undercover, to lie to her would be like bringing the world of gangbangers and dealers into her bed.

"Things are a little fucked up," I admitted. "The Feds are pretty uptight, their strategy is a risky one, and they're treating me like a head case. But it will work out all right."

"Risky for who?" The light tone was gone. "Are you safe?"

"Yeah. Of course. I couldn't be any safer. Mungo's looking out for me, you know."

"Seriously?"

"Seriously, Rebecca. It's cool. This is a surveillance job for me. No heavy lifting. But they're going to be putting Roberto out on the edge."

"That's where he likes it, isn't it?" she asked rhetorically, her tone a little tight now, the way it got on the occasions when my brother's name came up.

She didn't ask for more details, knowing that I couldn't answer. Even if she weren't a reporter, I still wouldn't tell her the details. Not because I didn't trust her, but because just like lying to her, it would be bringing it too close to home.

"How's our little girl?" I asked.

I imagined putting my head against Rebecca's warm little belly and listening for the beat of a tiny heart.

"No kicking yet. How come you're so sure it's a girl?"

"My mom. When I last talked to her, she'd been working the tarot cards."

Rebecca laughed. "I dig your mom. She's the only one in the family with any sense. I can't imagine how she puts up with you maniacs, your father included."

"I know she likes you. And that's saying something. Latino mamas don't often go for Jewish gringo girls. They don't want their fine, upstanding sons corrupted by all that big-city liberalness. But she knows you kick my ass, and she's lived with Dad long enough to know a lot of that's needed."

She laughed again. "You're telling me, Anton. So how's our big girl? Are you taking care of her?"

I looked around for Mungo and caught a silver flash in the moonlight. She was halfway up one of the slopes that ringed the camp. Her head was buried in a hole large enough to take her up to her shoulders—all I could see was a madly waving tail. Dirt flew out from between her legs.

"She's doing all right, as long as she doesn't wake up the badger she's after. I think she likes being back in Wyoming.

She doesn't keep her tail between her legs all the time the way she does in Denver."

"Poor thing. She has an awful self-image. She thinks people cross the street because she's ugly. She doesn't know it's because she's big and beautiful."

"Just like you."

"Ha. I weighed myself today. I finally gained a couple of pounds, and I think I'm starting to show. I've cut way back on the running."

"Good. Anyone giving you grief about being an unwed mother?"

"Don't start, Anton."

The playfulness had left her voice. A minute or two later we said good-bye.

My proposal had been accepted a couple of months earlier, but was then left hanging. It hadn't been made in the most auspicious circumstances. I'd gotten down on my knees on top of a ridge high above a forest fire, just minutes after watching the arsonist topple off a cliff to his death. The only witnesses had been Mungo and a naked B-movie actor who'd been trying very hard at the time to cuckold me. As I probably should have expected from such a start to an engagement, no date had yet been set.

Sitting up in my sleeping bag and still looking out the window, I recalled the entire conversation again and tried to gauge what the strain in her voice at the end had meant. Was she reconsidering her acceptance?

Nothing moved out there in the night. What the hell was Roberto doing? Shivering a little, my teeth close to chattering, I finally lay back down and zipped up the bag. I wouldn't get up and look for him. Maybe he'd managed to smuggle a little treat past the Feds. Maybe he was out there shooting up—howling at the moon, he called it. It was something I didn't want to see.

I fell back asleep trying very hard not to worry about both my brother and Rebecca.

When I woke up there was a ray of dusty light cutting through the small cabin. Roberto lay directly in its path, his face half hidden by his hair. He'd thrown the upper half of his bag off his chest despite the morning chill. He was breathing heavily, definitely asleep. I watched him for a minute.

He looked more vulnerable than I'd ever remembered seeing him. Muscular and powerful still, but diminished somehow. Maybe from the two years he'd spent caged before his escape—his longest stretch. Maybe from too many years on the literal edge. Or maybe it was just my imagination, sparked by having seen him submit to the Feds. But whatever caused it, it made me sad. The leather cord was tight around his throat like a collar, the turquoise stone looking back at me like a third eye. I examined what I could see of his bronzed, bare skin for a fresh scab and didn't find one.

Mungo was awake on her blanket below me. Every time I moved, her tail swished two or three times across the floor.

I could smell myself as I sat up in my bag. The sweet scent of yesterday's sun, wind, and sweat had been turned sour after a night wrapped in clammy down. Mungo leapt to her feet when I reached down and tapped her head. She danced over to the door, her tail wagging furiously now. I shucked the bag, put on a pair of baggy shorts, found a towel, then let her out.

I meant to take a shower in the main cabin's bathroom. But on the way there the sight of the ribs of sandstone on the crater's slopes pulled at me the same way the thorny weeds were tugging at my trailing shoelaces. I veered up toward them.

The rock walls lined the hillside in broken, irregular rows. Some of them stood as high as thirty feet and were as long as one hundred, and many of them were vertical or overhanging.

Between them were slopes of cactus, yellow sage, red dirt, and short, twisted junipers. There was also a trail of fresh-turned dirt winding up to a sheltered notch in the ridge. It was where Tom had lugged his surveillance gear last night. I decided to stay away from there—it was too nice a morning to risk running into that asshole. Instead I chose a rock on the southwest side of the crater where the early light was turning the sandstone into gold.

For a half hour I traversed the rock. Back and forth, finding small holds for my fingertips and the inside edges of my big toes. I stayed low, not venturing more than ten or fifteen feet off the deck. Going above that would be highballing, entering what's called the coffin zone, where a fall is likely to be fatal. It's an area I thought of as my brother's province, not mine.

I worked up a new sweat, feeling the familiar burn of lactic acid in my forearms, shoulders, and calves, feeling the muscles tear so that they could grow back stronger, and working out the sadness that had come over me as I watched my brother sleep. The air was very still—rare for Wyoming—and it was cold on my bare skin when I moved, then warm when I stopped.

"What are you doing?"

I looked down and behind me. Mary Chang was standing at the base of the wall, blowing on a cup of coffee she held with both hands.

"Just bouldering around," I told her.

"Why?"

"Training. You've got to do it to stay strong." I paused to look at her again over my shoulder. "And when you're feeling pissed off, it lets you work out your frustration."

Then I moved sideways, swinging lightly on the tiny holds, diagonaling down low enough so that I could drop to the ground without landing on a cactus or a sharp stone with my bare feet. I was embarrassed to be caught half-naked and spread-eagled on the rock. I was also annoyed.

"Do you do this every day?" she asked.

"I try to do something."

"It looks like a good way to break an ankle."

"Better than getting fed to a guy like Jesús Hidalgo."

On the ground now, the air immediately began chilling the sweat on my skin. I touched my hands together and bent them back in a praying motion to relieve the acid buildup while I glared at her.

She looked warm in a red fleece jacket. But like me she was wearing shorts, knowing what the day would be like later. Her legs were thin and smooth as butter. She'd obviously just showered, as her wet hair was pulled back into a ponytail. It steamed a little, like the coffee cup she held an inch from her lips as she blew on it. She looked no more than sixteen.

For a minute I could picture her as a young girl: very smart, very disciplined, very formal outside of the home to cover up for what I suspected was a deep-seated shyness. An only child, I was willing to bet. Her parents must have been puzzled by her career choice. I wasn't. What better way to make up for social awkwardness than to carry a badge and a gun?

"There's more coffee in the lodge. I made a full pot."

"That was decent of you."

"Come on, Anton. We're here to do something important. I know you local guys don't like the FBI coming into your territory and telling you what to do, but—"

"No. That's not it. What I don't like is the way you're using my brother. Sending him in there like . . . What's the expression? Like a sacrificial sheep? A sheep to the slaughter?"

"I think it's a lamb." She smiled over her cup. "And you can hardly describe Roberto as a lamb."

You're wrong, I thought.

Mungo, who had been hiding behind a bush where she was

playing her favorite game of You-can't-see-me-because-I'm-a-wolf, came out hesitantly and walked toward Mary and me. Her lips were lifted in her nervous grin—she probably sensed my anger and thought I was mad at her. When she hid like that I was supposed to call her name while looking around wildly, confused as to how she'd managed to disappear so completely.

Mary backed away uneasily. Mungo sidestepped around her, giving her plenty of room, and bumped her head against my thigh.

"You aren't afraid of dogs, are you?" I asked.

"No. Well, yes, I am a little. She's a lot bigger than what I'm used to. I used to have one but he only weighed five pounds."

"Are you sure it was a dog?"

This earned me a smile not unlike Mungo's. I felt myself starting to become a little bit likable, and I wasn't sure I wanted to be likable yet. I swung my arms in circles then arched my back to touch my toes. I spoke to my ankles.

"What's on the agenda for Day One, Agent Chang?"

Like last night, Mary had a mental checklist prepared.

"We're going to make sure we know everything about Jesús Hidalgo that Roberto can tell us. What he thinks, what his habits are, who he trusts and why. Then we're going to work up a way for Roberto to explain how come he'll be knocking on El Doctor's door after all these years. We already have some ideas about that. Later, we need you to go into town and set up a drop at one of the places where Hidalgo's men like to go. Someplace inconspicuous where Roberto can leave us a message. We also need to set up some kind of signal, some way Roberto can let us know if he's in trouble so that we can get him out if we need to. His safety, of course, is our first priority."

Right.

I stood up and let her read the disbelief on my face. She

had the grace to flush but also the intelligence not to try to either convince me otherwise or defend herself.

"Where's your partner?" I finally asked.

"He's up on the ridge. It's where he spent most of the night, I expect."

"The guy's a walking hard-on."

She smiled at the image. I almost smiled myself. It really fit him pretty well.

"He's not that bad, Anton. I've worked with him for two years now, and trust me, he's a thorough professional. He's just taken what happened to our colleague in Mexicali very hard. We both have. But Tom especially."

"Why him especially?"

She hesitated for a moment. The moment became so long that I thought she might have decided not to tell me something personal about her partner. I whistled for Mungo and started to walk back down the hill toward the lodge when her voice stopped me.

"They were close. Tom and the young agent who was killed. And a few months before what happened in Mexicali, Tom's half sister died of an overdose. She was a heroin addict, and they were estranged. But still, it was very rough on him. He'd been running his own side investigation, you see. Seeing where she got her stuff. Somehow he'd managed to trace it—through its chemical composition—all the way back to a truckload of Hidalgo's product that had been confiscated by the DEA. Then it was given to an undercover agent in Baltimore, who was working a gang thing there. This undercover agent sold it to some of the people he was trying to get to know and build a case against, and they eventually sold five grams to Tom's sister. Anyway, it's likely it all started with Hidalgo, even if, from a legal point of view, the evidence is tenuous at best. But sometimes that doesn't mean it's not true."

What she said at the end made me consider her again for

a moment. I wondered if there might be more to her than what I'd seen over the last twenty-four hours. It was possible that she wasn't such a rigid professional after all.

After showering, I locked Mungo in the cabin with my still-sleeping brother. I studied the sky dutifully before heading up for the ridge. There were no planes. Not even any contrails from high-flying cross-country passenger jets. The sky was completely cloudless and Wyoming blue.

The slope leading up to the ridge was about three hundred feet high and angled back at about forty-five degrees. It was interspersed with bands of sandstone similar to the ones I'd been climbing on the other side. There was no path leading up, but I didn't have any trouble picking out the fresh prints in the dirt. Tom's pointy-toed boots with their fancy riding heels made out a series of angry exclamation points in the sandy soil. Beside the prints there were two cables snaking upward. He'd kicked dust over them, and sometimes thrown twigs or dead branches, to make them hard to spot from the air.

The exclamation points and the cables angled back and forth as they rose, avoiding the rock bands, bushes, and clumps of cacti. They occasionally slid downhill because of the slick soles on the boots.

I was two-thirds of the way up the slope before I spotted the surveillance point.

As I did, Tom, who had been watching me from above, lifted an arm and called sullenly, "Here."

He'd set up the telescopic camera and the long-range directional microphone in a deep notch in the ridge. It was a good spot, shaded by junipers, and facing northeast. Looking in that direction I could see the red river below us and the pine-covered foothills to the Wind River Range rising up on the other side. The floor of the notch was relatively flat. A camouflaged pup tent had been erected and then decorated with more branches and a dusting of red sand.

Barely peeking out from the left edge of the notch, the camera and microphone pointed to the north. They were set on tripods and looked state-of-the-art. Both had cords running from them. The camera was apparently digital and sending images down to the computer screens in the lodge. The microphone looked like a Flash Gordon ray gun.

"Nice setup," I said.

Tom, who had gone back to peering through the camera, grunted, "Yeah."

"You want some coffee?"

When he turned I handed him the thermos of Mary's coffee I'd brought with me. I was feeling conflicted about Tom. I sympathized with him about his friend who'd been killed in Mexicali. And about his sister—*Christ, it was the government, his own agency, that sold her the drugs that killed her.* But I also still didn't like his attitude or the way he was about to take a gamble with my brother's life.

He unscrewed the thermos lid and sniffed it.

"I didn't poison it, if that's what you're thinking."

He looked back at me, considering. His eyes were tired but his hair was perfect. I guessed he'd been up all night playing with his toys. He probably still wasn't finished, as the computer screens had been dark when I was down there. After a couple of seconds he nodded thanks and filled the lid.

"Want to take a look?" he asked.

"Yeah."

He moved out of the way. I slid into his position and looked around the corner of rock over the barrel of the camera's lens. Hidalgo's mansion was visible. It wasn't what I'd expected, even after seeing the satellite photos the previous night. It didn't look like the hideout of a billionaire.

The old ranch house was nestled in a shallow valley that

descended down to the bank of the river. It was big, but not enormous. Maybe, when new, it had been impressive. But not anymore. Only one story high, its white paint was peeling from being sandblasted repeatedly by the gusts coming down out of the mountains. Some tiles were missing from the roof. The house formed a U around the swimming pool and the cracked flagstone deck. Both the deck and the pool were littered with tumbleweeds. Due to yesterday's high winds, there were more deck chairs in the pool than on the deck. The steep lawn that ran down fifty feet to the river's bank was brown and dry.

The only sign of life near the house was a man who was dragging the weeds and chairs out of the pool. He didn't look like your usual pool man, if such a thing exists in Wyoming. Gold flashed from his neck, wrists, and fingers, and his head was cleanly shaved. In addition to all the gold, he wore the bottom half of a fancy tracksuit, dark blue with a pair of white vertical stripes. The pants hung low on his hips while his underwear was pulled high. On top he showed off his tattoos and skinny muscles by wearing one of those tight, sleeveless undershirts known as a wife-beater. He didn't look like he was enjoying his job as he flung a wet tumbleweed onto the lawn then spat after it. The weed rolled down into the brown water.

Tom was looking over my shoulder.

"Who's that?" I asked.

"Dunno. He's a new one. Probably just some banger they picked up. Hidalgo likes to use them for his shit work—intimidation, not killing or anything serious. He usually keeps a pack of them around. Like pets. Most of them are American citizens. One of his lieutenants recruits them out of the barrios in L.A. and San Diego."

"How many of them are there?"

"Running around Mexicali and the border? Hundreds. Here, there's maybe ten. Most of them staying at those construction trailers by the mine entrance."

I adjusted the camera. About a half-mile back behind the house, up in the hills a little way, there were a pair of long white trailers. A dirt road led from them to the house, intersected halfway there by another, wider road that led off parallel to the river. Yet another dirt track led from the trailers, from this viewpoint, straight into a hill. That must be the mine entrance. There was no one around the trailers, but there were a couple of barbecue grills and a lot of empty beer cans.

"Hidalgo's lieutenants and his gunmen are probably staying with him in the house. Last night I saw a couple of them head into town with some of the bangers. The *jefes* probably go into town with them to keep those little maniacs in line."

"It's like a small army."

Tom snorted. "This is nothing. You should see what he's got around him in Baja. That's an army. Here, he feels safe. No one's going to come after him here. At least not the people he's worried about."

I saw something on one of the deck chairs that wasn't in the pool. Focusing in, I saw that it was a short, ugly gun. Tom noticed me zeroing in on it.

"It's an AK-47. Automatic rifle. Bet you that kid has no idea how to use it. But then it doesn't exactly take a lot of know-how or practice."

I didn't like the look of the kid. He looked a lot like the ones I'd killed in Cheyenne. He had similar tattoos on his arms and neck. I liked the gun even less. Despite having carried one for eight years—albeit only a handgun—since I was twenty-four, I'd never been very comfortable with them. I was required to carry my .40 Heckler & Koch, but for almost sixteen nervous months after Cheyenne, I didn't carry bullets.

The kid sat down on a chair next to the one with the gun on it. He dug way down into a pocket of his pants and came out with a short metal pipe. I watched while he picked a small yellowish crystal out of some aluminum foil and stuffed it into the pipe. He lit the pipe and sucked down the smoke. Although it was just my imagination, I could smell the acrid chemical odor of the methamphetamine. I could almost see it pumping out his veins, shrinking his pupils, and making him feel small and mean.

"Smoke up, son," Tom said. "Soon the big boys at Florence will be smoking you."

Florence was the site of the federal government's new maximum-security prison in Colorado. With luck, that was where he and his bosses would be in a few weeks.

I tried to make myself feel a little of Tom's excitement. This was *the hunt,* after all. The one I'd been on for eight years, and that—at first, at least—I'd found so much fun. Like climbing, a little risk in an investigation—not too much, just a little—made the adrenal juices flow. But God, sending Roberto in there, that was more risk than I would ever accept on a climb or an investigation. It wasn't adrenaline that was flowing in my veins, but fear.

"We're coming after you, and this time you're going down," Tom said, talking to himself, or maybe Hidalgo, who was somewhere in the house. "No more busting the little guys and letting the big fellows walk. This time the roof's going to come down. I'm going to cut off your fucking head."

"You know the story," I said after he'd apparently ended his monologue. "Another will grow in its place."

Tom twisted around so that he was looking at me from over his shoulder. His eyes were bloodshot and puffy, but I could see the passion burning in them.

"But at least I'll get to mount it on my wall, Burns."

And I finally managed to feel a little of the old excitement. For a while I even managed to feel a kinship with Tom and put out of my head the thought that we'd be sending Roberto in there.

FIVE

From the little I'd heard of Potash, and from what I'd glimpsed on our dark drive through it the night before, I was able to make an educated guess about the town's character. It was a sick, dying place, financed by the tight-fisted trickle of dollars from failed mines and hardscrabble sheep ranches, and populated by bitter people hanging on because they had nowhere better to go. Or nowhere else that would have them. Drinking would be the primary entertainment.

So I dressed accordingly.

From a crate of old clothes I kept in the back of the truck for just this purpose, I dug out a cheap Western shirt, a pair of tight black jeans, a wide leather belt whose silver buckle was stamped with a golden bull, and a pair of scuffed leather boots. I also found a sweat-stained cowboy hat that I was able to punch back into shape. A gold crucifix on a chain around my neck was the final touch. In my reflection on the Pig's side window, I looked just like a Mexican hand going to town on a Friday night. Or a mule ready to celebrate a successful delivery.

Mary, who had been talking, went quiet when I strutted

into the main cabin. Roberto and Tom looked up from the file-covered table where they were sitting. All three of them stared at me like I was a stranger.

Roberto broke the silence by letting out a low whistle then calling, *"Muy guapo!"*

Even Tom, who had dealt in the clandestine world for far longer than I had, was startled into nodding his head approvingly.

"Not bad, QuickDraw. Not bad at all. You look like you're here to cut the grass." Then, in broken Spanish, he asked, "You can talk Mexican as good as Argentine?"

I answered with a border accent, making it soft and a little slurred like Roberto's.

"Better than you, *chabacano.*"

The word I called him meant vulgar and low-class. Not that he'd know. But the insult, as well as my mimicking, made my brother grin.

The disguise probably wasn't all that necessary for just cruising through town and picking out a drop. But my face had been in the local papers and on the TV news too often in recent years.

The shoot-out in Cheyenne had been a major media event. In a state the size of Wyoming, taking out three citizens in a single night was taking a respectful-sized bite out of the population. And then there'd been that columnist screaming about planted weapons, an ambush, and generally fanning the flames with imaginative epithets like QuickDraw. The whole thing had heated up again a year later when the civil suit was settled, and then once more during the criminal trial of the state's governor-elect, when his attorney used the Cheyenne incident to try to impeach my credibility. The picture they'd shown on the TV screen—me looking outraged but also furtive as I dodged out of the courthouse—might have been fuzzy to the citizens of Potash over the rims of their beer cans and whiskey glasses, but with my brother's life at risk I didn't want to take any chances.

Mary Chang circled all the way around me. Then she examined me head-on, with a slight smile of her own.

"I guess you do know what you're doing."

"I've been doing this for eight years. I can be whatever you want me to be."

I wasn't bragging. All my life it had been easy for me to fit in with whatever clique or group I wanted to. Whatever natural ability I started with was enhanced by growing up on military bases, with a new school each year, and the desperate need to fit in. My mixed heritage—Indio, Spanish, and Anglo—didn't hurt. I could pass as either a light-skinned Latino or a dark-skinned gringo whenever it suited me. With a Jewish fiancée, my horizons might expand even further.

It wasn't all pretense, either. I'd become comfortable in these clothes—except for the boots, which hurt like hell—just as I was comfortable wearing a navy suit while testifying in court, or a tweaker's torn black T-shirt and Doc Martens, or my sandals, hemp shorts, and tie-dyes when hanging out with post-hippies. Working as a DCI agent in Wyoming for so long, I had been thoroughly immersed in the drug cultures of two races.

"Where are you thinking about placing the drop?" she asked.

"In one of the bars. There's not much else in town. I'll find out which one of Hidalgo's *sicarios* frequent and pick a spot or two. I assume whatever Roberto brings out is going to be small."

"Tom's idea is for him to communicate with us by placing notes on the inside of cigarette packs then casually discarding them."

It wasn't original, but I knew it would be effective. A

message could be written on the inside of the foil that lined the pack and then replaced.

"Uh-uh. I roll my own," Roberto said.

We all looked at him because of the firmness of his voice. It seemed like such a very small thing to need to be firm about. But I guessed he needed something to keep for himself. Smoking that foul Indian tobacco was an act of rebellion for him, something he'd only started when imprisoned in Colorado where it wasn't allowed. I thought it was probably symbolic.

It had been a long day for him. For all of us. It had been spent indoors, pulling out everything he knew about Hidalgo from his past, as well as cramming into him everything he'd need to know about El Doctor for his future. Roberto was feeling the tug of the leash around his neck. He fingered it now, touching the turquoise stone.

Tom glared at him, saying, "You're a Marlboro Man now."

"The fuck I am."

"Okay, okay. We'll work something out," Mary said, wisely giving in on this.

A brief argument followed because Roberto refused to smoke those "toxic rods." He seemed to think his pure tobacco was healthy. At least it was healthier than the needle and his preferred blend of cocaine and heroin. Mary finally agreed to get some bidis, all-natural Indian cigarettes. It was a better idea, really. Roberto could deposit them in a seldom-emptied trash bin and the exotic packaging would be easy to pick out later.

Mary gave me a long look before I left.

"Be careful, Anton," she said. "That town looked pretty tough, like something out of an Old West movie. Don't do anything to draw attention to yourself. And don't go anywhere near Hidalgo or his men. Remember: Don't take any chances."

"Yeah, that's my job," my brother said.

Then he smiled. "Have a cold one for me, *che*."

I was happy to be going, but Mungo wasn't happy at being left behind. She leapt in the truck while I was removing the license plates and then I had to drag her out by the collar. After that she loped after the Pig when I drove up the dirt track toward the gate. She seemed a little frantic in her desire to accompany me, but I was too excited at getting out to think much about it. I didn't yet know her well enough to understand that she could smell trouble. I let her in the truck, then drove her back to the camp.

She stood on my cot at the cabin's window after I locked her in. I could feel her yellow eyes on me until I was out of the hollow and through the barbed-wire gate.

I'd been tempted to take her, but I figured that she might draw too much attention. People in this part of the country have a thing about wolves. They think they slaughter cattle for sport and will run off with small children if given half a chance. The federal reintroduction of wolves had some ranchers calling for armed secession. And last month Mungo hadn't exactly done her part for the species' PR by biting an arsonist who died moments later falling off a cliff. Even though her role in the accident had never become public, the surprising autopsy results sparked a belief among many that the man had leapt off the cliff to escape an onslaught of wild wolves.

So I drove alone in the rattling Pig on the dirt roads west to Potash. In the rearview mirror the sun was red-faced and looking scared as it floated down onto the sharp spires of the Winds.

I came out of the hills and into town just as it was getting dark. I saw no people or moving cars until I hit the first bars. There were two of them anchoring the north end of the main street. The one on my left was called Wild Willy's. The one on the right didn't appear to have a name, and, unlike Willy's, it didn't appear to have much business. Both were squat one-story brick structures illuminated by only the neon beer signs in the windows.

Big dusty pickups and a couple of American-brand SUVs were parked all around Wild Willy's. A group of five Anglo men stood outside the door, wearing boots and Carhartt work clothes and baseball caps. They might have been talking, but as I drove slowly past they stopped and stared my way. I rode on, feeling suspicion and maybe a little menace in their gazes.

They once might have worried me, but I'd been in Wyoming long enough to know that the redneck attitude was mostly a pose. They might look xenophobic, but, on an individual level, people in Wyoming are pretty accepting. In Riverton, they'd put placards in their windows saying "Not Welcome Here" when the World Church of the Creator moved to town to espouse white-supremacist views. In Casper, they'd surrounded the church during Matthew Shepard's funeral and stared down the gay-haters from Kansas who came to celebrate the young man's murder.

The main drag was again empty of both people and cars. Its entire two-block length was lit by only a couple of scattered streetlights. The shops with their empty or boarded windows lined the street. Only a couple of pawnshops with heavily barred windows seemed to have much merchandise to offer—mostly guns and electronics. The largest building in town was an old theater, but its marquee was empty, and I noticed a piece of plywood nailed over the door.

A one-story sandstone courthouse faced the street. It had some graffiti prominently scrawled across the front to one side of the double doors. On the far side of the courthouse there was a separate entrance and a small lamp lighting a sign that said "Town Marshal." A patrol car was parked by the door. I knew that the town currently employed only one part-time peace officer. He had to single-handedly deal with the bar brawls and drunk drivers until the state highway patrol could arrive from Pinedale or Lander—both almost a hundred miles away—to back him up. From the vibe I was getting from this town, if I were him I'd just lock myself in there.

Under normal circumstances, I would have checked in with the marshal to get the lay of the land as well as to alert him that an operation was being conducted in his jurisdiction. But these weren't normal circumstances, not with the Feds involved and not with Mary Chang's mantra of *Take no chances*. I didn't know the man anyway—for all I knew he could be on a first-name basis with Señor Hidalgo.

There were two more bars at the other end of town, closer to the highway.

One was the place where the previous night we'd seen the vaqueros pissing on the hood of the marshal's patrol car. It was a tiny cubelike structure of dented brown stucco with Corona and Tecate signs flashing in the only window. At this early hour its dirt parking lot was empty but for crushed cans, cigarette butts, and a sleeping dog. Across the street, though, things were a little more active.

There a neon sign read "Señor Garcia's." The building was big and well-lit and painted white, with broad windows facing the street and allowing me to see into a place that was a restaurant as well as a bar. Despite the barred windows, it looked a lot friendlier than the Anglo places on the other side of town. There were some battered straw hats like mine inside and a lot of dark-skinned faces. Outside the front door were some planters that held bright flowers.

Among the trucks and cars in the lot was a slouching Oldsmobile sedan with Baja California plates. On its back window was a little sticker that caught my attention. It was a yellow smiley face, but instead of a smile there was the outline of a tongue hanging down beneath the two dots for eyes. Mary and Tom had mentioned that this was a sort of logo for the Mexicali Mafia—lots of the young bangers working for the cartel had it tattooed on their arms or chests.

I guessed that this was where Hidalgo's men would start an evening on the town. Across the street was probably where they would finish it. They wouldn't want to mess with the Anglo place on the other side of town, not if they were halfway smart. They would be looking for fun, not trouble. I hoped I was right, because I was going to go in there despite Mary's injunction of staying away from them. I wanted to get just a little whiff of what Roberto was getting himself into.

I drove back down the street a block and left the Pig there. I put my gun butt-out under the driver's seat, tapped it for luck—it had once brought me more than my fair share of good as well as bad—and set the alarm.

There were a lot of people in the restaurant. Couples and families for the most part, with a few kids darting around. A brown tile floor magnified the sound of voices talking in Spanish. It would have seemed welcoming if it weren't for the way everyone paused and looked at me. Even the kids slunk closer to their parents. When the talking resumed after a minute it was slightly more subdued.

I stood shifting in my too-tight boots until a girl came out of the kitchen in the back. She looked me over without smiling and motioned me toward the rear of the restaurant. I saw that there was a small bar there—six or more stools before a rail and a couple of high tables. Two men were sitting at the rail. Both looked like hard cases, and they were staring back at me. I was sure it was their car with the Baja plates and the little yellow sticker.

"I have come to eat, not drink," I told the girl in Spanish.

"You do not want to sit with your *compañeros*?"

"I am a stranger here. I know no one."

She shrugged and led me to a small table against one wall. I didn't look toward the bar area again but I could feel the two men's eyes on me. A lot of other eyes, too. She set the menu before a chair with its back to most of the restaurant and the bar. I sat in the opposite chair and pulled the menu across to me. She walked away without a word.

I studied the menu for a long time, trying to sit as still as possible and not look around. Slowly the families at the tables nearby began to relax as they grew used to me. But I still sensed a wariness among them. I eavesdropped as they talked about upcoming weddings, Miguel's new truck, a horse that something was wrong with but no one knew what, and whether the snow this year would be heavy. The whole time I could feel the gaze of the two men by the bar—the rest of the restaurant seemed aware of it as well. When I glanced that way, looking around for the girl to take my order, they both had their backs to the rail and were watching me.

The waitress finally came back. She was still acting sullen although I could see that she had laugh lines on the sides of her mouth. I ordered steak tamales. She again walked away without a word.

Even though it took less than ten minutes for my order to arrive, half the dining room emptied out in that time and the other half was getting up to leave. It was eight o'clock, and it appeared to be some kind of witching hour.

The girl brought my food and said as she put it before me, "Those men at the bar. They want to buy you a drink."

"I wish only to eat."

She looked at me directly for the first time, cocking her head to one side the way Mungo does when I try to give her a command she doesn't understand. Her expression softened a little.

"What are you doing here, mister?"

"I'm just traveling through. On my way north for a job."

"You would be wise to join them. Or leave and keep driving—there will be no charge for the food if you go now. Please understand."

She turned and hurried away without waiting for me to answer.

I looked at the two men in the bar. One of them grinned at me and showed some broken teeth. He gestured me forward. The other one, who was larger and had a long Pancho Villa mustache and a goatee, just continued staring. I nodded at them without smiling and held up my thumb and forefinger indicating the need for a few moments.

I ate fast while thinking even faster.

These were undoubtedly a couple of Hidalgo's *sicarios*. And they wanted to know about a strange young man in the neighborhood who looked like he might have something to do with the drug world. Mary Chang had ordered me to have no contact with Hidalgo's men—an order I would normally have felt free to ignore or follow depending on my mood—but now I realized the good reasoning behind the order. These were dangerous men. It was palpable in the air, in the way everyone had reacted when I walked in the door, thinking I was one of them. I shouldn't have dressed so flashy. That's what you get for showing off for the Feds.

There was nothing I could do about it now. If I bolted, it might make them suspicious. And I wouldn't be able to show my face in town for the rest of the operation.

I shoveled in the last bite without really having tasted the food. I wiped my mouth, drank some water, and put ten dollars on the table before standing. The grinning man nodded encouragingly to me as I headed toward the bar area. He slid over one stool, making a space between him and the other man. Pancho Villa just watched me walk over. His face was oddly swollen and his forehead seemed creased into a permanent scowl. I noticed that both men wore fancy dress boots with riding heels, not the work kind. Both had gold around their fingers, wrists, and necks. Broken Teeth had a silver automatic in his waistband, only partly concealed by his leather jacket. I was sure the larger man was armed as well, even though he was big and menacing enough not to need a gun.

"How goes it?" Broken Teeth asked.

Without waiting for me to answer, he patted the empty stool between them and called out over the bar for a drink.

I sat down facing the bar and both men turned with me. An old man came out of a side door. He was small and wizened, with scowling eyes beneath bristling eyebrows. There was a lot of Indian blood in him. Like the girl, he stood silent instead of asking to take an order.

Broken Teeth demanded a tequila and a beer for each of us and told the old man to hurry up. There were a lot of glasses in front of the two men, both mugs and shot glasses. It looked like they'd been here awhile and that the old man wasn't inclined to do much picking up after them.

"I'm called Zafado," Broken Teeth told me in a friendly manner. It was a nickname, meaning a crazy person. I could believe it, looking into his black eyes.

Then he flipped his hand past me to Pancho Villa. "This is Bruto. Tell me, my friend, what are you called?"

Bruto was another nickname. It meant someone who was coarse or uncouth. I could feel his eyes burning into the side of my head. As much as I disliked my own nickname, on its face, at least, it was better than either of theirs.

"Juan."

"Juan, huh? I haven't seen you around here before. You work here? In this town?"

The old man poured three shots of tequila and set about drawing three beers.

"No. In the north."

"Yeah? Where at in the north?"

While the old man put the beers before us, I named a ranch near Pinedale, a hundred or so miles toward Montana. I knew the guy who owned it, and I would call him later to make sure that if anyone asked, he would admit to hiring a Mexican hand named Juan.

"Yeah? You a real cowboy, my friend? Go on, drink up."

He picked up his shot. In the periphery of my vision I saw the silent, brooding Bruto lift, too. I picked up my own and poured it into my mouth.

It was very bad tequila. It scorched my throat and burned its way into my stomach. I tried to be cool in the way I reached for my beer but Zafado laughed all the same. Neither he nor Bruto touched their beers. I guessed it was a macho thing.

"So, you a real cowboy?" Zafado asked again.

I told him I was and he laughed, although I didn't know why. I didn't ask any questions. As usual in these kinds of situations, I played the near-mute. I wanted to let things ride and see what I could learn.

"What are you doing all the way down here, Juan?"

I explained that I'd delivered some horses to Green River. He asked if my trailer was parked outside, saying that he'd like to take a look at it, that he might like to buy it. I said no, it had been sold along with the horses.

I began to wonder whether these two were just stationed here to gather intelligence on strangers or whether they intended to roll me. Maybe both. Most illegal aliens can't open bank accounts in the United States, so they're stuck carrying large sums of money on their persons. And I'd just pretty much claimed that I was carrying cash from the sale of two horses and a trailer.

But Zafado seemed to have other things on his mind.

"You don't talk much, my friend. You're quiet, like Bruto there. That's good. Very good. Maybe you like to work for me sometime. I pay real good—better than what the gringos would pay you."

Before I had to answer, there was some raucous noise coming from the now empty restaurant's entrance. Shouts, whoops, and laughter. Seven or eight men were coming in. More of the Mexicali Mafia. Zafado stood and took a few steps, yelling out a welcome. Bruto stayed close by my side.

The pretty waitress hurried past us and into the kitchen. I thought the look on her face was one of both fear and distaste. She didn't return.

The majority of these men were dressed much the same as my friends at the bar. Lots of gold, designer jeans, and leather jackets. Slicked-back hair and the kinds of mustaches that are favored by cops and *narcotraficantes* alike on both sides of the border. A couple of the younger ones had shaved heads, tattoos, and wore expensive tracksuits. Like Zafado, few of them had bothered trying very hard to hide the pistols in their waistbands.

Carrying a concealed weapon is a crime—even in Wyoming—but I wasn't in any position to complain. I wasn't even armed.

With a bit of relief, I saw that at least none of them was Hidalgo. I wasn't quite ready to meet my brother's former friend, the man whose head, in Tom's words, we'd be cutting off. His eyes had been too penetrating in the photo I'd seen. And I looked just enough like my brother that meeting him would make me a lot more nervous than I already was.

The better-dressed *sicarios* and the street bangers rolled toward the bar at the rear of Garcia's like a summer storm that crackles with lightning and booms with menacing thunder. I sat on my stool, watching them come on in the mirror, with the immobile Bruto seeming to lean over me.

Zafado greeted them all by shaking hands, tapping fists, and clapping shoulders. The new men, every one of them, nodded respectfully at my silent companion. They ignored me except for a few questioning looks.

I drank my beer and listened to them talk about another boring day. They laughed at some others who were left behind tonight to guard the compound. They talked about the stink eye they were getting from the local gringos. And they talked about the lack of women in this part of Wyoming.

"Shorty wants to steal a sheep," someone said.

"Shorty's not tall enough to fuck a sheep."

Everyone laughed. Shorty, too, a little nastily.

He was one of the *sicarios*—I could tell because he was one of the ones dressed in jeans and leather and he didn't need to strut and posture like the bangers. Shorty's nickname was not the mocking insult mine was meant to be. He really was short. And grossly fat. The gold chains around his neck—he had as many of them as a rap star—were half buried by the fleshy rolls there. Lots of wavy dark hair framed his head. It was as perfectly groomed as Tom's.

"Shorty's going to rape some stringy gringo bitch if the boss doesn't bring in more women soon."

It was Shorty who said this, referring to himself in the third person.

The old man served them all without speaking or smiling. They drank down the tequila, whiskey, and beer faster than the old man could pour. It didn't look like he was keeping track of the tab. When one of them asked where his granddaughter was in terms that were far too familiar, the old man, to everyone's amusement, remained absolutely stone-faced. I assumed the granddaughter was the waitress who'd warned me off. Some more—even ruder—things were said.

I got up and slid through them toward the bathroom. Although they were still ignoring me, they were watching me, too. After checking it out, it would definitely be time to go. I already had a possible drop picked out, a place where it would be convenient and inconspicuous to make either a delivery or a pickup. It was a narrow ledge I'd felt underneath the bar.

I latched the door behind me in the bathroom and found a second possibility—a battered old trash can with flaking paint and a hinged lid. Then I washed my hands and face with cold water from the tap while I looked at my face in the mirror. It looked almost unfamiliar—cold and hard like the men I was among.

Bruto was waiting for me when I came out of the bathroom. He was leaning next to the pay phone in the dark hallway but not bothering to pretend to use it. I nodded at him and walked past. He followed. I intended to thank Zafado for the tequila and beer and then leave.

My looming shadow and I stepped back into the bar area just as the restaurant's front door opened again. Two young women, college-aged and very Caucasian, came inside.

They were obviously backpackers or climbers fresh from a camping trip in the Winds. Noticing the crowd of men in the back, they looked like they might be considering looking elsewhere down the road for their meal. Hidalgo's men looked back at them like they were the meal.

I tapped Zafado on the back as he talked and laughed about the two women with three men. When he turned I thanked him for the drinks.

"Stay and have another," he told me. "It's on me."

The men laughed at this. I didn't think they were paying for them in any currency but intimidation.

Then he introduced me. There were three more nicknames to remember, three more faces imprinted in my mind.

"I got to go," I said, but I was ignored.

Two men walked over to where the backpackers had seated themselves at a table. One of the men was Shorty, the other was a skinny banger. The table was in the far corner of the restaurant, all the way at the front and as far from us as they could get. The young women looked around self-consciously. They watched the approaching men with nervous smiles. The waitress came out of the kitchen, saw what was happening, and froze.

"I must go," I said again.

But I let someone put a beer in my hand.

Everyone was watching the two men who were approaching the two women.

"You hungry?" Shorty asked in English loud enough to be heard all the way in the back of the bar.

"He's asking if she's hungry," the man next to me translated into Spanish, apparently for my benefit.

One of the girls nodded uncertainly.

Shorty unzipped his pants and laid his penis on their table.

I was moving before I knew it. Beer still in my hand, passing men, then empty tables and chairs.

The women looked shocked and disgusted. But more than anything, they looked scared. They both stood up simultaneously.

"Where you going?" the skinny man asked, moving to block their exit.

Shorty pointed to his engorged member. "Try it. You'll like it."

He said this just as I grabbed the collar of his leather jacket. I yanked him backward and threw him on the floor. He took down a table and two chairs as he fell.

I said in broken English to the women, "Bar is closed. *Vamonos*. We go."

They didn't need any further encouragement. They scurried around us and half-ran for the door. Shorty was cursing on the floor, kicking away chairs and picking himself up. The other men were surging forward from the bar area. Shorty's buddy was staring at me with narrowed eyes and reaching under his jacket. I moved quickly after the women, herding them in real cowboy fashion.

I wasn't quick enough, though. They made it out, but I didn't. Bruto got to the door just behind them, intercepting me and slamming the door shut with his meaty shoulder. He locked it just as I was reaching for the knob.

I could hear more bootfalls on the tile floor coming up behind me as I looked up at Bruto. God, he was ugly. Beyond him, out the window, I saw the women get into a Subaru and tear out of the lot, heading for the highway. I didn't think I could win a stare fight with Bruto, so I turned and faced the room.

"Oh yeah, I'm going to gut you, Cowboy," Shorty said, coming at me slowly while the others stopped. He pushed a button on a switchblade knife, sending a thin blade out with a low *snick*. His partner in harassment stood grinning with a hand on the pistol in his waistband.

I took a cue from my brother's disreputable past and smashed the rim of my beer mug on the edge of a table. It splashed all over me but the glass base was comfortable in my palm, the jagged edge pointing up and out. There was something else I took from my brother—a sense of recklessness, of almost exhilaration. I let the feeling grow and spread over me because I knew that even if I evaded or outfought Shorty, there would be eight or ten more just like him who would be coming at me. Recklessness was all I had.

The restaurant was dead quiet now.

The silence was broken by a shrill female voice. It was the waitress, who stood in the hallway by the bathrooms and kitchen. She waved a cordless phone in the air as if it were a club.

"I will call the police!"

Some of the men turned and snickered. Zafado laughed. If I weren't about to get gutted or worse, I would have laughed, too, imagining the town's one deputy marshal trying to break up this kind of a brawl. If he was smart, he wouldn't be answering the phone on a Friday night.

The old man came out from behind the bar, firmly took hold of the phone with one hand and the girl's arm with the other. He pulled her out of sight into the kitchen.

Shorty began to swing the knife in the air. He made short slashing motions as he grinned at me. The knife was held the right way, coming out between the finger and thumb rather than the heel of his fist. You do a lot more damage slashing than stabbing and he, unfortunately, knew it.

"Cut out his heart," someone called, laughing.

"Cut off his dick!"

"Show him *la corbata de Jesús*!"

I can dive through the front window, I thought. *Dive through the window and run for the truck. Even in these boots, I can outrun these guys. There's no dishonor in running away. Not when there are so many of them. Not when they're all stone killers.* I was almost crouching to lunge for the sheet of glass when I remembered that the window was barred on the outside.

Shorty danced two steps forward and one step back as he grinned and waved the knife. He did it again, closing the distance between us, and moving with surprising agility for all his bulk. I stood rock-still with both hands upraised. The broken mug palmed in one, the other hand open, and me hoping I'd be fast enough to grab the wrist with the knife. Then I would hit him with the glass.

Shorty danced forward again, flicking the knife just in front of my forearms. I almost went for it, then stopped as he danced back again. I stared at his bright eyes—they glittered with the thrill. I was conscious of how hard I was breathing even though I'd barely moved. The knife flashed at my left side, backhanded now and coming high. I lunged to the right.

The blade drew back just as it almost nicked my wrist. If I'd dropped my hand it would have cut my cheek. The flush of hot adrenaline pumped through my veins. The men circled around us cheered.

"Let the cowboy go," a voice said through the applause.

The voice wasn't loud, but it was commanding. Commanding enough that Shorty's leering grin drooped as did his knife arm. It was Zafado who had spoken.

"Let the cowboy go," he said again to a chorus of disappointed groans.

I didn't know if it was a trick or not, so I maintained my pose. When the knife came next I wasn't going to try to grab it this time, but intended instead to smash the jagged end of the mug down onto the arm that held it.

Zafado walked into the circle and showed me all of his stained, broken teeth. He spoke to Shorty and the other men.

"I can't buy him a drink and then have it come out through his throat. He deserves at least to piss it out."

Then he looked at me.

"You are very brave, Juan. But very stupid, too. You are very close to tripping over your own balls, my friend. Shorty may not look like he's good for anything but eating, but he is very good with a knife."

He laughed and shook his head.

My field of vision widened as the adrenaline was soaked back up by the glands in the small of my back. I could see all the disappointed faces, the bloodlust evident in their expressions but also a casualness about it that was even more frightening. They had seen encounters like this a hundred times. Encounters where someone ended up forever on the ground. They'd seen men hacked to death—or worse, throats slit and the tongues pulled out—so often that it was nothing but a game to them. For me violence had always been about fear and madness. For them it was both work and recreation. That was what made them so scary.

"Where is your rig?" Zafado asked.

"Down the street," I managed through a very dry mouth.

"Perhaps I should escort you there? See that you get inside in one piece."

He waved Bruto away from the door. I waited to go for it until Bruto was well out of grabbing range.

"I'll be all right," I said, moving for the door faster than my pride wanted me to.

Zafado followed me out and firmly shut the door behind him. It was cold outside—colder than I remembered. I tossed the broken mug into the flowers by the door.

Behind Zafado's back, behind the big barred window, the *sicarios* and bangers were watching us, their faces pressed close to cut the glare from the inside lights. Shorty was grinning and tapping the tip of his blade on the glass. Another man was grinning, too, and making cutting motions across his throat while sticking out an unusually long tongue. Bruto was just staring.

"I have done you a favor," Zafado said.

It was true. And, sick as it was, I couldn't help feeling more than a little grateful. These guys scared me. And this Zafado scared me even more than Bruto or Shorty.

"So you owe me a favor now." He handed me a folded scrap of paper. "This is my phone number, okay? Call me in a few days, once my friends in there stop wanting to play their games with you. You must come work for me—I will pay you ten times what you make hauling horses and cleaning up their shit. A hundred times. Maybe a thousand times, for a man with balls like yours. And I will smooth everything out with my aggrieved friend in there. You think about it, okay? Then call me."

SIX

Guns lay on one of the picnic tables when I walked into the main cabin. There were two of them, and they were a lot more dangerous-looking than the simple pistols we carried at DCI, or even the shotguns we used when kicking down doors and executing no-knock warrants. These guns were both intricate and nasty, with long banana clips and skeletal collapsing stocks, and they were obviously capable of doing a lot of damage. I'd seen these kinds of weapons before, years ago, when they were slung over the shoulders of the Special Forces Pararescue soldiers my dad had commanded.

Immediately I wished I'd had one of these at Señor Garcia's. And the second one, too, with Tom or Mary or Roberto holding on to it as they backed me up. For an instant I indulged myself in a fantasy of spraying bullets through the windows of the restaurant and bar. Putting down the animals inside for once and for all—no warrants, no trial, no fuss.

"You'd better have a lot more of those, and a lot more Feds, when you want to go across the river," I said to Tom, who was cleaning the guns with oil and a toothbrush.

"Don't worry. We will."

Tom was wearing one of his too-small T-shirts and a pair

of jeans. He spoke without looking at me. He continued to scrub away, seeming to pay more attention to his own flexing triceps than the assault weapon he was working on.

"Did you find a drop?" Mary asked me.

She and Roberto were sitting at the other table, which was cluttered with files, water bottles, legal pads, photographs, and the two laptop computers. My brother looked bored. Mary looked tired and distracted.

"Yeah."

"You drink a cold one for me?" Roberto asked.

"Yeah. And a shot."

"Extra credit," he said, giving me a thumbs-up. "Thanks, bro."

Mary picked up a legal pad and took a pencil from behind her ear. Her eyes on the pad, she said, "Describe the drop."

I did. I described the trash can in the men's room with its swinging lid. Mary made a note, then pushed the pad across to me and had me draw a diagram, showing the interior of the restaurant and bar, and the exact position of the proposed drop. My hand shook a little as I drew. I was still feeling the aftereffects of a near-overdose of adrenaline and fear. I wondered why they couldn't see how white my skin must look, how wide my eyes must be.

"Did you see any of Hidalgo's men?" Mary asked after I pushed back the pad.

"Yeah. I had a drink with about ten of them."

Now she finally looked at me. She jerked her head up from her notes and stared. Tom left cleaning the guns and walked around to stand behind the paper-strewn table. He leaned on it with his fists. Roberto was smiling, nodding his head a little, his blue eyes lit up with amusement.

"Well?" Tom demanded. "What happened?"

I told them, sticking to just the facts and not going into just how much those guys had scared me. Mary began shaking her head almost immediately, saying, "You weren't authorized to have any kind of contact with them." I protested that I didn't have a whole hell of a lot of choice. When I went in there, I didn't know Hidalgo's men would demand that I have a drink with them. I didn't know that half of his *sicarios* and bangers would show up and be looking for trouble.

"I'm surprised you didn't just pull your gun and blast away," Tom said acidly. "For a guy with your history, that's showing some admirable restraint."

"Fuck you," I told him.

"Bet you didn't even take your gun. Right?" Roberto asked.

He was probably asking to make a point with Mary and Tom. To show them that there was more to his little brother— or less—than they'd read in their file on me.

Roberto knew that I didn't like guns. He didn't like them, either, but they held a kind of fascination for him. He'd once told me that they disrupted the natural order of the world. It was supposed to be about tooth and claw and strength and smarts. Guns made a conflict be only about who cared less about life. All you had to do was point one and twitch your index finger. It was too easy. But I knew that, for that same reason, guns also appealed to him.

"No," I answered. "I left it in my truck. And it turned out to be a damned good thing. If I'd pulled it in there, I'd be leaking all over the floor."

Tom snorted but didn't say anything else. Mary looked at me curiously, as if I'd done something not very smart. Or maybe she thought it was smart. I couldn't tell. Her hooded eyes were hard to read.

"These guys are dangerous," she said, as if I didn't know. "From now on we should all be armed at all times."

"Yeah? Cool. I want one of those things," Roberto said,

pointing at the partially dismantled automatic rifles on the other table.

"I meant all of us who have *not* been convicted of a felony," Mary corrected herself with a weary smile for my brother. "Providing a firearm to a felon is against the law, Roberto."

"That's discrimination," he said, sounding shocked. "I thought you'd be above that, being a fellow minority and all."

"I'm not a minority. I'm as American as you. More so, actually. Both my parents became citizens before I was born."

"Okay, Miss America. What are you carrying, anyway?"

She lifted the hem of her red fleece jacket, displaying a wedge of tan, flat stomach above her shorts, as well as the gun on the paddle holster.

"It's a Glock 9 mm."

"Know what a 9 mm is? A .45 set on stun." Roberto looked at Tom. "You?"

"Glock 29. That's a 10 mm. I guarantee it'll do more than stun."

I'd heard about the Bureau's vaunted 10 mms. My office had wanted us to use them for a while. Wyoming cops tend to like big guns. But they dumped the idea when they learned that, although the weapons looked impressive, the huge caliber of the bullet tended to be too much for the gun's subcompact frame.

"Those are yours, too?" Roberto indicated the machine guns on the picnic table.

"They're the Bureau's," Tom corrected him. "Heckler & Koch MP5s. They're *assigned* to me."

My brother gave him a pitying look.

"A 10 mm and a couple of machine guns, all for one guy. I'd say that adds up to a very small dick."

Tom's mouth opened but he didn't get anything out right

away. Instead he just turned redder. You could see the color rising up from his neck to his forehead.

"Gentlemen," Mary interrupted before Tom could think up a threat or a comeback, "although this discussion is very interesting, let's get back to the reason we're here."

I finished telling them about the end of the evening at Señor Garcia's, when Zafado followed me outside with his job offer and the note with his cell-phone number scribbled on it. I handed over the napkin it was written on. Mary bagged it then filed it away.

"I know that guy," Roberto said. "Bad teeth, skinny-fat?"

"Yeah." Zafado was skinny-fat. He had narrow shoulders and skinny limbs but also a belly that probably made it hard for him to zip up his expensive leather coat.

"Don't take him up on it unless the money's really good, *che*. Dude treats his employees like shit. I know firsthand."

Prodded by Mary, Roberto explained that back when he knew Hidalgo, almost ten years ago, Zafado had been the *bajador* in charge of organizing overland trafficking into Arizona and California. He was the one who recruited and paid poor illegal immigrants to haul fifty-pound packs of coke through the desert. "Those poor little guys were getting slaughtered. Thirst, or the heat, or rattlers, or, worse, the boys from Juárez looking to make an intercept. Zafado didn't really give a shit until enough started dying that it was affecting his profits. That was when he hired me to guide them."

For six months Roberto had led human pack trains through the desert. Finding them water and concealing them from the authorities and other dangers by day, then leading them on fast nighttime hikes. He spray-painted their clothes and packs black and had them tie strips of carpet to the soles of their shoes so they wouldn't leave tracks.

Mom and Dad would be so proud, I thought but didn't say. *Good use of all they taught us about living outdoors, bro.*

I often admired my brother. Sometimes I feared him—or at least feared what he might do to himself. But this was the first time I felt embarrassed by him. How could he have worked with those animals? Those men who killed with such abandon? Even though Roberto had been arrested countless times for acts of vandalism or violence, I'd always seen the higher justice—even if only in his own head—in what he'd done. This was the first time I'd heard details of him doing something for profit. But, I reminded myself, he probably thought it was fun. He probably convinced himself he was saving lives, not ruining them.

Mary wanted complete descriptions of each man I'd seen. She went through her files and nearly half the time was able to pull out a picture for me to positively identify. Some of the files were more complete than others. Some of them were unknown to the Feds, or I was unable to describe them sufficiently. Tom pulled up some additional snapshots on his laptop, pictures he'd taken with the telephoto camera throughout the day showing men either outside the house across the river or near the construction trailers. These were printed out and the nicknames or names I'd picked up were written on them and new files were created.

The one who called himself Zafado they knew as Ramón Méndez-Valle. He was a former Mexican federal agent. He'd actually been a member of the Attorney General's elite and later disgraced FEADS, Mexico's antidrug force, until two years ago, when their American counterparts insisted he be forced out for failing lie-detector tests and background vetting. Of course he'd been working for Hidalgo the whole time. Getting fired allowed him to make it formal.

The picture they showed me of Zafado had him in a braided uniform, grinning through his crooked teeth. Tom said he was believed to have been responsible for the murder of eighteen men, women, and children in Ensenada in 1998. They were thought to be the family members of a low-level Hidalgo *bajador* who had been selling information to Hidalgo's rivals in the Arellano-Felix cartel.

"Tom was at the scene," Mary said. "He saw the bodies."

"*La corbata?*" I asked before I could stop myself. I didn't really want to know.

"Just the men," Tom said quietly. "The women and children were forced to lie down. Each was shot once in the head. And then the bodies were raked with an AK-47."

There was a moment of silence. While it lasted I was reminded that Tom was not such a bad guy. At least he was fighting the good fight. My brother, on the other hand, had worked with these guys.

"If I'd known he was going to do shit like that, I would have killed him myself," Roberto said softly, no smile on his face now.

"You damn well should have," Tom growled at him. "Or, better yet, killed Hidalgo, who ordered it done. Instead all we're going to be able to do is arrest them, spend a lot of years and money trying them, and then put them in a cell for a few years. But hell, maybe we'll get lucky. Maybe they'll resist."

"Tom," Mary said warningly.

I knew what she meant. FBI agents needed to tread lightly—there'd been too many scandals lately where agents had crossed the line. Ruby Ridge, missing evidence about Oklahoma City, Whitey Bulger, the crime-lab debacle. They couldn't even insinuate things like that.

Tom lit a cigarette with a hard snap of his lighter.

To me Mary said, "Go on. Describe the others."

Big, bad, silent Bruto was Juan David Navas-Rodriguez. He was still a cop; his name remained on the roll of Baja state-police officers, where he was ranked a sergeant. His pumpkin face was partially hidden beneath a white cowboy hat in most of the surveillance photos they had of him. But the goatee, as well as his wide, powerful shoulders and self-contained manner, were distinctive. He was seen in the same Mexicali bar that the FBI agent—Mary and Tom's colleague—had disappeared from. Roberto didn't know him. He'd probably come into Hidalgo's full-time employ in only the last year or two.

Together Zafado and Bruto were believed to be the heads of Hidalgo's security detail. The fact that they were together at Señor Garcia's, a half hour or more away from the man they were paid to protect, indicated that Hidalgo wasn't worried about much in Wyoming. I pointed this out, and Mary nodded.

"That's true. He really has very little to fear here. We've been unable to indict him in the U.S. despite a decade of trying. He's too protected by the layers of lieutenants he uses. And, of course, by the threat of overwhelming retaliation. It's in Mexico that he's in danger. Not from the government, but from the rival cartels in Juárez and the Gulf."

Tom added, "The other cartels are too chickenshit to confront him north of the border. They're scared of riling us up, too." He meant the American authorities.

If it wasn't genius, at least it was impressive cunning. Hidalgo and the other narcos knew they were relatively safe in Mexico from their own government as long as they continued to pay the price and offer up the occasional token trafficker or load. Allow the *federales* to make the periodic bust, so that they could brag to their sponsor in the north that they were doing something about the War on Drugs. As long as the U.S. continued to supply the Mexican government with tens of millions of dollars in aid money each year, the cartels could transport drugs and kill one another with abandon while the politicians grew rich with them. But if they moved the violence north along with the drugs, the American authorities might be given a reason to finally react. Maybe even to demand that Mexico really do something to smother the cartels, like allowing American law enforcement to operate in Mexico with their weapons, or to extradite Mexican nationals indicted by U.S. courts on drug charges—something the Mexican government only rarely allowed. The narcos knew they couldn't afford to stir up that kind of trouble, so the north side of the border was a safe zone.

Killing Mary and Tom's colleague, even though it was done in Mexico, was a big risk. That was another supposed rule—*You don't mess with U.S. cops.* Mexican cops, of course, were fair game as long as they weren't in the employ of your friends. Hidalgo had made a mistake in ordering the murder of the FBI agent. Arrogance had turned to hubris. Tom and Mary were obviously serious about making him pay for it. But this still seemed like a very small, freewheeling operation for one that should have the full weight of the federal government behind it. It was strange that Mary and Tom would be given this much independence. But I wasn't given time to pursue the thought.

"Who's next?" Mary demanded.

I described the squat, round face and the rap-star jewelry of the one called Shorty.

They knew him, too. He was thought to recruit and control the many expendable barrio bangers Hidalgo used for both protection and intimidation.

Shorty had been with Hidalgo since the beginning of his drug operations, sometime in the early 1980s. They had tons of pictures of Shorty, but little information. Not even his real name. But he was said to be a sexual predator who preyed on the young American women who partied in Tijuana bars where the unenforced age limit was only eighteen. It was a way to impress the new recruits—give them some pretty white high-school or college girls that they could rape with impunity. The victims were drugged with Roofies or Ketamine and then driven away by Shorty and his boys, later to be dumped in an alley somewhere. Mary and Tom had spoken to several girls after they'd reported their victimization to the local Tijuana police, who turned them away ostensibly because there was no evidence, but really because they were either working for or terrified by Hidalgo.

Most of the others I described were either unknown to both the Feds and my brother, or I was unable to recall them with enough detail. Where I didn't have a nickname, Mary asked me to make one up. I wasn't too original. There was Punk 1, 2, and 3, as well as Pineapple Face for a young guy who looked like he might have had smallpox. A few I couldn't remember at all.

Mary made Roberto look at each file, whether there was a picture and other information or not, and repeat, memorizing, the names. He needed to know these guys so that he wouldn't have to describe them too much when he sent out his messages. Once I'd gotten past Zafado, though, and onto the guys he didn't know, he lost interest. Instead of paying attention, he just doodled on a legal pad he held close to his chest so that none of us could see it. It was something he'd been doing all day. When I'd asked him earlier what he was drawing, he had just grinned and said, "None of your business, *che*."

"How is it that Hidalgo is able to control these guys?" I asked when we were finally done with our rogues' gallery. "You'd think Shorty or Zafado or Bruto would get ambitious. Knock Jesús off and take over. Is it smarts or charisma or what?"

Mary answered, "We think he's both smart and charismatic, but there's probably more to it than that. He's respected. He makes things happen."

She was standing and shaking out the wrist she'd been writing with, letting the hand flop around on the end of her arm. Then she folded her right arm across her chest and pulled the elbow in with her left. It was an ordinary stretch, but it was done in a particular, practiced manner. The way a hotshot climber would. Or maybe a professional dancer. I looked again at the muscular delineations on her legs and decided she'd either been a dancer or a gymnast. And I wondered again what her immigrant parents must have thought when she joined the FBI.

"These guys aren't that smart. They're just ruthless," Tom said.

"Dude's got the power," Roberto said, surprising all of us, since he hadn't seemed to have been paying us any attention after we'd moved beyond the guys he knew. "He's plugged in, you know? Not one of those pricks could deal with the government bigwigs or army guys like Jesús can. It's like he's one of them. That, and he's loyal to those who are loyal to him. Except for those dumb gangbangers, he takes care of his people."

This was a better assessment than either Tom or Mary had offered. Tom knew it and blew out a lungful of smoke in my brother's direction. Mary nodded thoughtfully. Roberto put down the legal pad—facedown—and stood up. He wandered over to the table with Tom's guns on it.

"Stay away from those," Tom said, back in pain-in-the-ass mode. "You want a gun, get it from your buddy Jesús."

"Can I talk to you for a minute? Outside?"

Mary followed me out onto the porch. A sliver of a moon was rising over the steep rim of the crater. The stars overhead were high-wattage pinpricks, and you could clearly see the neon red of Mars. She stared up at the sky.

"I've never seen anything like this. How come it's so clear here? Is it the altitude?"

"It's just clean. No pollution. No city lights to reflect off all the dust particles in the air."

"Wow. It's pretty amazing."

I let her stare at the sky for a few minutes while I stared at her. Over the last twenty-four hours she had lost a little of the wall she'd tried to build around herself. She was loosening up, and I knew it was Roberto's doing, not my supposed charm. My brother was hard not to like unless you were a complete butthead like Tom. It wasn't just the way he looked. Sure, he made people nervous, but his wildness was so evident and so playful that you wanted to stroke him the way, giggling uneasily, you might stroke a tame tiger. You knew he was dangerous but you also knew he wouldn't hurt you. As long as you didn't cross him. But you feared what would happen to him. What he might do to himself.

He'd been gently teasing Mary throughout the day. Making fun of her seriousness, making light of her job. At first she'd tried to be as stiff as she'd been during the long drive up the day before. But I'd watched her iron spine weaken, her awkward, smart-girl's defenses melt, until she was teasing him back in an almost shy way. Like what she'd said to him about carrying a gun. Despite herself, maybe she was beginning to like the man she might be sending to a bad death. And that would be a good thing—she might relent.

"So, what did you want to talk to me about?" Mary asked now.

I took a deep breath, not wanting to say what I was about to say, and definitely not wanting to do what I was about to suggest.

"I want to be the one to go in. I want to take Zafado up on his offer."

"No," she answered automatically.

"Why not? I'm trained for this kind of stuff. I'm good at this. Wouldn't it be a hell of a lot better to have a cop in there? And Zafado himself, a top *capitán,* offered me a job."

"Because they'd kill you," she said simply. "You're too

well known, Anton. Someone would eventually recognize your face. And even if they didn't, these people are smart enough to check your background before they let you get close to anything they're doing. Your information would come from Zafado or one of the other captains and it would be useless for getting Hidalgo. And we would have to create a whole legend for you—here and in Mexico. We don't have the time or the resources. Your brother, on the other hand, doesn't need any story. He's already known to these people. He's a friend of Hidalgo's—he rescued him off that mountain and he's worked for him. He's an open book, with next to nothing to hide. We couldn't ask for a better confidential informant. He's perfect."

"Except that he's reckless."

"And you're not?" She smiled.

"He's a drug addict."

"He's been clean since we picked him up. We've made sure of that."

I wasn't so sure, but didn't say anything. I didn't have any proof, and besides, I was pretty sure that even if I did, it wouldn't matter. They seemed determined to run the operation through Roberto. Reckless druggie or not.

Reliance on a single confidential informant—especially one as lawless as my brother—was something that I knew was dangerous in an undercover investigation. They should have known that, too, after losing their friend and colleague in Mexicali. But now they were going to gamble another life. Another family, actually, but one they probably considered expendable. A junkie felon, a semi-disgraced state cop, and their expatriate parents. I didn't fault the Feds for that. Maybe I was being cocky, but I thought I could take care of myself. Mom and Dad and their vaqueros on Grandfather's ranch could look out for themselves, too, once they were warned. Besides, I really wanted to get Hidalgo. I wanted to do something important with my professional life. I was getting tired of putting dime-baggers in prison while the big guys skated.

My main criticism of their operation came down to just one simple thing: I didn't want Roberto going in there. It was a nest of vipers—I'd seen how those men were in the bar just an hour or two earlier. Hidalgo and his men were stone killers. But I had to admit that Roberto was a killer, too. His criminal history proved it.

I said something about how we should pull out—about how the whole thing was too risky. There had to be another way. Pressure the Mexicans. Someone had to be willing to testify against Hidalgo. Surely they could find someone he'd bribed or threatened who, with the right incentives and guarantees of protection, would be willing to talk.

Mary wasn't having any of it. She looked up at me, her eyes glittering in the light of the moon and the stars.

"Do you know how many deaths we believe Hidalgo is responsible for? Hundreds, at least. More likely thousands. And then there are all the people who buy his drugs, who overdose or kill someone else while under the influence or are rotted away by daily use. Hundreds of thousands."

"Hidalgo doesn't inject them or shove it up their noses," I objected, sounding not at all like a narcotics agent. But I thought I'd learned something over the years. "You can't blame him for the users."

"No?" she asked, raising her eyebrows. "Maybe you should ask Tom about that. Ask him about his sister. If people weren't selling the drugs, people wouldn't use them."

"Take out Hidalgo and someone just as bad will fill his shoes."

I was wussing out and I knew it. And Mary called me on it.

"Maybe. But we will have stopped *him*. Cut off his head and mounted it on the wall, as Tom likes to say."

As she said it she drew her hand across her throat like that guy in the window had, but she slashed instead of sawed. And she didn't stick out her tongue. I had to nod at her words, imagining Hidalgo and a whole row of his *sicarios* looking down from a long wall with dead, glassy eyes.

"What we've learned over the thirty years of the so-called War on Drugs is that although we will never win it, each time you lop off a head, the head that replaces it is weaker. Taking Hidalgo down will not only accomplish that, but it will also let them know that they cannot kill American agents with impunity. Right now they think they've gotten away with it. We need to teach them otherwise. They need to learn something about respect."

We watched each other for a minute. This time I was the one who looked up and studied the stars. It was getting cold out. I'd been hot and sweaty since leaving the bar, and the cold air felt good.

Mary, though, crossed her arms and shivered.

After a while she said, "This place is crazy. It's burning up one minute, freezing the next."

I didn't answer.

"Your brother is an extraordinary man, Anton. You know that, don't you? He can do this. I know he can. No one wants him to get hurt. That's not a price we want to pay just to get Hidalgo."

Oh? Would your partner agree with that? I didn't think so. *And if Roberto's killed, maybe even while being filmed on Tom's camera, then they can call in the troops and make an arrest for murder. That would sure be convenient, wouldn't it?*

But there was something in her voice that kept me from speaking. I studied her, feeling my head cock a little to one side the way Mungo's did when she was close to making a realization about some command I was trying to give her. It wasn't what Mary had said but the way she'd said it. The words had sounded far different from the professional way she'd been speaking to me.

"You're starting to like him, aren't you," I said. A statement of fact, not a question.

She kept staring at me with her glittering brown eyes. I imagined her blushing but it was too dark to see. I did see her stiffen, though. When she replied she sounded defiant.

"Yes. I am. If he hadn't gotten so messed up with drugs, he might have really made something of himself. He might yet."

"I'm scared that he's going to die in there, Mary," I said very softly.

Now it was her turn to look up at the stars.

SEVEN

When I woke up the next morning my whole body felt sore, as if it were still recovering from the tension I'd felt when Shorty came at me swinging that knife. My watch said it was eight o'clock already. Roberto was gone. His sleeping bag lay on the cot next to me like a snake's discarded skin. I expected to find him in the main cabin, where Mary would be making him cram for going across the river.

I would be driving him there later in the day.

The plan was that I'd take him across on the bridge that stood fifteen miles north of Potash, then drop him off high in the mountains. He would be carrying a pack and some of my climbing and camping gear. He'd spend twenty-four hours getting verifiably dirty and working his way down toward Hidalgo's place. The full day alone was also to give him time to, as Roberto said, get his head on straight, but I knew he intended to do a climb. Solo, of course. I'd lobbied to go with him but Mary had turned me down flat. And my brother didn't argue for me.

But they weren't cramming in the main cabin. I spotted them the instant I stepped out of the ramshackle little cabin. Mungo did, too. She headed straight for them, loping across the weeds and sage then running up the incline so gracefully it looked like she was floating.

Roberto was clinging to the overhanging rock I'd been screwing around on the day before. He was a lot higher than I'd dared to climb, almost at the upper lip. Because of the overhang and the way the hillside sloped away below, he was almost forty feet off the ground. Roberto was definitely in the coffin zone. Shirtless, the brown muscles in his shoulders and back coiled and uncoiled as he gripped tiny edges.

Mary sat below him, her back against a small boulder and her knees close to her chest. She was dressed as she'd been yesterday in khaki shorts and a red fleece jacket. The clothes were less incongruous on her than they'd seemed the day before. Something about her posture or the setting made her seem almost relaxed. She had her steaming coffee mug balanced on her knees. She was sipping from it as she watched Roberto moving high above her. For a moment I stood still, watching her watching him.

Then Mungo busted through the brush. The mug leapt in Mary's hands, and a brown spout rose a foot in the air before splashing down onto her shorts and legs. The spell was definitely broken. Mungo stood beneath Roberto, gazing up with tail wagging, while Mary wiped at her legs and looked at me with what might have been a scowl as I scrambled up the hillside.

My "Good morning" was answered with a curt nod.

"Where's Tom?" I asked. "Already up on the ridge?"

I couldn't see him. The shaded notch in the ridge looked unoccupied.

"No. He's gone to town. To look for those foreign cigarettes Roberto wanted."

"And the dude wasn't too happy about it," Roberto added, looking down over his shoulder. "Took off out of here like he was pretty pissed. I hope he's watching his blood pressure."

"He's going to have to go all the way to Rock Springs to find them, I bet." I wondered if Roberto had demanded the exotic bidis intentionally. Just to tweak Tom. The nearest store likely to have them was more than a hundred miles away. While I approved of the sentiment, I didn't like the thought of Tom cruising throughout the state in the obvious Suburban with its telltale antennae and California plates. Too many people would recognize a truck like that for what it was. "Did he take the Fed-mobile?"

"Would you give him your keys?" Mary asked.

"Uh-uh," Roberto answered for me. "No frigging way. What kind of car do you think ol' Tom drives in civilian life?" He was descending now to a safer height and swinging easily despite tiny holds that wouldn't accommodate much more than the tips of his fingers and toes.

"Tom doesn't have a civilian life," I said, thinking about it. "But if he did, he'd drive an identical truck, I bet. Smoked windows and antennae and all that. A guy like him needs to be the king of the road. And he'd have Harley stickers on the back."

"Not a Firebird or a Camaro, *che*?"

"Nah. When he was a kid, maybe. But now those are too Latin for him. He'd be afraid of looking like one of us greasers."

Roberto, on the ground now and shaking out his hands, nodded thoughtfully. He was smiling and I was, too. This was a game we'd played when we were kids. Guessing how far people would go to establish their identity, to fit into their chosen stereotype. It was intended to make us feel superior, I guess. A way of compensating with a new school on a new foreign base each year, with the same bullies and geeks and athletes. But it could be argued that we were guilty of it, too. The last thing I knew my brother to drive was a rebuilt Indian motorcycle from the 1950s. A stereotypical outlaw machine. And I drove my battered Pig, which was the quintessential climber's transport.

"You think he's queer?" my brother asked. "All that repressed rage and macho bullshit? The way the dude looks at me sometimes . . . I swear he's about to try and suck my face."

"Maybe," I said, laughing at the image.

Mary laughed, too. Her laugh—the first I'd heard from her—was a loud "Hah!" that she quickly gained control of. But still grinning, she said, "Come on. You guys stop making fun of him. He's my partner. And he's good at what he does."

"He's a pain in the ass," I said.

"You should make me your partner, *chica*. I make you laugh," Roberto said.

She shook her head and, looking like she was making an effort to be grave, said, "He might not be all that fun, but he is really good at what he does. And he's a true believer."

That quieted me down, the part about Tom being a believer. That was something I respected even when I didn't believe in the same things. Maybe that was why I respected it—because I didn't believe in anything anymore. Once I'd believed in the law as an instrument of absolute justice, but those days were long in the past. It was impressive that someone could be in law enforcement as long as Tom had and still keep the faith.

"What do you think Miss America here drives?" Roberto asked.

I looked at Mary. Her smile reappeared, but it seemed a little crooked. I don't think she wanted us prying into her personal life.

"She's got something sensible. Something, you know, federal and lawyerly. Like a nice, understated sedan. A BMW, or maybe an Audi."

Now Mary looked embarrassed. I was dead-on. And it was obvious I'd seen too far into her and viewed things that right here, right now, and in the present company, she didn't want known.

Roberto broke the uncomfortable silence. He said to Mary, with a mischievous grin, "Ask my bro what his fiancée drives."

Now it was my turn to look embarrassed. *Roberto, you prick.*

"You've got a fiancée?" she asked. "I didn't know that."

But I was glad there was something about me that wasn't in their file.

"Four months pregnant," Roberto said. "Just picked up a new car last month, right? C'mon, ask him what she drives."

"Okay, Anton. What does your pregnant fiancée drive?"

The answer was that she had recently bought a used poor-man's Porsche, also known as a Boxter. Unhappily, I admitted it.

"Flashy," Mary said, with her eyebrows raised. "I can't picture you with a woman like that."

I defended Rebecca's choice of automobile. "The pregnancy was unexpected. She says it's her way of coping with it."

Roberto laughed and punched my shoulder. "You know how many seats one of those things has? Two. No backseat at all. Where's Daddy going to sit?"

"There he is," Tom said, his face close to the camera's digital screen. I could hear him breathing. "Our boy. Looking sharp."

Tom had come back from his errand in midafternoon looking extremely pissed. He'd thrown a plastic bag with a dozen packages of bidis inside at Roberto then headed for the ridge without saying a word. He must have gone all the way to

Rock Springs. After a few minutes I'd followed him up. I was sick of having nothing to do.

All day I'd been listening to Mary coach Roberto: *Where were you on this particular day? On that? Who did you see? Who saw you? Why did you run from prison? Why did you come back to the States? What are you doing in these mountains? How did you know where to find Hidalgo? Why did you want to work for him again?* She had divided up the last twelve months of my brother's life into two separate lives, one fact and one fiction. The endless repetition of questions and answers was intended to turn the fiction into fact. Roberto had seemed to mind less than you would expect. He was having fun with Mary, drawing her out of her shell. He'd even gotten her up on the rock that morning, where she'd shown surprising strength as well as a not-so-surprising amount of determination.

"Let me see."

Reluctantly Tom yielded the camera and scooted backward beneath the canopy of juniper branches. I slid in behind the tripod. The camera was focused on the chairs beside the swimming pool.

Jesús Hidalgo had neither horns nor a forked tail, both of which I'd been expecting despite the photograph I'd already seen. There was no obvious menace in the man's appearance at this distance. He was certainly no *chupacabra*. He looked neither like a murderer—by whose order or by whose hand hundreds had died—or a billionaire. He was just a fat slob with slicked-back hair, a gold Malverde medallion around his neck, and a tiny swimsuit around an expansive waist.

It's hard to look dangerous in a pair of black bikini briefs—maybe that's why no one respects the French. You see how exposed a man is, how easy it would be to kick him in the nuts. Clogged arteries would kill him as easily as a silver bullet or a wooden stake. Looking down at him through the telescopic lens, I saw that Hidalgo was just a man who drank too much, ate too much, ran a stressful business, and casually adorned people he didn't like with neckties made of their own tongues.

He was lounging in a chair, wearing dark glasses. He held a newspaper that was flapping in the wind on his hairy belly. The other men had disappeared in order, I supposed, to give El Doctor his privacy.

"What does he do with all his cash?" I asked.

Behind me, Tom snorted. "He's not spending it on liposuction, I can tell you that. Not after what he had done to Carrillo."

He was talking about Amado Carrillo-Fuentes, the deceased head of the Juárez cartel, whom Tom had once chased. He chuckled. "You know the story. Rumor is Hidalgo was one of the 'doctors.' Wore a surgical mask the whole time so Carrillo's bodyguards wouldn't recognize him. That's really when people began calling him El Doctor. He didn't even own that chain of pharmacies back then. This was a couple of years ago, when Hidalgo liked to take a personal hand in these things. Anyway, it was nicer than what he did to one of Carrillo's top lieutenants. See, Hidalgo found out the guy's trophy wife was vacationing with their kids in San Francisco. So he flew up there and convinced her she'd be better off with him. They raided the lieutenant's bank accounts—took out something like twenty million. Then he cut off her head and FedExed it to Juárez. Imagine opening that package. Threw the lieutenant's kids off a bridge, too."

"If that's true, why didn't you get him for the murders on American soil?"

"The Coast Guard fished the kids out of the bay, but there was no evidence linking Hidalgo to it. Just rumor, as always. No one would talk. *La corbata,* remember?"

I stared at the screen, zooming it in on Hidalgo's face.

There was something disturbing about how normal he looked. How pathetic with his longish hair, his fat waist, and the stupid bikini swimsuit. I wanted him to take off his sunglasses so that I could see his eyes. I wanted to see the monster there. That was what was so disturbing—he looked like anyone. Anyone could be a monster. But after eight years of making arrests, I still didn't understand how one became a monster. Was it greed, or lust for power, or the simple lack of empathy?

"What does he do with all his money?" I repeated.

"A lot of it goes to bribes. The DEA estimates it at over a hundred mil a year from just Hidalgo's Mexicali Mafia alone, but there's no way to know for sure. But remember when Presidente Salinas's big brother Raul was seized by the Swiss? He had well over a hundred million bucks in just his Swiss account. The Brits grabbed another twenty-four million in an account he had there. The DEA thinks the Salinas brothers left office with nearly a billion. El Presidente, by the way, is now living in exile in a castle in Ireland."

The numbers sounded outlandish. But I knew that narcotics trafficking was Mexico's number one industry, estimated at thirty-two billion dollars a year. So Hidalgo, who transported about a quarter of all the cocaine, could easily afford to give the police, judges, and politicians there a hundred million a year. The Mexican government must love it. They get all that cash, plus almost another hundred million a year in clean money from the States for supposed antidrug aid.

Tom was still talking. "Hidalgo probably manages to wash a lot of it, but it isn't easy. He pushes millions through his pharmacies, grocery stores, mining operations, and hotel chains, but even that's tough to do. We think a lot of it just gets buried. That he makes a big hole in the ground and just stuffs it in."

I moved the lens up as I wondered about that. Every now and then a state highway patrolman would make a traffic stop and find a car filled with bundled cash. On its way to Mexico. You couldn't fit more than a few hundred thousand in a standard-sized car. It was less difficult than bringing drugs into the country—there wasn't any search at the border—but it had to be a pain nonetheless. The lens refocused automatically where I'd aimed it a half-mile back from the house. There were the long construction trailers, then beyond them a wasteland of dirt and debris, and then the entrance to the mine. Men were hanging around outside the trailers. Some of them were loading cardboard boxes onto the back of a pickup truck. The truck was pointed toward the mine.

Tom continued, "The bribes he pays are so big, and paid to people so high up, that he'll never be arrested in Mexico. And for the same reason a lot of people in our government don't want him arrested here. If he were to start talking, it would stir up all kinds of trouble for Congress the next time they have to recertify Mexico for foreign aid."

"Why do we care if everyone knows how corrupt the Mexican government is?"

Tom chuckled at my ignorance. "Because if they were to be exposed, they would stop even pretending to care about drug smuggling into the States. Because they are one of our biggest trading partners. Because without drug money, by far their largest resource, we'd have revolution to the south and a flood of refugees coming north like nothing we've ever seen."

I turned around and looked at him. "Then how come you want to arrest him here?"

Tom took a minute, staring back at me.

"Fuck him. Fuck politics. Fuck Mexico. This guy's killed a federal agent and he's going to pay the price."

Yes, Tom was a believer. I admired that even if I didn't like him.

I scooted back and gave up the camera. Tom resumed his post at the tripod, a pilot's notebook Velcroed to one of his thighs. I watched as he began to scribble obsessively in tiny, precise letters. He seemed to be documenting everything.

For a few minutes I amused myself by speculating about what he was writing. *Suspect reads Tijuana paper. Suspect has large mole on the left side of his chest. Suspect needs to cut his nails. Suspect has skinny ankles and an apparently unimpressive package.*

"You know this guy as well as anyone, right?" I asked after several minutes that were silent but for the scratching of his pen.

"Yeah," Tom said, not turning around. Still scribbling. "I've been on his ass for almost four years."

"What do you think he's going to do when Roberto shows up at his door?"

Tom shrugged, still not turning. But he stopped writing.

"He'll let him in. If your brother wasn't bullshitting us about dragging him off that mountain in Argentina. Then he'll sit on him for a while to give his security guys a chance to sniff around him. Then it's anybody's guess. Depends on just how good a bullshitter your brother is. They'll put him to work or they'll kill him and we'll get us a warrant. Either way, he'll get us in."

EIGHT

To get to the other side of the river, you either had to take the same route Hidalgo's men used when going home from a fun night out at Señor Garcia's or you could swim. We were going to stay dry.

From Potash, the land route involved taking a paved county road south twelve miles, then another paved road east to cross the wide, red river on a suspension bridge. On the other side there was a gravel road that ran all the way up to a trailhead in the mountains. There was also a dirt road paralleling the river that ran north and south. The way north was impeded by a cattle guard and a barbed-wire gate. Nailed to the posts that supported the wire were signs reading in English and Spanish, "Keep Out. No Trespassing. Violators Will Be Shot."

We kept out, staying on the gravel, which wound up through the foothills and then entered pine forests on the way to the high peaks. But as we passed the signs I couldn't help slowing and staring north, remembering from Tom's satellite photo the camper that was down that road, just out of sight. Hidalgo surely had a few armed men there, probably some lowly bangers with big guns.

Roberto didn't comment as we passed the narco's ten-mile-long driveway. He didn't even look that way. Instead he doodled away on one of Mary's legal pads, holding the pad in the crook of his left arm so I couldn't see what he was doing. The ride so far had been in silence, except for the José Cura disk that Roberto had slipped into the CD player. The spooky tenor's voice was starting to freak me out.

"You sure you want to do this?" I asked him, turning the music down.

Roberto didn't answer right away.

Outside the Pig's open windows was a pine forest. You could see the trees even with your eyes closed because their smell was so strong. Especially after days down in the high desert. Mungo was trembling in the backseat. She was dying to get out and run around in the forest. A small lake on the left reflected snowcapped peaks in the fading light. It was beautiful up here, but the music and our purpose somehow made it a little sinister.

"I'm going to do it," Roberto finally said. "Relax, bro. It's gonna be fun."

I slowed as the pavement turned to gravel. The washboards made the CD skip. Thankfully, I turned it off.

"You don't have to, you know. You can just take off. What are they going to do? Put out another warrant for your arrest?"

He was shaking his head, putting away the pad of paper by tucking it into the door's pocket.

He pointed out the windshield. "Is that Gannett?"

He was indicating a spirelike peak shrouded with glaciers.

"No. Gannett's a long ways north. That's East Temple Peak."

He stared at it. "It'll do."

I could see what he meant. There was a face that was easily a thousand feet high and, as far as I knew, was virginal, never been climbed. The face looked dangerous. A good part of it looked to be overhanging. The rock was black—maybe rotten—and the glacier on the summit dropped over the top with long daggers of ice.

Instead of asking if that was a good idea, I asked, "Are you going to have time for that?"

He nodded, studying it through the windshield. "I'll hoof it up to the base tonight, start early, and be down at Jesús's by midnight tomorrow."

It was a good ten miles or more cross-country to Hidalgo's property.

"You're going to be wasted," I warned him.

"If I'm late, I'm late."

"Did you pack enough gear for something like that?"

He just smiled.

We rattled and shook for fifteen more minutes. It had been a half hour since we'd seen the last car going down the other way. The trailhead was a fairly popular, as well as isolated, entry point for the Winds, but it was late Sunday afternoon and the vacationing climbers and campers were heading home. Roberto would have it all to himself.

"What do you do if there's trouble? What's the signal?" I asked him.

He smirked at me.

"Mary says I'm to get naked, go out on the lawn by the pool, and do the Macarena while you guys take pictures."

"C'mon, 'Berto. This is important."

Now he sighed.

"Stop worrying about me, okay? Everything's going to be cool. If things are looking bad, I go out on the lawn, put both hands behind my head, and stretch."

"That's the official version. What are you really going to do?"

"If I listen to my chickenshit little brother, I'll head for the hills."

"Good. Listen to your chickenshit little brother. Screw the Feds. You don't owe them anything. Especially not your life."

There were only two cars parked at the trailhead. One had green Colorado plates, the other white Californians. Both looked like they'd been there for a while. It was a wonder they hadn't had their windows broken. Greenies—Coloradoans—aren't that popular in Wyoming and Left Coasters are even less so. Too many of them were moving here. Mungo squeezed out the window before I could even open the door for her and sprinted into the trees.

Although it was cool, Roberto pulled his T-shirt up. He didn't take it all the way off but let the neck stay around his head, above his face, where it would hold back his hair. There had been a picture once in a climbing magazine of him using a shirt just like that. Two-thirds of the way up El Cap, two thousand feet off the deck. No rope. Looking, just like he did now, impossibly strong. It became trendy for a while for young climbers to wear their shirts like that.

Unstoppable, I told myself. *Remember that. He's even crazier than the narcos. He's lighter than air. If gravity can't touch him, they can't, either.*

I wanted to ask him why the hell he was doing this. But I held my tongue as I had held it the whole ride out and for the last three days. I just prayed that when it was all over, he would still hold his.

Without saying anything at all, we hugged and then he shouldered the pack we'd prepared. It held no transmitters, no cameras, none of the technological junk that Tom had wanted to put in there. Just camping and climbing gear and the packages of bidis Roberto would write us messages on. Mary had said Roberto's notes would be enough for a warrant, that we couldn't run the risk of Hidalgo having him searched. Tom had argued bitterly, but, thank God, to no avail. I didn't want to think what would happen if Hidalgo's *sicarios* searched the backpack and found a transmitter.

Mungo came back to stand beside me. She looked up at me, cocking her head, wondering why I wasn't putting on a pack, too.

Roberto bent and thumped her shoulders. Then he hit mine.

"See ya, *che*."

"Be real careful, 'Berto."

I had to hold Mungo's collar as he walked away.

What he'd been doodling on the legal pad was bizarre. I pulled it out of the passenger door's pocket as soon as he was out of sight, heading for the peaks.

On the first page there was a cartoonish drawing of a laughing wolf's face. Tongue lolling, lips raised in a happy smile, like Mungo after a run. I thought maybe it was a crude portrait of her, but there was a caption printed beneath it that read, "The Wolf Who Wanted to Be a Little Girl."

What the fuck?

Below that it said, *"Por mi sobrina, de tu Tío Roberto."*

On the following pages was a strange little story, written in pencil, with a lot crossed out and other parts erased. Crude sketches accompanied each part of the story.

"There once was a wolf who wished she could be a little girl. She watched the kids playing in the meadow and wanted to play with them."

The drawing on this page was of a wolf peering Mungo-like out of the trees on the edge of a field. Children were playing with balls and climbing around on rocks. I smiled. My brother was no artist, but he'd caught Mungo there, doing her you-can't-see-me thing.

"She wanted to run on her hind legs, to wear a blue dress, to laugh, and to make the other kids laugh. But she couldn't do any of these things very well."

A series of rough sketches showed a wolf trying to walk on her back legs, trying to nose her way into a dress, and, in front of a microphone, trying—I guessed—to tell a joke.

"She thought about it. What makes one a little girl? Two legs instead of four? Round ears instead of pointed? No tail? The wolf thought this might be the one big drawback to being a little girl. How do they warm their noses on a cold night?"

More pictures. Crude, but kind of cute. And definitely perverse, having been drawn by Roberto's hand.

"But the wolf was smart enough to know that it's not two legs, or hands with thumbs, or even round ears, that makes one a little girl. Those are only the outer manifestations of girl-hood. What makes one a girl is when you are there for your friends, when you make them laugh, and laugh with them."

"The wolf ran out of the forest and tried to join the children. At first they ran away. They screamed and called for their mothers and fathers. They were very afraid. But the wolf began running in circles, chasing her tail. The children stopped running. The wolf pulled up her lips and began walking around on just her hind legs. The children laughed. The wolf lay on her back and kicked her legs like she was riding a bicycle. The children came to her. They stroked her and petted her. She licked them and gave them rides on her back. And they laughed with her. And she with them. She never hurt any of them. She was their best friend, standing up for them when she needed to, chasing off the bad kids who wanted to hurt them. She became a little girl in all the important ways."

I mumbled one more *What the fuck?* The wolf looked like Mungo, but using the maybe true/maybe bullshit powers

about interpreting symbolism that I'd learned in college liter-
ature classes, I was betting that the wolf was Roberto. And he
didn't want to be a little girl, but he wanted to be one of us.
One of the kids. Playing our games, yeah, but also chasing off
the bad kids—like Hidalgo.

Holding the notebook propped against the steering wheel
with my thighs, I rubbed my face while looking down at it. My
throat felt a little tight. My eyes got a little wet. *Roberto. You
are a trip, bro.*

2

He clasps the crag with crooked hands;
Close to the sun in lonely lands,
Ring'd with the azure world, he stands.

The wrinkled sea beneath him crawls;
He watches from his mountain walls,
And like a thunderbolt he falls.

> — *"The Eagle"*
> *Alfred Lord Tennyson, 1851*

NINE

nterstate 25, running from Wyoming to Denver, is straight, flat, and all downhill. Traffic was light going south in the dark, and my gold-plated badge allowed my foot to lie heavy on the accelerator. Mungo leapt and spun around in the backseat of the Pig after testing the air. She realized where we were going. And who we were going to see.

I waited until I was past the stench of the cattle yards outside Greeley, Colorado, before I picked up my cell phone and speed-dialed Rebecca's number. She answered on the first ring.

"It's me," I told her, trying to rein in the excitement that I, too, was feeling. "I'm about an hour out."

"Good. I'm cooking."

She was a lousy cook, but that didn't put a brake on my anticipation. She only knew two dishes—one a sort of tofu goulash, the other a quiche—but I didn't care. In fact, I would gratefully lap up anything she put before me because I knew what could come later. Maybe even before. I didn't know if I could wait to feel her naked skin. To be engulfed by it. To run my hands over her belly and see if I could finally detect the swell of my growing child.

"I've got a surprise for you, Ant."

"Tell me."

"I guess you didn't hear me. I said it's a surprise."

"At least give me a hint, smart-ass. Is it something you're wearing?"

She laughed. "No. It's most definitely not something I'm wearing."

My heart rate picked up. My foot pressed a little harder on the accelerator. Rebecca always ran hot and cold when it came to me, and tonight it appeared I would be in luck. It definitely seemed to be hot.

"I need another hint. Some graphic description, maybe."

"No more hints. Hurry home. Drive safe."

Home. That sounded good. Almost as good as the bare flesh I was picturing in my head, the thick brown hair that hung in tangles to below her breasts and provided such dazzling contrast against her white skin. For the next twenty-four hours, I didn't intend to think about my brother or murderous drug lords or uptight FBI agents.

I found a parking space for the Pig near Speer Boulevard, only two blocks from Rebecca's loft in Denver's LoDo district. The early-evening crowd was everywhere on the streets, coming and going out of trendy restaurants and bars and, after getting a few dirty looks, I snapped a leash on Mungo's collar. No one but Roberto and me wants to see a wolf running loose on the streets of Denver.

I poked the elevator button in the lobby while Mungo tap-danced with her long nails on the marble floor. The elevator didn't come. I poked a few more times, Mungo danced some more, and still the elevator didn't come. So I hit the stairwell door and started climbing with Mungo lunging at my heels.

We burst out onto the sixth-floor hallway and barely missed knocking down a small child that belonged to the other loft on the floor. She was pulling a wagon full of stuffed bears, moose, and wolves.

"Sorry, honey," I yelled as we ran past.

The little girl stared at Mungo with huge eyes and a dreamy smile.

"Mun-GO!" she shouted.

The real wolf, trailing her leash, slicked back the girl's hair with her tongue as she galloped after me.

At Rebecca's door I took a moment to compose myself, trying to control my heavy breathing. I meant to take longer than I did—but picturing Rebecca somewhere behind the door had my knuckles beating on the metal after only two inhalations. I didn't use my key because I wanted her to be there, letting me in.

The door swung open before my hand was back down at my side. What stood before me was not my naked fiancée. Instead it was someone ugly and misshapen, someone looking malevolent and slightly obscene. His name was Ross McGee. He resembled Santa's evil twin, but instead of a red hat and a fur-fringed coat, he wore a pin-striped suit.

"QuickDraw," he rasped, the words followed by a familiar odor of whiskey and cheap cigars. "Is that your gun in your pocket or are you just happy to see me?"

I stared at my boss, saying nothing. All the excitement drained away. Beside me Mungo began to rumble.

Ross McGee grinned at the wolf for a moment, exposing his own large teeth, then held out his meaty hand for her to sniff. He held it in a peculiar manner, with his middle finger extended toward the dog's snout.

Mungo must have understood the gesture, because she refused to sniff. She backed away a step, growling louder, and slipped behind me.

"Ross," I heard myself growl. "What the hell are you doing here?"

"A man can't visit his goddaughter? Can't check up on his most troublesome employee? The same bastard who had the unbelievable audacity to impregnate her?"

I'd used up all my luck that night in Cheyenne two and a half years ago. Since then the karmic payback had been an unrelenting bitch. An investigation into my conduct, a lawsuit, the media condemnation, and the nickname . . . all that on top of what was going on with my brother. But the worst of it, at that moment, seemed to be that I'd fallen for the daughter of my boss's old comrade in arms from their army days together. Even if I were to finally quit my job with DCI, Ross McGee would still be around to haunt me.

"Surprise!" came a voice from behind Ross. I could hear a bit of irony in the exclamation.

Mungo stopped growling and darted past McGee. Although I tried, I couldn't help but smile as the wolf planted her paws on Rebecca's shoulders and bowled her onto the big velvet couch in the center of the room. There Mungo licked her cheeks and throat ecstatically, the way I would have liked to but couldn't in present company.

"Great surprise, 'Becca," I said, sliding around my boss. "All my Christmases have come at once."

I dragged Mungo off Rebecca then quickly bent and kissed my often-reluctant fiancée. Even though she'd played this dirty trick on me, I couldn't help but light up at the sight of her and the touch of her lips. Even though she was clothed.

She looked spectacular. She wore a sleeveless black blouse and a green silk skirt, both of which I was aching to lift off her. Her rich tangle of hair was pulled back loosely and her feet and legs were bare.

In a crowded room or at a party, Rebecca Hersh might not immediately draw a man's attention. That usually went to the loud bleached blondes with their fake tans, revealing clothes, and carefully applied makeup. But Rebecca would draw a second look, and then some talk if you were brave enough. And from that point on you'd be like me—absolutely hooked. Her brown eyes, when viewed up close, were a kaleidoscope of color. Slivers of gold, orange, and green danced within her irises.

"Hi, Ant," she said, giving me the full, up-close effect of the eyes.

McGee, who'd followed behind me, raised his cane sharply between my legs, making me jump.

"That's enough of that, Burns. You're going to make me sick. It's like watching an alley cat try and hump a Persian."

Rebecca got McGee and me seated across from each other over a silver bowl of crackers and a bottle of wine. She worked in the open kitchen, all the way across the big living room. She'd refused to let me help—not that I would have been able to do anything, but I would have liked to at least try instead of sitting across from my boss.

"What's happening in Podunk?" McGee demanded.

He meant Potash, which I'd heard him describe as Wyoming's rural ghetto.

I shrugged. I didn't want to think about it. Not here, not now. I looked around the room and tried to make myself feel at home in these modern surroundings. The big windows, the recessed lights, the bright art, the traffic noise below, and even the woman herself made me feel foreign. Even after more than a year of visiting her here. None of it was like anything I'd ever known or pursued. It was all exotic to me, a whole other world. Past girlfriends had been climbers, skiers, kayakers— all nature freaks. Their ideal homes had mostly been trucks and tents.

"Surveillance. Setting up a confidential informant. Nothing much," I said.

"Oh? Is that why you haven't reported in? You've been too busy?"

He was staring at me, leaning forward on the couch as if the weight of his gut were dragging him toward the floor. His blue irises were bright and hard even though they swam in wet, yellowish orbs. The long white beard was bristling, as were his wiry eyebrows.

"I'm attached to the Feds for six weeks, Ross. I don't work for you right now."

"Bullshit," McGee said. "Who signs your paychecks, ingrate?"

"The Wyoming Attorney General. Not you."

"You think he'd be signing them if I wasn't covering your ass? No, lad, you'd get an official pat on the back, an unofficial kick in the nuts, and a letter of termination so fast you wouldn't know whether to puke or cry. Now give it up."

He was right, of course. I was holding back only because of the subject matter, the place and time, and the churlishness that characterized our relationship.

Ross McGee had been a pain in my ass since I started with DCI—I nearly quit the first day I met him. The last two years he'd become an even greater pain since sparing me a political prosecution for what had happened that night in Cheyenne. He owned me now—there was no getting around it. The pain of his mentorship had magnified into almost agony since I began sleeping with his goddaughter. He was loathed by our superiors for the way he forced them to toe the line, was admired but avoided by his subordinates for his perpetual orneriness and off-color remarks, and, next to my brother, was probably the best friend I've ever had.

He'd once been a legendary trial attorney but age, ill health, and ever-increasing vulgarity had made him no longer effective in front of a jury. So he was relegated by the senior suits at the AG's office to riding herd over the twenty-six special agents. It was a saddle they hoped he'd soon die in.

I put it off for a moment longer by calling out to Rebecca, "I can't believe you told him I was coming down here."

"He called and asked if I'd heard from you. What was I supposed to say?"

"You should have lied. I thought you were more loyal than that. Bad fiancée."

McGee grinned at me. "You know what Chauncey Depew said? 'A pessimist is a man who thinks all women are bad. An optimist is a man who hopes they are.' "

"Who the hell is Chauncey Depew? Is he that skunk in the cartoons?"

McGee let out a wounded groan and muttered something profane about my ignorance.

I got up and went over to where Rebecca's small Bose stereo was installed on a built-in bookcase. Trumpety jazz came on when I hit the CD button. I turned it up high enough that I didn't think she could hear us across the wide-open space that stood between the chairs and sofa and the kitchen area. After looking out the floor-to-ceiling window for a moment toward the Front Range, I sat down again facing McGee.

I quietly told him about the mine purportedly owned by a Mexican City attorney, Jesús Hidalgo's residence there, and my brother going in as the Feds' confidential informant. Until now he'd known only what I'd known before arriving in Potash—that Roberto had turned himself in and they wanted my help in controlling him while they pumped him for information.

Listening, McGee looked even more appalled than usual.

"Jesus Christ!" came coughing out of his emphysemic lungs. "Putting in a murdering nutcase like your brother to act as a CI? An escaped felon and a drug addict to boot? They think anything he gives them is going to convince a judge to grant them a warrant? Who the hell's running this goatfuck?"

I hadn't really thought about that. Some judges—particularly federal judges who crossed their *t*'s and dotted their *i*'s—might have a problem with accepting the testimony of Roberto as McGee had described him. With CIs you had to give the deciding judge an opinion as to the informant's reliability. Some background regarding credibility. But I assumed Mary and Tom had thought about that, that they'd have some other evidence to back him up.

"An FBI agent named Mary Chang," I told him.

"Who's behind her?"

"I don't know. Why?"

"Because when my boss, our beloved Attorney General, asked where you are and why you hadn't been causing any trouble lately, he nearly had a shitfit. He'd just been at a meeting in Washington with the director of the FBI, where he'd been told that there were no current federal operations in the state other than the usual bank robberies and insurance fraud. With something this big, either the director was lying or he didn't know about it."

I was confused. I didn't understand why McGee was so worked up about this part of it. The director of the FBI couldn't keep tabs on every case his office was investigating. Not in these post-9/11 days when the Bureau was under such heavy fire. But this was, obviously, a potentially very big case.

"Who came to you to get me assigned in the first place?" I asked.

McGee had ordered me to meet the Feds in Salt Lake and work with them without explaining who had requested me to do so. I hadn't asked. I'd known it was about my brother.

"The same Mary Chang. After the Attorney General came back yesterday, I checked up on her. She's assigned to the San

Diego office. I called there. They said she was taking some personal leave."

What the hell? Maybe it was a cover.

"Did you tell them who you are?" I asked.

"Of course I did. That didn't change their answer, except to tell me that a colleague of hers had been murdered. She's not on assignment, secret or otherwise. She's freelancing. And dragging you into it. Christ! I'm going to make some calls and shut her down."

"Don't," I told him, my voice sharp.

It explained all those things I'd been wondering about. Why they didn't have more guys. Why Mary and Tom didn't seem to need to report to anyone, not even with a case this big. It wasn't right. I felt sick. And it might be too late to stop Roberto.

Rebecca called out, sounding just like Mary but smiling, "Eat, gentlemen."

The portions on the table were small, and the smell wasn't particularly pleasant, but I didn't comment and McGee only asked for hot sauce. This, something called Kick Yo Ass that Rebecca kept around just for him, he dumped all over the contents of his bowl. It wasn't long before beads of sweat were rolling down his freckled scalp and he was noisily snorting into one of my fiancée's linen napkins. I did my best to swallow the goulash and with it my rising panic.

Aside from that, the food, and the guest, Rebecca managed to make the meal agreeable. She did it by just being there for me to watch. And touch, as under the table she'd put one bare foot between my legs. With my left hand I rolled around and around the gold ring she wore on one toe. I barely said a word as she answered McGee's questions about what stories she was working on.

One story had me concerned—she was looking into hazardous chemicals at Shattuck, the chemical company's dumping ground outside Denver. This was a place that was allegedly brimming with chemical and radioactive leftovers. I didn't want her nosing around there, especially not with the child in her belly, and said so.

Rebecca responded by giving me a direct look and a half-smile.

"And what do you do for work and fun, Ant? Are you out there playing it safe?"

McGee snorted into his napkin.

"You've got more than just you to worry about," I said, giving the ring another gentle turn.

"And you don't?"

I kept myself from responding. But I wanted to say, *Not really, not when you won't talk about wedding plans. Not when you're out buying that ridiculous two-seater car. Not when you won't even give a clue as to where we're going.* Instead I smiled and let it pass.

"What do you plan on naming the spawn?" McGee asked, enjoying the show.

"Ross. Master Ross Hersh-Burns," Rebecca said with an alarmingly straight face.

"Sounds like heartburn," Ross said. His satyr's grin grew broader.

"Over my dead body."

McGee eyed me and stroked his beard. "That can be arranged, lad. That *certainly* can be arranged."

"Anyway, it's going to be a girl," I said.

Mom's tarot cards combined with Roberto's dedication of his strange story to *"mi sobrina"* made it seem like a safe bet. Besides, I thought, Fate wouldn't be so cruel as to give me a boy to take after his father the way Roberto and I had taken after ours.

"It's going to be one screwed-up kid, that's for sure," McGee mused. "Mom is smart and pretty and Dad is slobbering mad. She likes museums and ballet and he likes rocks and guns—"

"I don't like guns—" I tried to interrupt, but he was on a roll.

"—her job is to tell the truth and he's a professional liar." The litany continued. McGee finally wound down, shaking his big head and saying, "The poor kid's going to need me around to keep her straightened out."

Rebecca was watching him and smiling with what I guessed was fondness or amusement. I was watching him, too, not smiling at all.

"How much you had to drink, boss?" I asked.

"Not nearly enough, Burns. Something like this happens to your goddaughter and it keeps you stone sober."

"Good. Then you shouldn't have any trouble driving yourself home. Come on. I'll walk you out."

"So where's your lunatic brother?" McGee demanded when we were out on the street. "If he's in there, you're going to have a hell of a time getting him out."

"That's why you can't shut it down. Not yet. Not until I make sure he's safe."

McGee hobbled in silence for half a block, leaning heavily on his cane. There were fewer people on the street now. Those that were seemed to be mostly drunk fraternity boys. A couple of them howled at Mungo. Car tires squealed around corners, sirens sounded in the distance, and in an alley nearby someone was pouring a trash can full of bottles into a broken Dumpster. I wasn't sure I could ever get used to this. And there wasn't much hope of getting Rebecca to move to Wyoming.

McGee's car was in a lot only a block away, but it took us almost fifteen minutes to get there. We were silent for a while as my boss limped along and my wolf-dog sniffed at anything that protruded from the ground.

Finally McGee asked, "Well? Is he in there?"

"No. Not yet. But he's on his way. If I leave early enough in the morning I might be able to head him off." There wasn't any signal to abort, but I thought I might be able to catch him as he came down out of the mountains.

"Do it," he said.

"And Jesús Hidalgo's going to walk again." I shook my head. "He offed that Fed, you know. That guy in Mexicali that was in the news about two months ago? He was a friend of Mary Chang's and this guy Tom Cochran who works with her."

McGee grunted and stabbed the sidewalk with his cane.

"Not our job, QuickDraw."

"Why are you so sure they're freelancing? Maybe she has someone high up behind her. Maybe they're just keeping it quiet."

McGee stopped and looked at me as if I were an idiot.

"Because the Hoover Building would never approve it. The State Department would have conniptions. Don't you read the papers, Burns? This animal Hidalgo's seriously connected and Mexico's our best friend. Our little buddy to the south. No one's going to do anything to embarrass the administration there. It would make every politician from the President on down look like they were sanctioning a drug empire, which they are, by the way. But that's the best-kept secret in foreign policy and they're going to keep it that way."

"I can't believe they'd let him get away with killing a U.S. agent."

McGee chuckled. "They won't. I can guarantee you that

pressure's being applied to get the Mexes to clean up their own mess. They don't want him arrested up here where he can get a deal by threatening to flap his lips about who he's been paying and how much. He or his lawyer will talk to the media if the Feds don't offer him one, and they'll embarrass a lot of people in our government."

We were at his car, a Chrysler New Yorker. McGee opened the door and flopped down onto the seat. He continued to talk as he fought to get the seat belt around his waist.

"Most likely they're pressuring the Mexes to set him up for a hit by another cartel. All those big narcos use cops anyway, so it won't be a problem. Like when Ramon Arellano got whacked in Mazatlán by cops who probably worked for Hidalgo. Served three purposes: The Mexes got to claim they took down a big boy, Hidalgo got to knock off a competitor, and we got to claim all our antidrug money really is doing some good. But like I said, it's not our job. Thank God. It's a filthy business down there. Just like in Washington."

What I didn't understand was, if it was true that Mary and Tom were freelancing, what did they hope to accomplish. My best guess was that if they managed to arrest Hidalgo, and make it public, then the FBI and the U.S. Attorneys who prosecuted their cases would have no choice but to go along at that point. Hidalgo was too well known—too much had been written about him and his bloody dealings with the Arellanos just a hundred miles south of Los Angeles— for anything to be hushed up.

"Get your brother out of it," McGee said, finally getting the belt to lock. He was breathing hard from the struggle and glaring up at me with his fierce eyes. "And call me within the next twenty-four hours. I'll hold off on doing anything until then. And tell Ms. Chang I want to meet her in person before the Feds can her ass. Maybe I'll hire her. That woman, she's got balls."

When I went back into the apartment, Rebecca was standing across the room by the bedroom doorway. The room was lit only by a fire. She was smiling slightly, not saying a word. The jazz on the stereo had been replaced by Big Head Todd and the Monsters. It had a lot of bass and a slow, seductive beat. I think the song was "Turn the Light Out." She'd turned it up very loud.

I unleashed Mungo, who lapped at her bowl then lay down by the gas fire. I sat in one of the big chairs and, smiling, too, motioned Rebecca toward me. The music was too loud in the room for talk. But she didn't come.

Instead she lifted her thin arms and began unbuttoning the blouse. All thought about what was going on in Potash, Wyoming, disappeared by the time a black lace bra was exposed. *Roberto's going to be fine, right?* The world receded even further and the shirt was pulled off. She reached behind her, arching her back, and unzipped her skirt and slowly let it drop to her ankles. Her underwear was black lace, too. When she turned to the side I could see a slight roundness to her belly but the rest of her was as taut and supple as ever.

Leaning forward, she let her hair spill over her face and hide her smile as she slid her underwear off. Then she unhooked and lifted off her bra. Her breasts were definitely larger than when I'd last seen them. I motioned her toward me again, but still she wouldn't come. Instead she began to move to the music. You could see why she'd once been an aspiring ballerina as a young girl—she still had the moves.

I felt something like what my brother must feel when he pushes the needle's plunger with his thumb. It was a narcotic trance, heavy and thick. Just when I thought my worries about

Roberto and Potash might overwhelm me, I lay back in the chair and let my legs fall open. Probably my mouth, too.

Rebecca moved farther into the bedroom doorway. She began to slowly writhe out of sight. I didn't know if I could move. All that was visible was her shoulder and arm. Then her index finger cocked at me and drew me in.

Later, in bed and once our mutual panting had slowed, she said to me, "You've been away for a while, Ant."

"How could you tell?"

She chuckled from down deep in her throat. It sounded like it came from another person. She was like that in bed.

"Wow. We haven't done it like that in a while. You must have had some venting to do."

I nodded, saying, "Yeah, I just hope it was safe. For our little girl."

She laughed now.

"You're afraid of hurting the baby? You don't know much about female anatomy, Ant."

That reassured me, but still, I couldn't help worrying. We'd been going at it pretty hard. Feeling stoned in the afterglow, I now worried about having poked her in the head. Maybe even taking an eye out. Or making the baby's head look like a golf ball.

When I mentioned this to Rebecca she laughed again and wrapped her hand around me. She slid her head down my stomach and said to it, "You've got nothing to worry about, my little friend."

"Hey, what do you mean by that?"

She didn't answer but I could sense the vibrations of more laughter.

When Rebecca was feeling hot for me, she was on fire. It almost made me forget about the cold times. As far as I was concerned, she only had two faults. One was that she didn't like my brother—he absolutely scared the shit out of her. Not because of who he was or what he might do, she said, but because of what I felt for him. The other fault was a total inability to understand the thrill that came with getting your heels a thousand feet off the deck. She claimed to be utterly mystified by my addiction to it. She disliked my profession, too, of course, but that was okay—I was getting pretty ambivalent about it myself.

I clawed my fingers through her hair and thought that I should tell her that *this* was what climbing was about. This feeling of absolute rapture. But I kept my mouth shut. I didn't want to ruin the moment.

But my cell phone did just that.

It flashed a green light from the nightstand. My first thought was that it was McGee, calling from his car on the way to Cheyenne. Not with some new question or order, but just because he'd known what Rebecca and I might be doing right about now.

The phone stopped beeping, then started again. It seemed even louder this time. When it stopped, the message indicator chimed. I couldn't stop myself from gently lifting a hand from Rebecca's head and tilting the phone toward me. There was a text message on the digital display. It said FEDS, meaning the incoming call was from the number I'd programmed for Mary's satellite phone. After that it said 911 911 911.

"What are you doing, Ant?" Rebecca asked, lifting her head. Her voice was no longer low and seductive.

"Shit. Something's happened."

The phone started beeping all over again.

"I'm sorry," I said, closing my eyes hard and feeling a cold little rush of fear run through my overheated limbs.

Rebecca rolled off me and walked out of the room. Her back was stiff. She didn't look back. Out in the living room the music was cut off instead of just being turned down.

I hit the recall button, calling up the number for Mary's encrypted satellite phone. She spoke before I could even say hello.

"You need to come back. Now."

"Why? What's happened?"

"He went in."

"No. He's staying out tonight. He's not going in until tomorrow night."

"That's what he was supposed to do. But he went in early."

No, he's climbing, I told myself. *Up on East Temple Peak. Soloing that big gray wall with the glacier hanging over it.* But now I remembered the way Roberto had seemed unusually stressed the last few days. How he hadn't been quite himself. I'd been around narcotics long enough to easily recognize the signs of withdrawal. Why hadn't I been able to notice the obvious about him? Hidalgo would have drugs—that was certain. It was still hard to believe, though, that Roberto would put one addiction ahead of the other—getting high over *getting high.*

"What happened?" I asked again.

"I don't want to talk about it over the phone. This end's secure, but yours isn't."

"Is it critical?" I made myself ask. I felt like someone had kicked me in the stomach.

"Call it *intensive,*" she said.

TEN

The quality of the digital tape wasn't very good. The image twitched around a lot and the super-high magnification caused the night being filmed to appear grainy, as if a summer snowstorm had dropped down out of the Winds. Low-light enhancing gave everything a greenish hue. A counter ran in the lower-right corner of the screen. It recorded the time when the video was made, which it showed as a little after 0300 hours. Steam rising in spurts and leaps off the green glow of the swimming pool was the only other indication that this was a moving image. Then a light blinked on from a room on one wing that overlooked the pool. I knew from having seen the ranch blueprints that it was the master bedroom.

"*¿Sí?*" came a man's voice from the computer's speakers, startling me.

"*Someone has come to see you,*" another voice said in Spanish. I recognized the voice. It was Zafado, the grinning monkey with the broken teeth.

There was a long silence as I stared at the screen and the light blooming out of the master bedroom. Tom Cochran, who was playing the tape for me, filled it by saying, "I've run the video together with some communications we picked up on the digital scanner."

"Pause it, Tom," Mary ordered from where she was sitting next to me on the bench.

I looked at her. She was looking at her partner.

"I didn't ask you to do that."

"You didn't ask me not to."

"You need to destroy it as soon as we're done." Then she fixed me with her narrow gaze. "We'll keep watching, Anton, but forget what you hear. All right?"

"What are you talking about? Why?"

I didn't really care what they were bickering about. I only wanted the tape to continue. I had to know what had happened.

"We were testing the equipment," she explained slowly, giving her words emphasis. Very much a lawyer now. "Making sure that it worked at this range. We were *not* intentionally intercepting telephonic communications. We don't have a warrant for that. Not yet."

She looked back at Tom. "Destroy the audio after this playback. Go on."

As Tom pressed a button on a remote and started things rolling again, I understood that Mary had intended to exclude me from their extralegal activities, that she didn't fully trust me. I also understood that she wasn't quite the stickler for legalities I'd believed she was.

"Who is it?"

"We should not use names, Doctor."

A pause. Then, *"I see."*

"You met him on a mountain long ago. He is an old friend. He has done some work for us over the years. Work that I helped arrange."

Another pause. *"Yes. I believe I know the man. Where did he come from?"*

"From the mountains to the east. At least that is what this guy says. He approached where Barco watches. Barco pointed a banana at him and sent José to get me."

"I see."

Hidalgo's voice was odd—this was the first time I'd heard it. It was crude in tone and accent, but he spoke with meticulous precision.

"Do you want me to bring him to the house?"

"Please. The man was a friend, but I do not know if that remains the truth. I seem to recall that he is supposed to be in prison. And that he has a brother who is a policeman in this state. Please take necessary precautions."

"You do not need to tell me, Doctor. That is what you pay me for."

The crackle over the stereo speakers went dead. A few seconds later another light went on next to the bedroom.

"The bathroom," Tom said. He clicked a button to speed up the tape.

More lights popped on in various rooms as the tape was fast-forwarded. Sometimes passing shadows could be seen speeding around inside the house. I watched the time clock reel off fifteen more minutes before Tom returned it to normal speed. He slowed it down just as a pair of headlights came bumping over the hill behind the house. The lights disappeared then emerged again on the far side of the big U-shaped house.

A new sound came over the speakers. Not the crackle of a cell phone, but a low, continuous moan. Barely discernible beneath it was the sound of an engine. I remembered seeing the long-range directional microphone stored under a tarp up on the ridge. It had looked like a science-fiction ray gun mounted on a tripod.

"This wasn't an intercept," Tom confirmed. "We used the

mike. You can't hear anything for a while. It took a few minutes to get it zeroed in. Then the wind messes it up."

On the bench seat next to me Mary said, without taking her eyes off the screen, "Without a warrant. Again, obliterate and forget."

A flatbed truck parked near the house. Three dark figures could be seen getting out of the cab. The camera zoomed in.

"The second one is your brother," Mary commented needlessly.

The way my brother moved was familiar to me. Utterly easy, smooth, and unself-conscious, even with his hands cuffed behind his back.

The other two I also recognized from their shapes and the rhythm of their movements. One, getting out of the truck with lumbering menace, was the Baja state-police sergeant known as Bruto. The other, hopping quickly out from the driver's door, was another cop, albeit a former one—Zafado. I said as much to Mary and Tom.

Next to me Mary nodded. "His security *jefes*. Barco must be one of the bangers. One of the guys at the camper by the gate. That was where Roberto was supposed to go in."

Zafado led the way around the wing of the house. Bruto followed behind my brother, pushing him roughly past the pool to where a small, open cabana stood at the apex of the U.

Another one of Hidalgo's men—a boy I didn't recognize—joined them. He was carrying one of the short, ugly rifles. An AK-47. The faces were clearer now in the dim light emanating from the pool. A chrome-plated pistol was evident in Zafado's hand, pointing at the ground. His weapon and the other's automatic rifle didn't worry me nearly as much as the blade Bruto flicked open. The moan from the speakers began to sound like a scream to me.

The big man was standing behind my brother. He raised the knife high, and it appeared he was going to stab Roberto in the back of the neck. Slam down his fist and bury the blade to the hilt between my brother's vertebrae. I could almost hear the sound of metal scraping bone, the spine parting with stringy toughness like an old climbing rope.

But all Bruto did was slash the shirt off my brother's back. Then the pants. It was done with short, downward strokes as his free hand grasped Roberto's shoulder to hold him in place. My brother appeared to be struggling, but not very much. He twisted his head around, straining to say something up into the face of the man with the knife.

The microphone finally found its mark.

"Pendejo. *This turning you on, cocksucker?*"

If Bruto responded, the microphone didn't catch it. But there was a new level of viciousness in the way he hacked.

When my brother's clothes lay in tatters on the pool's deck, the big man grabbed one of Roberto's ankles and twisted it up and back, like he was shoeing a horse, and tore off the motorcycle boot and the sock. He did the same thing with my brother's other foot. This was smart, because if he tried to take off Roberto's boots from the front, I had no doubt that, handcuffed or not, and as big as Bruto was, my brother would kick his head in.

Now my brother stood handcuffed and naked in the digitally enhanced green light spilling out from the pool. Zafado played a flashlight over my brother's skin, probing and examining with the beam. It looked like they were arguing—my brother's mouth continued to move—but the sound of voices had been lost to the wind's amplified moaning. The boy with the automatic rifle suddenly reversed the weapon and slammed the butt into my brother's stomach.

I felt the blow deep in my gut. My legs went weak, my mouth dry, and my bowels heaved.

Roberto doubled over, then lunged forward as if to spear the young gangbanger with his head. But the boy was too quick. He stepped back and to the side and brought the rifle butt down again, this time onto the back of Roberto's head. His hair seem to splash upward from the force of the blow. He crashed to the ground, hitting first with his face and one knee. Like a bull following the final cut. He was struggling to get up when Bruto kicked his legs out from under him.

"Now this is my favorite part," Tom said. "Anyone want me to make some popcorn?"

"Shut up, Tom," Mary told him.

I looked at her and saw that her face was as white as mine probably was even though she'd undoubtedly seen the video several times already. The dark irises half-concealed by her narrow eyes looked hard and sharp. Unseen, under the table, her hand gripped my wrist.

I didn't fling it off. *Wait,* I told myself. *Just wait.*

What I felt, more than the rush of rage Tom's words stoked in me, was something approaching complete panic. I'd never seen my brother so helpless before. I'd never seen him powerless to strike back and wreak even greater havoc. Even when I'd seen him in prison, it was as if he were still in control, still dangerous. But on the tape Bruto was sitting on his prostrate form while Zafado went through the contents of his pack.

Then the screen lit up as the outdoor lights around the pool came on. The scene retracted as the camera lens pulled back. Jesús Hidalgo came walking out from the house. He was dressed in a flannel shirt and blue jeans. The shirt was tucked in. His hair was wet and looked as though he'd just finished combing it.

The *narcotraficante* made a great show of marching up and exhibiting complete surprise at what his men were doing. He seemed to be demanding an explanation. My brother managed to roll onto his back and, scissoring his body, began to get his feet beneath him. Seeing my brother's face, Hidalgo's jaw dropped open in mock surprise.

Then he was gesturing wildly, waving the men off and away from Roberto. With my brother still handcuffed, Hidalgo pulled him to his feet then hugged him. He kissed both my brother's cheeks. Roberto appeared oddly rigid, like a branch about to snap back with the force of a whip.

Hidalgo must have noticed, because he didn't tell his *sicarios* right away to take off the handcuffs.

"Return to this man his clothes," he said instead, the microphone again finding its mark.

Roberto nodded toward Bruto and appeared to spit. *"Fatass there cut them up."*

"Then give him your clothes," Hidalgo ordered Bruto.

"No thanks," said 'Berto. *"That fucker stinks like a pig."*

"Then you can wear my clothes, old friend. We will go inside and you will choose some. A refreshment, too. Whatever you wish. I recall that you always had some specific tastes. Take off those restraints," Hidalgo now commanded, apparently having decided Roberto wasn't a physical threat anymore. Not to him, anyway.

The handcuffs were removed by Zafado. While he was taking them off, my brother stared at Bruto, then the boy with the rifle. He stared at them for a long time until Hidalgo called to him. Then he followed the narco into the house.

"That was the bad news. Here's the good news," Mary told me, letting go of my wrist.

She'd been gripping my arm under the table ever since the ugly part of the tape began, with her fingertips on the inside as if she were taking my pulse. I didn't know if it had been her intention to restrain me or to offer compassion.

Tom began fast-forwarding again, speeding through the

departure of the three *sicarios*. Bruto and Zafado disappeared into the wing of the house where Hidalgo's chosen slept. The skinny gangbanger moved off to some unseen guard post in the shadows near the front of the house.

The good news was far briefer and far less dramatic than the bad news had been. It was only a minute or so of tape. As the lights finally went off throughout the rest of the house, they came on in one room in the wing Hidalgo kept for himself. It wasn't directly visible from the camera because the window was on the far side of the house, but you could see a dim glow reflected on the flagstone by the pool. It came on for fifteen seconds, then disappeared for fifteen, and then came on again for a final fifteen before going out for good.

"That's the signal," Tom said. "Everything's peachy." He shut down the video.

I didn't feel much relief despite the signal, and despite the fact that, for the moment at least, my brother was safe.

For some reason I was reminded of a photo of him that had been published as a poster in a climbing magazine almost ten years ago. Roberto had been sitting on a ledge no wider than a bookshelf. Below him was more than two thousand feet of space. There was no rope or gear attaching my brother to the wall. He wasn't wearing a harness, either. Yet his posture was relaxed, like he might have been sitting on a park bench. All he wore was a pair of cutoff jeans, and his muscles looked like they'd been carved on him with a knife. The wind was blowing dirty black hair halfway across his face. He was slumped, feet crossed at the ankles, holding up his hands as if examining the bloodstained athletic tape that was wrapped around them. His blue eyes, though, had fixed on the camera. There was definitely something unworldly about his eyes—the color and the heat in them. The guy who took the picture once told me he'd been accused of touching it up. I knew, though, the source of my brother's rapturous gaze. It was all the space beneath him. And, if you looked close enough, you could see the pinpricks on the inside of one lean arm.

He was most alive when he was on the edge. That's where he was now. It scared me. And it sickened me a little, because I knew the feeling all too well. Also, because I had helped these fucking people put him there.

I stood up, pushing back the bench and Mary's slight weight on it.

Turning, I looked at Tom, who stood behind us now. He was leaning against another table and sipping from a coffee mug. It took me only three steps to reach him. I grabbed a handful of his shirt and threw him toward the door.

I didn't mean to do it gently, but even I was surprised by the result. With coffee slinging an arc in the air, Tom spun through the blanket covering the door, crashed through the door itself—it opening rather than breaking—and staggered, lunging, out onto the porch. He almost regained his balance there. But then either the sudden light or his high riding heels caught him up and he went—bent forward almost ninety degrees and with tangled legs churning—down the steps to hit the dirt face-first.

I was out the door right after him, into the heat and the wind. I was aware of Mary shouting behind me but didn't bother to listen to the words. I stood at the top of the steps and waited for Tom to get up.

He did so slowly. He got to one knee and then his feet, dusting his palms on his jeans as he rose. His eyes were fixed on mine.

"C'mon, QuickDraw. I've been looking forward to this."

He motioned me forward with both hands, then took a sideways karate stance.

"*Hai!*" he grunted.

I felt a grin tightening my face. *A karate-boy. The most ridiculous of all street fighters.* I remembered Dad's advice about them. *Get close and they're finished.* My field of vision grew wide, taking him in entirely and ready to perceive the slightest attack or feint. Sound faded under the building roar of pounding blood.

In my head I instantly calculated how I would block and step around the expected side kick. How I would knee him in the groin as his leg was still in the air, how I would bang my right elbow into his jaw.

As I stepped forward off the porch to do these things, I was grabbed from behind. The arms wrapping around my arms and chest were surprisingly strong. They lifted me back, pulling me off-balance. Dragging me back toward the door.

I jerked my arms up and easily broke the hold. Behind me, Mary grunted. Then she darted around me before I could take a step back down toward Tom, who still held his kata pose. Mary shoved at my chest with her hard little fists.

"Stop it!" she yelled at me. "Stop it! Or you won't be able to help your brother! We'll have you taken out of here!"

"Who's going to take me out of here? You two? You have no authority to be doing this in the first place!"

Her face changed colors. To a paler shade. She looked over her shoulder at Tom, then back to me.

"We have authority," she said in a quieter voice. "You need to listen to me now."

ELEVEN

Before Mary Chang was sent to San Diego, all she'd ever done was Financial Crimes. She was good at it—good enough to be a rising star within the Bureau. Paper-chasing corporate bad guys made big headlines, and the Bureau has always loved headlines. Among her coups was a Senate investigation of U.S. banking giant Citibank, which was criticized for policy lapses that allowed the laundering of drug money from Mexican kingpins and politicians. It goes without saying that a female Asian American also looked good representing the traditionally white male agency on both the perp walk and the witness stand.

She spent two years in the New York field office, and then another three in Washington that came with a promotion. Her gun was useful to her only as ballast for her purse; her primary weapon was an HP business calculator. The quarterly firearms testing on the range was a formality, like the sexual-harassment training all agents had to sit through.

They wanted to promote her again, but someone high up thought she might need a little seasoning—some street experi-ence—in order to round out her résumé. There was a position open with the joint task force of narcotics agents in San Diego, so they pushed her in that direction. She went there knowing next to nothing about drugs or violence, but fully aware what a trophy Jesús Hidalgo's head would be if the task force brought him down. It would make an already promising career go from gold to platinum.

For several years already Hidalgo had been eluding the American authorities. Ever since he destroyed his primary rivals, the Arellano-Felix organization, he'd become the Feds' main target in the War on Drugs. The task force, of which Tom Cochran had been a member since its inception, believed he was responsible for a quarter of all the cocaine and methamphetamine shipped into the United States via the Border Region. But even though they knew who he was and what atrocities he'd committed, in two years of trying they'd failed to find a shred of admissible evidence that could be used to secure an indictment against him.

Three things kept him beyond their reach: the layers of lieutenants, *bajadors,* and mules he used for transporting his drugs; the menace of the *sicarios* and bangers he employed for threatening or killing those suspected of talking about him; and his generous "donations" to Mexican government and judicial officials who, even without the influence of fear and bribes, were loath to extradite Mexican nationals to the United States. Hidalgo appeared untouchable.

Mary helped develop a plan, though, that got them close.

Rookie agent Damon Walker had grown up in the barrios of San Diego. It was the place the man known as Shorty, Hidalgo's primary headhunter, used as a recruiting ground for gunmen and mules. Damon had been a troubled kid, and he'd run around with gangs before his mother yanked him out of the neighborhood and sent him to live with his grandparents in New Jersey. There he straightened up, spent four years in the Air Force, another four in college, before he went through the Academy and became an FBI agent. Mary's plan was to send this rookie back into the neighborhood he'd originally come from, where he was still remembered, and where he could begin to make buys that he claimed he was reselling to connections in New Jersey.

As he established a reputation as a dealer, he began purchasing larger and larger amounts of cocaine, heroin, and crank. The bigger loads got him meetings with people higher up in Hidalgo's organization. He was working his way through the messy hierarchy with money, élan, and enormous courage. He was hunting for the one the Feds could pressure into turning.

Damon would meet with the agents who worked as his handlers—Mary, Tom, and two other, older agents—every third night. On these occasions the drugs were bagged and tagged and Damon was given more cash for both flashing and making the next buy. His statements about his activities were videotaped. Likely candidates for conversion were discussed.

These debriefings took place in an apartment Mary rented in San Diego. Living there, she played the role of his wild *chino-gringo* girlfriend. To get in character the young Financial Crimes analyst had her black hair streaked with blond, picked up a new wardrobe of short skirts and leather, and had her eyebrows pierced. She even pricked the insides of her arms with a pin to make it look as if she enjoyed shooting up and didn't mind flaunting it. After the debriefings, Mary and Damon would substantiate their cover by hitting local bars. There they would make sure they were seen acting very much unlike federal agents: dancing, drinking, fighting, and pretending to make out in darkened booths.

It was fun. It was a thrilling game for a previously shy, introverted girl like Mary.

Tom and the other two handlers on the team would follow Damon in relays, not tailing him but looking for tails that might indicate he was suspected. The rest of the time, like when Damon was making his buys, the surveillance was either very loose or nonexistent. Nobody wanted to risk a slip that might clue Hidalgo's men in to the fact that Damon was really a cop. So there were no hidden cameras, no body mikes, no eyes in the sky. All there was to document the operation were the videotapes of the debriefings and the purchased drugs. The only person the team reported to was the Deputy Assistant Director of the Criminal Investigative Division of the Bureau.

The operation was so secret that none of the other federal agencies involved in the task force were told about this part of it. No one was trusted outside of Mary, Tom, the two other seasoned FBI agents, and the top executives at the Hoover Building. Not the DEA, not the Border Patrol, not the local police agencies, and certainly not the cooperating Mexican agencies. In the process, through all the tension and excitement, the tiny team became close and intimate. They all became friends.

Then one night Damon didn't come out of the Mexicali bar Tom had watched him go into. After four hours Mary was called to the scene. She prepared to go into the bar with her streaked hair, flashy clothes, and the attitude of a jealous addict, demanding to know where the hell her man was. It was the first real undercover role she was to play—this was the real thing, not just covering Damon and the meets by publicly dancing and fighting with him. Mary was keyed up as well as scared. But when she blew in through the barroom door, there was no one there. Not even a bartender.

Apparently everyone had slipped out the back, which hadn't been watched as a standard part of the intentionally loose surveillance.

Despite frantic searches, despite pulling in every witness they could think of and coming down on them hard, and despite bringing in the DEA and finally even the Mexican authorities, Damon didn't reappear for a week.

That was when they found his body draped over a fence north of town. He was bent over it backward, his upside-down face looking toward the border. His throat was cut, of course—*la corbata*—and his spine had been severed with a blow from a chisel. The coroner said he'd drowned on his own blood. There were other evident signs of earlier torture, too.

A brief whirlwind of indignation degenerated within days to finger-pointing at the Hoover Building and even the White House. The faces there were red, not from anger, but embarrassment. A lot of government money had been invested in the operation. Millions of dollars, in fact. Millions that had been used to buy drugs and fill a drug lord's coffers. And the other agencies were furious that they hadn't been trusted with the details of the operation in the first place. If they had been allowed to participate, they insisted, this never would have happened. An FBI agent would never have been killed. The Bureau had bungled it, they claimed. Yet again. Just like all the Bureau's other recent disasters. For the suits in charge, the loss of face was worse than the loss of an agent.

Until then the killing of an American law-enforcement officer had been taboo. Only once had a cartel killed an American cop, a DEA agent a decade and a half ago, and the resulting pressure had nearly destroyed their industry. Since then, it had become a line that even the most arrogant of the cartels didn't dare cross. The fact that Jesús Hidalgo now had crossed it—leapt over it and pissed all over the ground without any apparent concern for the potential consequences—was the greatest blow of all.

So the operation was shut down as quietly as possible. A plan was set up to minimize the damage to the FBI's reputation. It was easy to do because the team was so small, and the only evidence was the tapes and the drugs and a whole lot of missing money.

The cover-up was simple: Justice Department sources told the media that the dead agent had been turned by the narcos, and that he had been the target of an investigation himself. He had died as the Bureau was readying to arrest him.

Mary and Tom and the other agents protested vehemently. They were told to shut up and follow orders. For the good of their country. Someone came in from the Attorney General's Office to explain to them that the risk of further embarrassment to the FBI was too great—as was the risk of embarrassing our NAFTA trading partner by exposing the way Hidalgo lived and trafficked south of the border with impunity—for the Feds to pursue the murder. Things would be better this way. And even more important, they later learned, the political party in charge was doing everything it could to recruit Mexican-American voters before the next election, and the party leadership knew they would fail to do so if they embarrassed the government of the immigrants' ancestral home. It would make them look anti-Mexican.

It was shut down, but it wasn't over. At least not for Mary and Tom. The two older agents resigned in protest—they both had more than twenty years in and a pension—but Mary and Tom were too young and too ambitious. And too outraged.

They made a pact: They would get Hidalgo, no matter what. Even if their bosses, along with Jesús Hidalgo himself, had forgotten that it was the cardinal sin in the world of crime and punishment to kill a federal agent, Tom and Mary would remember. To them this was about law and justice, not politics. That was their authority: justice.

Although the case was more or less dropped by the American government, Hidalgo did take some heat in Mexico for the murder. It angered the other cartels who were unaware of the Justice Department's laxity. They feared it would bring down more pressure from the antinarcotics agencies. So when their own *sicarios,* their purchased *federales* and state cops, and even their hired *generalíssimos* in Mexico's armed services came looking for Hidalgo with renewed intensity, he fled north to the safety of the country where he sold his drugs and whose agent he had murdered. If he was careful, he would be safe not only from violence but from the law as well. And he could live off his riches until Mexico welcomed back its most outrageous narco lord.

This, of course, was outrageous in itself. It was obscene. The man tortures and kills an agent of the United States of America and then takes refuge in one of those very states.

Mary and Tom had known for months about my brother's pending immunity deal with the Attorney General's Office. The entire task force was aware of it even though Mary and Tom and their supersecret operation weren't a part of the negotiations with the lawyers in Buenos Aires that Mom and Dad had hired for Roberto. The two agents learned the details as they were placed on indefinite leave to grieve for their colleague and recover from the several frantic weeks that had followed his death.

They'd intercepted Roberto before he had a chance to turn himself in per the agreement. As far as the Justice Department was concerned, he was still a fugitive who'd reneged on his deal. Mary and Tom stashed him in a hotel room while they finished gathering the surveillance equipment, renting the hunting camp, and deluding my office into detaching me to join them.

In essence they'd kidnapped my brother. It was almost funny. FBI agents kidnapping a fugitive who was trying to turn himself in. McGee was right—she had balls.

"You know the old saying, better to ask forgiveness than permission?" Mary said toward the end of her story, her voice tight and pleading. But her apology was not meant for me or

Roberto. "That's what we're doing here. We're betting our careers that we can bring in Hidalgo. As a fait accompli, which will make everything okay. They'll have to prosecute him. The Justice Department won't have any choice. It would be more embarrassing to let Hidalgo go than to accept the political fallout. Once we have him in custody, on good, solid charges, they can't let him go. His name has been in the newspapers for almost a decade. Everyone from the Attorney General to the Secretary of State has publicly called him the most notorious drug lord in the Western Hemisphere."

"But we've got to have a case against him," Tom said sullenly. "And your fucked-up brother is the only one who can deliver that."

"We're already racing the clock here. There's not much time. Any day now they're going to figure out what's going on." She meant the Justice Department. "Then they will come here and shut us down for good."

I listened to the entire story in silence. I wasn't surprised by the tale. I knew too well about the slimy entanglement of politics and justice. And I wasn't surprised that these two uptight but ill-matched agents would risk their careers to do the right thing. They might break the rules—as I'd seen them do that with the listening devices, and as they had done by grabbing my brother in the first place—but they believed they were serving justice.

It was ironic that I thought of myself as one of them—good, righteous, an enforcer of the law—while I knew from what was in their file about me that they believed, or at least strongly suspected, that I was just the opposite. That I was very *bad,* in fact. Even now, listening to their story, it seemed a little strange that they'd want to ally themselves with me. I had to wonder if they were finally telling me the whole story. I didn't like some of the looks they'd exchanged during the telling. I didn't like the way Mary watched me, waiting for my reaction. And they'd lied to me before—by omission, at least, and by letting me believe that this was a fully sanctioned Bureau operation.

But what I mainly felt was something quite different from sympathy or suspicion. For the first time in my life I wanted to strike a woman. As for Tom, I wanted to tear off his arms and beat him with his own pale limbs. Yeah, they were risking their careers. But they were risking my brother's life. And mine and my family's. But even over my own outrage, I was still able to sense theirs. I couldn't help admiring their relentlessness.

With their four eyes boring into me—two blue and two narrow and dark, I picked up my cell phone and called McGee as I'd promised him I would.

"I need you to keep your big mouth shut for one week," I told my boss.

"Now we need you to do your part," Mary said. "Tell us what your brother is thinking and feeling. How he's going to respond to a greeting like the one he received last night."

It was something I should have been asking myself. Why hadn't Roberto exploded? How had he kept his famous feral nature in check? He was *destraillado*, as Mom said. Unleashed. Unable to contain himself. Yet somehow he had. It must have taken a great gathering of will to do it.

"I don't know," I told her. "He's going to be pissed, there's no doubt about that. There's going to be a reckoning with Bruto and that kid who hit him with the gun. But he kept his cool. I think he'll keep it." I didn't say anything about my suspicion that he was still riding the horse.

"Better than you did, I hope," Mary said with a tentative smile.

I let that go.

Another question came into my head. How well did Hidalgo know my brother? Would the lack of an explosion on his part be suspicious to the *narcotraficante*?

Mary was evidently thinking along the same lines.

"Is it possible your brother doesn't know him as well as he says he does? It seems strange that Hidalgo would allow an old friend to be strip-searched and beaten like that."

"Burns could be shining us on," Tom said, nodding. "Guys like him lie about everything."

"My brother's not a liar."

"Right. He's just a junkie and a killer."

I stood up. Tom did, too.

"Damn it, Tom!" Mary said. "Cool it! Both of you!"

Tom and I looked at each other. The relief on Mary's face that I'd noticed during my short talk with my boss had never registered on his. He showed no appreciation that I was allowing their charade to go on—not that I really had any choice. He still wanted to put me in my place. Especially since I'd thrown him in the dirt a half hour earlier.

"Why is it that men are such children?" Mary berated us, the cautious smile gone. "We're trying to do something significant here, and all you can think about is fighting each other. Squabbling like kids. Tom, your friend—our colleague—was murdered by this guy, but you're so worried about being top dog that you keep forgetting that. And Anton, your brother is in there with that monster. Yet you seem to think guarding your precious machismo is more important."

I suppressed the urge to say, *He started it.*

But I wasn't sure I'd be able to choke out an apology if she demanded it. Saying *I'm sorry* to the man who'd clearly reveled in my brother's beating would be a betrayal of my blood. As would any act of contrition toward the two people who had put him in that situation. But I was relieved that our mutual aggression was being reined in. I imagined that it was finished now—that Tom and I would be able to work together with a sort of icy efficiency. We were pros, after all. I think Tom was relieved as well. He should have been. I'd really wanted to hurt him. I still did.

Instead of demanding that apologies be traded, Mary only insisted that we suffer the indignity of shaking hands. We did it, demonstrating our newfound maturity and professionalism by not seeking to grind each other's finger bones. I was tempted, though, because I knew my climber's grip could crush the bigger man's hand.

"Now, is there any chance your brother could be playing us?" Tom asked.

"I know him. He's not," I said flatly, as if it were incontrovertible.

But what if he was? What if this whole thing was one of his games? What if he was just pimping the Feds, and what if his intention all along was to inform Hidalgo that he was being watched, make a game of it, then simply return to South America where he remained untouchable to American law enforcement?

If that was his plan, then he might get us all fired, or maybe even killed. Roberto had to know that. Even if he didn't, I remembered what he'd said to me when we talked about Hidalgo. *He's gotten twisted, he's messing with women and kids.* I knew Roberto would never tolerate the abuse of women, children, or animals. I couldn't explain it to the Feds in a way they'd believe, but I knew my brother. So I dismissed the possibility.

Mary was nodding slowly, looking at Tom. "Anton's right. He wouldn't turn on us," she said in the same tone I'd used.

Tom didn't say anything. He didn't look convinced.

"We don't have any choice but to assume that he's with us, and that Hidalgo doesn't suspect him," Mary said. "The call from the embassy bears that assumption out. If we're wrong, there's nothing we can do about it at this point anyway."

"What call? What embassy?"

She explained that she'd had Roberto's NCIC file flagged. Anyone seeking to access information about him from the Bureau's National Crime Information Center would trip the flag and she would be notified. Word had come in this morning—the morning after Roberto's arrival at Hidalgo's compound—of a request from a senior law-enforcement official in the Mexican Embassy for verification of Roberto's status as a fugitive. Of course the foreign official was assured that Roberto Burns was still a wanted man.

I didn't bother to ask if it was really possible that such a high-level Mexican official could be on Hidalgo's payroll. Yes, I knew from what I'd learned over the past few days, one could easily be that dirty. And the request proved it.

It also proved that Hidalgo was as suspicious and smart as the Feds had assumed when planning this operation. As expected, he was checking up on Roberto. All according to plan. My brother's infiltration of Hidalgo's operation in Wyoming rested on the belief that the drug lord was smart, but that we were smarter.

"When did you get that call?"

"Two hours ago," Mary said.

"Not long before that, someone across the river used a cell phone to call Mexico. That call was encrypted, but another one wasn't. We picked it up on the scanner. Jesús has got a plane coming in this afternoon."

"What does that mean? A plane?"

They both shook their heads. "We aren't sure."

TWELVE

I spent most of the afternoon up on the ridge, where I squatted in the junipers' shade while peering through either my binoculars or the powerful camera's viewfinder. For once the wind wasn't blowing. Mungo lay at my side, panting hard in the dry heat that reflected off the sandstone.

I'd suggested that the inbound plane might be full of drugs, but Tom scoffed, telling me not to count on it. Planes were extremely suspect in a post-9/11 world, while the remote border remained wide open. The narcos were smart enough to know that. If drugs were coming north to disperse east and west along I-80—the so-called vein of evil running through the state—they'd come by car or by truck. So a plane meant something else.

We'd speculated on the possibilities. It could be more of Hidalgo's men coming north to relieve his current soldiers. It could be some of the lieutenants who were running the business in their boss's absence. It could be his lawyer, the one in whose name the property had been purchased. It could be someone coming to make a deal—one that we'd hopefully learn about and use to nail Hidalgo for conspiracy. Or the plane could be coming to take Roberto south, either to kill him or put him to work.

That was my brother's pitch: that he could negotiate the purchases of raw product from the South American syndicates better than anyone else. Nobody would mess with him, and, because of our dead grandfather's lingering influence in that part of the world, he would be safe from interference by the governments there. Who would be better to negotiate on Hidalgo's behalf than someone who couldn't be arrested? Who was too crazy to double-cross? The only thing he would have to fear would be a kidnapping by American authorities similar to what Tom had done in Juárez several years ago.

That was funny. Roberto had already been kidnapped, only no one knew it but me.

As the day wore on, my worries began to ease. The household's three maids, who must have been the only servants in Wyoming to wear black uniforms trimmed with white lace, swept the sand from the flagstone around the swimming pool. One of the bangers swung a net through the water when he wasn't groping himself the way rap stars do on MTV. The maids later tied cushions to the iron chairs and lounges and set up a couple of umbrellas. Stacks of towels were laid out, and a table to serve as a bar.

I noticed that all of the maids were older, plump, and matronly. They might have been the bangers' mothers. If men like that had mothers.

Clearly there was going to be a party. That meant that it was someone important coming north to pay a visit, not to take my brother away. Hidalgo was trying very hard to create a refined atmosphere in his isolated Wyoming home-away-from-home. I fantasized about Roberto sitting in on some major cocaine deal, dropping me a note, and the whole thing being wrapped up in just a day.

Mary had offered to bring me lunch, but it was Tom who scrabbled and slid up to the ridge in his cowboy boots. He threw a plastic-wrapped sandwich at me when he reached the notch. He threw it low and hard, just inches above Mungo's head. I managed to catch it but not before Mungo, with a sudden lunge, nearly snatched it from the air.

I wished Roberto were here to see it—he loved it when Mungo showed some spirit.

"It's gonna be girls," Tom predicted.

Squatting before the tripod, he began to fiddle with the camera.

"Picture's off," he explained.

"Be sure to get it just right, Tom. You can jack off to it later."

He turned to fix me with his close-set eyes. I closed mine for a moment and ground my teeth, remembering Mary's lecture about cooperation.

"Sorry, Tom," I said. "The heat's getting to me."

He took out one of the small walkie-talkies and switched it on.

"All right?" he asked into the mouthpiece.

"A little to the left," came Mary's tinny voice. "More. Now back. That's it. Wipe the lens now. Thanks."

"What's she doing?" I asked.

He didn't answer for a minute while he carefully dabbed at the lens with a small white cloth.

Then, turning to look at me again, he said, "She's watching the monitor, QuickDraw. What do you think? Been there all morning. Doesn't want to miss seeing her boyfriend."

He had a sly smirk on his face. As if he meant something more than just an offhand remark by "her boyfriend." I wanted to ask what it was but I held it in. Instead I raised my binoculars and stared off past the house to where clouds of dust were drifting from the mine entrance. A pickup truck was heading into the mouth of the tunnel, which was just out of sight behind a shrubby hill. What was in those cardboard boxes? Drugs? Cash? I knew that potash mines are usually miles deep and I couldn't help but envy the driver's courage. The one time I'd been that deep under the ground, I'd been absolutely terrified.

Tom was apparently disappointed that I hadn't asked what he was talking about. I felt him watching me for a few more seconds before he headed back down the hill without another word, sliding and scuffling in his slick-soled shit-kickers.

Mary came up the slope a little later. She wore a sleeveless T-shirt, shorts, and, being smarter than Tom, a pair of light-weight hiking boots with lugged soles. She also was carrying two canteens, one of which Mungo and I made quick use of to wash down the peanut-butter-and-jelly sandwich we'd shared.

"You've been watching?" I asked her when I could work my mouth.

She nodded, making a seat for herself next to me by moving some small stones. We sat more or less facing each other, our backs propped against furry juniper trunks. Mungo had moved off into some bushes, where she pretended she was invisible just like a real wolf. Whenever I looked her way, she lifted her lips in her shy Cheshire grin. Her tongue snaked in and out, trying to rub the peanut butter from the roof of her mouth.

"It looks like it's going to be quite a party. Any sign of your brother yet?"

Roberto hadn't shown himself amid all the pre-party activity. Other men had been milling around the house along with the maids, but neither Hidalgo nor Roberto had shown his face. Another pickup had driven up to the mine and then down into the tunnel. Neither had come back out. Curiously, this one had been loaded with cases of bottled water. I wondered if Hidalgo was paranoid—if he was building some kind of shelter in the mine. Wyoming was full of bomb shelters awash in food and guns, but I'd never known a Latino to buy into end-of-the-world conspiracy theories. It had always seemed a peculiarly Anglo phobia.

"Nine Mexican nationals have been processed through Immigration in Salt Lake, but their names were unavailable to us. We don't even know yet if they're male or female," Mary said.

"Tom's hoping they're female."

"I expect he's right. Hidalgo's been known to fly high-priced prostitutes from Mexico City to his ranch in Baja. We know he has a taste for big-haired blondes."

"That should make Tom happy. I'd guess that's his type. That is, if Roberto was wrong about Tom being gay."

Mary looked at me with her dark eyes.

"What's your brother's type?"

I shrugged.

"All types. Just not bleached blondes."

"Does he have a girlfriend?" she asked, still staring.

"He's had two that I know about. One left him because she said he didn't have a future. The other said he'd break her heart, so she broke his first."

"Only two? I find that a little hard to believe."

"There's been lots of women, but only two he cared for. You have something other than an idle interest, Mary?"

Now she looked away.

I'd seen this happen before. Several times, actually. There'd been a female rookie cop in Denver. A probation officer in Durango. A Deputy District Attorney in Boulder, fresh out of law school. Even an Air Force doctor—a major—when my brother was still a teenager. Women of a certain type—those that believed in rules and regulations above all things—were fascinated by Roberto. He was from a kind of opposite universe. He was an outlaw. An anarchist. And for some reason the women who fell for him the hardest tended to be those for whom such an attraction would seem the most repellent.

But Roberto's thing had always been the broken birds. The fellow addicts, the abuse victims, those who had nothing left to them but a fragile beauty—they were the kind he'd gone for. And rebuilt into strong, confident, independent women. Who would then leave him.

As good as he was at climbing and general self-destruction, he didn't have a clue when it came to women—not that I do, either. But I did know that with his looks he could have blown through them like a tornado, notching a thousand bedposts and breaking a thousand hearts. But he didn't. It was *his* heart that had been broken twice too many times. Girls wanted to be with him for the moment, for the excitement and immediate gratification, but for the future they wanted someone more securely attached to the earth. It was true they lusted after him, but they didn't love him. So he'd learned to keep them at a distance, only occasionally getting intimate when his physical needs became too great. Or, maybe, when he was high.

I explained a little of this. While I did, Mary reviewed our surveillance position. Checking to make sure the lenses were properly concealed, that the camouflaged tarps were covering any human sign on the ridge. She pretended to be only mildly interested in what I was saying. She even took the precaution of unwrapping a desert khaki poncho and pulling it over her T-shirt. She didn't say a word, and I would have felt like I was talking to myself if it weren't clear just how intently she was listening.

It wasn't really surprising that she was more than a little curious about him. As uptight and serious as she appeared when I first met her, I should have predicted something like this might happen.

For a minute it worried me, so in my explanation I hit hard on the fact that it was the broken—not the rigidly erect—that he was drawn to. But I was beginning to see that maybe she saw herself as a little bit broken. Despite the camouflage poncho and the gun clipped to her hip, I saw again what my brother must have seen. An awkward, shy girl, working hard at coming off as a tough, ambitious FBI agent.

And that realization led me to understand that, from a selfish point of view, her interest in my brother might make him a little safer. She might bring him out sooner, once we had the smallest piece of necessary evidence, rather than leave him in too long in hopes of something better.

It came from the south, a silver bird steady in the sky, far in advance of the jet noise that trailed it. Like the mine entrance, the airstrip was out of our sight. According to Tom's satellite picture, it was in a valley just beyond the first hills behind Hidalgo's house. We could tell, though, that the plane was heading for it.

We both watched the plane through binoculars as it zoomed toward us. The pilot had obviously been here before, as he didn't bother to circle the private strip. We'd been worried about that, and had taken extra precautions to be sure we couldn't be seen from the air. But he just roared straight in, disappearing from view with the wheels down.

Mary and I heard the chirp of rubber hitting pavement, then the sound of the reverse thrusters being engaged, and finally the low roar of a taxiing jet.

Some of Hidalgo's men came pouring out of the house. They headed toward where the cars and trucks were parked in the driveway. I recognized a few of them from Señor Garcia's and others from our surveillance. The boy with the assault rifle who'd twice struck my brother was among them. He startled me by taking out a handgun and firing several shots in the air. Bruto grabbed him roughly and appeared to chew him out.

All the men were strangely dressed—it was as if they'd put on their best clothes. Most of them looked like a bunch of *Sopranos* wannabes. I'll never figure out who is emulating whom—the real gangbangers or their TV and music-video counterparts.

For the low-level bangers the height of fashion was track-suits worn halfway down their asses, tight, sleeveless under-shirts, and a lot of tattoos and gold jewelry. I'd always appreciated the crack-exposing trend in pants, as it made them really easy to run down when they ran from a bust. For the older Mexicans—the true *sicarios,* the hired guns, the killers—the fashion was more cowboy-inspired.

Bruto, for instance, wore a clean white hat, a black leather jacket despite the heat, and black jeans. His skinny-fat and far smaller partner, Zafado, was dressed identically except that his hat was black. Shorty was dressed even more extravagantly than the others. He wore a wide-sleeved guayabera shirt un-buttoned to his waist and a pair of shiny gray slacks. His fat neck and wrists glittered with what must have been pounds of gold. He was going to be in trouble if he fell into the pool.

Dressed as they were, I hoped that tonight would be a going-to-town night once this outdoor party wound up. I des-perately wanted word that Roberto was all right.

Tom was right—it was girls in the plane. Eight of them. They were far outnumbered by the men. Several cars and trucks ferried them from the airstrip to the house. The women were dressed up, too, with a lot of big blond hair as promised. Their clothes appeared at first to be expensive until I looked closely through the binoculars and could see that everything was a little too tight, a little too short, and a little too revealing.

None of them looked older than thirty. Several looked younger than twenty. They seemed nervous but like they were trying not to show it as they chattered among themselves and ignored the leers of the men escorting them into the house.

The men came out and gathered around the pool. Traditional folk music played over the outdoor speakers by the swimming pool. Mary and I could hear it all the way up on the ridge. It prevented us from using the directional microphone. The kid I'd seen cleaning the pool was now grilling tamales, husked corn, hamburgers, and hot dogs on the built-in brick grill. The black-clad maids disappeared after laying out a full bar on one table and a spread of snack foods on another. The men stood in small groups, laughing and fidgeting and fingering their groins.

The *sicarios* and gangbangers seemed overly eager, like junior high school boys. It was almost laughable to see these cold-blooded killers, drug runners, and thieves acting so shy while posing so hard, as if this were their first prom. It was funny. For a little while, at least.

The girls came out en masse from a wide sliding-glass door on the wing opposite where Hidalgo slept. They were wearing swimsuits that were really only small patches of cloth tied together with long, thin strings. Tattoos and flashy jewelry colored their skin. They came out of the house strutting with confidence—they were determined to remain in control. For their sakes, I very much hoped they would.

For the first hour the surface of the pool was unmarred even by the wind. The men clustered in small, tight groups around one or two of the women, pressing drinks upon them while running their eyes over all the too-tan skin.

Hidalgo came quietly out of his bedroom door. He was dressed even better than his men, in a gray Western-cut suit and pimply black ostrich-skin boots. His dark sheath of hair was slicked back but looked as if it had been casually tousled before a mirror.

A few of the bolder girls hurried to him. They fawned and

pranced as they greeted their host, each one seeming to vie for his attention. He appeared polite but not affected by their displays. He settled himself onto a lounge chair and casually waved the girls back to his men like a good *patrón*. Someone brought him a drink. He sipped it while watching the show from behind his sunglasses.

Roberto wandered out a few minutes later. From the same door, which we assumed was Hidalgo's private suite. He was wearing only a pair of blue swim trunks that he must have borrowed from the narco, because they were far too big around the waist. His black hair hung in tangles around his face. He stood to one side and looked at the party. Then he looked toward the ridge where I was watching his face through my binoculars. He grinned, shaking his head a little.

He was definitely high. Stoned out of his mind.

"Something's wrong with him," Mary whispered.

His eyes were hidden behind dark lenses, but I recognized the slack smile, the disengaged way he stood so perfectly still as he surveyed the party. Then he stepped forward and I saw him wobble a little.

Everyone—men and women alike—instinctively kept a wary eye on him as he wandered over to the makeshift bar and made himself a drink. No one approached him. That the men would be wary of him was understandable. There was a coiled violence in him, like a spring cranked way down. But I was surprised by the wariness of the painted women. He was no threat to them, and it should have been obvious by the way he ignored them. It was as if they knew he was something far different from what they'd come here for. Maybe it shamed them.

Roberto walked over to where Hidalgo reclined on a lounge chair. He slumped onto a chair next to the narco.

"You're going to put him in some place with a methadone

treatment program, right?" I asked, meaning when the operation was over.

She nodded.

"The written deal only requires a minimum-security country club, but I'll make sure it's one with a rehab facility."

She said this as if Roberto weren't still a fugitive, as if the Attorney General's Office would actually honor the deal. Maybe they would. If we brought in Hidalgo.

As time passed and drinks were downed, the men seemed to be losing their shyness. The leering and closeness to the women grew more pronounced.

One was thrown into the pool. She screamed as she went in and the men all laughed. She came up smiling, but the smile looked fake as she patted her ruined hair. The makeup made black streaks down her face. Another woman followed. Soon they all were going in, the later ones having their tops pulled off by the men doing the pushing.

"This is going to get ugly," I said. "You sure you want to watch this?"

"Do you think I'm too delicate to watch?" Mary asked huffily. "You're a lot like your brother, you know. You're chauvinistic. You think women need to be protected. Those women know what they're doing, and I know what I'm doing."

"I didn't know you were a feminist."

"I'm a federal agent, Anton. I spent six months one time going after the bank accounts of a bunch of child pornographers—I doubt anything I'm going to see here will make me faint."

"Okay. Sorry."

The women in the pool got into the spirit of things quickly enough. They were pros, after all, and they didn't really have any choice. Soon they'd all lost what little clothing they'd started with. They splashed and giggled and squealed while the men cheered them on from around the swimming pool's edge. Two of the women hugged each other in a tight embrace and began kissing, to much applause. A third woman joined them, pressing her front against another's back.

One of the young bangers was shoved in after them. Soon half of the men had entered the pool to cavort with the prostitutes. The men took off only their boots, shirts or jackets, and pants. Most were still wearing their undershirts and underwear.

Things became more frenzied. Hidalgo sat forward on his chair to watch. Roberto, next to him, never even looked at the pool. Instead his sunglasses stared across the river in our direction.

At one point he took out the pack of the bidis Tom had bought him and shook one out. He smiled at us. *Maybe there'll be a drop tonight,* I thought.

I noticed that only two of the youngest bangers appeared to be on guard duty. One had been posted by the cars at the front of the house, and another on the cabana facing the river. The one by the cars had come all the way around the side to stare enviously at the action. The one by the river kept his back turned to us and instead drooled in the direction of the pool. When I focused in on him I saw that his hand was moving in his pants. There wasn't much of a perimeter now. If we had a warrant and a Bureau SWAT team, we could wrap up the bunch of them.

Hidalgo stood and plucked two of the prettier girls from the pool. He led them toward the sliding-glass doors outside his suite. They disappeared inside, giggling at what they probably thought was their good fortune.

With the boss gone, so were whatever remained of the inhibitions. The men began touching the women, and the women, the men. Someone turned the music up. Someone else turned on some outdoor lights because it was getting dark, then shut them off again. A brown paper bag containing more than twenty joints the size of cigars was dumped onto a table. A long line of cocaine was placed on a woman, running from her throat to her pubic region.

It quickly became an orgy. I put down my binoculars. Mary did the same.

"We could get a warrant," I said. "That stuff's in plain sight. We could be in there in two hours."

She pointed at the fancy camera with its long, powerful lens.

"I'm not sure this qualifies as plain sight."

"This is Wyoming. Not New York or California."

I meant places where liberal courts give emphasis to such restrictions on law enforcement. But then I thought about it, and knew that in Wyoming the courts often give those kinds of restrictions even *more* emphasis. People here—and the courts—are serious about the rights of the state's citizens to do whatever the hell they want on their property. Plus Wyomingites tend to be even more suspicious of law enforcement than people on the coasts, not out of bleeding-heart liberalism, but snide, self-righteous conservatism. Especially federal law enforcement, as many federal employees over the years have had the misfortune to discover.

"Besides, you want him on a minor possession charge?" Mary went on. "He's not even present. And he'd claim he didn't know the drugs were in his house. We need to get him red-handed on an 841(b)(1)(A) or an 848 violation. We need to catch him with either a ton of narcotics or at least conspiring to import them."

By 841(b)(1)(A) she was referring to the federal statute about manufacturing or distributing cocaine or heroin. The minimum penalty for really large amounts was ten to twenty years. An 848 was the so-called Kingpin Statute, providing for up to life imprisonment—possibly even the death penalty—

for those who procured huge amounts of drugs and had people killed while doing so. The amount of cocaine we'd seen on the woman and the bag of blunts that had been passed out wouldn't amount to much of a sentence even if we could tie Hidalgo to them.

"But it would get Roberto out of there."

She shook her head. Reluctantly, I thought.

"He's safe enough. Hidalgo obviously accepts him. He knows he's a fugitive after having checked him out on NCIC. Your brother's safe enough as long as he doesn't get in any trouble with Hidalgo's men."

I glanced back downriver toward the orgy by the swimming pool. As if on cue, I saw my brother getting up from his lounge chair. I grabbed the binoculars.

Roberto was facing toward where the tables were set up—where one of the women had lain on her back as the men snorted cocaine off her bare skin. There now, amid coupling couples and threesomes and foursomes, one girl was getting more than she'd bargained for. She was the smallest of all the women, and also the youngest-looking. She could be anything from thirteen to twenty years old. She was bent over the table, facing the river, and the expression I could see on her face was definitely not contrived rapture. Tears were running down her cheeks and her mouth was opened wide in pain.

I thought that it had to be a fine line to walk. Give the men what they want, but try to stay in control. Be the whore but also the master, parceling out your favors and remaining in charge. In Mexico City there would be bodyguards and bouncers. Here she was on her own, a long, long way from home.

Behind her was one of the bigger bangers. His expression wasn't rapturous either, although he was clearly in control. His lips were pulled back in a snarl and a vein throbbed in the side of his shaved head. Both his hands were so hard on the back of her neck that his steroid-pumped triceps were rigid and flexed. He was riding her cruelly. His body was bucking with savage jerks.

"Oh no," Mary said.

Roberto was walking that way.

"Oh no," I agreed. But I didn't mean it. *Yes, 'Berto. Sic 'em.*

For once my brother wasn't smiling. His movements were no longer stoned and uncertain. Instead he walked with the old feral grace that I'd always admired. He took off his sunglasses and dropped them on the flagstone.

Some of the other men and women stopped what they were doing. As if even over the loud music and rampaging hormones, Roberto somehow projected an energy force that grabbed their attention.

He stalked straight up to the big gangbanger. The meaty triangle of muscle on the left side of his back inflated suddenly as he drew back his arm. Then he hooked the banger in the throat with his left fist. The punch was thrown so hard that the guy blew backward. He was lifted right off his feet. Off the girl, too, and then through a glass door.

We heard the glass break all the way up the river. From our viewpoint we could see the banger go sliding backward across what appeared to be a kitchen floor. He hit a counter and stopped, both hands holding his own throat now. Roberto stepped barefoot in the empty doorway amid the shards of broken glass. He stood there with his hands on his hips. He might have been saying something to the crumpled figure who had seconds earlier been brutally violating the young girl.

I had to smile. The banger didn't look so vicious now.

Catching myself feeling a satisfaction that was premature, I quickly scanned the pool area and saw that the girl had disappeared. The half-naked men were gathering around where my brother stood gazing into the kitchen with his back still turned to them. It looked like some of them were shouting at him. The girls picked up their discarded swimsuits and scattered. One of the banger's compadres found his pants lying on the flagstone and reached inside the pocket for something.

I focused in on his hand. He was trying to tug a small automatic from the cloth. I wanted to stand up and shout a warning to my brother. Mary was gripping my arm.

The banger got the gun free and began to push his way into the crowd.

Breaking Mary's hold on me, I jumped over the camera and stood on the very edge of the notch, fully exposed. I drew in a great breath and got ready to shout my brother's name.

But Zafado beat me to it. He stepped in front of the kid with the gun and grabbed his arms. He was wearing only his black cowboy hat and an undershirt, but he still apparently commanded authority. The boy stopped trying to push in the direction of my brother. Bruto was there, too, grabbing the kid's shoulder and jerking him away.

Roberto turned and walked back toward Hidalgo's wing. No one tried to stop him as he picked up his sunglasses, put them on, then disappeared from our view. He left a series of bloody footprints on the flagstone.

"Your brother is something else," Mary said to me when I got back under the junipers' cover.

"He's a sociopath. But he's good, you know?"

She nodded slowly without looking at me. "I know."

She was looking across the river through the camera's viewfinder. She felt my gaze and glanced at me. Our eyes met for a moment before she went back to the camera and adjusted the lens by a fraction.

"He's in real trouble now," I told the back of her head. "You know that, too, don't you?"

THIRTEEN

Tinted windows are a threat to cops. At least for the uniformed type. They are a wall of darkness that a man with a gun can hide behind when you pull a car over late at night on some lonely, high-plains road. For an undercover cop, though, they're a blessing. They let you sit and watch without being seen. But for me, they were also a pain in the ass. That was because I'd tinted them myself after a friend assured me any idiot could do it.

The first bubbles and cracks appeared two weeks after I'd applied the sheets of dark tint to the Pig's windows. Over the years Wyoming's wildly fluctuating temperatures had continued to spiderweb the smoky tape, then turned it into a fractal collage of white and black. At least it matched the rest of the truck, with the dents and dings and flaking holes of rust. Now the bubbles and cracks trapped against the windshield's glass floated huge in the binoculars' lenses, obscuring my view into Señor Garcia's Mexican Restaurant and Bar.

I couldn't see in, but at least we were equally invisible to those inside. I'd parked the Pig a little ways down Potash's main drag, where we were shaded from the stars and moonlight by a cottonwood's dense canopy. Tom sat next to me gnawing on a PowerBar I'd given him. I was trying to be extra nice, belatedly hoping to make him want to do everything he could to protect my brother. Mungo's ax-shaped head drooled between us.

"See anything?" Tom asked.

"It's like looking through beer bottles," I told him, handing the surveillance expert the binoculars so that he could try his luck.

Almost all of Hidalgo's men had driven to the restaurant shortly after sunset. We'd watched them from the notch in the ridge as they'd piled into only four vehicles—lowriders and pickups with crew cabs. Like circus clowns, five or six men staggered into each vehicle, and then a few squealing prostitutes were shoved in through the open windows. It seemed impossible that so many people could fit into so little space.

Hidalgo stayed behind again, probably still cozied up with the two girls he'd plucked from the pool. Only two of the younger shaved-heads remained to stand guard. Just two—Hidalgo was feeling very safe in my state, which was something that now pissed me off more than ever. The banger Roberto had punched in the throat was either dead or convalescing. Neither Tom, nor Mary, nor I really wanted to know which it was.

After the fight, I didn't believe Roberto would join the men and women heading out for a night on the town. But he had, walking out alone from the house and squeezing in just before the last car pulled away. I could almost feel the unwelcome response he must have received when he slid in.

We'd waited an hour before following them into Potash. We figured it would take them at least a half hour longer to reach it, as they would have to drive all the way south to the suspension bridge before they could turn west and north on the road to town.

So they had already been inside for a while when Tom and

I pulled up. I was a little worried they might have gone all the way to Casper with its better nightlife, but we found the four cars with their Baja California plates parked haphazardly in front of Señor Garcia's. They were probably too drunk and drugged to drive any farther.

"Nothing," Tom said, dropping the binoculars in my lap. "We can ease up in front, or maybe across the street, but they might spot your truck."

Zafado and Bruto would be in there. Of course they'd come along to keep the more reckless young narcos from causing too much trouble. I didn't think anyone had seen my truck on my previous visit to Señor Garcia's—I'd parked it more than a block away and was pretty sure I hadn't been followed—but I was reluctant to take the chance. Any chance. And I didn't even want to pull up in front of the restaurant, as one of the men inside might notice it and wonder why no one was getting out.

"Or we can wait till morning to see if he's making a drop," Tom said. "I just hope they don't take out the goddamn trash at night. I'm not going to go crawling around in some filthy Dumpster."

Meaning I'd have to do it. But I didn't want to wait for the morning, either. I wanted to know what my brother had to say right now.

"I can't go in there. Some of them don't like me too much," I said, thinking of Shorty. "Besides, they think I work on a horse ranch up near Pinedale. If I walked in again tonight, it might seem like too much of a coincidence."

"Then I'll go," Tom said. "Ask if I can use the toilet or something."

I didn't think that was a good idea. Tom was too conspicuous in his New Jersey cowboy getup. And he was too much of an asshole. There was no one else in the bar but the *sicarios,* the gangbangers, and the prostitutes, and I remembered the fun they'd tried to have with the backpacker girls who'd come in for a meal. I didn't want Tom going in there looking like a white, well-fed, obnoxious tourist in search of a bathroom. I had to admit, though, once again, that he had balls. Even if he lacked brains.

"Let's do a drive-by. See what's going on," I suggested.

I started the engine and drove down the street. Señor Garcia's was on the left, and there were only the narcos' cars in front. One big, sagging Oldsmobile, an equally aged Cadillac, and two pickups, one whose frame had been lowered to within inches of the ground for some dumb reason I've never been able to understand.

I braked a little in front of the restaurant, putting on my left blinker and easing around the corner. We were able to get a good view through the large, barred windows on two sides of the restaurant.

The narcos had pushed aside some tables in the dining area and made a sort of small dance floor. It looked like all of them, or almost all of them, were seated in a loose semicircle around it. Two of the prostitutes were dancing—embracing, really—in the open space. Two others appeared to be grinding on men's laps. I didn't see Roberto at first, but then spotted him all the way in back. He was at the bar, talking to the old man.

As we passed around to the backside, I saw a tiny orange glow emanating from the darkness behind the kitchen. Staring hard and driving slower, I began to make out the shape of a girl—the waitress. The one who'd been kind to me. Who'd warned me to get out of there a few nights earlier.

"I've got an idea," I told Tom.

We circled the block and went back to our old parking space under the cottonwood. Leaving Tom and Mungo there, I hopped out and walked a block north, so that I would approach the bar from the rear.

She was there. Sitting hunched forward on a broken concrete step in front of a screen door that led to the kitchen, still smoking.

I purposely made some noise when I was twenty feet from her, kicking some gravel. She jerked her head up and stared at me in alarm. She looked as if she might run. It was dark where I stood, the only light coming out through the door from the small kitchen. I moved closer while holding up my hands.

"Hey. It's okay."

I said it in Spanish, and softly, even though, with the loud music that was also coming through the screen door along with the dim light, there wasn't any chance we could be overheard.

"Remember me? I was in here last week. You told me not to mess with those guys inside."

She stared at me for several heartbeats, her expression something like a startled deer's. I could see she was twitching to turn tail and run. But then I was standing within the dim circle of light and the jumpiness left her.

She gave me a small smile as her hand touched her chest.

"Hey. Yeah, I remember. You didn't listen to me. You messed with them anyway."

I gave her a smile of my own and put down my hands.

"How come you aren't inside? Are you taking a break?"

"*Sí*. A long one. Papa doesn't like me working when those foul goats from across the river come here."

"Smart. Why don't you just go home?"

She frowned, shaking her head. "You think I'm going to leave him alone in there? Out here, if they start messing around with him, I'll run down to the marshal's office and get help."

Like the one-man police force in Potash would be able to do any good.

"You're going to be here all night," I told her.

She shrugged.

Brave girl. She couldn't have been more than sixteen or seventeen. At that age most girls only think of themselves. But there she was, sitting out alone in the dark, keeping an eye on her grandfather when she must have had a thousand things she'd rather be doing.

"So what are you doing back here? You afraid to go in because of those guys?" she asked.

"Yeah. They didn't like me too much last time."

She giggled and covered her mouth with her hand. Before she did I noticed that her teeth were bucked and crooked. Other than that she was very pretty. Or she could easily have been if her bangs weren't ironed a half-foot into the air. Like the lowered trucks, crotch-grabbing, and body piercing, this was another youthful style in the state that I didn't understand. It made me feel old.

"My name's Antonio."

"I'm Lupe. Are you hauling another horse? I overheard that last time. If you are, I'd like to see him. Someday I'm going to buy a horse."

"No horse tonight. Listen, Lupe, can I get you to do me a favor? Something you've got to keep secret?"

Raising her eyebrows, she now gave me what might have been a teenager's idea of a seductive gaze. She lowered her hand from her mouth and looked at me through her lashes, her smile now slight but willing. Her voice became throatier.

"Sure, Antonio. You're a good guy. I saw that the other night. Anything you say."

"Okay. I need you to take out the trash. From the men's bathroom only."

She looked at me straight again, grimacing. Her voice became suspicious.

"Are you kidding me? The trash? You want me to take out the trash?"

"Yeah. I think I accidentally threw something away."

It was a weak, half-assed effort, but I didn't really think there was anything I could say that she'd believe. And I was right.

"You weren't here earlier today. I would have seen you. And if it was from before, you should know we take out the trash every night."

"Just do it for me, okay? A favor. Do it when no one's in there. I'll watch through the door and tell you when it's clear."

She watched me for several seconds. Studying me closely, from my head to my feet and then back up again.

Then she said, "You're that cop, aren't you? The one who was in all the papers two or three years ago?"

Shit. I was burnt by a teenage girl—I wasn't going to last much longer in this job. I had to admire her acumen, though. What fifteen-year-old kid in a ghost town like Potash reads the papers? I wished I'd worn the cowboy hat and the too-tight boots.

"Hey, are you going to do me that favor or not?" I asked, smiling and not answering her question.

She didn't need an answer.

"It's the scar," she said, laying a finger on her own cheek. "I recognize it, because I cut out your picture from the time when it was in the paper. You're that policeman that got everyone so upset. But I thought you were cute. I was fifteen years old back then."

I didn't say anything.

She went on smiling, too, then frowning a little. "Papa didn't like it when I put it on the wall. He said you were a killer. That you murdered three Hispanic boys in Cheyenne for no reason. I didn't think it was true. It's not, is it?"

"No. It's not."

Whatever her reason for not believing it, I was truly grateful all the same. Everyone else in the world just assumed it was true. Even the FBI.

"I thought so. Papa's kind of an activist. He used to organize the local miners, you know. He thinks everyone's out to get the brown man. Anyway, I've been thinking about joining the police somewhere when I get out of school. You think I should?"

I told her I would give her a card when I was done with what I was doing in Potash. That I would stop by and talk to her and her papa about it, but that I couldn't do that right now.

"So why didn't you just shoot that bastard when he pulled that knife on you? You're a cop—you got a gun, right? What that guy did to those two Anglo women . . . that was really gross."

"It doesn't work like that. . . . I'm sorry, Lupe, but I'm in a big hurry," I told her. "We'll talk about it later. Another time. I promise. Will you do me that favor?"

"Yeah, Antonio—if that's your name. I'll do it." She gave me a seductive look again. "But you keep that promise, okay?"

She flipped the cigarette away into the alley. Brushing her hands on her jeans, she stood up.

"Hang on a sec."

I could see that the bathroom was empty because its little beveled window faced us. It was lit from the inside. I wouldn't have been able to make out the identity of anyone in there, but I would be able to tell if someone was moving around. I checked it again. Then I looked through the screen door. Beyond the kitchen was a hallway with the bathroom doors and then the bar. I worried that someone would notice the girl in the hallway, going into the bathroom marked *"Toros,"* and follow her. I'd seen how the narcos treated girls. And if anything happened, and if I then had to go in there after her, all hell would surely break loose. Roberto would then do something, and everything would come apart.

"Okay. Go."

She looked at me funny and went.

Nothing happened. No evil luck or bad timing occurred. The girl, Lupe, simply ducked in, grabbed the trash can, and strolled back out. Not even her grandfather, presumably behind the bar, noticed.

She wrinkled her nose when I used a stick to push aside some damp paper towels and a filthy condom—used—to get down to where a bright, crumpled pack of bidis rested in a nest of more towels. I plucked it out and stuck it in my pocket.

"Glamorous, huh?" I said to her. "You sure you want to be a cop?"

"That's all you wanted?"

I nodded.

I emptied the trash for her into a Dumpster and handed back the dented metal can.

"Wait until they're gone before you take it back in. Your papa's right—believe me, you don't want those guys even catching sight of you. You're a pretty girl, Lupe. Smart, too. Thank you for your help."

Be something good, I prayed as I walked back to the Pig. *Be something good enough to get a warrant, to finish this and to get Roberto out of there.* I hurried down a narrow causeway between two dark, abandoned buildings, crunching over beer cans and kicking through old papers.

I was about to step into the street and cross it when something made me stop. I froze on the sidewalk, turning right toward the sound of loud voices. They were very close. Then I saw them.

Five or six young men were coming down the street from

the direction of the small park in the center of town. And from the direction of the cowboy bars on the other side. They filled the sidewalk on my side of the street, three of them abreast in front and more of them behind. They weren't more than thirty feet away from where I'd stepped out from between the two buildings.

"Going to beat some Mexes," one of them was calling out in a singsong voice.

"Gonna *kill* us some Mexes," another corrected in a louder voice.

"Fuckers think they can hang in our town."

"Fuckers think they *own* this place. But they're gonna learn."

I had just started to step back between the buildings when they noticed me.

"Hey!"

"Who's that?"

I hesitated.

There were six of them. Young men—boys, really—in jeans and boots, T-shirts, and tightly curled baseball caps. They gripped beer bottles in their hands. I could smell beer on their collective breath even from ten feet away. One of them, in the second row, held a pool cue. Another held what looked like the pump handle of a car jack.

"Looks like one of them Mexes squirted out of there," a boy in the lead slurred.

My first thought wasn't for my own safety, but for what would happen to these boys if they confronted Hidalgo's men. These were Wyoming boys. Ranch kids. They might know guns inside out, but they fought with only fists or bottles or maybe, like these, with jack handles and pool cues. I would have bet that they weren't even armed with anything that goes *bang*. I knew, though, that Hidalgo's men were. And that at least two of them were former Mexican federal police officers who had used the guns that I saw tucked into their waistbands and wouldn't hesitate to do so again. If these young cowboys went in there, it was likely some of them wouldn't be coming out. Not even Roberto would be able to stop that.

"What are you doing out here, Mex?" one of them demanded. Two of the others stepped to the left, blocking me from going into the street. Another two stepped to my right.

I almost answered in Spanish, or at least accented English, having just come from talking with Lupe in that language. But I remembered in time to say, in a Western drawl, "Who you calling a Mex, kid?"

No one said anything for a minute as they scrutinized me through bleary, red eyes. It was hard to take these boys seriously even though they were older than the bangers recruited by Hidalgo. They just lived in a completely different world. The kid in front of me, the apparent leader, scratched his ear and took a swig from his bottle. *He's in high school, probably,* I thought. *He'll go on to college. Play football. Get married and get a job as an accountant.*

"If you're looking for trouble with Mexicans," I continued, "there're some of them in a bar down there who'll give it to you. In spades. I've never seen so many guys carrying guns."

"You sure as hell look like a Mex," one of them slurred.

"They got guns?" a less aggressive voice asked. "Shit. Weren't 'specting that."

"Well, if you ain't a Mex, what the hell are you?"

"You aren't from around here."

"Shit, he's a Mex," the leader drawled to the others. "And I bet he don't got no gun. Let's start by kicking his ass."

He threw the beer bottle down on the sidewalk. It shattered at my feet. Glass shards and foam pelted my pant leg.

I wanted to yell at them, *I'm a cop!* But there was no way I could. Word would get around. Fast.

I could have pulled my gun and threatened them. Maybe

even chased them off. Scared them so they wouldn't ever again even think of doing something this stupid. But then I remembered that I'd left the gun in the truck—there was no place to conceal it without a jacket and I hated wearing an ankle holster.

Run right through them. But which way?

I hesitated for a second too long.

The big guy, the leader, stepped forward and punched me in the chest. The blow knocked me back two steps and took the air from my lungs. Despite the anger that bloomed in me, there was no real pain, as I'd been hit a lot harder and in a lot more sensitive places. I made up my mind. I would defend myself and fight and probably take a beating from a bunch of kids.

God, how embarrassing.

A voice came from behind me. "Marcus? What are you guys doing?"

The boys froze.

I didn't turn around. I recognized the voice, but it sounded so different now that it was speaking English. Lupe sounded like just another American teenager.

"Why are you guys, like, messing with him?"

"We're gonna kick this wetback's ass," one said.

Another shoved him from behind. "Don't say that, dude. Shut up."

A third said, "Hey, Lupe. We're, like, uh, gonna get those guys who've been hassling your granddad. And this guy, he, like, just stepped out of nowhere."

She laughed.

"You morons. He's not one of them. He's a friend of mine. Leave him alone, okay?"

"What was that all about?" Tom asked when I climbed in the truck.

"Kids." I shook my head.

Was I ever that stupid and innocent? I knew the answer: an emphatic yes. I didn't thank Tom for getting out and trying to help. It was something he hadn't done.

"Well? Did you get it?" he demanded.

I took the crumpled pack out of my pocket and turned on the overhead light.

Carefully, I removed the cellophane. The packet came apart with a slight tug. Written on the white paper inside was dense, neat script.

Don't know if you caught it on TV, but shithead had me searched and knocked around. Then took me inside and offered me some blow. Everything's cool now.

Yeah, right, I thought. *A guy's either very sick or very dead because of you, and I bet his buddies aren't too happy about that.*

Saw a bunch of the stuff, maybe a quarter of a kilo. Said he has more. Not buying from Colombians anymore—getting out of that business. Said something new was up, kept talking about `new opportunities,' and a bunch of crap about how the old days were done. Global warming, he said. No more snow. Said the future was X, high-quality Nazi meth, and roofies. Said it could be made *right here in El Norte, no more worries about crossing over. I said stuff's cheap, so how do you make money on it? He said quantity. Big quantity. Claims he can make up fifty pounds in a single cook. Underground, no chance of getting caught. Trick, he said, is getting it on the road. But he said that problem was almost fixed. Later he said he'd show me something in a couple of days maybe. I asked some of the boys about it but they won't talk to me. Hidalgo trusts me, but his dogs told the others not to talk.*

I turned and looked at Tom. He was smiling back at me. Not his usual unpleasant smirk, but a big, toothy grin. A vengeful grin.

"We've got him!" he said. "We've got the bastard. He's cooking meth in the mine."

FOURTEEN

Tom Cochran was still smacking a fist against a palm when we walked into the main cabin.

"We've got him," he said. "We've got him!"

Mary Chang looked off into space after reading the note. A slight smile came onto her thin lips. Other than that, there was no celebration. No hand-shaking or high fives or champagne. But there was an air of righteous victory in the main cabin.

It seemed like an astonishing thing. One little slip of paper and Hidalgo was gone. Vanquished. Blown away. This would not just be a legal love tap of simple possession, but a grand slam with the club of the Kingpin Statute. Things were looking better than any of us had imagined. Some of the prostitutes were surely underage, too. We'd hit him with some state and federal charges for that. Procurement. Minors across state lines for immoral purposes. Some of the weapons possessed by his men were definitely illegal. We'd hit him for that, too. But it was the mine that was going to be our El Dorado.

And Roberto would not only get out, but he would no longer be a fugitive from justice. The sweet deal the U.S. Attorneys had originally offered him would surely be honored—

they wouldn't have a choice in the face of the risks he'd taken. They would send him to the equivalent of a Club Fed in Colorado where he would be close to Rebecca and me, and where he would receive some kind of treatment for his addiction.

The tension that had been present in my muscles and joints for the last couple of days was released. *The wolf's going to come out of the woods.* I cuffed Mungo's shoulders, then stooped to touch my forehead to hers. She rasped her sandpaper tongue against my throat.

With Hidalgo locked up, along with his top lieutenants, the drug lord would be as good as dead. His remaining compatriots in Mexicali would be too busy fighting over the pieces of the cartel to worry about avenging their onetime *jefe.* I would be safe. We all would. And Mary, Tom, and I would have a trophy we could brag about in our old age. *We struck a real blow.*

I smiled into the wolf's golden eyes. She lifted her lips and showed me some teeth, giving me her hesitant grin. The desire to call Rebecca and tell her that everything—*everything!*—was going to be all right was almost overwhelming.

It was too good to be true. And I should have known it then. Good luck will drop into your lap like a warm kitten, but the karmic payback is always a bitch.

The first hint that the world wasn't completely golden came when we began jointly writing up the application for a no-knock search warrant. Mary sat before a computer terminal and called up the template. It surprised me when the template she pulled up was not headed by the words "Federal Bureau of Investigation," but by my own outfit, "Wyoming Division of Criminal Investigation."

"What's that?" I asked, even though I knew what it was.

I'd written up scores of them over my eight years as a state cop.

Mary didn't turn around to look at me. She just kept typing, filling in the spaces. Tom didn't even take the opportunity to ride me by saying something like *It's called a search warrant, QuickDraw.*

My question hung there over Mary's clicking fingertips until she finally said, "Tom and I think it might be better if the original warrant came from the state."

She turned slowly to me when I didn't respond.

"You see, all warrants by federal agents must be approved through the Hoover Building. Through the Deputy Assistant Director in charge of the Criminal Investigative Division, specifically. If we ask for permission, there's still a chance we might get shut down. Remember? Take no chances? So this needs to be a fait accompli, Anton. You guys don't have the same kind of bureaucracy."

"We need Hidalgo in a cage before we make that move," Tom said, almost too quickly. "And with state charges already pending, the government won't be able to hold back or cut a deal. Don't worry—aren't you state guys always complaining about how the U.S. Attorneys swoop in on all your big cases?" He then grinned at me as he repeated his and Mary's other mantra: "Better to beg forgiveness than to ask permission, right? You're going to look like a big guy, Burns. You and DCI are going to get all the initial credit for taking him down. And guess what else? We're even going to let you be in on the bust."

"Thanks, Tom. That's real generous of you."

This wasn't right. He was too smug. And the Feds are never that generous. I understood and appreciated Mary's take-no-chances posture, but surely the federal government could and would take things from here. They would never try to screw around with a case this solid. And were Mary and

Tom really so unambitious, so selfless, that they were willing to step aside at this point and let DCI make the biggest of busts? I knew them better than that, or thought I did. They were serious about avenging their friend and colleague, but they were equally serious about advancing their own careers in the Bureau.

Something stank.

The Bureau has always been famous for snatching credit. It was a skill they'd been perfecting ever since the days of J. Edgar Hoover. Anytime we, the yokels in Wyoming, happened to stop the right car on Interstate 80 and make a major bust, the Feds would more often than not swoop in within hours to take control. And to take credit. Their PR flacks would trumpet the arrest, the charges, and eventually the conviction, without ever mentioning the state officers responsible for the whole thing. Not that we minded all that much—federal mandatory-sentencing guidelines for drug crimes made our own laws look like a mild spanking. But it could be demoralizing—not even getting credit for the initial hook.

The only time I'd seen the Feds turn down a major case was when I caught a guy flying into the Cheyenne airport with a kilo of heroin in his gut. He'd managed to swallow it all in tied-off condoms—almost two and a half pounds of the stuff—and I'd learned of his impending arrival through six months of undercover work. It was the largest heroin bust in the state at the time. The U.S. Attorneys were begrudgingly notified as usual as soon as I had him in the jail, where I gave in to his begging and bought him a carton of Ex-Lax. I expected the Feds to be down at the jail, as usual, in minutes from their office across the street. But they declined. I couldn't believe it. It meant that I had to babysit the mule for six hours as he hunched, groaned, and cried over a toilet I'd had to dismantle so that it wouldn't flush.

It wasn't until the ordeal was over, the filthy evidence

bagged and cleaned, that the Feds changed their minds. Only
then did they come across the street to take him.

I didn't say much more while the affidavit was typed. Tom
and Mary argued about wording. Mary scanned Roberto's
note, printed out a copy, and attached it to the document. I
read through the whole thing before signing it and found one
flaw. The affidavit is supposed to contain all the relevant information for the judge to consider, exculpatory as well as in-
criminating. Roberto, described for his—and my parents'
future safety—only as a Confidential Informant or CI, just in
case, was described as a felon working in conjunction with
state and federal police in return for consideration upon sentencing. The deal was outlined. No mention was made of his
ongoing drug use. I argued for full disclosure of my brother's
name and addiction. After all, Hidalgo in the bag wasn't a
threat anymore, right? But I was overruled by Tom and Mary.

"We don't know for sure that he's still using," Mary said.

"Why confuse the judge? The judges in this state just
rubber-stamp these things anyway," Tom said. "Hell, I doubt
if they can even read."

He spoke with the arrogance that has become a part of
the FBI's image. It was exactly the kind of statement that gets
the Bureau in so much trouble every couple of years.

Tom went on, "Besides, I know you cowboys up here
have a thing about property rights, but Hidalgo isn't even a
voter. And he's a Mexican, anyway. The judge is just gonna
give it a glance and sign off."

It was four in the morning by the time we were finished.
Mary already knew the name and the number of a district-
court judge—the only one—in Pinedale, the county seat. She
picked up the phone and handed it to me.

"Let's wait a couple of hours," I suggested, still trying to
identify what it was that reeked so badly. "Let the judge have
his sleep. Let's not risk pissing him off. Besides, we aren't go-

ing to storm right on in there, are we? The narcos have us out-numbered almost ten to one. Even with those things over there"—I pointed to Tom's H&K MP5s—"we'll get our asses kicked."

And Roberto very well might get killed.

"You need to call in your Fed SWAT team or whoever does this kind of thing."

As I should have expected, Mary and Tom already had a plan mapped out for this, too.

"Tom said you were going to get the credit. Your office. As soon as we get the warrant signed, you can call your boss. He can send over whoever he wants to make the bust. His agents, deputy sheriffs, state patrol, whoever. You guys will be in charge. Until Hidalgo's locked up, we're just along for the ride, okay? Let's get this warrant signed first."

FIFTEEN

S ince it was my state and my judge, I made them wait until 7:00 a.m. before I dialed Judge Ronald Koals's home telephone number. His wife didn't sound pleased when she answered the phone with a sleepy voice. I identified myself and she sounded even less pleased.

"Good Lord," she said. "Can't you people ever call at a decent hour?"

I didn't have an answer to that, and I didn't get the chance anyway. A gruff, also sleepy voice came on the line.

"Just bring it by my house like you guys usually do," the judge said. "I'll be here until eight-thirty, when I leave for court."

"Where do you live, Judge?"

There was a pause. He sounded more awake now.

"What did you say your name was?"

"Antonio Burns. I'm with DCI."

Now there was a longer pause.

"Never mind. I'll meet you at the courthouse, Agent. You can find that, can't you?"

I wondered what he meant by that. Pinedale is tiny. Just a few thousand people live anywhere near the town, which has one main street. And the fact that he apparently had recognized my name wasn't exactly auspicious. He hadn't wanted me to meet him at his home, where warrants were usually signed.

"I think I can find it, Judge. It'll take about an hour to get there."

"Then why are you calling me now?"

I didn't get to answer this question, either. He'd already hung up on me.

The judge's chambers were as unkempt as the man who occupied them. The small room was crowded with file cabinets, counters, and chairs, all piled high with stacks of statute books, binders, and assorted papers. I guessed that his chambers probably also served as the county's law library. The man himself was small and old, bald but for wisps of white hair that stuck out in all directions, and he had eyebrows that stood like lifted wings, as if his head were about to take flight. He had not put on his robe but instead wore a frayed flannel shirt and a suspicious expression.

His desk, though, was uncluttered. The entire oversized surface was clear.

"I've read about you, Agent Burns," he said to me when I walked in the door with Tom and Mary following. "I can't say it made for pleasant reading."

He didn't get up from behind his desk.

I met his gray eyes and held them, trying not to appear insolent, only honest.

"I'm afraid the press was misinformed, Judge. A lot of what they wrote about what happened in Cheyenne was fiction."

I hoped that Tom wasn't smirking behind me.

"Is that so?"

His question seemed to be rhetorical. The tone wasn't exactly challenging or disbelieving, but it didn't sound entirely convinced either. He held my eyes for a long time.

Mary broke in by introducing herself, then Tom. They both held their credentials out to him in their left hands the way they were taught at the academy. The judge rose and leaned over his desk, first studying the proffered badges and ID cards then solemnly shaking their extended right hands. He didn't offer to shake mine. Nor did he need to see my credentials—my face having been already seen enough on the front pages of Wyoming papers.

"I wasn't aware the FBI was operating in this county. To what do I owe the honor of your presence?"

He had yet to smile. I wondered if he was just taciturn by nature or whether he liked having the Feds in his county even less than he liked having me in it. The federal government isn't exactly welcome in a lot of parts of Wyoming.

Mary had handed me the application with the attached affidavit and the copy of Roberto's note before we'd walked in the door. I now handed it to the judge. He spread the eleven pages out on his expansive desk in two rows, aligning them side by side.

"This is a joint operation," Mary explained modestly as the judge squared the edges of the pages. "We're working in conjunction with Mr. Burns and the Wyoming Division of Criminal Investigation. That application should help explain the reason we're here and the importance of this investigation."

"What I mean is, Ms. Chang, why are you seeking a warrant from me? Why not the federal district court in Casper?"

The man was bright. It only took him seconds to ask questions that I should have been asking days ago. He was cutting right to the heart of the matter, without even having yet read the application. Without even knowing who we were investigating. It wasn't a particularly good sign—smart judges tend to be suspicious of law enforcement.

"Your Honor, we thought perhaps this case would best be pursued on a local level. At least initially," Mary said.

The judge looked at me. "I take it then that Mr. Burns will be left holding the bag if anything goes wrong with your investigation?"

No one said anything.

The judge went on, "And am I to understand that this case will be charged and prosecuted in my county? In my courtroom?"

Now there was a hint of mockery in his tone. Again, no one said anything. Mary stood very prim and still with her eyes focused somewhere out the window behind the judge. I glanced over my shoulder at Tom and saw that his jaw was tight. His face was growing darker, too. It was pretty clear the judge didn't like us. Not any of us.

"Our primary concern at this time, Your Honor," Mary said, still looking out the window, "is to arrest a drug kingpin and murderer who is hiding out in your county. No one's given much thought yet as to who will get the credit for the eventual prosecution or in what jurisdiction it will finally end up. That will have to be worked out between your District Attorney and the United States Attorneys."

"Of course," replied the judge. "Of course." He let a moment of silence pass, disbelief thick in the air. Then he said, "Have a seat. Give me a moment to read this."

While he bent to study the application, Tom, Mary, and I looked around at the chairs. There were three of them, but they were all piled high with papers, binders, and books.

"You can set those on the floor," the judge said without taking his eyes off the pages aligned so perfectly before him.

It wasn't easy to find room on the floor, but as he read we

managed to get the three chairs in front of his broad desk and ourselves in them.

This judge didn't just pick up a pen and sign the accompanying order like they so often do. Most of them scarcely even bother to read them. Some will even give you permission for a warrant over the phone after simply being told the barest facts and conjecture. Judge Koals, however, took a red pencil from a drawer beneath his desk and actually began making marks on the application.

Now it was Mary turning a darker shade of tan. She probably felt like she was back in law school. And *Professor* Koals was jabbing at her with the Socratic method. She managed to keep silent, although it looked like it was taking some effort.

Finally the judge looked up at the three of us.

"I find it hard to believe that Mr. Hidalgo, a Mexican drug 'kingpin,' as you call him, would move to this county and to this state."

Mary launched into an explanation.

"Your Honor, Jesús Hidalgo has been having considerable trouble in Mexico over the past year. And his problems have been increasing these past few months. He recently fought and won a war with the Arellano-Felix cartel, but now the other rival syndicates are targeting him as well as the surviving Arellano brothers. Additionally, the new Mexican government under President Vicente Fox has sworn to finally end the corruption in that country—the corruption that has allowed Mr. Hidalgo's 'Mexicali Mafia' to flourish for so long. His operations have been subjected to raids by the various Mexican drug task forces, and as a result, his own cartel, based in Mexicali, has been forced to go to war with them, too."

The judge nodded. "I believe I saw a mention of this new attempt to rein in the cartels on CNN."

"Yes, sir. There's more, though, than just President Fox's efforts. You see, we had an FBI agent working undercover in

Hidalgo's Mexicali Mafia." Her voice was beginning to grow tight with rare emotion. Her words were coming clipped and fast. "He was working his way up toward exposing the leadership. He'd been under deep cover for more than a year, and we believed he was quite close. Somehow, he was discovered. Or perhaps just suspected. It makes little difference when you're dealing with an organization like Mr. Hidalgo's. He was murdered—"

The judge interrupted.

"If this is a vendetta by the FBI, Ms. Chang, I don't want to hear about it."

"No, sir. Excuse me." Mary took a moment to compose herself, then went on. "After the death of Agent Walker, the DEA, FBI, ATF, and other American agencies, in conjunction with their Mexican counterparts, began to turn things upside down. It's our understanding that all this added scrutiny did not please the other kingpins with Hidalgo. They are already suffering due to the increased border security since 9/11. It's also our understanding that the bribes they pay to border guards on both sides of the line went up astronomically due to this new, additional scrutiny. The other members of the cartel thought killing a U.S. agent was a stupid and reckless thing to do—they've told us as much, wanting us to know that they do not condone what Mr. Hidalgo did or had done to Agent Walker. Increased attempts were made on Hidalgo's life and his operations—perhaps in part to appease the United States. In any event, Mr. Hidalgo fled here, where, frankly, he's a lot physically safer than he's ever been in Mexico. And we expect he's going to stay here until it's safe for him to go back—until his rivals have been assassinated by his own men."

"How come Mr. Hidalgo hasn't been charged and arrested for the killing of this Agent Walker?"

"I'm afraid we don't have any direct evidence. Hidalgo operates through layers and layers of associates."

"Ah, so this is a variation of the Capone stratagem," the judge said.

"To be candid, Your Honor, we expect a lot more serious charges against Mr. Hidalgo than tax evasion. All we're asking for here is a search warrant for his home and the mine on his property."

I wondered where she was choosing to draw the line on her candidness. Something still seemed wrong.

The judge asked, "You're asking for a warrant that will allow you to fish for those 'more serious charges,' correct? Such as the murder of Agent Walker, which could even result in the death penalty for Mr. Hidalgo under the federal government's Kingpin Statute?"

Mary didn't need to say anything to confirm it. Her fierce expression said it all.

The judge went on, nodding at the documents now. "I see that you are alleging that Mr. Hidalgo is in possession of cocaine and marijuana within his house, and that you suspect he may be operating a clandestine methamphetamine laboratory in this defunct mine on his property."

"Yes, sir. That's what our confidential informant has told us."

"Do you have any evidence of that, other than the word of your CI?"

Tom, who knew drugs from his time in Juárez with the DEA, answered before Mary could.

"No, Judge, but it makes sense. In the Midwest, crank sells for about twenty thousand dollars a pound. Say Hidalgo can make, as our informant says he claims, fifty pounds once or twice a week, allowing time for cleanup. That's one to two million dollars a week. On meth alone. And no worries about getting it across a heavily patrolled border. He wouldn't even need to go back to Mexico ever if he didn't want to."

I threw in my two cents.

"And with each pound of meth he's producing five to seven pounds of highly toxic waste and dumping it under the ground, Judge. Right here in your county. Down near the water table."

Tom surprised me by saying, "Yeah. That's right. It doesn't help that your state has the most liberal pollution laws in the country."

Tom's green? I hadn't known he was an environmentalist. And I didn't know if the judge was, too. In Wyoming, the odds were against it. But it still seemed like a clever way to push the judge in the right direction.

I added, "There wouldn't be much obvious evidence of a lab in an abandoned mine. It's really the perfect setup for a clandestine lab. The toxic and highly volatile waste is how we usually find them when we don't have an informant. Either somebody smells them or they explode. In a mine, though, you could just dump the waste down a shaft and forget about it. It will dissolve into the rock and the groundwater. We've seen before that it can make a lot of people sick, and no one knows the long-term effects."

"Perhaps you and Mr. Cochran should call your state representative, Agent Burns," the judge said wryly. "I'm sure he'd love to hear from you."

Nope, the judge wasn't green. I shut up and Tom did, too. "QuickDraw" Burns was the last person a state politician would want to hear from. And an environmental appeal wasn't going to score us any points from this judge.

"So besides trying to appall me with this threat of water pollution, you're asking me to hang my hat on the word of your CI and what 'makes sense.' I've found that when it comes to crime, what 'makes sense' does not very often turn out to be true. And I need more than 'making sense' to find that there is probable cause for a search of private property."

Oh shit. I almost couldn't believe it. He was turning it down.

He pushed the papers across the desk toward us.

"I want to hear about these drugs firsthand from this felon, your informant. I want to consider his veracity myself while I look him in the eye. And I want his sworn testimony as a part of the four corners of this affidavit. Then maybe I'll reconsider my ruling."

"We can't do that, Judge," Mary protested. "It would be extremely suspicious to pull out our informant right now. It would put him in grave danger."

The judge just looked at her with his gray eyes, holding out the papers until she took them.

SIXTEEN

There was no conversation on the ride back to the hunting camp. Mary sat next to me in the front passenger seat, perfectly still but radiating heat. Behind us Tom fumed more volubly by working his jaw and muttering curses. Mungo kept batting at his face with her tail whenever she stuck her head out the window, and then stepping on his thigh when she forced her way up between the front seats. When he tried to shove her away, she would push her snout at him apologetically and lick his face.

It was at almost the peak of the midday heat by the time we got back to the camp. Even in the main lodge the temperature was high enough that Mungo couldn't stop panting. Mary fetched us sweaty bottles of Snake River Ale from one of the ice chests.

"Goddamn hick judges," Tom said, opening one of the beer bottles and throwing the cap across the room. "That yokel doesn't know his head from his ass. Now we'll just have to run around him. Give it to a judge who knows what the hell he's doing."

While in a way Tom was defending my brother, confirming his veracity, his words caused me to bristle. The judge was right. Perfectly right. If I were in his shoes—not knowing the parties, not knowing that Roberto wasn't a liar despite his other faults—I would have ruled the same way.

Mary was shaking her head at Tom.

"We can't, Tom. You know that."

U.S. law on the issue is the same as Wyoming's. When one judge rejects your application, you can't just go knocking on some other judge's door. Not without attaching a full and complete statement concerning all previous applications and explaining why you've already been shot down and who had done the shooting. No judge is going to sign a tainted warrant like that. Judges don't do that to one another—it would be a professional insult. Plus it would create all kinds of hell at a later hearing to suppress whatever evidence was obtained via the once-refused warrant.

"You think a federal judge is going to care how some yokel in the sticks ruled?"

"Yes. I think any judge will care," Mary replied.

Tom pressed his hands against the sides of his head and squeezed shut his eyes while making a face.

"Christ, Mary. Do I have to spell it out? Forget the notice of a prior application. Fuck it. Don't mention it. We should have gone federal in the first place."

Mary shook her head harder.

"Without the approval of the Deputy Director? Without bringing in the U.S. Attorneys? Without revealing what just happened with Judge Koals? No. No way."

Suddenly Tom was almost shouting.

"Yes! Yes way! Once we get in there, no one's going to give a shit how we got the warrant signed! The Deputy Director will be jumping out of his socks to take credit and cover his ass at the same time! Hidalgo's operating the biggest lab anyone's ever seen in there, and when that comes out, none of this preliminary shit is going to matter!"

There was a moment of silence before Mary answered him, speaking low, but with her tone and emphasis on each word she might as well have been shouting right back.

"This is my operation. I am the senior officer here. We will not take shortcuts. We will play this game by the rules."

I almost leaned back, away from the quiet force of her words. Tom was glaring at her, so red in the face that I thought he might have a heart attack. He stared at her for a long moment, his close-set eyes bulging, then he kicked through the blanket and the door and stormed out into the daylight.

"Fuck!" I heard him yell.

I'd kept out of the argument. I didn't like it, but Mary was right. At least from a legal perspective. She was also right about it being a game.

"It's not going to be easy," she now said to me. "How are we going to get Roberto out of there long enough to testify without people getting suspicious?"

"We put up the abort flag."

That was the signal for Roberto to run—a bit of black cloth would be tied to a juniper branch not far from the notch. If he saw it, he was supposed to get the hell out, as fast as he could.

"No. We can't. Then he couldn't ever go back in."

"Good. Let's do it."

"No, Anton. What if the judge insists on getting more information, or if the warrant gets overturned at a suppression hearing? What about you and your family? Hidalgo will certainly know who informed on him if your brother bolts. And that's only a small number of Hidalgo's men across the river. Even if we manage to arrest and hold them all, others will come after you. That's Hidalgo's signature. Retaliating against the families of those he suspects."

La corbata, she didn't need to say. His other signature.

We had thought it would be so easy. We'd send Roberto in and he'd smuggle out the necessary observations for us to get a warrant. Then all we'd have to do would be snap the ammo clips onto Tom's precious submachine guns, call in a few more guys, and crash through the gate. It had made a lot of sense at the time, when you didn't think about a Wyoming judge's obstinacy and suspicion.

"Shit," I said.

I didn't say anything about how maybe this could have been avoided if they'd let me in on everything at the beginning. If they'd told me from the start that this was an unsanctioned operation, that they would need Wyoming warrants and law. But if I'd known, I might not have let my brother go in there. No, I definitely wouldn't have. I couldn't really blame them. And I think I was beginning to want Hidalgo as bad as they did.

So how to get word to Roberto that he needed to slip out for a day or two?

"You have any ideas?" Mary asked.

"Let me think about it."

I whistled to Mungo and followed Tom out into the daylight. The heat was visible, wavering to a height of six feet off the red earth like high, transparent grass. I could hear Tom scrambling up toward the notch but I didn't look after him. Pulling off my shirt, I instead headed for the rocks. Thankfully, the one Roberto and I had chosen as our bouldering wall had fallen into the shade. Touching the places my brother had touched two days earlier, I moved onto the rock. Even shaded, the stone was still hot enough to make my fingers tingle. I traversed the rock for a half hour, until my fingertips were bleeding, my toes were aching, my skin was dripping, and my mind was clear.

Then I sat close to Mungo and panted for a while as hard as she was.

God knows I didn't like him, but at least Tom's way of doing things would keep Roberto safer. But it also might blow the case against Hidalgo in court. If the warrant was found to have been issued without sufficient probable cause, or if it was discovered to have intentionally left out the fact of an earlier ruling against, all the evidence discovered subsequently would be suppressed.

It had happened to me before. And there is nothing worse than having overwhelming evidence on a perp and then seeing it suppressed, the charges dropped, and the case forever dismissed.

Although I hadn't intentionally hidden anything, what had happened then still shamed and infuriated me.

One night in Rock Springs I was riding in a patrol car with a uniformed cop. He was helping me look for a guy I had a warrant on. Then, right in front of us at a stoplight, a big pickup coming at a right angle toward us blew the light and slammed into a car pulling out of a fast-food joint. The collision was enormous—it tore half the back end of the cheap Japanese car right off. One of the pickup's oversized desert tires went wobbling down the street. As I was throwing open the door to go help, the pickup backed off, the wheel-less axle grinding into the asphalt, and tore down the street.

Inside the compact was a man in the driver's seat, a woman next to him, and three children without seat belts in the backseat. The ones who weren't unconscious were bleeding. There was blood and glass everywhere.

The local cop and I did what we could until an ambulance arrived. Rage built in us both while we tried to calm the screaming children and their parents. How could anyone just cream an entire family and drive away? It was so fucking arrogant. So outrageous.

Finding the pickup's driver was easy. The cop and I followed an inch-deep gouge in the asphalt for about a half-mile until it ran up a driveway and into an open garage. There was the pickup.

We walked up the driveway. It was the pickup. There was no doubt. A missing wheel, the front end smashed, the windshield spiderwebbed in the shape of a head. Absolutely no doubt. The engine was still ticking as it cooled off. Green fluid was puddling beneath it. There was also an interior door leading into the house.

"This guy," the cop said through clenched teeth. "This guy. I'm going to fuck him up."

I grabbed his arm before we stepped under the open garage door.

"No. This is clean. The court's going to fuck this guy up for us."

I pounded on the door. A woman answered it. She was small and scared-looking, not willing to meet my eyes. She was unmarked, too—she obviously hadn't been the driver.

I didn't have to say anything. She motioned us into the house without saying a word, then she turned and led the way. I walked behind her into a kitchen that was cluttered with trash, and she pointed through it to a filthy living room where a man was slumped in a chair. Blood from his face ran down his neck and had soaked his shirt. You could smell the liquor on him from all the way across the room.

"Shit," he said, holding his ruined face. "Didn't see the damn light."

We took him clean. No sneaky sucker punches to places where bruises wouldn't show, no "popcorn ride" in the back of the squad car—breaking and accelerating to throw our prisoner all over the cage. It was totally by-the-book. Eight months later I appeared in court to testify at the standard suppression hearing. I'd studied the motions in the County Attorney's office before going into the courtroom. They were the usual bullshit: a motion to suppress the arrest (and all evidence arising from it) for lack of probable cause, a motion to suppress any and all statements because they'd been coerced, etc. I was looking forward to seeing the judge deny these outrageous motions. I always hoped the judge would order the defense attorney horsewhipped for having the nerve to file such frivolous paper and waste the court's time, but judges tended to take it as just another part of the game—an exceedingly hopeful roll of the dice by the defense attorney or simply a way to bill the defendant for more in-court time.

What was strange was the way the defense attorney wore such a wicked smile when he asked me about entering the garage and then the house—as if he were accusing me of breaking down the door instead of being waved in by the defendant's distraught wife. The prosecutor, like me, seemed to think it was just the usual theatrics. I didn't like that grin, though.

It wasn't until the closing argument that I learned what was behind that smirk.

"I've got a case for you, Your Honor. Decided last month. An officer may not make a warrantless entry into a suspect's garage."

He handed the County Attorney and the judge a thin sheaf of papers. It was a slip opinion—not yet published.

I gripped the table while the County Attorney first argued that the garage was open, that I'd been invited inside. The judge shook his head sadly—the Wyoming Supreme Court, in their infinite wisdom, had been clear. Even if it were just a carport with no walls whatsoever, an officer may not cross the threshold without a warrant or consent.

"Emergency exception," I'd hissed at the County Attorney.

He tried to claim it, stating that I had reason to believe

someone was critically injured inside the house, but the judge wouldn't buy it. We'd crossed the threshold without permission. Motion granted. Charges dropped. Case dismissed.

The defendant walked out of the courtroom laughing. No doubt to go get drunk again and run over somebody else.

The County Attorney, of course, blamed me for somehow not knowing, eight months in advance, the contents of a future state-court decision. The suits at the AG's office called me in for a gleeful ass-chewing. Not one bothered to call the family—who had no insurance, one of the children still hospitalized—and I had to do it myself.

Mungo lifted her head and looked down the slope. Mary was coming up. It was almost dusk, and the sun was turning a little red over the river as it got ready to impale itself on the Winds' sharp peaks.

"Have you figured it out yet?" she asked. "How we're going to get him out of there long enough for him to testify?"

"Yeah. Listen, he'll tell Hidalgo that he's going climbing in the Winds. Going to go do a big wall up there or something. He can even invite Hidalgo to go with him. You know that Hidalgo used to think he was a climber?"

She nods.

"Roberto told us."

"Well, Hidalgo won't go. So Roberto will just head out on his own."

"How do you know Hidalgo won't want to go? Maybe he still thinks he's a climber."

"He won't."

He'd never been a climber. Not even the time Roberto met him on Aconcagua, when Hidalgo was so foolishly dressed in his designer alpine wear. And I'd seen the gut pushing out over his belt and heard my brother say that he'd gotten fat. Even if he wanted to go, he would never be able to keep up with Roberto.

"I'll pick him up somewhere in the mountains and lead him to where we'll have a car waiting. With the judge in it, if he's willing. Roberto can wander back down to Hidalgo's place after that. Then we'll either kick in the doors or be back to square one."

But the question still remained: How to get Roberto word that it was time for him to head out, purportedly to climb?

While we discussed options, Tom fast-forwarded through the surveillance tape that had self-recorded while we were visiting the judge. It showed a few of the prostitutes splashing—with swimsuits on this time—in the pool. They cleared out when Hidalgo came out to do his morning laps. A little later they were escorted in a caravan of cars back to the airstrip beyond the hill and the plane took off. Apparently a night and a day's debauchery was all Hidalgo would allow himself and his men.

Roberto was visible for what the camera's timer showed as almost an hour. He wasn't with the others, though, around the pool or taking the girls to the airstrip. He was out of their sight, hidden by a wing of the house. He walked halfway up the hillside to boulder around on a shelf of rock there.

One of the young bangers had followed him at a distance with an automatic rifle over his shoulder. He watched Roberto cruise the rock for a while, gaping, and doubtless wondering why anyone would fool around like that ten to twenty feet off the ground. Then he sat down, apparently bored. It was obvious, though, that he'd been told to watch Roberto, as he didn't go back to the house until my brother was finished.

It sent a clear message: Roberto was an honored guest, allowed to sleep in Hidalgo's wing of the house, but either Hidalgo himself or his security chiefs wanted him watched. So he was a prisoner, too.

"You Burns boys certainly have a thing for rocks," Mary said.

"It's all they've got in their heads," Tom said, managing to be almost witty.

"It's training," I told them. "It makes you strong and confident. So that you can do the same moves hundreds of feet off the deck."

I took the controller from Tom and reversed the tape. I watched my brother walk backward past the guard without a glance or a word. I slowed it, watching him leap fifteen feet straight up onto the rock. I then watched him traversing the upper lip of the long shelf, torquing his fingertips and toes into tiny cracks.

"That's how we'll tell him," I said, pointing at the screen. "We'll just leave him a note. Right there, where no one else will find it."

SEVENTEEN

om took charge of things. I had to admit that he had a lot more experience than I did with this type of operation.

And being in charge made him—for a little while, at least—less obnoxious than usual. He even began to tell me some stories of surveillances in the Mexican desert and in the Colombian highlands before he realized he was acting out of character. Then he stopped, took a mental look in the mirror, and frowned his way back into the carefully crafted persona of the hard-boiled Federal special agent.

From a crate he drew out a cellophane-wrapped pair of gray-and-black-patterned fatigue pants and threw them at my chest. A matching long-sleeved shirt followed a few seconds later. Unlike what you see on TV, these were the kind of FBI-issue clothes that did not have FBI stenciled in yellow letters on the back. These were meant to make one invisible at night.

We tested radios—fancy Motorola Sabers—that were far smaller and more advanced than the kind I was used to. A state like Wyoming doesn't have the budget for equipment that's not bulky or out-of-date. These were encrypted, and each had an earpiece receiver. The wire you taped to the inside of your collar and then down the inside of your left arm. The transceiver wrapped around your wrist like a watch. The radio itself you clipped to your belt.

I didn't want to carry any weapons—I didn't relish the idea of getting caught and possibly charged with armed trespass. But Tom and Mary insisted.

"Getting charged is the last thing you'll have to worry about if we get caught, QuickDraw," Tom said, sneering at what he perceived as my wimpiness.

At sunset Tom and I left the camp in the Pig and drove north. I turned off the headlights and left them off once we were on the other side of the river.

We pulled off the road at what I judged to be about five miles from Hidalgo's ranch. The road was the one that led to the high trailhead, not his private and likely guarded driveway. Murmuring an apology to the landscape, I drove over sage and cactus until we were about a hundred feet off the road and concealed between some boulders and a cottonwood.

Tom took out a tin of charcoal paint and we both smeared some onto our faces. I felt silly, like I was playing soldier, but did it anyway. Tom faced me after he pulled a watch cap over his red hair and asked me to "touch him up." I managed not to laugh. It was weird to be caressing his face; weirder still when he caressed mine. I thought about the way he'd been treating my brother and me and would have liked to poke him in the eye.

I knelt on the ground next to the Pig and studied a topo map with a penlight. I memorized the hills and valleys, the ravines and ridges, that would take us down to Hidalgo's property. I memorized the compass headings, too, just in case. For some reason I've never had any trouble navigating outdoors. Even at night, even on unfamiliar ground. But in the city I might as well be blind and dumb. It never failed to make Rebecca giggle when I got lost between her loft and the highway less than a mile away—something I'd done a thousand times but still couldn't get right.

I tried to move like my brother once we got going. I imagined myself as a phantom, gliding a foot above the ground, or as a coyote, tiptoeing over the earth. I expected the hike to be deadly serious, as what we were doing was a little risky, but it turned out to be almost comical.

Tom kept up with me, although he made a lot more noise. It was a little disappointing—I'd hoped to bury him. I'd imagined the pleasure of hearing him gasping behind me, panting to keep up, and finally having to beg for a break. But he did well, stamina-wise, although in another way he was a mess. He'd insisted on wearing his ridiculous cowboy boots—he said he was worried about snakes. Two times early on he caught his pointed toes or riding heels on something and went down face-first. Each time I was there to pick him up, glad the night was dark enough to hide my smile.

It reminded me of a good time with Roberto. Long ago, when we were very young, we'd gone camping in Yellowstone with Dad and a bunch of other kids from the Warren Air Force Base. Each night we played a game called Bear with a Flashlight, which was a little like tag in the dark.

During the day Roberto and I found a place where a small sapling had fallen and lay across a trail. We raised its tip up a foot and a half by placing some rocks under it and wedged it between the trunks of two other trees. Then we went back to the campfire for dinner before the game was to begin. Probably ten times that night we led the Bear—one of the fathers—to the trap, running like hell, leaping at the last minute and running on, then trying not to suffocate with laughter when we heard the crash behind us.

Wham! Tom went down again, and this time a chuckle escaped my mouth. I tried to turn it into a cough. He ripped his arm from my grasp when I tried to lift him up.

After that he wore his night-vision goggles. I'd refused the pair he'd offered me. In Wyoming, in open country, the stars are all you need. At least if you're smart enough to wear something other than cowboy boots on your feet.

Until we got within a mile of the house, the only things I was really concerned about were rattlesnakes. It was about the time they would be most actively hunting mice. But all we came across were a couple of skinny deer that went pounding away from us into the brush. I wasn't particularly worried about Hidalgo's men—from what we could tell, they weren't vigilant enough to post guards out in the country around the house. But I was a little worried that Tom, seething as he slipped around on his slick soles right behind me, would put a bullet in my back.

I checked my topo one more time when I judged we were getting close. I was lightly sweating and feeling loose and good. As we descended into one last valley before rising up onto the final one that dropped away to Hidalgo's, I began to move slower, taking greater care in placing my feet.

Tom thought I was moving too slow. He tailgated me just like he had when he'd first followed the Pig into Wyoming from Salt Lake. Not using the radio yet, he hissed for me to pick it up. But I wouldn't hurry. I was the one who was going to have to slither down the slope above Hidalgo's house. And there I would be within sight of the guard posted by the front door and within easy rifle range as well.

On the crest of the hill was a well-worn path. We paused on it to study the house below.

I decided I was glad that Tom had brought the night-vision goggles. Using them, he was able to clearly see the guard on duty at the front of the house. To me he was just a gray shape, features discernible only when he lit the occasional cigarette. Tom, though, could see everything he was doing and even which direction he was facing. He whispered this information into the radio when I began descending the slope.

Unfortunately, Tom was also able to see who had drawn the predawn posting. I'd assumed it would be one of the young shaved-head bangers, who seemed to get all the scut work around Hidalgo's place. I wouldn't have worried too much even if it were Bruto or Zafado, or anyone at all who might have had the brains to investigate a snapping twig before pulling a trigger. But it wasn't anyone I suspected had even the tiniest bit of brains. It was Shorty, the most unhinged of all Hidalgo's men. He was the kind of drooling idiot who would happily shoot at a random noise in the night. He was too dumb to consider that he might wake up one of his *jefes*. Tom informed me that he had what appeared to be an AK-47 on a strap over his shoulder.

I went down the slope on my hands and knees. Heavy leather rappelling gloves protected my palms as I gingerly groped my way through a prickly pear cactus that was too spread out for me to go around. My knees, though, felt each short, red-hot spine that pierced through the canvas fatigue pants. They ground into my skin each time I placed my weight. I longed to go for the tweezers in the hip pack that was tight against my belly. But it would have to wait.

Initially it was easy. Shorty was lolling on his feet, probably half stoned and exhausted from having spent most of the previous day and night with the imported girls. He would face one direction while he smoked a cigarette. When he'd burned it down to his fingers, he'd throw it on the ground and walk in a small, staggering circle for a couple of minutes. Then he would stop, face a new direction, and light a fresh smoke. Tom buzzed in my ear like a mosquito, telling me to *"Go"* or to *"Stop."*

Midway down the slope was the protruding shelf of rock that I'd seen Roberto working out on. I wanted to go around it, to get underneath the overhang and find a likely spot to hide my message, but that would take too long. Tom's stumbling around in the sage had taken up too much time. The first rays of the sun would be curving over the earth in less than a half hour.

So I waited behind a bush for a *"Go"* from Tom. Then I crawled a few feet farther and lay chest-down on top of the rock. I took off the gloves and reached over the edge. At first I couldn't find any holes or cracks. But I knew they were there—I'd seen Roberto swinging along on them.

I rolled to the side and reached down again. Nothing. I rolled a third and a fourth time along the shelf. Still nothing. Maybe I was rolling the wrong way. Maybe I was all mixed up. Maybe I was on the wrong rock. Maybe I would have to drop down after all to figure it out. The sky was turning to steel gray beyond the mountains.

Then, on the fifth roll-and-reach, I found it. My fingertips brushed an edge that disappeared. I felt it with both hands. It was a crack, a very narrow one that would only allow my fingertips. I got the tiny note from my pocket and leaned out again.

"Stop!"

Tom's warning was an electric slap to my ear. I looked up in time to see the glowing cigarette bursting in a tiny orange explosion from where Shorty had flicked it away from him. He was moving, beginning to turn in another staggering circle.

I made the decision to go for it. In another few minutes it would be too light. With the folded paper pinched between my index and middle fingers, I stabbed it deep into the crevice. My cheek was on the cold stone as I reached and strained, my eyes fixed on Shorty's silhouette. He stopped walking. He was staring right at me.

For a long, long, moment it was like our eyes were fixed

on each other's, staring in alarm and surprise and recognition. His hands began to rise.

But the automatic rifle wasn't in them. I saw his hands going to rub his eyes just as Tom hissed *"Go!"* far too loudly in my ear.

I lunged back into the moon-shade of a bush. The leaves rattled like cellophane as I scurried among them. When I looked again, Shorty was still peering at me.

"Stay. Stay. Stay. Motherfucking stay," Tom was saying.

It was hard to believe that Shorty couldn't hear him.

The *sicario* took out a flashlight. It wasn't one of the big, long, black Maglites like cops carry, but a cheap aluminum one. I could see the moon reflecting on its shiny length. He switched it on and shone it right at me. The distance diffused the weak light, but it didn't diffuse it enough.

Shorty looked for a long time. He stared and stared and stared, swinging the light back and forth over the bush I was crouching in. I held my breath, but I was starting to shake. He was going to call someone. He was going to shoot. Even if he didn't hit me—even if I managed to sprint over the ridge crest and into the valley beyond—they'd know someone had been there. They'd look for signs and find the note. Then they'd kill my brother.

But then Shorty began to turn. He clicked the light off. I took my first breath in minutes. Then he whirled back, snapping the light back on. But I knew now that he couldn't see me. Still, I didn't move. Except to lift my middle finger in an invisible salute.

I waited five minutes to calm down before I began crawling back up the slope. Shorty had lost interest in anything but smoking and walking in circles to stay awake. It wouldn't take much of a noise, though, to get him whipping around and shining his light again. So I moved very, very slowly, the gloves still off, testing the ground above and ahead for twigs, dried leaves, or anything at all that could make a sound.

I moved slowly despite the way the yet-unseen sun was brightening the east. I knew that even if it got light enough for me to be viewed with the naked eye, Tom's radioed instructions about which direction Shorty was facing would keep me safe.

I was only halfway up the slope when I heard a noise behind and below me. It was a lock turning. A door opening. Then there were voices.

Tom buzzed in my ear, *"Wait."*

Turning my head with the speed of an iguana, I looked behind me.

The front door to the house was open, spilling soft light out onto the flagstone driveway. Two men were coming out, walking toward Shorty. One was Hidalgo, dressed in a sweatsuit with reflective stripes running down the arms and the legs. The other was one of the young bangers. Carrying an automatic rifle like Shorty's.

The kid trailing behind, Hidalgo walked rapidly up to Shorty. I couldn't hear their distinct words, but it sounded like small talk. The kid was rubbing his eyes irritably, obviously unhappy to be awake at this hour.

I wondered what the hell Hidalgo was doing up at five-thirty in the morning. On the tapes, he'd never appeared outside before at least ten o'clock. But the tracksuit, and the way he began waving his arms in circles then trying to touch his toes, explained it. Maybe Roberto and his overwhelming physicality had sparked an envy in the narco king. Maybe one of the girls had teased him about his gut. It was a noble, and probably doomed, objective, but now—when I was still fifteen feet from the top of the slope—was definitely not a good time.

I crawled a little higher when Hidalgo began jogging down the driveway. Shorty was watching him, and probably chuckling, because El Doctor only made it about a hundred feet before he slowed to a walk. The kid had slung the short, blunt assault rifle over his back and was straining to keep up.

I was high enough to see Hidalgo turn right—not left, which was the direction that would keep him on the road toward the mine. With a sick feeling I realized he was heading up for the path that ran along the ridge above me. The path that Tom was probably lying across.

"He's coming up the trail," I whispered into my wrist.

"I see him."

Above me I heard a scrabbling noise as Tom slithered under some cover.

The impulse was strong to jump up and run for it. There was little doubt that we could get away. We could easily outrun these fat bastards. But there was no doubt that we would be seen and heard. So while the night sky continued its transition to gray, I stayed still.

"You could take him out. Right now."

It was whispered in my ear. For a second it seemed like my own thought. But it was Tom, over the radio earpiece.

"Think about it. No warrants. No trial."

Is he kidding? I wondered. *He doesn't sound like it.*

Is it a test? To see if I'm that QuickDraw of rumor and legend?

"Go on, QuickDraw," Tom whispered. *"Do it."*

It would be so easy, I thought. *To just drop him, right here, and slip away into the hills. He deserves it. El Doctor. La corbata. Shit. No one would know. No one but Tom and Mary and my brother.*

It seemed a lot longer, but it was probably only three or four minutes before I could hear sneakers thumping and scratching along the path above me. A half-minute later I could hear the sound of two men breathing hard. I had slipped my gun out of the paddle holster on my hip.

"I'm getting tired, boss. I need to rest," I heard the kid whine.

"You will rest when I do," Hidalgo commanded him.

I didn't doubt that Hidalgo had chosen one of the fatter bangers for this very reason. It wouldn't do to be run into the ground by one of his more muscular hirelings.

"My heart," the kid continued to whine, closer now. Very close. "It's going to burst, man."

"All right," Hidalgo gasped. "You may rest."

The tread of tennis shoes stopped. All I could hear was the ragged breathing just a few feet above me. So close. As much as I felt a dread of discovery, I also felt a thrill at being so close to Hidalgo. I could just stand up and shoot him. The kid, too, before he got anywhere close to getting the gun off his back.

QuickDraw.

I glanced up at the sky and saw that it was so light that the stars were only barely visible.

Then there was the sound of water being poured on the ground. Not poured, but sprayed. One of them was urinating.

"Feel better?" Hidalgo asked after a moment.

"Not really."

"Come. We continue."

And then they were gone.

When I got to Tom five minutes later, he was trembling with rage. And he smelled of piss. He'd taken off his shirt and was rubbing it vigorously against the back of his head and neck.

"You pussy!" he hissed at me.

EIGHTEEN

"You want me to swear on a stack of Bibles or something?"

"That won't be necessary, son," the judge told my brother. "This isn't a formal hearing. But I expect you to tell me and this tape recorder here the truth."

The "son" sounded disingenuous. From the way Judge Koals was looking at my brother, Roberto was not the kind of son the judge ever wanted to have.

We were back in the judge's chambers in Pinedale. He'd once again preferred meeting here to at his home. And he'd refused Mary's request to convene with Roberto in any other nonjudicial location, concerned that it would make him appear a party to the sought-after warrant rather than an independent arbiter. It was long after regular court hours, though—we hadn't wanted to bring Roberto in when people were likely to be around.

With the addition of Roberto to the small room, as well as the weird energy that accompanied him everywhere, it was so crowded that I could barely breathe. The four of us were not across the desk from the judge but gathered all around it, like it was a conference table. Mary—in a courtroom skirt, blouse, and jacket—had managed to shoehorn herself into a chair between the wall and one end of the judge's desk. I stood at the other, leaning against the wall. Roberto and Tom sat close together and opposite the judge, who was peering at my brother over the top of his reading glasses. He wasn't wearing his robe, but there was no doubting that he was judging us all.

"Ms. Chang and her cohorts here would rather I not know your name," the judge said, speaking to Roberto. "That's their prerogative with confidential informants. But they are required to convince me that your information is reliable, and that's why I exercised *my* prerogative to have this little talk."

It was evident from his tone and his gaze that he wasn't pleased so far with what he saw. I wasn't either. Roberto's tangled hair was spiking out from his head. His cheeks were creased with a slack grin. The pupils in his blue irises were so small they were hard to find. Above his faded and torn T-shirt, his neck muscles were tight against the leather cord with its turquoise stone.

"We've explained it to him, Your Honor. He understands why he's here," Mary said needlessly.

She sounded anxious to speak for my brother. She'd been anxious ever since we'd picked Roberto up that afternoon, way up at the trailhead in the Winds. I wasn't sure if Mary's unease was from concern about him or concern for her warrant.

"Thank you, Ms. Chang. Then we've both made it clear," the judge said, intending to shut her up. "Now let's start at the beginning, son. What's your relationship to this fellow, Jesús Hidalgo-Paez?"

Roberto shrugged. "He's just a guy I met 'bout twelve years ago. Down in South America, where he was freezing to death on this mountain he was trying to climb. I got him down. We got to be friends, sort of. Anyway, he makes a lot of money selling dope, and he thanked me for saving his butt by giving me some."

"Money or drugs?"

"Both."

"When you say he sells drugs, do you mean he sells them on the street?"

Mary spoke up, before Roberto could answer.

"As our warrant states, Your Honor, Mr. Hidalgo-Paez is a distributor of cocaine and heroin on a scale that is truly—"

"Please, Ms. Chang. Let me speak with your informant. I asked him here so I could talk to him, not you."

Mary colored and shut up. The judge turned back to Roberto.

"He's not out there slinging dime bags, if that's what you mean," Roberto said in his soft, slightly slurred voice. "He runs what he calls a *sociedad*—like a corporation. Hidalgo's the CEO. The Man. He doesn't get his hands dirty. The guys who work for him—the *capitáns*—have other guys, who have other guys, to do that kind of stuff. You know what I'm saying?"

The judge nodded. It was a good explanation of how Hidalgo operated so successfully. It was also a good explanation of why he'd never been indicted. That and *la corbata*.

"Tell me more about how he runs this corporation."

"Like a dictator, I guess. It's just him, you know—there's no board of directors or anything."

"No, I mean, how does he run it? Give me an example of how things are done. Something you know about firsthand."

"Okay," Roberto said, nodding. "Sure. The way it works is kind of like this: Couple of years ago, Jesús asked me to talk to this guy who works for him. A *capitán* who goes by the name of Zafado. Anyway, Jesús doesn't say anything about drugs, but I know that's what it's about. This guy Zafado tells me he knows a way to make me some scratch, tells me how much, and asks me to talk to someone else. He doesn't say anything about drugs, either. So then I talk to the little guy, way down low on the chain, and he's very open because he's such a little guy. Telling me about how he's having trouble getting his loads of black tar—that's heroin—across the border in Arizona because his mules keep dying. Heat, snakes, hijackers, vigilantes, all that. Guy says he heard El Doctor—that's Jesús—thought maybe I could help, and that his boss, Zafado, will make it worth my while. So then somebody else drives me to Sonora and has me show these mules how to get through the desert and into the States. I was, like, their guide. Each time I got a bunch of them through, all the way to Tucson, I got paid ten grand. That's how it works. I made the run on foot 'bout five times."

The judge was nodding.

"When was that?"

"I don't know, seven years ago? Maybe less. I only did it those couple of times. I got out of it then. I saw how the mules—the real little guys—were being treated and I didn't like it. So I took some money and split."

"How were they being treated?"

"They were mainly just kids," Roberto said, not smiling now. "Boys and girls in their teens. Going north for jobs and school and to hook up with relatives already there. This guy who worked for Zafado would drive around in Mexicali and Nogales and just pick them up. They knew better than to say no. There were a lot of bodies in the desert. Word had gotten around not to refuse. They were supposed to be paid a few hundred bucks for humping a pack through, but usually a truck would meet us in Tucson to pick the kids up and drive them back south. They never got paid and they had to do it all over again. Some of them who did a second trip with me told me what that truck ride back south was like. They weren't treated too well."

Roberto had already told us about this, when Tom and Mary had been debriefing him. The girls were often raped. Sometimes the boys, too. Once back in Sonora or Mexicali, they were locked up like beasts of burden—real mules—to await the next run north. He didn't elaborate now for the judge, but what he meant by them not being treated too well was evident on his face.

So far, so good, I was thinking. Even if nothing Roberto had said so far was exactly damning to Hidalgo for the current case. There was nothing to connect him to it but Hidalgo asking him to talk to Zafado and then another guy, but I was pleased all the same. The whole drive in I'd pounded on only one thing with Roberto: Don't be a smart-ass, don't be a smart-ass. I knew he didn't respond well to authority. Especially in the form of judges. So far he was doing well.

"So you 'split,' " Judge Koals said, using Roberto's terminology, "seven years ago or less. Tell me what your relationship with Mr. Hidalgo-Paez has been like since then."

"We didn't stay in touch, if that's what you mean. No Christmas cards. Then I just showed up at his place a few days ago. Said I was on the run, which is sort of true. He'd heard about it. Out of friendship, he said he'd help get me out of the country. He still owes me for how I helped him off that mountain. So he said he'd figure out a way in a week or two, but to hang with him until then."

"Even though you hadn't seen him in seven years or so?"

Roberto lifted both hands, palms down, and let them waver a little.

"Like I said, I was never a *capitán* or anything. I was just a guy who saved his ass one time and who he thinks can keep his mouth shut. A friend, sort of. Someone he can talk to about stuff other than business. See, Jesús doesn't have many friends. Not even among his *capitáns*. Everyone's too afraid of the dude. Afraid he'll tell someone to cut their throats for knowing too much about him."

"And you aren't afraid of him?"

Roberto smiled.

"I'm afraid of my own shadow, Judge."

The judge actually smiled back at Roberto. Seeing the judge amused by my brother's comment—the way it was so contradictory to my brother's appearance—both Tom and Mary chuckled politely.

"Anyway, Jesús—he's real careful these days. He's been having some trouble down in Mexicali, and had to come up here for a while before someone put an extra hole in him. I showed up unexpectedly—his old pal, you know—and asked him for help getting out of the country. Said I could do some work for him, too, make a little money to get on my feet again. I said I could deal with the guys he buys uncut coca from. Down in Colombia, Peru, and Uruguay. Negotiate on his behalf, you know? For a piece."

The judge's eyes had narrowed a little. I knew what he was thinking—entrapment—but wasn't worried. That wasn't where we were going.

"He knows I'd be good at it. Nobody hassles me down there."

Mary broke in, explaining, "Our informant has some high-level connections with various South American governments. These connections make it unlikely he would ever be harmed or extradited from a South American nation."

This was Grandpapa's—my mother's father—proud legacy, I recalled bitterly. He'd earned it by being a murdering bastard during the Dirty War. Although he'd been dead for almost fifteen years, the world would have been a far better place if he'd never been born.

"Is that right?" the judge asked Roberto.

Roberto again shrugged, then continued.

"But he said he was getting out of that business for a while. The cocaine business, that is. Said he knows something that's going to be a lot more profitable and that can be produced right here in the States. No worries about getting it in. He was talking mainly about crank—"

"He means methamphetamine, Your Honor," Mary put in.

"Yes, I'm aware of that," the judge said, his eyes staying on Roberto. "Go on."

"About how it's the thing now, and that blow and rock are going out of style, and since those motherfuckers from Saudi Arabia did that shit—9/11—it's been too hard to move it across the border anyway. Jesús said he can make huge amounts of crank right there on his ranch and get it out and on the road without any trouble at all. Then he said he'd show me something in the old mine that's near the house."

Now we were getting to it. I felt myself growing excited. But also wary—Roberto was becoming too loose. He was using more profanity, and his soft slur was growing more pronounced. But Mary and Tom didn't seem to notice it. They were perched on the edges of their seats, eager to see how the judge would take what Roberto was about to say.

We'd all been frustrated and nervous over the last two days. Mary had worked—editing the application again and again—with an even fiercer intensity. Tom moaned and bitched and either watched the camera or played with his guns. When I wasn't with him—both of us barely tolerated each other's presence—I attacked the short rock walls surrounding the hollow, climbing until my fingers bled. Working out the anxiety and getting strong. Some sixth sense told me I needed to be strong.

During that time we'd seen Roberto leave the house across the river, escorted by Hidalgo himself, as well as Zafado and hulking Bruto, and driven down into the mine. That caused a brief flurry of excitement for us—the secondhand hearsay knowledge Roberto had alluded to in his note was about to become firsthand. I'd watched with my eyes glued to the binoculars as one of the narco's big SUVs was swallowed by the hill that held the mine's entrance. It returned two hours later. Roberto sat by the pool after that. At one point he raised his sunglasses and I think he winked at me.

"What did you see in the mine?" the judge asked.

Roberto blew out a puff of air. "The place is huge, man. Tunnels everywhere, big rooms, equipment, and stuff like that. In this one big room there was this fence. On the other side were all these tables. With lab stuff on them, and big jugs of Coleman fuel and cartons of ephedrine. There were some people, too. Mexicans. Behind the fence, with the tables. They were some chemists Jesús had snatched in Mexico and brought here."

"We believe he's kidnapped them," Mary said. "That he's holding them as prisoners. They are a slave-labor force."

"Did you see anything that substantiates what Ms. Chang just interjected?" the judge asked Roberto. His voice was sharp.

"Yeah. Some of the guys who work for Jesús were down there, too. With guns and shit. They were keeping those other guys on the other side of the fence."

The judge was getting excited, too. He was leaning forward, looking at Roberto straight on. No longer peering at him disapprovingly over the tops of his reading glasses.

"Did you see them actually manufacturing drugs?"

Roberto shook his head.

"They were, like, sleeping. On cots. Nobody was doing much. I was only down there for a little while."

"But Mr. Hidalgo told you they were there to manufacture methamphetamine?"

"Yep."

Judge Koals leaned back. He picked up a pen and turned it with the fingers of both his hands. *He's going to sign,* I thought. The judge reached forward and made sure the recorder was running.

In an official voice he said, "We're here because Ms. Chang, Mr. Cochran, and Mr. Burns have submitted to me for my approval arrest and search warrants pertaining to Mr. Hidalgo-Paez and his property here in Sublette County. Can you tell me what you know about illegal drugs that are on his property right now?"

"Yeah, all this crank they're getting ready to cook in the mine," Roberto answered a little irritably, thinking probably that he'd just gone through this and not understanding that this portion of the tape would be transcribed and attached to the warrant applications.

"I mean actual narcotics. Not just precursor chemicals and laboratory equipment."

Roberto thought for a minute. "In his house he's got some horse that I've seen—"

"That's heroin, Your Honor."

"I know that, Ms. Chang. Please continue."

Roberto had done more than see it, I guessed. Although he was still doing well, I was worried. His pupils were pin-pricks in the blue irises. They looked as blank as the stone on his throat.

"There's some blow, and some pot, too. Jesús stays away from it, for the most part. It's a couple of his guys who showed me the stuff. Not a lot of it. What they've got, it's mostly for personal use. He told them to show it to me and that I could take what I wanted."

Next to Roberto, Tom was scowling. He had wanted Roberto to say the mother lode of drugs was in the house it-self. *Good, Roberto,* I thought. *You're doing good. Stick to the truth now.*

"Aside from these small quantities in the house that are 'for personal use,' as you say, have you seen anything with your own eyes that would indicate Mr. Hidalgo intends to distribute narcotics within this state?"

"Yeah. I told you. The lab stuff. Propane cookers and vats and all that kind of stuff. All the ingredients, too. Like I said, crates of bottles. Chemicals, you know? Ephedrine. That shit."

It sounded good to me. To Mary and Tom, too, who'd barely been able to contain their exhilaration on the drive in when Roberto told us what he'd seen. *Seen,* not just heard about. This was the way probable cause was supposed to sound. Not a certainty, not proof beyond a reasonable doubt, but, as the law books say, "reasonable grounds, based on trustworthy information, that a crime is taking place or is about to be committed."

The judge, however, wasn't jumping all over it the way we'd expected him to. He ducked his head lower and went back to looking at Roberto over his glasses.

"But no large quantities of actual narcotics? In a condition that is ready to be sold?"

"Nope. Just the ingredients. The other stuff—the drugs in the house—it wasn't what you'd call large."

There was a long pause. The judge put down his pen.

"Now tell me a little bit about yourself, son. What is your arrangement with these three police officers here?"

Mary answered before Roberto could.

"For information he provides us about the illegal activities of Jesús Hidalgo-Paez, and in consideration for the risks he has taken to assist us, our confidential informant is to receive a reduced sentence for charges pending against him. An additional charge, in a neighboring state, will be dismissed. He will be granted immunity for all crimes committed up until this date. It's a very standard deal, Your Honor. One our office, in conjunction with the U.S. Attorney's Office, made enthusiastically."

The judge considered this for a minute. He picked up his pen again. *Sign,* I ordered him, but not out loud.

Then he asked Roberto, "Tell me something, son. What have you got against Mr. Hidalgo-Paez? You were once friends, you said. He obviously thinks you still are. And I assume you could find your way to South America if you so desired, where you would be safe from interferences from our government?"

Yeah, I thought, *why the hell are you doing this, bro?* But I knew the answer. I'd read the strange little children's story my brother had written and knew what it meant.

Roberto looked at me. Directly at me. His smile didn't change, but his gaze lit me up. I felt the hair rise on my arms. The blue light of his eyes was like a warm bath for a moment. Then he turned back at the judge and shrugged while considering his response.

The judge was looking at me with narrowed eyes. They seemed to open wider after a couple of seconds. Then he glanced at Roberto, then at me again. Maybe seeing, for the first time, a family resemblance. *He knows,* I thought. *Or at least suspects.*

"Guy's an asshole," Roberto finally said. "Word is that he's killed a lot of people. A lot of them women and kids."

"I've been led to believe that he's been doing that for a long time. Surely you were aware of that before you began your relationship with him."

Roberto looked almost sheepish—a way I didn't ever think I'd seen him look before. He dropped his eyes and spoke to the table, fingering the turquoise stone at his throat.

"I knew he was a bad guy. And I heard some of that *corbata* shit. But I didn't think too much about it."

"But now you don't mind betraying him? You've worked up some indignation since those days?"

There was an edge to the judge's voice. It was an edge I was too familiar with. That of a cross-examiner, poking the way lawyers love to do at an evident wound.

Roberto glanced at me. "I was whacked a lot of the time back then. But I've been waking up."

The judge still held his pen. *Just sign it. Don't put him through this.*

In a more judicial tone the judge said, "Part of my job, son, is to assess your credibility before deciding whether I should find that this tale amounts to probable cause. That includes consideration of just how credible a witness you are. I take it that you've had more than a little trouble with the law in your past."

Trouble with the law, both specifically and philosophically, I thought.

Roberto looked up and grinned suddenly, showing white teeth.

"Yeah. You could say that, Judge."

I wanted to groan now. Suddenly we were losing ground. And I could see that my brother was feeling mischievous. The judge had embarrassed him by asking—in front of me—why Roberto had tolerated, and even profited from, the friendship of a murderer seven years ago, then compounded it by suggesting disloyalty and betrayal. And Roberto had been holding it in too well, and for too long, and now it was starting to sneak out.

"Have you ever been convicted of a felony?"

"Oh, yeah. Couple of times."

"But never one that involved perjury or false statements to authorities, Your Honor," Mary broke in, speaking quickly. "Our informant has always taken responsibility for his actions. In fact, he has never even been to trial."

"Is that so?"

Roberto grinned wider.

"Then either you're not very bright, son, or you're very reckless."

"I 'spect it's a little of both," Roberto agreed.

"Did any of these crimes involve drug use?"

"Most of them."

"Only misdemeanors, Your Honor," Mary interjected. "The felonies our informant was convicted of all involved either crimes of violence or vandalism. An argument could be made—not a legal one, of course—that the victims of his crimes deserved—"

It wasn't exactly a great save. Or even a good attempt. I guessed that she, too, could feel the ground slipping away and was willing to take a chance. But the judge ignored her. He was leaning forward, staring at my brother.

"Are you under the influence of any narcotic substance at this moment?"

Shit. His eyes.

"I'm high on life, Judge."

"I mean, have you been partaking in any illegal narcotics? In the last twenty-four hours?"

Roberto, still grinning, sort of shrugged and looked at Mary. I interrupted, speaking for the first time.

"Just tell him the truth," I said.

"I'm high on life and high on a little *chieva*."

"She-va? That something like heroin, son?"

"Something like it, Judge."

"Injected?"

"Smoked." Roberto put his fingers to his mouth and blew on them, like blowing a kiss to the judge. "A-bomb. You dip a joint in it."

And the ground dropped away. We were all falling. The room was like an elevator whose cables had been cut.

It was silent for a while before the judge spoke again, still looking at my brother.

"Let me see if I can summarize this, son. Please tell me if I'm incorrect. You are a multiple felon and an abuser of Schedule 1 narcotics?"

" 'Fraid you got me there."

"You stand to have charges against you reduced, and others quashed, if Mr. Hidalgo is convicted of a state or federal crime?"

"The agreement requires the informant to testify truthfully—" Mary tried to interrupt one last, desperate time. But the judge held up a hand to silence her.

"You come into my chambers so that I can make a determination regarding your credibility, and you come in here stoned?"

"Sad but true."

"He's an addict, Your Honor," Mary protested, her voice rising. "He's come to us to seek treatment! He's trying to get his life straightened out!"

Judge Koals turned to her. I was surprised to see that he didn't look angry. I would have been. But his tone remained thoughtful and judicial.

"Ms. Chang, in this state we have standards for determining the reliability of witnesses who are brought before the court. These include past convictions, mental state, and possible motive. Your informant's testimony here tonight is extraordinary." He paused, shaking his head, then continued. "Yet I cannot find it trustworthy to the standard required by law. Based on his testimony alone, without corroboration, I cannot find that there is probable cause to believe that there is a clandestine laboratory manufacturing methamphetamine more than a mile below the surface of the earth, being worked by 'slave labor.' Nor can I find that the subject of your warrant has narcotics in his home other than those that your informant has taken there himself."

Okay. Hidalgo's going to walk. For a while, at least. Then somebody'll catch up to him. Roberto's going back to jail. This is bad. Very bad. I knew that in prison again Roberto would burn himself up. I couldn't help, though, feeling a little relief. It could be worse.

Then the judge named the thing that could be worse.

"But I'll tell you what I will do, Ms. Chang. I will reconsider my ruling here today provided that you can bring me film or recorded conversations corroborating the story your informant has told me. Attached to your application, of course, so that it is within the four corners of the affidavit. This material must be legally obtained, under Wyoming law. That is to say, whoever makes these records must have consent to be on the property, and must be a party to the conversation being recorded. If there is any truth to this story, that way it will come out. You bring me lawfully recorded pictures and sound to back this up, and I'll sign whatever warrant applications you give me."

"No," I said, speaking up for the first time. "That means sending him in there with a camera and all that, and I won't let him do that. They searched him the first time he went in. They'll do it again. It would be a death sentence."

The judge stood up.

"That's your choice, I'm afraid. Now, if you will excuse me, officers, Mr. Informant, it's quite late."

NINETEEN

A re you protecting that fucker?" Tom demanded outside in the hallway. He was talking with his mouth a few inches from the back of my brother's head. "Are you? Whose fucking side are you on?"

Roberto turned to face him. He was standing loose and still smiling. He cupped a hand to his ear. I waited for the cupped hand to turn into a fist, and then for Tom's head to snap back. But it didn't happen.

"Excuse me?" Roberto said, hand to his ear.

"You heard me!" Tom roared in his face. "Whose side are you on?"

I pushed in between them. It felt like I was entering a zone between two powerful, maybe radioactive, magnets. Mary forced her way in next to me with sharp elbows and sharp words.

"You want to fuck me or fight me, Tomás?" my brother asked. "If it's fight, we can go anytime. If it's fuck you want, you're going to have to find another *chupate*."

Tom tried to hold it but he couldn't. He spun around, away from the three of us, and punched the wall. His fist left an imprint in the plaster.

"Goddamn junkie!"

Mary let out a hiss.

"That's enough, Tom!"

Tom stormed down the hallway and blew out the court-house door. I looked at the dent on the wall, which was smoking with chalky dust, and wondered if the judge was still in his office. He might have heard the impact or felt the reverberation. If he had, I hoped he would make Tom pay for the repair. I would gladly rat Tom out. But the judge didn't appear in the hallway.

"That guy's losing it," Roberto told Mary.

"We all are. It's been a tense couple of days, and this is not what any of us was expecting."

Roberto chuckled. "Tense for you guys? What, you afraid you might lose your job? Your buddy Tomás there will lose his anyway if Mr. Ashcroft finds out that he's got a gay guy working for him. And you, Mary, you don't belong in this business anyway."

Mary colored. Her heavy eyelids squeezed into slits. She looked fierce in her courtroom clothes with her hair pulled back so severely. She stared up at him, stepping close—as close as Tom had stood a moment before. They were nose to chin, only a few inches apart. The energy between them was just as intense as it had been with Tom but it was different somehow.

"Don't you tell me what business I belong in, Roberto."

I had the feeling they'd forgotten about me even though I was right there with them.

"Easy, girl. Easy now," my brother soothed.

"You think I shouldn't be doing this because I'm a woman? You think I'm too soft? Not big and strong like you? Not a filthy addict who knows nothing about self-restraint?"

"Cool down. Don't blame me, *mariquita*. I told the truth just like you asked me to."

Mary didn't look like she wanted to cool down.

"My God, Roberto! You think you did what we asked? Smoking heroin? Telling the judge about it? You've ruined everything. Not even to mention that you're going to kill yourself."

"If you guys don't get me killed first."

That was my opportunity to remind them they weren't alone.

"We need to shut it down," I said to Mary.

She stepped away from my brother and glared now at me.

"We aren't shutting anything down." She stabbed her index finger toward Roberto's chest, poking him. "Your brother hasn't fulfilled his end of the bargain. There's still a good chance we can redeem this operation."

"No," I said. "It's too dangerous. There's way too much risk."

"I thought you brothers weren't afraid of anything. That you hang by your fingernails, climb mountains, do bad things to bad people. I thought you were tough. The Fearless Burns Brothers."

"Not me," I said.

"Hell, I'm scared of my own shadow," Roberto said meekly. "Remember? You heard me tell the judge."

"Yes. I heard that. And I heard you say some other things in there that didn't need to be said," she told him. "How many people do you think Hidalgo is going to kill if we don't finish this? More women and children, maybe? Not that you'd care. How many more lives is he going to ruin with that shit he peddles? Now, you are either going to finish this operation or you are going to go to prison. A real prison—not the rehabilitation center I would like to get you into."

"I can run. No way you can catch me in those shoes." Roberto pointed at her high heels.

"We'd get you sooner or later," Mary said hotly, not realizing he was teasing, that he still wasn't taking this seriously. At least not outwardly. But I suspected her jab about women and children had stung him. "You wouldn't make it out of the country. And even if you did, we would find you in South America. Your friends down there won't help you if there's a large enough price on your head. Forget about extradition— we could kidnap you and transport you north. It's been done before and we'll do it again."

Roberto held up his hands in mock surrender.

"Hey, all right. I guess I'm your man, then," he purred at her. "Sounds like you own my ass, Mary. I guess you can do whatever you want with me."

TWENTY

T he camera was a commercial one. Tom found it at a Circuit City store in Casper and paid for it out of his own pocket. There wasn't the time—or even the ability—to get something more surreptitious and impressive from the Bureau. And Wyoming DCI, of course, still used big, inefficient 35 mms.

It was digital rather than film, would capture short video as well as still images, and was about the size of a deck of cards. It would also record sound. I was given the job of concealing it.

"Up his ass," Tom suggested.

Roberto demurred with a smile at Tom but didn't make any of the obvious comebacks.

Before deciding where to put it, I studied the recorded video showing my brother's previous welcome to the compound. I watched all over again as Roberto was stripped, searched, and beaten. Roberto told me that he'd only been searched that one time, but he didn't know if the same was true about his belongings. So the tape was all I had to go by in order to get a feel for how seriously the search was taken. Figuring out how to work the enlarger on the laptop, I zoomed in as Zafado dumped the contents of Roberto's pack on the flagstone by the pool.

Zafado's search was surprisingly thorough. But then I figured the narco probably had a lot of experience concealing things. In about two minutes he'd examined all the stuff on the flagstone, taken apart the small camp stove, shaken out the sleeping bag, and patted down the empty pack. He also took Roberto's wallet from the pants that had been cut off him and went through it with particular care. I noticed that it was about a minute after this that Hidalgo finally—conveniently—showed up, pretending surprise and joy at seeing his long-lost friend and reprimanding his men for roughing him up.

Zafado hadn't taken out the foam insert that gives shape to the part of the pack that lies against your back. It also protected your flesh against sharp objects inside the pack. Maybe Zafado didn't know that the foam could be removed in climbing packs so that you could sit on it during an unplanned bivy on some icy ledge. The idea was that the foam would insulate your butt from the cold rock, and then you could shove your legs into the pack itself for warmth. I'd spent a lot of happy nights that way with Roberto. I hoped to spend a lot more.

I took out the sheet of foam. It was about three-quarters of an inch thick. I folded it tightly, then made an incision with a razor blade. After a little bit of careful shaving I was able to slip in the camera. It barely made a bulge.

The plan was that once he was back inside the compound and the house, Roberto would transfer the camera into his wallet. The wallet was already fat and messy, stuffed with cash in the currencies of four nations, some scrawled phone numbers and business cards that various girls had pressed on him during his South American sojourn, and other scraps with comments and illustrations—called beta—that described climbing routes.

Roberto approved of the plan.

"Better than Tomás's idea, anyway," he said loud enough so that Tom could hear. "Guy's got a thing about asses."

Mary gave the instructions.

"All we need is a picture of the laboratory in the mine. Take a series of them if you can. We don't want the judge to think we're trying to fake anything. That's all you have to do, Roberto. Then you can leave the camera in the rock where Anton and Tom left you the note. We'll pick it up there and take it to the judge."

I didn't like that part. But then I didn't like any of it. Maybe, though, if I was very lucky, Tom would get peed on again.

After reading the instruction manual and downloading software onto one of the computers, Tom gruffly showed Roberto how to use the camera. How to shut off the flash, how to aim and focus, how to silence the beeping noise the camera would otherwise make, and how to delete the images in a hurry. Then the agent got away from my brother as soon as he could. He headed up to the ridge to monitor the surveillance equipment there.

For a little while Roberto ran around the main cabin like a hyperactive kid, taking practice pictures of everything from odd angles. Pictures of me, focused on the scar on my cheek over the rim of a coffee cup. Another picture of me, this time showing him my middle finger. A close-up of Mungo's yellow eyes looking up at him just inches above her head and looking something like a furry halibut. A portrait of her nervous, toothy grin. But mostly he filled the disk with shots of Mary. Close-ups from different angles, all catching her unaware.

He was pretty good with the little camera, getting shots of things I hadn't seen. For instance, I would see Mary sitting erect in front of the computer screen, her narrow eyes clicking back and forth as she read lines of text. *Snap*. Roberto would catch her tucking a strand of hair behind her ear, looking suddenly vulnerable and pretty. I would see her writing hard and fast on a legal pad in tiny, precise script. *Snap*. Roberto's close-up of her hand showed small, elegant fingers caressing a page.

Mary finally got annoyed with his clowning around. She insisted that they get busy with serious matters. For the next four hours—the rest of the afternoon—she went over every detail of his two-day stay in Hidalgo's house. Mary recorded every facet. Everyone he had spoken to, every word that was said. Next was a discussion of what ruses Roberto could use to get back into the mine for another tour. Then there was endless coaching on the exit strategy. How Roberto should allow himself to be arrested along with the others when we finally raided the place. How he should say nothing about his status as an informant to anyone. How the suspects would be separated in a yet-undetermined federal facility and, after a few days, she would come for him. How she would remove him on the pretext of taking him to Colorado to face the still-pending escape charges there.

The optimism disturbed me, but didn't affect my brother.

"Better not forget about me, Mary" was all he said.

That was the only time all afternoon that she cracked a smile. It was a polite smile, not a true grin. Otherwise she was all business, as uptight and furiously professional as she'd been on the drive in from Salt Lake a week earlier. None of Roberto's gentle joshing seemed able to soften her. She was a federal agent preparing an unreliable source for a hazardous operation. Nothing more. This had become a distasteful job, but she would do her duty. The only concession she'd made to any sort of informality was to change back into her shorts and a white sleeveless T-shirt.

I wandered in and out, fretting. I couldn't get over a sense of impending doom.

As dusk was falling, Roberto was finally allowed outside. All day Mary had insisted that he stay indoors. To work, and also because of the fear that Hidalgo's plane could return unexpectedly. "No risks" was still her official motto, but it had worn pretty thin with me.

Mungo and I were sitting up by the bouldering wall when Roberto emerged from the cabin. The air had cooled only a little since the sun dropped behind the tail end of the great Teton Range. The red earth and the gold stone had soaked up enough heat during the day that they would radiate like a furnace for half the night. Even sitting still I was sweating. Beside me, Mungo's head was bobbing, keeping beat with her panting.

Roberto saw us and headed up.

"You working out?" he asked.

I shook my head.

"I was waiting for you."

He laughed.

"You wouldn't want to wear yourself out before I got up here, right, *che*? Want to look strong for your big bro."

I rolled my eyes, but it was true enough. Some kind of adolescent carryover that the years couldn't shake. Something I hadn't lost even though I was a full-grown man, a college graduate, an eight-year veteran of Wyoming's investigative police force, and responsible for the deaths of four other men, all of whom had been shot in self-defense even if no one believed it. Posturing for my brother was one of those things I would never grow out of.

As a kid I'd done everything I could to impress him. I remembered how every morning, for something like ten years, I did pull-ups on first waking, trying to get strong enough so that I could keep up. I would push myself hard on the climbs we did together, often taking ridiculous chances with gear and strength, to show him I could be as fearless as he was.

"Go ahead," he said now. "Get on it. Show me something."

Sitting in the shade, staring at the rock for a good part of the afternoon, I'd figured out some problems. Places where the overhanging shelf of stone had only tiny pockets like bullet holes for your fingertips and edges no thicker than dimes for your feet. We worked these for a while, one of us "spotting" with upraised arms while the other clung to the rock. The darkness grew until half the challenge was just finding the holds.

Roberto, as usual, kicked my ass.

Taking a break to shake out the lactic acid, I asked him, " 'The Wolf Who Wanted to Be a Little Girl'? What the fuck, 'Berto?"

He laughed. "You like?"

"Yeah. The drawings were pretty good. But the text—it was good, too, but it creeped me out a little, bro."

He slapped my shoulder. "Give it to your daughter. Tell her it's from her Tío 'Berto."

That was all he'd say about it.

After a little while he told me, "I think I'll sleep up here tonight. It might be a while before I get to sleep outside again, you know?"

I knew all too well. For the next few nights he would be in Hidalgo's house—the lion's den—then, if all went really well, he'd be in a jail cell for a few more days to weeks. Long enough that hopefully Hidalgo and his *sicarios* wouldn't suspect him of being the rat.

"You mind bringing me my bag?"

"I'll bring it. I think I'm going to get something to eat. You hungry?"

He shook his head.

With Mungo loyally dogging my heels, but looking back over her shoulder at my brother every few steps, I walked down the slope and into the cabin that held our bags and cots. I threw Roberto's bag over my shoulder and went back out. I stopped on the porch, though, seeing Mary hiking up the hill toward Roberto and our rock wall. The timing was such that she must have seen me come down. She must have been waiting. So I didn't follow her back up. I didn't really feel like talking to her, anyway. It was her decision to put Roberto at grave risk. As if he weren't already risking enough in his life.

Instead I left the bag on the porch and climbed up the other side of the crater to the notch in the ridge. I expected to find Tom stewing there, and, unfortunately, wasn't disappointed. He didn't say anything—didn't even turn around—when Mungo and I pulled up to the rocky platform in between the junipers and stone walls. My greeting was answered with a grunt. I sat, waiting to be offered a peek through the camera, but Tom apparently didn't feel like sharing.

So I picked up his low-light binoculars and looked across the crater to our bouldering shelf. I found Roberto and Mary, both glowing and green.

They must have made some kind of a truce, because I could see that he'd gotten Mary up on the rock again. I focused the binoculars on her. She was hanging onto some fat edges with her fingers, and her profile seemed to be scowling with concentration. Her thin calves were pumping up and down with the onset of sewing-machine leg. It comes with the first spurts of adrenaline, that nectar that my brother and I have spent almost all our lives chasing. She probably didn't know it, but she wasn't in any danger. Roberto stood beneath her, spotting, his bare arms upraised. I could see his mouth moving as he offered some half-mocking encouragement.

Mary slowly peeled off the rock. She dropped, turning for a moment into a green streak, a shooting star, before Roberto caught her under the arms. He bounced a little from the impact of her slight frame then put her on her feet. But she didn't step away from him like I expected her to. And he kept his arms around her. They stayed motionless for a moment, her back to his chest. When she did move, she still didn't step away. She just turned around in his arms to face him. It looked like she was still trembling the same way she had before she fell.

I put the binoculars down and smiled. For a few beautiful minutes, I was no longer scared. Not of Hidalgo, not for Roberto, not for what would happen between Rebecca and me.

After a little while I picked up the binoculars again. What I glimpsed in the green light before putting them down for good was pretty X-rated. This time I didn't just smile—I laughed out loud and slapped Mungo's butt.

Roberto was on his back, reclining on a boulder. Mary was crouched over his hips. Shorts gone, shirt pushed up above her small, high breasts. Her head was thrown back, her eyes—if they were open like her mouth—totally unseeing.

Feeding the Rat, I supposed, thinking of my brother's term for getting a fix. In this case the expression had an interesting double meaning. She was taking that rush of sweet adrenaline she'd found on the rock even further. Feeling the blood pounding in her veins, feeling her stomach high and light in her rib cage. Involving herself with a guy like my brother was taking a big dose. It was probably only her second taste—and it was a gulp rather than a sip. Leaving the Bureau to start this whole thing with Hidalgo would have been the first taste. Now she was jumping right in, all the way. Next thing she'd be wanting to go with him to Yosemite or Patagonia.

How far would she push it? I had to wonder. *How far would she push 'Berto?*

TWENTY-ONE

As if to mock all my fears, they didn't immediately search Roberto when he turned up from his "climb" back at Hidalgo's compound. It looked like they might not search him at all.

I'd had a nightmare about watching it through Tom's monitor as they discovered the camera. About being across the river and a half-mile downstream, totally helpless to do anything about it, unable to even shout a warning. In the dream I could see—looming large—the happy-faced sticker with the tongue hanging out that I'd seen on some of the narcos' car bumpers. Only the face wasn't anonymous and yellow with just dots for eyes and a wide slash for a grin. Instead it was a lot more like my brother's.

Roberto was escorted to the front of the house by a banger with an automatic rifle. Presumably he'd picked my brother up on the several-mile-long driveway that led from the Forest Service road to Hidalgo's compound. We knew that there was the camper parked by the road, and this seemed to confirm that it was manned. The kid wasn't holding the rifle but let it dangle on its shoulder strap.

"Looking good," Tom said into his radio.

Tom was squatting next to me in the notch, monitoring the camera and working with the microphone. I was using a pair of low-light binoculars. Mary was in the cabin below us, watching on the computer screen. She'd wanted to come up, too, but there wasn't enough room for the three of us plus a one-hundred-pound wolf in the notch. Tom had to be there to run the equipment, and I'd insisted on being there so I could be as close to my brother as possible.

Roberto looked suitably scruffy. Just like he'd been doing a serious climb high in the Winds. I'd coached him about a route called Red BVD on Schiestler Peak that I'd scaled two years before. His hands were convincingly torn from bouldering the previous afternoon, and I'd kicked his nylon windpants and T-shirt in the dirt. I'd even cooked some oatmeal with the little camp stove in his pack and left remnants glued to the side of the pot.

Zafado came out of the house. In his role of security chief, I supposed. It looked like he was talking to my brother. Interrogating him, but nicely. Tom tried to get the long-range microphone zeroed in but couldn't quite get it right. The house was between us. It, as well as the wind, seemed to be blocking the sound.

But everything looked all right. Roberto was nodding and grinning, raising his hands as he described imaginary moves on his imaginary climb. I could only see the back of Zafado's head but he was nodding, too. Maybe even laughing.

"He's going to be fine," Tom informed me. "I'll say this about your asshole brother—he knows how to bullshit."

I said, with less good grace, "Shut up, Tom. Get that microphone on them."

And I told myself, *Relax. Everything's fine. No worries.*

Then Bruto came out of the front door.

He looked a lot less pleasant than Zafado did. But that didn't mean anything—he was such an ugly bastard with his big, swollen face and creased forehead. He stalked up to stand next to his *compadre*. Roberto greeted him, probably saying something smart-ass.

The talk in front of the house went on for a few minutes. Bruto and Zafado standing between Roberto and the front door, the kid standing off to one side and fiddling absently with his gun and his crotch.

Then a car seemed to come out of nowhere. It was one of the big black SUVs. A Cadillac Escalade, all polish and chrome. The headlights were turned off. I'd been so focused on my brother and the gathering in the driveway that I hadn't seen the car coming. It must have been rolling with its engine off, because Roberto didn't seem aware of it, either.

It came on fast, jerking to a stop just behind Roberto. He turned to look at it. As he did, a rear door popped open. No one got out, but Bruto stepped forward. He wrapped his huge arms around my brother and lifted him, pinning his arms to his sides. He carried Roberto two or three steps to the truck's open door.

What the hell is going on?

The last thing I saw before Roberto disappeared into the SUV was his head snapping back. He seemed to throw it back with all the strength in his powerful neck. The back of his skull smashed into Bruto's face. The big man paused, staggered, then roughly shoved Roberto into the truck.

The kid with the cheap machine gun—the one who'd been fondling his gun and groin—was suddenly bouncing up and down in excitement. Yelling something, too, but I don't know what because Tom couldn't get the damn microphone working. Zafado was grinning his toothy grin. He had his chrome-plated automatic out now and was pointing it into the SUV. Beside him Bruto was holding his face and staring balefully into the truck's interior.

Shit! Shit! Shit! I wanted to scream. But I couldn't make a sound.

Zafado climbed into the backseat with his gun leading the way. Bruto got into the front passenger's seat, the truck sagging with his weight. Its lights still off, but the reverse lights filling the binoculars with a blaze of green, the truck turned around in the driveway.

Then, slow as a hearse, it headed up the road that led into the mine.

I flew more than ran down the steep slope. Being stupid, I knew—risking a broken ankle or neck—but I couldn't help it. There was no putting on the brakes.

Inside the main cabin I was dazzled by the white light from the three bare bulbs. Mary's face looked white as a ghost's. She sat in front of an open laptop, staring at the monitor. The radio headset was over her ears and I could hear Tom's tinny voice coming over it. Mary wasn't responding.

"Did you see?" I wasted my breath by saying, or maybe shouting.

It took her a moment but she nodded. She didn't turn to look at me, though. Mungo was pressing hard against my hip. I could tell the wolf sensed something very big and bad was happening, and that I hadn't just leapt down the steep hillside for kicks. She'd never seen me this panicked. I tried to calm her—and myself—by stroking her head with a shaking hand.

"They took him, Mary. They took him. We've got to go in there. Now!"

Mary went on staring at the screen.

Tom came into the cabin. He was out of breath, too, and had the decency to look as shell-shocked as the rest of us.

"Is the camera still on?" he asked.

Mary slowly nodded.

"The car go into the mine?"

She nodded again, managing a quiet "Yes. One minute ago."

"Holy shit!" Tom said.

I wanted to shout at both of them—*I told you it was too risky. Too dangerous. But you sent him back in there. You made this happen.*

But I still held on to enough sense to know that accusations and recriminations didn't matter right now. I could play the blame game with them later. The thing to do right now was to get my brother out.

"We've got to go in there. Now," I said again. "Call whoever you've got to call. Get them out here now!"

Without really knowing it, I was moving toward the table where Tom kept his toys, the scary-looking assault weapons. I had no idea how to fire a gun like that, but I intended to take one of them along anyway. They were both locked in their hard plastic cases. Tom had grown sick of Roberto ridiculing them and him.

"Give me the key," I told Tom. I was jerking on one of the small padlocks.

"No."

It was Mary who said it. She'd managed to both find her voice—barely—and turn away from the green screen. Her eyes looked almost wide.

"No," Tom echoed. "Listen, Burns. We don't know what the hell just happened. They might want to talk to him some more. Or have him do something in the mine. If we go in there with guns blazing, they'll definitely kill him. No doubt about that. And there's only one way we know of to get into that mine. They'll know we're coming from a mile away."

For once the tough-guy growl wasn't evident in his voice. He sounded like a pro now. For the moment. God, I hoped he really was. And I hoped he really knew how to shoot those things.

"Give me the key," I repeated.

He shook his head. I let go of the padlock and faced him, torn between pleading with him and hurting him. At my side Mungo was so freaked out she was starting to growl. Her blade of a snout darted this way and that, looking for the threat. But Tom didn't look like a threat. He stood ten feet away from me, his hands spread out with the palms toward me.

"No. We need to—"

I moved toward him. I'd take the key.

"Anton! We can't go tearing in there," Mary said, rising and standing in front of me.

Her chin was trembling. But her voice was stronger. I saw her fingers reach out to touch my shoulders but my flesh was completely numb.

She shook me. "We don't know what they're doing, Anton. We don't know what they suspect or why. Or what they intend to do. The very worst thing we could do is go charging in there."

That didn't sound right to me. But I tried to listen. She was smart—I knew that. And I also knew that, unlike Tom, she liked my brother.

"We're also grossly outnumbered here. And what we saw through the camera was illegal to view without a warrant. We have no legal authority to enter Hidalgo's property. Not yet."

TWENTY-TWO

Getting into the mine didn't look that tough.

It was an hour and a half later. I was standing on top of the brush-covered hill above the tunnel entrance, looking down at a wasteland of broken stone. The mountains of debris had been dragged from the earth's belly and strewn for acres around the gaping wound that was the mine. It seemed obscene to expose the subterranean rock this way. To eviscerate the hills. I knew the deed was done years before Hidalgo had come here, but now he was like an infection in the wound. He'd crawled into it and was spreading around in there like some toxic bacteria.

He's got a lab in there, I remembered Roberto saying. *Slave labor. Kidnapped chemists. Men with guns guarding them.* And now my brother was in there, too.

I kept seeing what I'd seen through the light-enhancing binoculars. Roberto escorted to the house by the kid with the gun. Zafado coming out, grinning and nodding. The Escalade pulling up silently. Bruto grabbing Roberto from behind. My brother's head arcing back to smack into Bruto's face. Zafado's chrome automatic. The kid dancing with excitement. Then all of them disappearing into the dark car.

The two long construction trailers that were the quarters for Hidalgo's second-rate bodyguards and gunmen were almost a half-mile away, beyond the edge of the enormous slag heap. They were too far away for anyone inside to hear if I moved with something less than Roberto's grace. Since it was three in the morning, I wasn't surprised to see that all the windows were dark.

What I couldn't see below me was whether the entrance was guarded. I didn't think it was—we'd never noticed anyone hanging around it, or the trucks even slowing when they sped into the pit. But still, this wasn't a time to be clumsy. I crouched onto one knee and then the other to tug tight the laces of my approach shoes.

Then I checked my weapon one more time.

The clip of the .40 pistol was full, and a peek beneath the slide showed a brass cartridge in the chamber. An extra clip was heavy in my left pants pocket.

Thirty-one shots, I thought. I would have felt better if I had one of Tom's nasty-looking guns with me. But the keys remained in his pocket, across the river and far out of my reach.

I closed my eyes and took a breath. Then another.

Until now, Mary and Tom and I had more or less followed the law. The occasional tiptoeing forays over the line and onto the dark side had been harmless. The results would never see the light of a courtroom, and therefore would not prejudice the precious rights that were the very reason Mr. Hidalgo had come into this country. The tapes from the long-range camera would be destroyed. The same for the sound recordings from the Flash Gordon listening device that only occasionally worked. Then there'd been the single literal tiptoeing incursion when I'd come onto Hidalgo's property to leave the note and get Tom pissed on, but that, too, had been harmless. For Hidalgo, at least. Less so were whatever stealthy administrative moves Tom and Mary were making to keep the operation from coming to the attention of their superiors too soon.

But what I was about to do was way over the line. I was going to bring my brother out. Whatever it took. They could sit back there and wait to see what happened, but I was going to make something happen.

If I were to analyze the situation coolly, I might have been able to at least understand Mary's point of view. I was a trespasser here. An armed trespasser, acting without a warrant or the color of authority. If something bad happened to me in that hole, a conservative Wyoming jury would find Jesús Hidalgo and his employees well within their rights to blow me away. Once, of course, the lab within was removed or dumped into some bottomless hole. Cop or not, in this state you don't go fooling around on another man's property.

But I wasn't cool enough to understand. I sure as hell wasn't cool enough to wait and see what happened.

I wondered if they were watching.

Up here, exposed on top of the hill, it would be easy to spot me using the enhanced starlighting of the long-range camera or the space-age binoculars. They had to know I was here. I'd torn out of the crater in the Pig after locking Mungo in the small cabin where I slept. I'd driven fast up to the bridge and across it, but not fast enough that the Fed's Suburban couldn't overtake me. The Pig was old and rattling—the Suburban was sleek and powerful.

But they hadn't come. And they'd let me go. Now I didn't let myself wonder why.

The silver river below was running like mercury in the moonlight. I picked out the spiny ridge beyond. I studied it until I could see where some stars cut deep into a half-hidden recess. The notch. I raised my right hand high and extended my middle finger.

Even on the purely emotional level that I was operating

on, I could understand that Tom hadn't wanted to come. He didn't give a shit about my brother or me. He'd said it once before—Roberto would get the information to burn Hidalgo or they'd kill him, and either way, we'd get to go in. My upraised middle finger was mainly for Mary. She'd just made love to my brother less than twenty-four hours ago. Now she was sitting back there and waiting to see what happened to him. The two Feds might have had the courage to violate administrative policy and legal technicalities to do what was right and avenge their dead colleague, Damon Walker, but they didn't have the courage to follow through with what they'd started.

I didn't want to think about it anymore. I started down through the brush.

The hillside was heavy with cactus and sage. Slipping in and out of the night shadows, I made no more noise than a small animal scurrying around. When I stepped onto the slag, though, and took my first step up the twenty-foot pile before me, suddenly I was a bull in a china shop.

My weight started a small avalanche of clattering stone. Then another and another as I half swam up to the summit.

Shit! The backside was mostly sand, thank God, and I staggered down it praying that the debris shifted and slid all the time. And that if there was a guard at the entrance, he was either asleep, very used to the noise, or drunk off his ass.

My prayer was in vain.

I heard a clattering from beyond the bulldozer-made mountains ahead of me. Someone had heard me. Someone was coming, looking for me. Two someones by the sound of it, maybe three. There were no voices, only the sound of boots scrambling around on the loose rock. *Shit!* I was going to get captured or killed before I even got into the mine.

If I ran for the cover of the brush on the hillside, they would be sure to hear and see me. If I stayed where I was, they'd be sure to find me. Moving as softly as I could, I slipped behind some bigger rocks and crouched down, trying to make myself about two feet tall. Carefully, silently, I began to pile more stones on top of those in front of me and to the sides and rear. I tried to dig myself into the dirt and stone.

I listened to them coming, working their way over the miniature mountains, ridges, and valleys. They moved without speaking—and that made me wonder if they might be Hidalgo's more professional men. Zafado and Bruto, the two who scared me the most. I took out the pistol and held it two-handed, my forearms flush against my thighs, and my chin, mouth, and nose cold against the top of my gun.

I waited, not knowing what the hell I was going to do.

I expected Bruto's cowboy hat to be the first thing I saw, but it looked like some kind of old-fashioned TV antenna.

What the hell? Then, *Antlers. Fucking antlers.*

A bull elk staggered over the ridge and half slid down into my little valley. He stopped no more than thirty feet from me. Bending his gigantic rack low, he brandished the sharp spikes toward me as if he were preparing to charge. Then an impossibly long tongue slipped out and slurped at a rock.

Feeling like an idiot, I realized that all sorts of animals would come here to lick at the exposed minerals. To taste the salt. It was something that Hidalgo's men had undoubtedly grown used to. A nervous laugh came out of my mouth.

The elk froze midlick and lifted his head. His tongue sounded like Velcro as it peeled off the rock. He snuffed the air, raising then lowering his enormous rack to catch different levels of the atmosphere. Finding my scent, he wheeled around and stormed out of there. He made enough noise for a marching band.

Ten minutes later, I lay on top of the last debris ridge and stared at the hole that had been ripped into the hillside. No light emanated from it. It was the most perfect black I'd ever seen. A literal black hole, like the ones in space that suck in and digest everything in their path.

We have no legal authority to enter Hidalgo's property, I heard Mary's voice saying.

There was no one guarding the entrance. I guessed there was really no reason to—the whole compound was so remote, and there was only the one road leading into it unless you went a long, long ways overland the way I had.

God, I didn't want to go in there.

I'd only been under the ground once before. About five years before, in southwest Colorado. That time Roberto and I had rappelled off the end of a rope into a chamber that resembled the mouths of those beasts you see in *National Geographic* pictures of life thousands of feet beneath the ocean's surface. Fanged stalagmites and stalactites looking as if they wanted to snap together. To get out, we'd had to crawl through a passage the diameter of a coffin for more than a hundred yards. It had almost crushed me—not my body, although that was a near thing, too—but my soul. I didn't want to go down there again. I belonged in high, wide-open spaces without even the ground to press in on me.

But this man-made hole turned out to be nothing like the coffin crawl. It was a tunnel sloping gently downward, easily thirty feet wide and just as high. There were no fangs hanging from the ceiling or rising up from the floor. Only a road of flat hard-packed earth and some kind of conveyor belt on the right side.

From my hip pack, I took out the night-vision goggles I'd taken from Tom's kit. I switched them on, and the tunnel was bathed in green light. The walls were rough stone bursting with edges. The road ahead seemed to wind slightly as it snaked into the earth. I could only see ahead to the next curve. Over my head and to the sides were steel beams bracing the roof, and, every hundred feet or so, the shape of an overhead light switched off.

The lights made me nervous. What if they were to come on? Or, worse, what if one of the trucks came roaring up this underground avenue? There were few places to hide. The conveyor belt was only two feet high. From the high cab of an SUV I'd be obvious, even lying down. The walls, although very rough, were more or less regular. Only occasionally did they cut in deep enough to offer a shallow space into which I might be able to fit my body. In the light it would be like trying to hide behind a streetlamp.

The green glow of the night-vision goggles grew dimmer and dimmer as I jogged. I fiddled with the adjustments, but I couldn't make them pick up much light. *Piece of FBI shit,* I thought. Maybe the batteries were dying. But then I realized why they're called low-light goggles. They magnify tiny amounts of ambient light, and down here, as I went deeper, there was no ambient light. No stars, no moon. The thought of it made my stomach lift a couple of inches.

My one-man illegal assault had so far been ridiculously quixotic. My brother might be being beaten or worse. . . . And here I was, racing to the rescue, and I'd nearly been smothered by an avalanche of slag, then almost gored by an elk, and now I was lugging two extra pounds of headgear that was as useful as a Halloween mask.

I tore them off, and considered ditching them. I ended up stuffing them back in my hip pack with the flashlight, water, and energy bars.

The tunnel went on and on, descending at the same slight angle. I was moving fast but awkwardly. One hand traced the wall at my side and the other wavered in front of my face so I didn't smash into a wall. Occasionally I lost my equilibrium and staggered.

I wanted to look at my watch to see how long I'd been running, but was afraid of what its soft blue light would do to my night vision. But then I realized I didn't have any night vision down here anyway. I was totally blind. So I went ahead and hit the luminescence button and saw that it had only been twenty minutes. It felt like hours. The tension did that, I guessed. The blue glow faintly illuminated the wall next to me, and for a moment I was bathed in a warm, blue light. I periodically began to use the watch—Roberto's watch—to move even faster.

The darkness was a physical presence, much more than just a lack of light. As I moved through it I felt a resistance that couldn't be explained by the faint wind following me down. I could sense its pressure against my bare arms and face. Against my eyes, too, which seemed to be open impossibly wide, as if they were bulging with the need for light.

The tunnel and the darkness and my passage through it went on and on. The only sound other than my breath was my shoes occasionally scuffing on the dirt floor.

This is my brother's world, I told myself. *He's going to be all right. He doesn't need me down here. I should turn around. Get the hell out. Turn around and run.*

But I kept running downhill.

There was a faint vibration in the dense air. A low sort of rumble that at first seemed like it might be my imagination. It was growing almost imperceptibly louder.

Maybe my eyes were somehow adjusting to the total dark—*Maybe they're growing stalks*—because it seemed, after a long while, that I could see a little better. The walls my hands touched were a dimmer black. After a little while longer I began to imagine I could make out the steel beams. I didn't know what was real any longer. The darkness had invaded me. Hypnotized me. I made myself stop and groped at one imagined beam. It was there. It was real. I touched my eyes and they had not grown out on stalks—there was light coming from farther down the tunnel.

I stopped and spent a long moment shaking off the hypnotism. With a force of will I drew back into myself and gathered my senses. I also slid my gun out of its plastic paddle holster.

I began to move faster, no longer shuffling my feet through the well-packed dirt. Lighter, too, renewed with purpose and a sense of self. The rumble grew louder. A generator, I thought. It had to be. No way to tell how far off, but I was definitely getting closer. The walls really had grown clearer, more visible. I could see the irregularities and the protruding stone. I could see where the tunnel wound gently into yet another curve up ahead.

I checked the time again. It was 4:30 A.M., so I'd been jogging for only an hour and a half. Eight or nine miles, maybe—I was never much of a runner. *Jesus.* My sweat turned cold. *Eight or nine miles into the earth.*

The rumble grew louder still. The darkness was receding. I switched sides, crossing the road, and climbed over the conveyor belt. Gun in hand now, I started to move more carefully.

The first room was enormous. As big as a football field, and a ceiling that had to be fifty feet high. I crouched behind the conveyor and studied it for a couple of minutes before entering.

There was no sign of life other than a pair of enormous machines. They were tractors of some kind, but different from each other. Both machines were quiet and still. Sleeping, maybe. This was truly another world. Like *Land of the Lost,* a TV show I'd watched as a kid.

One machine resembled—in size and general shape—a yellow brontosaurus. Instead of a head, it had huge circular blades mounted on a long neck. It looked like it had been frozen in place while taking a bite out of the ceiling. There was a dark, narrow hole up there that was probably a ventilation shaft. The other machine was a bulldozer on steroids with a cab up a ladder at least twenty feet off the ground.

There were other holes in the walls of the great room. These were other tunnels rather than vertical shafts, and all but one of them were black. They led, I didn't doubt, into a maze. But only one of them drew my attention. It was the one the numerous tire tracks headed into. It was also the one that both the light and the rumble of the generator came from.

I slunk along the wall, past the sleeping monsters, and entered it.

This side tunnel curved, too, but after five minutes I was braced behind a protruding slab of rock and then peering around it into another big chamber. The light was bright here, so bright it was like a surgical theater. The light came from freestanding posts with arms that held a blazing array of bulbs. There was a long camper/trailer that had been hauled down from the surface. Beside it was the hearselike Cadillac Escalade.

But there was no noise other than the constant chugging of the generator. No one walking or standing around. No sign of Roberto or anyone torturing him.

I couldn't see into the trailer. And I couldn't see anyone peering out at me. The windows were tinted, and it looked like the curtains had been pulled. Whoever was inside it was probably sleeping. Anyone wanting to sleep down here would have had to pull the shades to keep out the brilliant light.

I half ran, half tiptoed with my gun in my hand across thirty or forty feet of open ground to the front of the trailer. Crouching with my shoulder against the fiberglass, I listened and felt for movement inside. There wasn't any that I could hear over the generator's constant chugging. Still crouching, I moved around to the side the door should be on.

I lost interest in the door, though, when I saw what was beyond the trailer. A hundred feet away was a chain-link fence topped with razor wire. And beyond that were tables littered with laboratory supplies—vats and beakers and green Coleman camp stoves. Just like Roberto had said. There were cots, too, which from my view looked like they had body bags lying on top of them.

One cot was on my side of the fence. On it, too, was a body bag. Or what, I realized when my heart climbed down out of my throat where it had been choking off a scream, might be a sleeping bag. And hanging off one end of it was lank, black hair.

I knew it was him. Even though I couldn't see his face or any part of him other than the hair. I knew the way he slept—like at any second he'd yank away the lip of the bag and be staring right at me. With a slight grin, saying, "Hey, Ant. Been waiting for you." All-knowing, like, "Almost got gored by an elk, eh, *che*?"

I had the sense to check the trailer behind me once more before I went to him. I was horribly alone. There was no one to shoot.

I hesitated for a long moment before I touched the bag—it was a sleeping bag. *Please, 'Berto.* I touched it at the shoulder.

He rolled over to see who'd poked him. I could feel the relieved grin tightening my mouth at the first twitch. And I glimpsed the backpack on the other side of the cot. It had been dumped out, the contents strewn, but the foam insert was still in place.

Then I felt the grin freeze.

His eyes were wet and glassy, the pupils mere pinpricks. All around them his flesh was blue-black and swelling. Dried blood lay caked in the creases of his eyes. He didn't look at me. Instead he looked past me. Behind me. And for once he wasn't smiling.

"Shit, Ant," he groaned.

I turned my head.

Zafado was standing not ten feet away. He had the chrome-plated oversized automatic in his hand. It was all shiny angles except for the small black hole. The smallest of any I'd journeyed through lately, but drawing me into it nonetheless.

"Put down your gun, *mi amigo*," he said.

TWENTY-THREE

The guy from the restaurant . . . Juan, right? Not that it's
your real name. I told you that you should come work for
me. And now here you are. You come to fill out an application, no? Take me up on my generous offer?"

Zafado was grinning widely, showing me diseased gums
as well as crooked teeth.

My head was reeling with too many ideas, with too many
possibilities, with too many terrible outcomes. I couldn't get
them lined up or sorted out. But I made a try.

"I came looking for you, boss. To see about that job. Saw
you drive into the mine and so I walked down here—"

His nasty grin was growing impossibly wider as I talked.
He was shaking his head, laughing a little, not believing a
word of it.

"I thought . . . oh, forget it," I said. In English I added,
"And fuck you."

I looked back down at my brother because I didn't want
to look at those teeth or, especially, at the black hole on the
muzzle of his gun.

Roberto was shaking his head, too.

He said again, quietly and with a small chuckle, "Shit, Ant."

"You even brought your own pistol," Zafado said. "That was ambitious of you, no? You must have been very sure I would decide to hire you. Or maybe you are a cop."

The passenger door of the shiny Escalade opened. Bruto stepped out. His nose was misshapen and his eyes were blackened from the vicious head-butt I'd seen Roberto deliver three hours earlier. It made his features even more menacing. He cradled a sawed-off shotgun in his huge hands.

Zafado kept on talking.

"We've been waiting for you, of course. We knew this fellow Roberto had friends who would come for him. And Bruto did a beautiful job of placing a line in the tunnel and connecting it to an alarm. It was fishing line, thin as a spider's web. Absolutely beautiful."

Bruto didn't smile at the praise. His face remained locked in that deep, dark scowl.

There was some movement on the other side of the fence. There were seven or eight people there on cots. They lay in sleeping bags or were wrapped in blankets, not the body bags—I could see now—that I had feared. I saw some dirty faces peer at us through the fence. They disappeared quickly when Bruto glanced their way.

"So this is your brother, no?" Zafado asked. He was speaking to Roberto now, who was sitting up and squirming in the bag. "We heard you had a brother with the state *policía*."

Roberto got the bag down to his waist but kept on wriggling. I realized his feet were shackled as well as his hands.

"This dude? Never seen him before in my life," Roberto said.

Zafado laughed.

Then to me he said, "Kick that gun over here, brother. Then that small sack around your waist, too. After that you can put your hands up above your head, okay? That's right. Keep them right there. Reach for the sky. Isn't that what they say in the American West? Only I'm afraid there is no sky down here."

He was circling around us, keeping the chrome-plated automatic on us both. Checking to see, I realized, that there was no one else in the side tunnel backing me up. That was probably why Bruto had waited a little while before getting out of the Escalade. He had me lift my pant legs and then my shirt, too, to prove I didn't have another weapon concealed.

God, these guys were good.

Bruto remained sullen and silent by the truck. I realized I'd never heard him speak—not in the bar, not on the long-range microphone, not now. I wondered if he was damaged in the head somehow. He certainly looked like damaged goods. And he scared the shit out of me. Even more than grinning little Zafado did.

Still watching us, Zafado picked up my gun and then my hip pack. He talked while he went through the pack. His eyes darted from us to the items he was examining, but Bruto's never faltered, or even seemed to blink. He seemed to know exactly how desperate I was. Or how desperate I should be.

"Roberto, Roberto, you are a ridiculous piece of shit," Zafado went on. "I told El Doctor you were up to something. I told him that the very first night you showed up. Why would you choose this moment, when we're having all this trouble down in Mexico, to come visit your old friend El Doctor? 'He's come to kill you,' I said. For the money being offered up by his competitors. But did he believe me? No. He said I was being paranoid. He said that Roberto Burns was his friend. How can you protect a man like that, I ask you? A man who believes in friendship?"

Roberto had managed to get all the way out of the bag. He was wearing just his shorts. His hands were cuffed in front of him. Two pairs of handcuffs had been used on his ankles so that he could walk a little if he had to. His face looked awful, and there was more bruising all over his chest and stomach and thighs. The bruises were shaped like a fist. A big fist, as big as Bruto's.

Zafado found my wallet.

"So, who's your little friend, Roberto? Tell me he's your brother. Tell me who this guy is, wearing these military clothes, okay?"

He shook open the wallet with one hand. My badge flashed brightly in the light from the spotlights, like a glittering chunk of gold. Zafado held it up and studied it.

"Ah, Special Agent Antonio Burns. The same surname as yours, Roberto. A certain resemblance, too. Although the special agent doesn't have your mad eyes, Roberto. And he's not so handsome, of course. This is really quite shameful, no? Tsk-tsk. Shameful. Working with the *policía*!"

Roberto cocked his head and squinted at me.

"That you, bro? Didn't recognize you. What the hell are you doing down here?"

This really cracked Zafado up.

"You are a funny man, Roberto. A little crazy, but really very funny. So, do you want to tell me what you fellows are up to? I'd really like to know who you're working for."

I said in my most confident voice, "The FBI, asshole. There is a team of agents surrounding the compound right now. Put down your guns and step back. You're under arrest."

Now he thought I was even funnier than Roberto. He slapped his leg with his free hand as he laughed.

"You two are really funny. Terrific. You should be on a stage somewhere. Now stop making me laugh like this. Of course you are here for the money that's on El Doctor's head. I'm afraid, Special Agent Antonio Burns, that I know something about you. You are *not* the kind of man your FBI would like to work with, no?"

He was right. It did seem unlikely. And these guys, being former murderous cops themselves, thought they knew the whole story.

"Roberto wasn't too talkative last night," Zafado said. "That's why we decided to wait for his friend to show up. The one I saw in that old truck when he was picked up at the trailhead. But I couldn't see who he was. The invisible man, no? You are him, of course."

He was packing my wallet and the other items back into the hip pack as he talked. My gun included. He walked over to Bruto—careful to stay out of the shotgun's line of fire—and put the small pack in the Escalade.

"You see, Roberto doesn't like to talk when you beat him. No matter how much you beat him. He's stubborn that way. But he's the kind of guy who might talk if we beat someone else. Especially if that someone else is his brother. And Bruto can really make them sing. Let me tell you, he's one hell of a conductor. This is very wonderful, Special Agent Antonio Burns. I'm so very glad you could join us!"

He climbed into the truck behind the driver's seat.

"Now you two stay right there, okay? Talk with Bruto to pass the time. I want El Doctor to be here for this. I want to show him I was right about Roberto Burns. He'll enjoy what we do after that. And maybe, if the two of you put on your comedy show, and if you beg and plead convincingly, maybe he'll show some mercy."

He laughed again before closing the truck's door. Then he rolled down the window as he started the engine.

"You know El Doctor's rule, right? The whole family must die. To make a point, yes, and to make sure there are no blood feuds. Simple and effective, okay? You have made it very easy. Thank you. The two brothers right here, having come to us. Someone will have to fly down to Argentina, I suppose. Maybe Bruto and I will be the ones to visit your parents. I've been praying to Saint Malverde for a vacation, after all. Would you like for us to give them a message before they die? *I'm sorry,* perhaps?"

TWENTY-FOUR

Notwithstanding the other prisoners on the other side of the chain-link fence, we were left alone with Bruto when the truck accelerated into the tunnel and then disappeared.

"Put down the gun," I said in Spanish, doing my best to sound commanding. "FBI agents will be all over this place soon, Bruto. If you cooperate I'll see to it that—"

"Don't waste your breath, *che*. That *pendejo* isn't going to help us out."

The *sicario*, his face as impassive as ever, used the shotgun to wave us toward the nearest rock wall. I assumed he didn't want us anywhere near the trailer, which one of us might be able to duck behind while he was shooting the other one. I spat in the dirt but then walked when he pointed the twin barrels at my groin—it almost made my gut heave. Roberto, with his shackled legs, shuffled and staggered along in the dirt beside me.

"Christ, Ant. You're like a chick, you know? No patience. Can't wait worth a damn," he joked in English. "If you'd hung on and really raided this place, you might've been able to do something."

Reading my thoughts, he added, "Don't worry about shit-head over there. He doesn't speak English. Probably can't even speak Spanish."

"What the hell happened, 'Berto?"

He shook his head ruefully. "Who would have thought that Zafado could run and track? That the skinny-fat little fucker could keep up? He followed me when I rendezvoused with you. To go see the judge. Saw me get into your truck when I said I was going climbing."

There was broken rock on the ground by the wall. I pushed some out of the way and sat down heavily.

"I'm sorry, bro," I said. "I messed up."

He was facing me, his back to Bruto. He was too amped up to sit.

"Don't sweat it, *che*. This whole thing was messed up from the start. Your pals Mary and Tom don't have anyone behind them, you know. Those guys are freelancing. Mary told me."

"I know. So why didn't you walk?"

He shrugged and laughed.

"I kind of like that Mary. She's got some depth to her, you know? I wanted to see what she'd do."

I wondered if he was on something right now. Maybe they'd given him something to increase the sensation of pain while Bruto was using him as a heavy bag. His eyes were so swollen that I couldn't really tell. I couldn't see his pupils.

"You know I'm solo, right?" I told him, wanting him to be serious. "Mary and Tom didn't follow me. They said it would be making an *illegal entry*."

I said it bitterly. I was angry. Angry at Roberto for obviously liking the federal agent who screwed him and then sent him to get screwed. It had been sort of cute when I'd caught them, but it sure as hell wasn't cute anymore.

"They might wait a few days before they try to do

something," I went on. "Even then, they're going to have a hard time doing anything. They can't get a warrant. They aren't likely to get much support from their colleagues. They're too chickenshit to come in here themselves. We're pretty much on our own."

Roberto shrugged. He didn't seem to mind.

"So we've got to do something. Now," I said in the same aggrieved tone although I wanted to whisper it. I hoped Roberto was right and that Bruto couldn't speak English.

The big monster had moved up behind Roberto. He was standing at a safe distance, about fifteen feet behind my brother, twenty or twenty-five from me. I studied him as he stared back at me. He held the shortened shotgun loosely in both his hands, pointing it in our general direction. I couldn't really read any malevolence in his massive pumpkin face. There didn't seem to be much there. And that made him even scarier.

"We're damned if we do and way more than just damned if we don't," Roberto agreed.

I broke off my gaze with Bruto and tilted back my head. Bouncing it off the rock wall a couple of times and gritting my teeth in obvious frustration.

"Did he do that to you?" I pointed at my brother's chest, indicating all the massive bruising.

Roberto turned his head and grinned at Bruto, nodding. Bruto stared back at him.

"Yeah. Guy can punch. I'll give him that."

I put my hands behind my butt to shove away some of the uncomfortable stones I was sitting on. I palmed a long rock about the size and weight of a stapler. As if clearing more stones, I pushed it into the back of my pants.

When I looked up again Bruto was still staring blankly at Roberto. I tried to figure out what I would like most to do to him. I wanted to punch the shit out of him like he'd done to my brother, but I doubted I could do enough damage that way to his enormous body, sheathed as it was with so much muscle and fat. With his shotgun, maybe, I could really hurt him. Hold it by the barrel and use it as a club. That's what I would do, I decided. If I ever got the chance.

"Was I ever any good at baseball?" I asked my brother as I stood up and dusted my hands on my pants. Arching my back and rubbing it, as if the stone floor were too uncomfortable.

Roberto broke off the stare fight with the monster to turn to me. Hopping with his handcuffed ankles to change directions. His expression was curious and amused.

"No. You sucked. Only kid I ever saw strike out at T-ball."

"Thanks for reminding me. I could throw, though, couldn't I?"

"You were all right at that," he allowed.

He lowered his head and raised his eyebrows. As if to ask, *Now?*

I nodded.

Roberto lost his balance, half shuffling and half staggering to one side. The shotgun twitched to follow him. That was when—trying like hell to live up to my hated nickname—I whipped out the rock and threw.

My movements seemed to take an ungodly long time. It was like slow motion, like being underwater. Getting my hand up under the tail of my shirt. Lifting out the rock. Cocking back my arm. Throwing while making sure to get a lot of hip into it. I almost couldn't believe Bruto didn't point the gun at me and fire. It seemed like he had all the time in the world.

The rock flew truer than I had any right to expect. It covered the twenty or so feet between Bruto and me without arcing, without even dipping. It caught him flush in the mouth.

The breaking teeth made a distinct crunching sound an instant before the room exploded.

The noise in the cavern nearly crushed my eardrums. My hands instinctively clasped my head. I don't know if I screamed or not.

With the gun still aimed in the general direction of my brother, Bruto had reflexively pulled the trigger. At the periphery of my vision I saw that Roberto was no longer there. *Blown back by the blast?* But no—he was in the air, flying forward. Like a rock himself. He'd stumbled into a crouch then leapt toward Bruto the moment I went for the stone. He'd been trying to keep the gun on him instead of me.

Roberto speared Bruto's gut with his head. The monster doubled over and dropped the shotgun. Then I was on him, scooping up the gun and swinging it by the hot twin barrels—just the way I'd fantasized. The oak stock smashed into the side of Bruto's head. I felt the blow reverberate all the way through me. I swung it so hard that the gun broke apart in my hands.

I wanted to swing it a second time but I only held two skinny, awkward pipes. There wasn't any need, anyway. Examining him, Bruto's big head was severely dented at the temple. He was still breathing, but I doubted he'd be doing so much longer. Blood was leaking out of his ears, nose, and mouth. It was pooling beneath the wound.

Roberto pushed himself to his feet with his still-shackled hands. When he spoke it was hard to hear him over the roar of adrenaline and the high-pitched ringing in my ears.

"You don't suck quite as bad anymore," he said. "Maybe you can swing after all."

"You okay, 'Berto?"

He worked his neck around in a circle, then nodded. "Shit yeah. You?"

I nodded more carefully. My head felt like Bruto's because of the shotgun blast. But at least I was conscious. At least I wasn't leaking onto the floor.

But we were still in a lot of trouble.

Bruto had a big ring of keys in one of his pockets. Using them, I helped Roberto take off the handcuffs. He stretched out his arms even wider than his grin. Despite the bruises and swelling, he looked like he was feeling good. I was going the other way—I was starting to feel pretty sick.

"Well?" Roberto asked. "What's the plan, *che*?"

"Are there any weapons in the trailer?"

"Don't know."

We looked. There were filthy dishes, filthy clothes, filthy magazines, and some filthy beds. But no guns. No knives, even, other than kitchen utensils.

Roberto brandished a butter knife, slashing the air and trying to make me laugh. It didn't work.

"We need to get out of here," I said. "Is there another way other than that main tunnel?"

"Nope. Not that I know about, anyway."

We obviously couldn't just go running up the road. Zafado and Hidalgo and who knew who else would be coming down it anytime now. And they'd be armed with a lot more than butter knives. The other choice, it seemed, was to hide somewhere in the mine. Hide and wait for Mary and Tom to do *something*.

This chamber that we were in only had one entrance and exit, but I'd seen a bunch of others in the big cavern with the machines in it. I tried not to think about what hiding would get us. We had no flashlights, no weapons, no food, no water, no idea of where to go. It felt like one of those dreams. Where you can run but not very fast, where you can't fight because your arms feel like lead. Those were the worst dreams. Mom called them *sueños de parálisis*. Paralysis dreams.

I kept searching the trailer while Roberto opened a

padlock on the fence with Bruto's keys. He yelled at the men on the cots. A few of them looked at him then ducked back down into their bags or blankets. I heard Roberto yelling at them in Spanish. His words echoed off the walls. Over the generator that was keeping the huge lights lit, and over the ringing in my ears, I couldn't hear what he was saying.

"They're like sheep. They say they want to stay," Roberto said disgustedly when he returned.

"What will happen to them?"

"They're Jesús's little moneymakers, so he probably won't hurt them. If they run, he'll kill their families."

"We've got to move. We don't have that kind of choice."

With me leading, we jogged into the central chamber. The light was much dimmer here after the brilliant glow in the other room. There was no sign of headlights coming down the tunnel, but I knew it wouldn't be long. I took a second look at the huge, sleeping machines. And I had another fantasy, kind of like the one about clubbing Bruto.

This one involved the yellow tractor with the long neck. The one with the rock-cutting blades on the end. In my fantasy, I started up the machine and then used the whirling blades to chop apart the Escalade when it returned. I cut up Hidalgo and Zafado, too.

I ran for its ladder and climbed up to the Plexiglas cab. The flimsy door was unlocked. I ripped it open and slid into the dusty seat. In front of me were dozens of levers and switches and pedals. I had no frigging idea how to use them. There was an ignition box, too, with a keyhole, but no key. I stared at it stupidly for a minute.

Roberto appeared outside the cab.

"You think this is some action movie, *che*? Get real. Just follow me, okay? It's been too long since we did a real climb together. Time to feed the Rat."

Instead of climbing back down the ladder, or even jumping to the ground, Roberto started shimmying up the machine's long neck. Up toward the ventilation shaft in the high ceiling.

The notched blades on the end of the neck stopped short of the shaft. You couldn't just stand up and climb up into the rock—instead it took a long reach. To do it, Roberto had to balance on the big circular blades and stretch one arm all the way out. Feeling his way as he searched for a good edge to grip.

He found one, because suddenly he was hanging with his body parallel to the ground. Feet still on the blades, but with both hands now in the black hole. Then one of his hands dropped back out. But the other one held. He looked at me down the length of his body and chuckled. He showed me his free hand, which held a rock.

"Little loose," he said.

"Oh shit," I replied.

"Feels kind of like the Big Horns, you know? Same kind of crappy rock. I think it'll go, though."

He tossed the stone down. It fell for what seemed a long time before it hit the ground fifty feet below. We hadn't even started climbing, and already we were a long way into the coffin zone. I definitely didn't want to do this. But I didn't have a choice.

Roberto pulled himself up—both legs kicking free before they swung up and in and found purchase—and then he wormed out of sight.

Sweating, I made the same long, awkward reach from the blades of the machine. The edge I felt was surprisingly good. But there was no way to see it, to test it. I just had to hope it was the same one that had held my brother's weight. I grabbed it with both hands and let my feet drop off the blades. Doing a pull-up, and at the same time twisting my body and swinging up my legs, I managed to wedge myself into the shaft. Small stones pelted me from above.

There was no little speck of blue far off in the distance. That meant that either the cylindrical shaft curved like the tunnel below or that it dead-ended. Or maybe it was still night. I didn't push the indigo button on my watch—I didn't want to know. All I knew was that the shaft was blacker than anything I'd ever seen. Just four or five feet wide, it seemed to go on and on forever, ever farther from the light instead of toward it.

But the rock didn't feel that bad. Despite being a little loose, it was full of edges. And the texture was rough, like good sandstone. Perfect for climbing, as if the rock had been coated with grip tape. The sticky rubber of my approach shoes grabbed well when I began smearing and edging with my feet as well as my palms. After that first move off the blades, when there was nothing for your feet, the climbing wasn't all that technical or strenuous. All you had to do was stem—put one foot and one hand on each side of the shaft. Even without a good edge or hold, your weight alone held you in place.

My fear of the shaft dead-ending lessened, too, as I began working higher. There was still no blue dot above, but there was a breeze rising up from underneath us. The shaft was definitely for ventilation. It had to lead outside somewhere. The looseness was the only problem. Stones and sand continued to rain down as Roberto, just above me, scrambled higher.

"Piece of cake," I heard him say.

It had to be a little harder for him in his bare feet and with his bruised—maybe broken—ribs. But he'd pulled himself in without a problem, so I guessed he could handle it.

"Maybe you ought to let me lead," I said. "You're knocking all kinds of stuff down on me."

My eyes, even though they couldn't see much in the diffused light around us, were stinging from the salty sand that was raining down.

He laughed. "You'd better hurry up, Ant. I've got to take a piss."

I heard myself laugh, too.

The technique was easy. Supporting your weight with your hands, you set your feet higher. Then you replaced the hands higher still and repeated. The soft, steady wind seemed to be lifting me. It made a gentle, almost inaudible moan. That was the only sound for a few minutes except for the occasional grunt or the soft scuff of our feet. Soon the weak light from the far-off generator was nothing but a dusty pool below.

We were maybe fifty feet up the shaft and a hundred feet off the deck—what would be less than a single pitch if we were using a rope—when we heard the sound of a motor riding up on the wind. Above me, Roberto paused to look down. I did the same, pasting my feet to good edges on opposite walls and trying to shake out the muscles in my chest, shoulders, and arms.

A car of some kind, headlights blazing, drove directly beneath the shaft. Then another. Then a third. And a fourth. Jesús obviously wanted to put on a show. Make a demonstration to scare the young bangers. I was glad we weren't down there to perform for them.

I looked up at my brother's barely discernible shape above me. After a few seconds I could make out his smile.

"They're going to think we're magicians or something," I said, almost laughing—but a little wildly. "They'll be searching the tunnels for days, scratching their heads."

"C'mon, Ant. Keep climbing."

We did for less than a minute—maybe gaining another ten or twenty feet—when suddenly the engine noise came back. We froze instinctively, not wanting to send down any

stones. I wondered now if any had hit the windshields the first
time they passed under.

And then I was literally transfixed by a powerful light.
Looking down, I couldn't see anything but the light. It must
have been one of the searchlights I'd seen mounted on some
of the Mafia's trucks, the kind that could be used for spotlight-
ing deer on backcountry roads. I could imagine what they
were seeing: Roberto and me lit up, almost spread-eagled, directly over their heads. I could hear them yelling at one another. I could picture guns being pointed.

And at least one gun was.

A single shot shattered the wind moaning through the
shaft. I heard it strike rock somewhere well below me, then
zing-zing-zing as it ricocheted off the rough stone. The men
below began shouting louder, like men who've just about had
their eardrums nearly blown out. I knew how they felt—my
ears were still ringing from when Bruto pulled the shotgun's
trigger.

*Stupid bastards will have to find something to put in their
ears before they shoot again,* I thought.

But I knew they would find something, and that they
would start shooting again.

I looked around me. While the walls were full of protruding edges, there weren't any that stuck out more than a few
inches. In the shaft there weren't any side passages, either.
Nothing to get behind. Nowhere to hide. But it would have to
be a very straight shot, fired directly overhead, for the bullet
not to hit a side and begin ricocheting. And the assault
weapons the narcos carried weren't made for that kind of
sniping.

I looked up. I could see a long way in the light so thoughtfully provided from below. Roberto, ten feet above me, wasn't
even in my shadow because of the way the light bounced off
the tan walls. Beyond him, I could see nothing but the shaft

going on and on. There was no end in sight. It must go for a vertical mile.

"Shit, Ant. Only thing I hate worse than getting beat up," Roberto grunted, pushing himself higher, "is taking a bullet up the ass."

"Or getting your wing-wang shot off," I answered, following him again.

Below us they weren't yelling anymore. No, now it sounded like they were laughing.

A voice called up.

"Eh, Roberto. What are you doing up there, my friend? Come down and bring your brother. I would like to meet him."

"That's Jesús," Roberto said. "Look out."

He spat. The blob fell past me, and I hypnotically watched it sway down then disappear into the light.

I tugged on a rock, trying to work it free so that I could drop it and maybe take out that light. Or maybe hit one of them on the head. But the rock held. I tried for another but it was solid, too.

"Keep climbing, Ant."

And we did. Faster than before. With less caution, too—the thought of falling to my death was suddenly less terrifying than the thought of getting shot and *then* falling. The light remained fixed upward.

A thunderstorm of noise was unleashed from below us. Someone had switched from single shot to full automatic, I guessed before the deafening sound overwhelmed my thoughts. But I could still hear ricochets zinging and chunking into the stone seemingly all around me. I paused for a couple of seconds, then decided that none of the *chunk*-ing sounds had been a bullet *chunk*-ing into my flesh.

"They'd be better off with a rifle," I panted up to Roberto. "Shoots straighter."

Roberto made a grunt of acknowledgment. I arched my head up, expecting to see his grin lit up by the spotlight. But for once he wasn't smiling. While I took in this fact, something hit my face. Something wet. It was coming in spurts. Spilling right out of his stomach.

" 'Berto?"

He wasn't moving. He was very still, spread-eagled just over my head, looking down at me.

"Roberto!"

"Oh, no," he said.

His voice was strange. A lot softer than usual. His arms and legs were quivering.

"Keep moving, Roberto! We've got to keep climbing!"

He shook his head at me, his wild hair swishing around his face like he was trying to shake something off his head. His limbs were starting to quiver, and the quivering became more substantial.

"Can't," he said. "Shit."

"Roberto!"

He managed to croak out, "Look out, Ant. Gonna fuck 'em up for you."

And then he was falling toward me.

My brother's weight hit me like a sack of cement. I caught him with my shoulders and head more than my arms. I held him with the pocket of one of my elbows between his legs, the other under one of his arms. *Christ, he's heavy,* I remember thinking. *All that prison muscle.* I think I was in shock. I'd never seen Roberto like this. Although I'd always feared what would someday happen to him, a part of me had never believed anything but that he was bulletproof.

He began twisting in my grasp. He was getting slippery, too: The blood pumping out of his stomach was running all over me.

"Leggo, Ant," he grunted.

"No."

"Let go."

He said it calmly the second time, without a grunt or any kind of force in his voice. I couldn't answer. The muscles on the insides of my thighs, tired already from the steady stemming, were screaming with the effort of supporting our combined weight. Three hundred and fifty pounds of it. I wanted to move up with my hands, or at least spread them to take some of the weight off, but that would mean letting go.

Roberto's cheek was pressed against mine. "Let go, Ant. You can't hold us both."

I didn't say anything. I couldn't.

His voice was just a whisper. Soothing and as soft. I felt his lips on my cheek. I felt his breath.

"Let me go."

My brother contracted in my arms, spasming. Then he was sliding through them. Then he was gone. I stared down and saw nothing but a black shadow growing smaller as it fell into the light.

" 'Berto!"

There was shouting from far below. I guessed it was Hidalgo and his men scurrying out of the way.

" 'Berto!"

There was a crashing thump and the sound of breaking glass. A sound I knew I would never forget. The light went out, leaving me in complete blackness. I didn't scream again. I didn't dive down and try to follow him. I didn't even weep or fall apart. I just started stemming on up the rock. Not thinking. Not crying. But hearing in my head that thump and crash. Feeling the impact of *my* flesh on glass and metal. Again and again.

TWENTY-FIVE

The shaft opened up to a sky touched with orange and pink. Somewhere to the east, way out over the dry plains of the Red Desert, the sun was waking up with a smile for the new day. Birds were calling to one another from the brush and stunted trees around me. The sky would soon be that Wyoming blue I loved so much. The sun would rise, and with it the wind and the temperature, but I knew I would remain locked in the night. In my heart it was pitch-black, cold, and as still as death.

Roberto.

A chain-link fence surrounded the shaft. To keep dumb animals, unwary hikers, and half-drunk hunters from falling in, I supposed. There was no need to climb it, as a portion of it had collapsed long ago. I walked over it and the links sprang and jingled beneath my feet. Within a few hundred yards I could see three other similar squares of rusty fence. I passed two as I began to run. More ventilation shafts, more lances into the earth. My brother's dried blood stretched and cracked on my skin.

Roberto.

What became a race through the hills was a blur to me.

Sage and willow branches tugged at my pants and tore my shirt as I crashed through the brush. They whipped across my face and arms and then my chest once I'd ripped the sticky shirt off. They scratched and sliced my flesh. Tiny droplets of blood welled up in the thin wounds, mingling with what had poured out of my brother's stomach. I welcomed the pain. Any sensation. But I barely felt it.

Roberto.

I slid down a steep bank, stumbled onto some gravel, then dove into the river's ice-cold water. The air left my lungs as if I'd been hit in the chest with a baseball bat. But still I didn't feel it enough. Not nearly.

I stroked so hard my arms were like windmills spinning in a tornado. Anyone watching would have assumed that I was totally panicked, that I was drowning. And more than anything I wanted to be panicked. Drowning. To feel anything but the solid, black weight lying in my chest like a twenty-pound tumor.

Roberto.

My hands slapped into the soft mud on the far side. I splashed to my feet and slogged toward the high brush that hung far out over the water from the bank. Pushing my way through it—with it shoving me back—all I wanted to do was find an open spot so that I could curl up on the ground. The urge was almost overwhelming. It was as if the earth were dragging down on me with a magnetic force. As if my shivering body were willing itself into a hard, tight little ball. And as if that ball wanted to sink into a grave.

I forced myself to keep moving, to keep pushing. Through the dense brush that lined the bank, then through the wet red earth that clung to my shoes. I started climbing the slope toward the notch in the ridge above me. I made no effort at concealing myself from any sharp eyes down and across the river at Hidalgo's hacienda. They were surely pouring out of the mine by now, hoping to seal off the shafts. I didn't care if they saw me—I hoped they did. Saw me running, and wondered whether I would be coming back. But when I stared over my shoulder, there was no one in sight.

Roberto.

The slope steepened until it was almost a cliff. The earth was sandy and loose. I pulled myself upward by grabbing barely anchored rocks and the snakelike roots of eroding shrubs. My feet slid on the soil, sending down little avalanches of stones and gravel. My breath came in high, sharp little gasps.

It got steeper as I got higher. The soil became more solid. It brought me no joy, no little thrill, to be on the open rock where I usually felt the most comfortable. I scaled upward without bothering to look very hard for hand- and footholds. I was ascending like I was a part of the rock itself, like a geologic thing, a creature made of stone. Moving as a part of it. The way my brother did.

This is what our bodies are made of, I told myself. Minerals and cells and water. They form up just right and then we walk and breathe. When we die, they come apart—an unbonding, that's all it is—and those that aren't eaten or inhaled by other creatures—from the microscopic to the mammals—fall back to become a part of the soil and rock. A part of the earth. This is what we are. All we are.

Roberto.

A thin, strong hand grabbed my wrist. It seemed to come right out of the rock. I looked at it in a sort of panting stupor. The hand was tan, like my skin, but a different shade. A lighter, more translucent brown. Different kind of cells, but the same, too. My brother probably had some of his cells still inside her.

"My God, Anton! You look like you've been flayed!" Mary said as she tried to pull me into the notch.

I didn't need the help, but she grasped and tugged at me anyway, her fingers slick on my body. I was still dripping with blood and sweat and the river.

"What happened, Anton? Is Roberto okay?"

Her words came fast. She was breathing as hard as I was.

I looked at her for what seemed the first time. She was so small and fragile, standing before me under the low branches of the junipers. She held her palms toward me, as if she were incapable of letting them rest at her sides. The whiter skin there was stained with my blood. She was trembling, too. Her eyes were wide and scared and . . . guilty.

My focus spread, taking in the camouflaged tarps and the camera on its tripod and the Flash Gordon listening antennae. *The last time I was here I watched him make love with her,* I thought. The last time I was here I'd seen him happy. It was a place of possibility for all of us—from this place I'd seen the wolf in him take a big step out of the forest. A step toward joining the rest of us children.

I tried to say something but it came out garbled. I tried again and this time nothing at all came out. My teeth were locked down tight.

I managed to shake my head. Then I pushed past her and started running and sliding toward the cabins in the crater.

Halfway down, Mungo hit me hard enough to make me stagger. She buried the flat top of her head into my belly and almost took me to the ground. She was making whimpering noises, maybe reprimanding me for leaving her behind yet again. Maybe she sensed something else. Her feet were dancing and scratching in the dirt. I allowed myself to pause for a moment, holding on to the ruff of her neck and holding her head against the flayed skin of my stomach. Then I pushed her away and kept running down the hill toward the lodge.

Tom stood on the porch. He'd seen me coming and opened the door, letting Mungo out.

"What's going on?" he demanded as I headed toward him. "What happened? Is Hidalgo dead?"

When I didn't reply, he barked, "What the hell were you thinking, anyway, Burns, going in there last night? We've been freaking out here! You've blown the whole goddamn operation! Now tell me! What is going on? Is Hidalgo dead or not?"

You let me go, I thought. *You sent my brother in there.*

I pushed by him, too, and then through the blanket that covered the doorway. He followed me. As did Mary and Mungo. I headed straight for where Mary's satellite phone sat on the picnic table. I picked it up and started stabbing the buttons.

"Who are you calling?" Tom demanded.

I didn't answer.

"If it's your boss, we called him last night."

I looked at the phone shaking in my hand and hesitated with my index finger on the SEND button. I put the phone down.

"You called McGee?"

My voice was surprisingly steady. Surprisingly calm.

"I called him on his twenty-four-hour pager after we figured out where you'd gone," Mary answered.

She paused, seeing something in my face and taking it for anger, I guess. It wasn't. It was instead a faint, fierce kind of thrill. *McGee, the old warrior,* I was thinking. *Maybe he can make it right.*

"I'm sorry, Ant. We had no one in the federal government we could call, so we called him."

"What did you tell him?"

"That we thought you were in danger. That you'd gone to get your brother out of the mine."

"What did he say?"

Here she almost smiled. I could imagine what my boss

would say upon hearing that I'd gone alone into a mine, armed and trespassing on private property, and amid south-of-the-border killers. I could imagine the colorful obscenities he'd summon up—far stronger words than *impulsive* or *stupid*.

"He cursed a lot," she confirmed. "He called you some names. Then he said to give you until eight o'clock this morning. That in the meantime, he was going to call the state patrol's SWAT team in Rock Springs and put them on standby."

I checked my watch and tried not to think of the fact that there was a similar watch on Roberto's wrist. It was seven-thirty. McGee was always in the office by seven. Too old and sick to even sleep properly, he had nothing else to do with his life but hound me, harass my fiancée on the phone, and work.

I started to pick up the phone again then stopped. I needed to put off calling him for a few minutes. I wanted the SWAT team wheeling this way in a half hour. I didn't want McGee rethinking things because I was out and my brother, the worthless felon, was not.

"Is Hidalgo dead?" Tom demanded again.

I shook my head. Tom let out an angry sound.

My attention turned to focus on the two metal cases on the otherwise empty picnic table. Guns. Big guns. The padlocks were still in place.

The sight of the cases, and knowing what was inside them, made a tiny crack appear in the stone that sat heavily in my chest. Desperate to feel something, anything, I put a crowbar to it. The stone opened up. What spilled out was molten lava.

"Give me the key."

"Why?" Tom said. "You tell us what's going on. Tell it—now!"

My first impulse was to go for him. Beat the shit out of him and *take* the keys. All he cared about was Hidalgo. But I closed my eyes and breathed. I tried to keep the lava bottled. I tried to center myself the way Rebecca had taught me in her morning yoga sessions. But that was another life. That was another person who had been laughing with her.

"The mine," I said, looking at Tom because it was easier than looking at Mary's guilty face. Then, working to get the words out, "They've got maybe nine people in there. Prisoners. Hostages. Slaves, I don't know. They've got them cooking high-grade meth."

"Is Hidalgo in there?" Tom asked.

I nodded.

"Where's the camera?"

"I don't know. But I saw everything."

Tom shook his head.

"No good, Burns. You were on Hidalgo's property without a warrant. Without consent. You're a peace officer and you know that's no good. Where's your brother?"

You mean, Where is his body.

For the first time I made myself consider the question. Could Roberto have survived his fall? Thinking about it made me suddenly feel very sick. How far had he fallen? Maybe a hundred and fifty, two hundred feet. Had he smacked into the walls of the shaft, slowing his descent? The part of his fall I could see before he was engulfed by the light was free. Had the roof of the car acted as a cushion or had it speared him with metal struts? There was no way to know.

I asked myself again: Could he have survived that fall? No, almost certainly not—and I wanted to retch. But maybe he did. My brother was a tough motherfucker. There was a chance—A chance in ten? A chance in a hundred? A thousand?—that the roof of the car I'd heard him hit had broken the fall. But it would have broken him, too.

What I could do is not place a bet on that chance, whatever it was. Any chance. What if he was alive? Dying slowly from his wounds? What if he was there, right now, right this second, still breathing and being tortured by Hidalgo and his men? Or, just as bad, what if he was dead—what would they be doing to his body to make an example for the troops?

The lava burned through my veins.

"He's hurt. Probably dead. They've got him, okay? Now give me the key."

"No," Tom said firmly. "There's a SWAT team on standby. If anyone is going in there, it's going to be them."

Five heartbeats of silence. The heat and pressure climbed and climbed and climbed.

Then, "Give him the key, Tom."

Mary's voice was very steady. We both looked at her.

"Give him the key," she repeated.

Tom shook his head again. When he spoke his voice was flat, for once not the demanding bray.

"Listen. We need to think about this first. Roberto went in there with Hidalgo's consent. You didn't have that, Burns. Or a warrant. You went in there on a hunch. Nothing you saw or heard will be admissible in court. What's our basis for going in now?"

"The emergency exception," Mary said. "We know our informant's in trouble. We have no time to chase down a warrant. Give him the key."

Tom was shaking his head vigorously.

"If we go in there, anything we see is inadmissible. Because you"—he pointed at my chest—"created the emergency, didn't you? Therefore whatever happens afterward, whatever you see and whatever we find, will be thrown out of court."

What I should have felt was shame. *I created the emergency*. But some internal filter channeled it into rage.

"Just give me the fucking key, Tom."

I held myself very still. I wanted to go for him, to take

him—to take anything—apart, but I held it. The menace, though, the closeness of the edge, was clear in either my voice or my expression, because Tom took a step back. When I didn't jump for him, he sidestepped around the picnic table with the computers on it and put the table between us.

Mary spoke. She sounded mechanical, either numbed or almost like what she was saying had been rehearsed.

"It's uncharted territory, as far as I know. I don't remember any case law on point. But this isn't about cutting off heads anymore, Tom. We'll go in on the emergency, get our informant out, make the arrests, and let the Assistant U.S. Attorneys sort it out."

"Don't worry about not getting your heads, Tom," I told him. "They're going to resist."

He stared at me for a long moment. He glanced at Mary, and then at me again.

"It's true, isn't it? What they say about you. QuickDraw, right? Tell me it's true and I'll give you the key."

It wasn't. Factually, at least. Not the way it was meant—that I killed three gangbangers in cold blood, then planted guns on them to make it look like I'd been ambushed. But I guessed it was a little bit true, too. *QuickDraw*, meant sarcastically, scoffing, like *Yeah, sure, you drew and shot three men who already had their guns on you. Snicker snicker. Right!* But that part was true. I had done it. It wasn't quickness, really, but just unbelievable luck. The last I could expect in this life, I'd always joked to myself. The joke now was more bitter than I'd ever imagined.

I had gone into the house wired for sound, with the intention of gathering enough evidence to put the bastards in prison. Failing that, I was going to provoke them into doing something. I'd already been warned that my cover had been burned, so I knew it wouldn't be too hard. It might sound too cowboy, too suicidal, but the possibility of dying was the last thing on my mind that night. It was anger and anger alone that pushed me through the door.

I nodded at Tom.

He smiled back at me. It was a pitying grin, full of condescension and distaste. But also satisfaction, in that all his suspicions had been confirmed.

"Told you," he said to Mary.

He dug in his pocket and threw me his ring of keys.

"Okay, we'll do it. It's probably illegal as hell, but we'll do it. We need to wait until the state patrol's SWAT team gets here. If they're willing to go in there without any paper, then we can, too."

Turning and crouching, I plugged a short, thick key into the lock of the top case. The case popped open. There, lying on the shaped foam, was one of the wicked-looking automatic rifles. It appeared more like a pistol, but giant and skeletal. I picked it up and a curved magazine from beside it. Guessing, I slapped the magazine onto the gun where it looked like it ought to go. There was a satisfying click as the magazine snapped home.

"When they get here, you can tell them where to find me."

Before leaving, I made a phone call. It should have been to Rebecca—the woman I loved, the mother of my child—but it wasn't. I would pay for that later.

"Christ, Burns, what the hell have you been doing?"

"I went to get my brother."

McGee could chastise me in all sorts of ways, with all sorts of insulting twists. Surprisingly, though, he didn't.

"You get him?"

"No."

"Then where the hell are you now?"

"With the Feds. At the hunting camp outside Potash."

"With the Feds," he mimicked, unable to resist making his voice a high-pitched parody of mine. "Both of them, from what I understand, are in some very hot water."

"Hotter than you think."

"That's pretty goddamned hot, then. Where's your brother?"

"Still in the mine. He's . . . hurt."

His voice was unsympathetic.

"What a clusterfuck. Jesus Christ. What do you want to do?"

"Send in the state SWAT guys. Immediately. Have them seal the house, the construction trailers, and the tunnel. Then get them to work their way into the mine with an armored vehicle. There are hostages in there. I'll be standing by with the Feds to direct them in. Tell them we'll meet them at the suspension bridge."

And for once, for the first time in the eight years I'd worked with him, McGee didn't argue with me.

"All right. You stay the hell out of that place, understand? That's an order. Leave it to the pros. You and your outlaw friends have already screwed the pooch enough."

I told him I would.

TWENTY-SIX

I was lying, of course.

I wasn't going to wait for them to go in there shouting over a bullhorn, *Police, put your weapons down!* I didn't think Hidalgo's men were the type to put their weapons down. Not when there was so much evidence lying around. Not when there were so many live witnesses about. They would have to make a decision at that point, and I had little doubt what their decision would be. They would hold off the state patrol, shooting if they needed to, and neaten things up as best they could.

"Oh my God."

Tom was on hands and knees before the shaft. He stared down into the blackness.

There's something about edges that literally brings people to their knees. You think nothing of standing on a curb, don't even consider stumbling or falling, but when the edge is this high, when its sheer space sucks at you like a gaping mouth, you have to get down on your knees before approaching. That feeling is increased when the abyss leads not over but straight down into the earth.

"How far down did you say it was?"

"Somewhere around a quarter-mile."

"You sure you want to do this?" he asked, twisting his head around to look up at me.

Like I had a choice. I didn't bother to give an answer.

I carefully flaked out the ropes to clear any knots. I had four sixty-meter ropes of varying ages and degrees of wear, as well as an eight-hundred-foot reel of skinny 5-mm cord. The pink cord had been a gift from a friend at a climbing shop, where it was sent by mistake. A 5-mm diameter is not much thicker than furry yarn, but the numbers printed on the side of the cardboard spool indicated a breaking strength of eight hundred pounds.

Ropes flaked, tied together with double fisherman's knots, and then tied to the loose end coming off the spool, I began shoving the whole mess in a backpack. I didn't want the rope hanging down into one of the chambers ahead of me, so I intended to pay it out as I descended the same way you do when rappelling a mountain in a gale. I shimmied into a harness, then shrugged my way into the pack. It weighed at least fifty pounds.

Tom handed me his precious MP5 submachine gun, to which he had thoughtfully attached a strap. I slung the ugly gun around one shoulder and my neck. Tom also provided me with two extra clips that were shaped like large, black bananas. These I shoved into my pockets.

I tied the loose end of the rope around the only thing nearby that looked suitable, which wasn't very—the base of a twisted juniper. I put my weight on the rope, tugged a few times, then started backing toward the hole.

Tom watched me with a rare grin. He looked pleased.

"You may have the morals of an alley cat, QuickDraw, but you've got balls. Happy hunting. You get the fucker."

I would have liked to think he was referring to my brother. To bringing him out alive. But I knew it was Hidalgo he was talking about. And *alive* probably didn't describe very accurately what he meant.

Careful not to dislodge any loose stones near the lip, I walked backward over the edge. Into the darkness.

For the first ten feet it felt like I was still a part of this world. But I was leaving it slowly, like a snarling badger backing into his burrow. Every inch of rope sliding through my hand and then the belay tube took me farther and farther from the sun and the wind and whatever order exists out there.

After fifty feet the sky seemed very far away. It was just a distant blue orb, a porthole far out of my reach. And that was good—that was where I wanted it to be.

At two hundred feet the sky was a single bright star.

The knot connecting the first two ropes snagged as I tried to tug it out of the pack. Yanking on it with my free hand, I felt an unreasonable twinge of panic when it didn't come free. For a minute everything threatened to break loose. *Shit. Shit. Shit. Calm down, Ant.* I'd dealt with knots and jams before, even when dangling thousands of feet above the ground. *But never in a bottomless pit!*

Cracking open the stone in my chest again, I let a little of the lava seep out.

I wrapped the short length of trailing rope around one thigh a couple of times to lock the rope through my belay device. Now I could use both hands. I reached behind me for the top of the pack, dug around in what felt like a mass of dead snakes, and found the knot. Gently lifting it out, I unwrapped the rope from my thigh and let it once again start sliding.

Down. Down. Down. Like a venomous spider, I told myself. Going to bite the ones who tried to squash me and my kind.

The second knot and then the third and the fourth passed

without snagging. But the 5-mm line was cutting through my
hand. I managed to take some of the pressure off by wrapping
the line once around my thigh, but it too quickly heated and
then began burning as it worked against the nylon. I switched
to braking with my left hand to keep my trigger finger intact.
That hand soon became wet with blood. I could smell the
acrid scent of melting nylon and burning flesh. *Hellfire and
brimstone,* I thought.

There was no light below. Not even when I guessed I was
two-thirds of the way through the 5 mm. And that was both
good and bad. A part of my psyche desperately needed some
light, but I wasn't going to risk turning on my headlamp. But
no light below also meant I wasn't heading into an occupied
chamber. And besides, right then I preferred the dark.

Some extra sense told me quite suddenly that I'd dropped
out the bottom of the pit. No faint wind was rising up from
underneath me. There was just the slightest moan as the ex-
pelling air wrapped itself around the pit's edge on a cavern's
ceiling.

And I could hear distant voices, ringing very lightly off
the mine's walls.

I lowered myself slower now, and felt a magnification of
my senses of sound, and, unfortunately, touch, because my left
hand was on fire.

Then my feet hit solid ground.

I staggered. My legs were weak from hanging. I began to
fall, but caught myself with the rope and managed to lower
myself to a sitting position. Popping open the belay device, I
released the cord. A sick thought made me want to turn on my
headlamp and look at it—it had to be streaked with blood and
pieces of flesh—but I managed to suppress the temptation.

I lifted the stays on the pack's shoulder straps and let the
straps slide free, and the pack slid off my back without my
needing to take off the gun.

Then I started stalking through the darkness, drawn by the sound of those far-off voices.

It's strange that the descent was so memorable. Strange, because what happened next is hard to describe or even recall. Like the night in Cheyenne a couple of years earlier, I have a hard time putting together the pieces. There was silence then incredible noise, darkness then flaring light. If I were to try and describe it, it would start to sound like an action movie's climax. But this wasn't a movie. No one was acting.

What I felt is even harder to describe. It's hard to admit, too. Because for a little while I lost myself completely. All those things I'd once sworn to uphold—rules and laws and civilization itself—climbed into the backseat and shut their eyes. If I were trying to excuse it, I would say that Roberto's spirit invaded my body. But it wasn't my brother. It was me. And this version of me would return. Not just in a nightmare, either.

The facts of what happened would haunt me periodically for a long time to come. For the rest of my life probably, I knew. For several months I would have to live with it daily. I was forced to relive it in official interviews, depositions, Internal Affairs Review Committees, as well as other panels, such as those for reviewing officer-involved shootings and those for recommendations of disciplinary action. The questions would be inevitably asked by lawyers whose job it was to destroy me.

I really hate lawyers.

Here's what you need to know: I found only three of Hidalgo's men in the mine. But not Hidalgo himself, or Zafado, or even my brother's body. The three I did find were in the trailer, making up a meal of rice and beans for their prisoners before I shut off the generator. Two of them were kids—gangbangers. One of them was the rapist called Shorty.

I shot them all. And someone shot me.

TWENTY-SEVEN

My head felt like it was about to explode. Or like maybe it already had. It was leaking—that was for sure. Running down my neck and soaking my shirt. If I hadn't seen the muzzle flash from the trailer above me, I would have sworn somebody had snuck up and hit me with an ax. It felt like the blade was still in there, with the weight of the handle causing it to bite and grind into my skull whenever I made the slightest move.

On top of that, the gong of a tremendous bell rang non-stop in my ears. It made it hard to think.

Many large men dressed all in black were sitting on me or crouching around me. They had flashlights mounted on the barrels of their guns and they were swinging the beams all around. These men were bulky from lifting weights and too many steak dinners and all their body armor. In the glare of the headlights coming off some kind of van nearby, I watched them opening and closing their mouths with rapid snaps like goldfish on speed. I knew they were yelling at me, but I had no idea what they were saying.

I tried to talk.

"Where's my brother? The informant? Have you seen him?"

The man closest to my face winced and drew back. I decided it wasn't my breath but my volume. I hadn't been able to hear my own words. He put a finger to his lips and pumped his palm up and down a few times, indicating for me to lower it.

I tried asking again. And he tried answering. His mouth opened and closed less rapidly, but still mutely.

One of the other men finally drew my attention. He pointed at his face with two fingers of one hand. For a minute I thought he was going to very slowly poke himself in the eyes. Then he panned the fingers out at the darkness beyond the beam of the headlights. I understood. They were looking.

"Thank you," I mouthed.

I was carefully bundled into the back of what turned out to be an armored bank car, not a van. It was lit from a tiny dim bulb on the roof. *Let me stay,* I told them soundlessly. *I can help you find him.* But from what I could tell, they just ignored me. I tried to resist, to get out of the back of the armored car, but there were too many of them, and they were all too big to fight, and I was feeling pretty weak.

I was pushed down onto nylon bags that were stiff with coins. They hadn't taken the time, when borrowing the truck, to empty out the money. I noticed and appreciated that. But I didn't want to be here. I wanted to be back out in the darkness.

All but one man—who was especially large—jumped out. I felt a sharp pressure in my ears when someone slammed the door. The sensation made me open my mouth. Maybe I screamed, maybe I didn't. There was no way to tell. For a minute my eyes watered too much to be able to read the remaining man's face.

A little later some bumping and jostling indicated that we were moving. Turning around, I guessed, judging from the back-and-forth rocking, and then accelerating into the tunnel.

The left side of my face was stiff and sticky. A wetness ran down my neck and back and into my pants. I took a weird comfort in all the blood running out of me. My brother had had blood running out of him the last time I saw him.

I'm just like him. Almost.

The man sitting opposite me peeled a large gauze bandage out of its paper wrapper. He put it to the left side of my head then wrapped my head around and around with adhesive tape. It was the same kind of tape Roberto and I used for protecting our hands when climbing fat cracks. His mouth moved as he worked but I couldn't hear a word of what he was saying.

Again I said, *Thanks.* Again I said that I should be back there, looking for my brother.

I couldn't tell what he said in return, but the truck didn't slow or stop. It just vibrated on up the tunnel road toward the real world.

Weak light began to seep in through the tiny bulletproof windows. Then, suddenly, it became bright sunlight. *Back in the real world.* The doors at the back of the armored car swung open and even more light flooded in. Blinding light. There were more people here. A lot more. There were something like twenty police officers in uniform, and twenty more in jeans and flannel shirts.

Maybe my eardrums hadn't been blown out. My head was still ringing unbelievably, but I could now hear faint voices. I was helped out of the van and led to the passenger side of a patrol car. The rear door was opened and I was seated inside. I wondered why I hadn't been put in the front.

Am I being arrested? For what I did down there? No, they would have handcuffed me. They must not want to get blood in the front seat.

There was a lot of activity. More cars pulled up into the wide area at the tunnel's mouth. People stood around in little groups, individuals peeling off to walk a little way then stand in other groups. No one tried to talk to me. Everyone, though, glanced my way every few minutes. I watched the armored truck turn around again and speed back into the mine.

Finally an ambulance came down the road.

"Can you hear me?" a paramedic said into my face, but from very far away. I could feel the vibration of her words more than I could hear them.

"Yes."

She drew back from my affirmation—I must have been shouting again. She smiled, though, pleased. She was a Nordic princess. Blond hair, blue eyes, a little heavy, but definitely an angel.

She touched my neck with fingertips encased in a latex glove and stared at her watch for a little while. Counting the beats of my heart. *I didn't know I still had one.* Then she put her cheek next to my mouth as if waiting to receive a brotherly kiss. Counting my respirations, I realized.

"What's your name?"

"Antonio Burns."

"Where are you?"

"In Sublette County, Wyoming. At a mine entrance. About a mile west of the Roan River."

She smiled again, pleased so far. I was doing well on the test to gauge my orientation, my mental state.

"What day is it?"

I had to think about that. I honestly didn't know. I tried to surreptitiously glance at my watch but she caught me. She frowned.

"The last couple of days have been pretty hairy," I explained. "I don't think I'm concussed, though."

She gave me a look that said she'd be the judge of that. But I managed to pass the rest of the test.

I knew she was trying to be gentle, but my head burned and my eyes watered when she pulled away the tape. She stared at the wound for a moment then sprayed it with a saline solution and studied it again. She probed it lightly with the tips of her fingers. Her fingertips came away smeared with my blood.

"Looks like it was just a graze, Antonio, but we'll need an X-ray to be sure. It's already starting to clot. You're lucky."

Right.

She began to bandage it back up.

I was oddly disappointed. It didn't feel like just a graze. It felt like that ax was still hanging off the side of my head. She smeared some goop on my burned palm and bandaged it, too.

A few police officers came over to check on me. There was true concern on their faces. Not the sarcasm, or the distaste, or even the misplaced envy for my reputation that I'd become so used to. By looking at their uniforms, I saw that they'd come from all over the central part of the state when they'd heard there was an officer in trouble. Driven fast, at high speeds, I knew. I wanted to cry.

"Okay, Antonio. Let me help you to the ambulance. We're going to put you on a stretcher and take you in for those X-rays."

It was my blond angel. The words came from maybe only a hundred feet away instead of miles. My hearing was returning.

"No. I'm staying here. Thanks, though."

"I'm afraid you've got to come with me. We need to get a better look at your head."

"I'm afraid not."

She argued for another minute, the smile fading, trying to look stern. Then she spun and stalked off toward the ambulance. Tearing off her gloves and throwing them onto the dirt. Washing her hands of me, I guessed.

I got up from the backseat of the patrol car. Then I stooped, braced myself on the trunk with one hand, and vomited by the rear tire. Nothing came up but bile. I waited for the nausea and dizziness to pass. When I stood, more or less upright this time, I nearly vomited again when I saw my reflection in the car's window.

I wobbled and swayed over to a small group of uniformed state-patrol officers. High-level, judging from the ribbons and brass on their shoulders and chests. Those who saw me coming turned to gape. The others noticed and turned, too. One of them was a gray-haired man they'd all been anchored around. I recognized him as the commander of the state patrol.

"Antonio Burns, right?"

"Yes, sir. Thank you for coming out and bringing your men."

He nodded reluctantly. McGee had ordered him to send in the SWAT team. This guy didn't really have a choice, although he didn't have to come in person.

"What's the situation, Commander?"

"We've secured the house and trailer, where eleven men were taken into custody. Most of them were either armed with illegal weapons or were trying to hide them. One of them speaks some English, and he's demanding his lawyer, of course. Says his name is Jesús Hidalgo."

I felt a little something—a small rush of relief.

Good. The motherfucker's in custody. But it would have been so much better if he'd been down in the mine.

"The SWAT, as you know, is still in the mine," the commander went on. "They've got six more people in custody down there. Unarmed. Three or four of them are in pretty bad shape, in filthy clothes and looking half-starved. Probably those hostages we were warned about, but right now we aren't taking any chances."

"Are any of them wounded?"

"No. Not that I've heard about. But there's three bodies down there, too. In a camper or something. I'm told it looks like you were the shooter. And the shootee. There's some people who are going to be wanting to have a lot of long talks with you, Burns."

I nodded. I knew the drill. I knew it far too well. Cheyenne was going to come back and haunt me all over again.

"Only the three bodies?" I asked.

He looked at me strangely.

"You shoot anyone else down there, agent? Never mind—I don't want to know. Those three in the camper are the only bodies I know about."

No Roberto. No Bruto.

"Now if you don't mind, Burns, I have a crime scene to maintain."

"Wait. I need to get back in there. Into the mine."

He shook his head.

"No. We're pulling our officers out, along with the suspects we have in custody. We're leaving the bodies. It's too dangerous to continue searching in there right now. There could be booby traps. Or cave-ins. Or more armed suspects running around in the dark. We're going to back out and put together a plan to safely search the area. Get some thermal or infrared sensors, or something like that. Night-vision goggles apparently don't work."

"I know. Just give me a ride back down. Or lend me a car."

He looked at me, openly annoyed now.

"Something wrong with your hearing, Burns? I said no.

We're pulling everyone out and we're sealing the mine for the time being."

"My brother's in there."

"My *men* are in there. And I'm not putting any police officers at further risk. They were risking enough by going down to bring you out."

"I know. I can't tell you how much I appreciate it. But I need—"

He turned on his heel and walked away from me.

I staggered back to the rear of the empty patrol car and gingerly lowered myself onto the seat. I wondered if I could steal it. But there were no keys, either in the ignition or on the seat. I could steal another car—surely one of the ten or fifteen parked around me had keys in the ignition. But several of the commander's men were watching me closely. Maybe expecting just such a rash act from a blood-covered guy who'd done something very dark and ugly a quarter-mile under the earth.

I could feel my muscles getting chewed up by the mixture of worry, rage, grief, and adrenaline that was still flowing through my veins in the place of all the lost blood. I was stiff and sore and I hurt all over.

I sat, trying to think with my bruised and ringing brain, while the activity around me started to increase. More people were coming in. A second ambulance arrived, whose crew joined the two from the first in the hope of finding someone else in need of medical attention. I saw the angel frowning in my direction, as if I'd deprived her of something. A search-and-rescue truck from another county arrived. Then more patrol cars. Then an old station wagon listing to one side that said Señor Garcia's Mexican Restaurant on the side. Lupe Garcia was behind the wheel and one of the boys who'd tried to assault me a few nights ago for being Mexican-looking sat next to her. She either didn't see me or didn't recognize me with all the dried blood and bandages on my head. I overheard a cop say that the restaurant had offered to bring free food for the officers involved in the raid.

Soon the broad dirt area in front of the mine had an almost festival atmosphere. People stood in groups everywhere. Talking. Eating. Sometimes even laughing. The commander was surrounded by his men, and they studied a map on the hood of a car. I decided to go talk to him again. To plead, if necessary. And to scope out the arriving cars for keys left behind.

I only managed to stand up and combat a new wave of nausea when another car came rumbling down the dirt road past the construction trailer.

It was my car. The old Pig lumbered along, looking big and aggressive with its front-mounted winch and its dark windows. But it also looked a little silly, because Mungo's long face hung out one window and her tongue was flapping in the wind.

The battered Land Cruiser braked to a halt alongside me. It leapt up and down in either expectation or, more likely, from some inexperienced driver lifting his foot off the clutch too soon. The engine died. Mungo licked at me from two feet away, whining frantically.

I patted her cheek and moved closer so that the wolf could smell me, and could be sure I was all right. She started licking at the blood on my throat. The driver's window came down and it was Mary at the wheel. Tom sat beside her. Then he got out and walked around to get a good look at me. Mary just stared.

"They've got Hidalgo," I said to Mary through the open window.

For some reason I could speak to her, but not Tom. She, at least, had the grace to look guilty. I knew that she had liked

Roberto. But not enough, apparently, to want to keep him from risking his life for her ambition and her version of justice.

"I know," she said softly. "They're going to turn them all over to us as soon as some U.S. Marshals arrive from Casper to help with the transportation."

Beside me, Tom punched a fist into his palm. The gesture, the noise it made, was supposed to be the righteous smack of justice. To me it was stupid and hollow. So were his words.

"I'm finally going to get to put that bastard's head on my wall."

"At least his mug shot," Mary corrected her partner, not bothering to try and match his enthusiasm. Then to me she said, "You can sit in when we question him, Anton."

"No. My brother's still in there." I pointed at the mine's dark entrance.

Mary looked down at my feet.

"We've heard that they've rounded up six people in the mine. All alive. Hidalgo's chemists, we think. And—oh, Anton, I hate to tell you this—there are three bodies."

"Roberto isn't one of them."

She looked up, confused.

"Mary, I know about the three bodies. Roberto isn't one of them."

"Then they're still looking?"

I shook my head and felt the ax swing.

"No. They're pulling out. Until they can figure out a way to search it safely. They think more of Hidalgo's punks might be down there."

"And you think Roberto's still down there?"

"Yeah. I need to find him."

"Will they let you go in? To look for him?"

"They can do what they want. I'm going back down."

"How?"

"Get out of my truck, Mary."

My meaning was clear to both of them.

"Oh, now, that's real smart," Tom said. "You're going to disobey these guys who just saved your ass, and maybe get shot again in the process? At least a few of Jesús's boys are still unaccounted for, you know. They're probably in there."

"I'm not getting out, Anton," Mary said, ignoring Tom. "You get in. You're in no shape to drive."

For some reason her words hit me like a punch to the throat. It began to constrict. I felt myself choking up. And I felt moisture welling in my nose and behind my eyes.

"No," Tom said when I began to walk around to the passenger side. He pointed at Mungo. "You get in the back, Burns. I'm not riding back there with that thing."

I stopped and glared at him.

"You've got your man. Now why don't you get the fuck out of here?"

Tom brushed past me, saying, "My man's still in that hole. If you're going to look for him, then I'm going to help."

He opened the door and climbed into the passenger seat.

I put my hands on the hot hood for balance. Then my forehead. I'd managed to hold it all in for so long. First by being numb, then enraged. But now, because of Tom Cochran of all frigging people, I started to sob.

•

TWENTY-EIGHT

I couldn't hear most of what was shouted at us when Mary crept through all the cars and people and drove us toward the mine. That was all right—it was probably nothing I wanted to hear anyway.

One man—the commander—stepped in front of the Pig with his hand upraised. He jumped back at the last minute when Mary didn't slow. Through the window, I saw him looking almost comically bewildered that someone would ignore his order to stop. People didn't do that to a guy like him. In a minute he'd remember to get mad.

Sorry, I would tell him later. *But, you see, my brother's still in there.*

Mary flipped on the headlights as we ramped down into the big tunnel. It was the first time I'd seen it lit up like this. The walls were as coarse as I remembered, but for some reason it all looked very different. It was less menacing, safer. But then as the daylight receded behind us, it started to feel even more confining. Mary shifted gears and accelerated.

Ten minutes later we saw lights ahead. Another vehicle was coming toward us from the depths. It was the borrowed bank truck. Its high beams were flashing on and off as it rolled closer. Swinging to the left, onto what was our side of the road, then wide to the right again, it rolled to a stop a little bit sideways so that the truck was effectively blocking our path. The driver got out and waved his arms at us. The commander must have radioed from the tunnel mouth. The tunnel was straight enough that the call had gotten through.

"What do I do?" Mary asked, slowing.

"Pull around him to the right."

"I can't. There's all the metal there."

She meant the rusting frame of the conveyor belt.

"Just drive over it," I told her.

The Pig's big bumper hit metal and screeched, lifting a long portion of the conveyor's frame up and turning it over. The truck bounced and crunched on the section as we stomped over it. Then we passed the waving SWAT driver and were back on the packed dirt. As Mary accelerated again, he showed us his middle finger. It was too tight for the armored truck to turn around, so he couldn't follow.

It took another ten minutes of driving more than forty miles per hour down into the earth before we reached the first chamber.

It felt like we were in outer space, with the Pig our lunar lander. Mary and Tom and Mungo and I all craned our necks to see around the room. This place had been lit, distantly, by the generator in the far chamber the two times I'd been here. Now the only light came from the Pig's twin beams.

The atmosphere outside the truck felt thick and oppressive. The two giant mechanical dinosaurs were still frozen in rearing, violent poses. The big saw-blades on the end of the crane were still in the process of taking a bite out of the ceiling.

Beneath it, in the center of the room, the headlights framed a pickup truck. Its windshield was smashed, its hood dented. The roof was partially caved in, too. The light sparkled on the thousands of diamonds that lay on the hood. A lot of them were stained red. And somewhere in the black space over our heads was the ventilation shaft Roberto had fallen from.

"Pull up to the pickup," I said.

Mary rolled forward through the chamber and stopped twenty feet from the smashed truck. I opened the door and got out. I reached into the back to take a headlamp from a crate of climbing gear. When I turned it on, its light was swallowed by the darkness without even touching any of the walls.

Tom and Mary got out, too, neither of them saying a word. They each had long, black Maglites, which, when they swept them through the darkness, managed to touch the far walls. No one said anything. No one moved more than a step from the Pig. The hazy glow of the dome light held us all like a tether to a spaceship.

Then Mungo began to whine. I'd been standing in front of the open door, blocking her in. Now I turned to her and cupped her head in my hands. I gently massaged the thick, coarse fur behind her ears. I put my mouth close to hers and stared into her yellow eyes.

"Find him, Mungo. Find Roberto."

Mungo leapt from the truck. She didn't hesitate. She didn't pause to snuff the air. She didn't even look to me for further explanation.

She hit the ground running and streaked forward through the blaze of the headlights. Her head turned slightly toward the crushed pickup as she passed it, but she never slowed. Within seconds she was lost in the darkness beyond.

I didn't hesitate, either. I started running after her. Even though my head seemed to detonate with each stride and the nausea was once again pumping my stomach like a bellows.

The headlamp bounced wildly on my forehead, its beam jerking crazily up and down and from side to side. Every now and then I caught the flash of silver fur far ahead of me.

She was heading to the left—not straight ahead into the tunnel that led to the trailer and meth lab. And that was the last direction I knew. My focus on following her, on not vomiting, on not falling down due to the dizziness, on not fainting, pushed every other consideration from my mind. I didn't even know if Mary and Tom were following me. Only occasionally could I hear one of them shouting in the distance.

We entered a tunnel, then another chamber that may or may not have been as big as the first one. It was impossible to tell—it was a universe of cloying blackness. Then another tunnel. This tunnel was far smaller. Big enough for trucks, but not for the mechanical dinosaurs. Mungo was picking up speed. The flashes of silver I glimpsed were farther and farther away, and timed farther and farther apart. I was attacked by two new fears, adding to all the others. I was going to lose her. I was going to lose myself.

I ran on. Panting and choking on what was crawling up my throat and staggering from the dizziness. The thought nudged at the edge of my focused concentration: *Wrong turn. Somewhere back there I made a wrong turn. I've lost Mungo.* I ran for another minute before doubt and the dry heaves forced me to double over. When I stood up, I was crushed by the darkness. The headlamp showed nothing but two walls, a rounded roof, and bookends of solid blackness on each end. Weighted by total silence except for my own ragged breathing.

Panic welled up in me like a tidal wave. Cresting, falling, at a hundred miles an hour toward my head. It was going to wash me away. Crush me. Pulverize me.

Then there came the most extraordinary sound I'd ever heard in my life. It knifed through me, electrified me, and devastated me worse than the darkness and the silence and the panic.

It was a wolf's howl. It reverberated off the walls and through the earth. More than mournful—more than frightening—it was some kind of primitive, fluid sob from the very depths of a wild thing's soul. Fresh tears leapt out on my cheeks.

I staggered in the rough direction of the sound, back the way I had come. Pulled by the howl, I looked left and noticed a black hole I hadn't noticed before. It was, I assumed, an exploratory shaft. It cut down at a sharp angle and was barely larger than an upright man. The floor was a litter of uncleared rocks. The sound was ripping out of there.

The narrow walls, like all the other surfaces down there, were a light tan in the crazily jerking beam of my light. I noticed a brown smear on both sides at shoulder height. The smear glinted a little. It was wet and fresh. Something or someone had recently been carried through this passage at shoulder level.

The walls narrowed and the ceiling dropped. Soon I was running half-stooped, and with one shoulder pointing forward and the other pointing back. The smears were bigger here. Wider and darker. The howling was far louder. It cut right through me.

I went down hard. Not from pain or exhaustion, but because I tripped over something large that had been dumped there. I got up on my hands and knees and twisted my head to shine the light behind me. It fixed on Bruto's thick body, and then on his dented skull. I looked away.

There was a flash of silver ahead. Mungo. Tail no longer waving like a wind-torn flag, but tucked between her legs. She turned and stared at me, yellow eyes glowing green in the light, her black lips making an O and that unearthly sound coming from them. Beyond her the passage ended in a wall of jagged rock. Something pale was curled there.

I pushed Mungo out of the way—grabbed her and shoved her behind me. Then I focused the Cyclops beam on the paleness. And the tears started to run down my cheeks. My breathing made a pumping sound in the hole—I couldn't seem to fill my chest. My knees hit the stony floor but I didn't feel the bite of the sharp edges.

Oh God. Oh God. Oh God.

Roberto was curled into a fetal position. His skin was striped and smeared with blood. The long black hair covered most of his face. But I could see the brilliant blue of his eyes. Staring somewhere far beyond me. There was a faint smile on his lips. Or was it a snarl?

My brother—my mad, beautiful brother—was unleashed at last.

3

So, we'll go no more a-roving
So late into the night,
Though the heart be still as loving,
And the moon be still as bright.

—*"So, We'll Go No More A-Roving"*
  Lord Byron, 1817

ALLEGED DRUG KINGPIN IN U.S. CUSTODY

CASPER, Wy., August 23—Federal agents, assisted by officers of the Wyoming State Police, yesterday arrested Jesús Hidalgo-Paez, who is believed by some law-enforcement officials to be the head of a multibillion-dollar narcotics empire. He is expected to be charged with conspiracy to manufacture and distribute methamphetamine.

The FBI announced the arrest following a raid on an isolated estate in Wyoming's Wind River region. Four men were killed there in the clash with police, and one Wyoming officer was wounded. Property records indicate that the estate is owned by a Mexico City attorney named Paul Olivas.

Twenty-two additional Mexican nationals were taken into custody along with Mr. Hidalgo-Paez, six of whom were hospitalized for malnutrition. Another man, of dual Argentinean/American citizenship, is in critical condition after receiving a gunshot wound and other injuries. He is not expected to survive.

Mr. Hidalgo-Paez has strong ties with key officials in Mexico's government. He served as a campaign chairman for the Party of the Institutional Revolution, or PRI, from 1996 to 1999. A party spokesperson called the arrest "extremely unfortunate and erroneous, as Mr. Hidalgo has no ties to any illegal activities. We anticipate his imminent release."

Yet Mr. Hidalgo-Paez has long been suspected by some American authorities of heading one of

Mexico's most notorious drug-smuggling cartels. A source at the Justice Department alleges that Mr. Hidalgo-Paez is responsible for possibly hundreds of murders in Mexico. He is also believed to have ordered the slaying earlier this year of an undercover FBI agent in Mexicali.

According to an FBI spokesman, the raid on the Wyoming estate included some arrests made in an abandoned mine on the property. Evidence was found there of a large-scale methamphetamine laboratory. It was in this underground location that the gunfight occurred, during which the four suspects were killed and the police officer wounded.

Mr. Hidalgo will be arraigned Monday in federal court in Denver, Colorado. Warrants for his arrest have also been issued in Mexico.

TWENTY-NINE

The modern courtroom wasn't very large and it was less than half-full. But what mattered to me was that it was reporters who were half-filling it. As I watched them getting out their notepads, I felt like nodding my approval and even appreciation. It was very different from the way I'd felt about them just a year earlier. Then they'd been *frigging muckrakers* and *bullshit artists* and *goddamn liars*. My Rebecca excluded, of course. Then it had been about me. Now I wanted to cheer them on as they clicked their poison pens and got ready to do their worst to Jesús Hidalgo.

Over the last few days I'd been unable to get out of my head—which was still ringing—all the reasons Mary and Tom had previously told me about why the U.S. federal government did not want to see Jesús Hidalgo prosecuted. Those fears stayed with me day and night. They shut out all other thoughts. But with the reporters closely following the case, I felt there was a chance that justice—at least the kind of justice offered by the courts—would be done.

A high-publicity case gets everyone a little worked up. The prosecutor takes his job a lot more seriously. But so does the defense. Both sides are likely to grandstand far too much for my taste—for reasons personal, political, and in the hopes of influencing any potential jurors who might see them in the papers or on the news. But they do their jobs. At least when they're not preening for the cameras out on the courthouse steps.

This particular courtroom had a solemn dignity that Wyoming courts lacked. The flag and the seal of the United States of America were the only decorations. The walls were all dark wood. The ceiling was high. The room was furnished in a subdued, modern fashion that told the parties and the spectators alike that this wasn't a place to be screwing around. You don't do that before this flag, this seal—this wasn't Mexico or any of the other corrupt narcocracies south of the border. This was America. As a result everyone acted very deliberate. Very professional. Very cool.

Except for me.

But I tried. *I am an ice cube,* I told myself repeatedly. Then I had to strain like hell not to melt all over the marble floor.

I sat behind the low oak wall that separated the gallery from the court's well, and just behind the prosecution's table. In front of me was a young Assistant U.S. Attorney I'd never met. He looked a little forlorn, sitting there all by himself, but I didn't introduce myself. My focus was locked on the other side of the courtroom.

Across the aisle and over the wall, just fifteen or twenty feet away, sat El Doctor, Jesús Hidalgo. I had never before been this close, except for the time when I was lying on my face in the dirt and he was unknowingly pissing on Tom Cochran's back. But I'd studied Mary and Tom's pictures of him at length. And I'd seen him at a distance over the long-range camera and heard his voice on their illegal microphone.

He was, as usual, the center of attention. Dressed in orange coveralls with INMATE stenciled on the back in big, bold letters, he was the only one in the room who seemed like he didn't belong. Everyone else, including me, was in a suit. A courtroom is one of the few places left where people wear them, and I was relieved that Hidalgo had not been allowed to dress as a part of our society.

His ankles were shackled together with two feet of thin steel cable. The jailhouse clothes and the chains should have taken something away from him. But Hidalgo was not hunched and defeated. Instead he was leaning back in an expensive chair, looking amused. His thick brown hair was swept back and his mustache was neatly trimmed. A retinue of attorneys surrounded him, whispering and chuckling happily when he whispered a response.

"All rise," the clerk called.

Tom nudged me with a sharp elbow. A little late, I followed him to his feet. The judge stalked in from a door behind the bench.

I liked the look of him. Grim-faced, dark-haired, tall, broad, and cloaked entirely in black, he looked like a judge who could parcel out punishment with his own hands if he wanted to. He wore a cop's mustache, too, thick and square, and that didn't hurt, either.

I generally like federal judges. They're appointed for life, so they don't have to worry about playing up to a fickle and biased electorate. This judge immediately asserted his authority by taking his chair without a word—leaving all of us standing—and frowning intently while shuffling through a sheaf of papers he'd brought with him.

"Be seated," the clerk said for him after a few awkward moments.

This produced some quiet laughter to which the judge, still shuffling away, appeared oblivious. I also barely noticed. I was still staring at Hidalgo. Tom tugged hard at my sleeve and I followed him back down onto the pew.

I'd run into Tom out in the hallway. The hallway was

modern too, with an all-glass wall that looked out on the mountains as well as steel pillars and white marble benches. I hadn't expected to see Tom, and I was a little confused as to how I should feel about him. It wasn't something I'd really considered—it was just that when he came walking toward me, I wasn't sure if I should punch him or hug him. In the end I stuck out my hand.

I'd said, "Hey, Tom, I've been meaning to tell you something. . . . I'm sorry I was such an asshole up at the mine."

He looked at my hand and then at me. It was the same look of distaste he'd given me the first time I met him, in the hotel room in Salt Lake. Only a week and a half earlier. I didn't understand why he should be so bitter—he had gotten his man, after all, that head he'd always been talking about—but I was too wrapped up in my own world to pay much attention.

He took my hand reluctantly.

"Sure," he'd said, letting go after an instant without returning my grip.

He was looking at me like he blamed me for something. Like I had done something wrong. It should have been the other way around. I'd wanted to punch him then. But I didn't. I was still too weak, too fragile, plus I was storing up all my hate. Instead we ended up sitting next to each other on the bench behind the prosecution table, the one that's reserved for victims' families and cops. I was twice entitled.

"*United States* v. *Jesús Hidalgo-Paez,*" the clerk called out in a booming voice, hoping to get the judge's attention.

"Counsel, enter your appearances," he ordered while he continued with his papers.

A defense attorney beat out the prosecutor, even though the A.U.S.A. stood up first.

"Jeremy Horton, for the defense."

The young prosecutor started to speak but he was beaten again.

"Julie Watts, also for the defense."

It happened twice again. Two more defense attorneys chimed in before the A.U.S.A. got to say, "Mike Davadou, for the United States."

In the silence that followed, there were a few more quiet chuckles from around the room. I noticed that Hidalgo smiled.

The lonely prosecutor added, "I'm afraid it's just me, Your Honor."

I hoped that he was speaking with low-key confidence instead of embarrassment. I seemed to be worrying—obsessing—about every little thing. I was placing all my chips on a number I knew from eight years of hard, demoralizing experience only occasionally paid off. I was counting on the court and the law to do justice. I felt like an atheist prostrating himself before a god he long ago stopped believing in. Begging for salvation. If only I could summon up the righteous passion I'd felt in those early years.

"Who will be serving as lead counsel for the defense? I don't intend to have you all responding on the record."

More quiet chuckles, although there was no humor in what the judge had said.

Horton said, "I will, Judge. If none of my colleagues here objects."

There were smiles and nods and bows from the other members of the defense to their leader. I didn't know why, or at what, and I felt my aggravation grow. Horton talked with a bullshit country accent and he stood slouching with his hands in his pockets like some folksy politician. He had long, gray, blow-dried hair and wore a bow tie instead of a necktie. I wondered if that was intentional, just for this case and client. All three of Hidalgo's male attorneys wore bow ties. I suspected they didn't want anyone looking at them and thinking about what Hidalgo and his *sicarios* did to the people and their families who were suspected of informing on him.

The judge began the advisement by asking Mr. Hidalgo to please stand. Horton pulled back Hidalgo's chair and gave him a courtly wave to rise.

"Do you speak English, Mr. Hidalgo?"

"I do. Thank you."

It was said with an appreciative little smile. Hidalgo's eyebrows were slightly raised. There was a polite smile on his bland face. To me it looked superior and condescending, as if he were humoring the judge and all of us by taking part in this bit of theater.

"Are you aware of the complaint against you?"

"Yes, I am. Thank you."

"Have you received a copy as well as the affidavits filed with it?"

"Mr. Davadou was good enough to provide them," Horton answered for Hidalgo. "My client will waive a formal reading."

The judge nodded approvingly. "Very well."

Our dad, the former commander of Special Forces commandos, had taught Roberto and me never to hit with our fists. *Always use a knee or an elbow or, better yet, a weapon.* But my spare gun had been taken away from me by courthouse security, and all I could think of was what it would feel like to bury my fist in Jesús Hidalgo's mouth.

I could see his eyes blink as my knuckles drew near. His little smile flinch. Then his lips exploding, his teeth breaking, his jaw jamming then popping.

Maybe I was breathing too hard, or beginning to froth like a rabid dog, because Tom whispered in my ear, "Cool it. If you wanted to do something about it, QuickDraw, you should have done it up in Wyoming."

I looked at him. He was staring right back at me with his mirror-practiced gunfighter's glare.

"What the fuck are you talking about?" I whispered.

"Shh," a reporter from behind us hissed, drawing the judge's attention.

I received the stink eye from the bench for a moment before the proceeding continued.

"You are charged with violating 21 U.S.C. 841, conspiring to manufacture and/or distribute more than one hundred grams of methamphetamine. How do you plead?"

"Most certainly not guilty, Your Honor."

It was said with that same assured smile.

I'd learned that the six kidnapped chemists had refused to say a word against Hidalgo. That was no surprise, really. So the only charge against him was conspiracy to manufacture and distribute methamphetamine. Some of the others had been charged with possession of illegal weapons and possession of small amounts of drugs in addition to the overall conspiracy, but Hidalgo was only facing the single count. So far, anyway. Others could and would be added later. I tried to cool off by reminding myself of the stiff federal penalties. In this case a conviction would result in a ten-year minimum sentence. Hardly justice, but a start.

"Fine," the judge said. His clerk handed him a leather-bound book. "We need to go ahead and set a trial date, then."

He studied the book for a long time, and whispered back and forth with his clerk while covering the microphone with his hand. He lifted the hand and suggested a date. The entire defense team consulted their own smaller leather-bound books and PalmPilots and someone shook his head. An apology was offered. A new date was suggested. Another shake of a head, another apology. People began to chuckle out the apologies. I breathed deep, my head aching, my ears still ringing.

It wasn't the judge who ended this game, but Hidalgo himself. He pulled Horton to his side, cupped a hand over his mouth, and spoke in his lawyer's ear. Horton looked back at him, surprised, and then told the judge that an already refused date would be acceptable after all. The surprise, I guessed, was that his client wanted to expedite things rather than playing the usual defendant's delaying game.

Hidalgo must think he has a chance.

"Could we set a date for a suppression hearing as well, Your Honor?" Horton asked. "I expect that such a hearing might even make the trial date we just set academic."

There were more quiet laughs, but no one was really surprised by the defense attorney's optimistic prediction. It was part of the game. They shouted out their client's innocence and bragged that they would prove it all the way until a sentencing hearing, at which time they exaggerated their client's sad, abusive childhood, minimized their client's involvement in any crimes, and extolled his genuine, heartfelt remorse. Defense lawyers who lie like that should be horsewhipped.

After a similar discussion about dates—one that everyone again seemed to think was funny—one was set for an evidentiary hearing in six weeks. The attorneys were told they each had ten days to prepare motions.

"Your Honor, if we could get to the issue of pretrial release now. It would be unfair to keep my client in custody when we firmly believe the motions hearing will prove dispositive to the charges against him."

Fuck you, Horton, I wanted to say.

Davadou spoke up. "Your Honor, I believe that issue is moot. Warrants for Mr. Hidalgo's arrest have been issued in Mexico, and we are holding him on those as well, pending a possible extradition."

Good. Hidalgo getting bailed out had been one of my biggest fears. I could imagine him just disappearing, fading away, back into Mexico. But now Mexico was seeking his extradition. That had to be good. The corrupt politicians there must have finally decided that they no longer had anything to fear from him. That the days of the Mexicali Mafia and *la corbata* had come to an end, and that they could switch their allegiance and open their pockets to another cartel.

Another hearing, in two days' time, was set to consider the extradition issue. Then a preliminary hearing as well, to determine whether there was probable cause to keep Mr. Hidalgo in custody on the present charges. The words kept coming, all very formal, all very polite except for Horton's good-natured grumblings that all these dates would prove unnecessary.

Finally it was over.

I found myself standing up as Hidalgo and his attorneys and the rest of the court rose for the judge's departure. Three marshals approached Hidalgo to take custody of him. As he turned to meet them, his eyes finally met mine. He had never seen me before, but I knew he knew who I was. It had to be written all over my face.

We stared, his black eyes seeming to grow nearer, and I waited for the smile to flinch. It did.

Then I was suddenly being shoved backward. Two elderly but beefy marshals had taken hold of my arms and were dragging me back. I hadn't realized how close I'd gotten to Hidalgo. I hadn't realized I was moving at all. His face was just three feet away when I was propelled away from him. His smile bounced back. It actually grew wider.

I was out on the street, where I'd been deposited by the marshals after stern talking-tos by the judge, the Assistant U.S. Attorney, and the marshals themselves. I was told I wouldn't be allowed back in the courthouse without a subpoena to testify.

Great, Ant. Brilliant move.

I was standing in the late-day summer heat with my back to the glass-and-steel courthouse. I was looking out on downtown Denver. Cars were going past, as were bicycle messengers with enormous chain locks over their shoulders. The other pedestrians were dressed for summer and they all seemed to be smiling and laughing. I was trying to remember where I'd left the Pig. Or had I walked from Rebecca's loft? And where was Mungo? In the truck, in the loft, or tied to a pole somewhere?

Tom approached me then. He must have been waiting for me.

"What the hell was that?" Tom asked. "You're going to go for the guy in the middle of a federal courtroom? You want to make sure he doesn't forget about you and your family?"

My family, I thought. *Mom and Dad. Shit.*

"What did you think you were doing in there?" he demanded again when I didn't answer fast enough.

"I don't know. I just lost it," I tried to explain.

"Christ, Burns. Your timing sucks. You could have taken the guy out in Wyoming anytime you wanted. Stopped him for good. But no, you've got to wait until you're in a federal courthouse and he's surrounded by lawyers and marshals before making your move. It's a wonder you're still around, Quick-Draw. They should call you *SlowDraw*."

I didn't get mad. I was too tired. Too sick. And maybe I was getting used to Tom. Maybe this whole butthead show he put on was simply who he was.

"What did you think? How did it go?" I asked.

I only wanted his perspective because I didn't trust my own. And he was the only one who'd been there that I could ask, after pissing off Davadou, the Assistant U.S. Attorney.

He shrugged then smirked.

"A total whitewash. What'd you expect?"

"A whitewash? How?" *What was he talking about?*

"You think this is going to go to trial, QuickDraw? Don't be stupid. This was all a show for the press. Make it look like they're really going to nail the guy. But the charges are going to be quietly dismissed for lack of evidence or some such bullshit. Then they're going to announce they're sending him back to Mexico to face those supposed charges there, which will also be quietly dismissed. Or maybe just allowed to linger for years and years while everyone fills their pockets. Hidalgo owns the courts down there. Has for years. He wants to get extradited, you dumb-ass. So everyone will be happy. Everyone who isn't happy will have forgotten about it by then. And he won't be opening up his mouth about the people in the Mexican government who've been signing treaties with us."

"Bullshit."

Now he laughed.

"Wait and see, my friend. Wait and see."

THIRTY

Tubes, sensors, cords, and cables festooned my brother's wrecked body. He was plugged into at least a dozen bags and machines. Either the fluids that were pumping into him or the injuries themselves had bloated his face to such a degree that his features were unrecognizable beneath all the swelling and yellowed bruises. His cracked skull had been shaved, bolted, shunted, and bandaged with bloody gauze. There wasn't a trace of life in the half-opened eyes—the once spectacular irises were watery and faded. There was no brightness left. Nothing.

A particularly fat tube was rammed down his throat. It clicked and huffed as it shoved air into his chest. I followed the wires from his temples to a machine with a computer monitor and saw a flat line on the screen.

"He'll be all right once he wakes up," I heard a voice say. *"The outlook for a full recovery is quite good."*

This was my imagination, not a real doctor's words.

"He took quite a fall, and that gunshot wound to the abdomen didn't help. But he's young and strong. He'll be fine in a couple of weeks."

Reality intruded. I made myself face it and turn away from the fantasy I'd been working so hard to construct.

He won't be all right. Not when he wakes up. Not ever.

The catalog of injuries was enormous. The doctors and nurses I'd spoken to said they'd never seen anything like it. Nearly every bone in his body was broken. Three disks in his neck had exploded. There was a bullet hole through his stomach and one kidney. His skin had been almost entirely lacerated by the sharp edges of rock that had made climbing up so easy. He had a fractured skull, a burst spleen, and a burst appendix from landing on the roof of the pickup. Flailed chest, as well, the ribs having perforated the lungs. His legs and arms and hips were broken in every conceivable way. They estimated he'd lost two-thirds of his blood. Infection was already setting in.

If he wasn't already in a coma they would have induced one. He was hanging by a thread, they'd said, and that had almost made me smile. My brother the soloist always liked hanging by a lot less.

The worst wound—the one that made breathing for me an act of will and caused all the blood to rush into my head when I considered it—had been deliberate. Not that the bullet hole was not, or the injuries from tumbling down the shaft, or the impact of landing on the pickup. But this wound had been inflicted post-fall.

What was thought to be the dull blade of a machete had been dragged across his throat. Somehow the arteries had not been severed—either the muscles of his neck or perhaps the turquoise stone had protected the twin hoses there. His tongue had not been yanked through the gaping wound, either. They'd probably figured there was no point, since Roberto wasn't going to be dumped along a road somewhere to serve as an example. Even they wouldn't dare do that in the United States. So he'd just been dumped in that exploratory tunnel along with Bruto's corpse and left to die.

He'd been all but gone when Mungo found him. A Flight

For Life had helicoptered him to Denver, pumping fluids and oxygen, Roberto dangling by that proverbial thread.

I'd been allowed ten whole minutes this time. I stood next to the bed—there were no chairs here so that visitors wouldn't be tempted to hang around too long—and stared at him blankly. I couldn't seem to feel anything but the rush of blood to my head and the difficulty with breathing. I looked through blurry eyes. I didn't want to see. Or hear. Or feel.

I tried to again become that block of ice. I wanted to be academic, philosophical, to coldly assess the circumstances and outcomes instead of having my heart burn like a blowtorch in my chest and melt everything around it faster than I could freeze it.

I needed to sort through all my conflicting hopes and dreads. The hopes were few. Besides Hidalgo getting convicted and sentenced to a long prison sentence, then shanked sometime during his stay, I hoped Roberto would open his eyes and wake up for just a single minute. Just long enough for me to tell him that I was sorry. That I loved him.

Then I hoped that he would hurry up and die.

There would be no more climbing. No more shooting up. No more making love to confused women like Mary Chang who were drawn to him because he was the opposite of everything they'd wanted to believe in.

Just die, 'Berto. Spare yourself. Spare me. Don't make me pull the plug. I don't know if I have the balls to do that.

I was ashamed of that, of being so weak. And I was ashamed of a lot more.

I hadn't told my parents that their wayward firstborn was going to die.

I'd dialed the ranch, not sure what I was going to say or if I'd even be able to say it. The phone was answered by their cook, who finally recognized my gagging and throat-clearing, and managed to get the ranch manager on the line. He was a guy who had been running the ranch even in my grandfather's

time, long before my father was court-martialed out of the
United States Air Force and went into exile in my mother's
country. Bronco, we called the ranch manager, because even
though he usually wore a fancy suit, he would still break new
horses on the ranch. I suspected he'd broken a lot of people,
too, working for Grandpapa during the Dirty War.

My parents had taken mules—the four-legged kind—on a
camping trip, I was told. They weren't expected to return for a
week. Should he send someone after them? I told him no. I even
made myself sound a little like my dad, making it into a command. Did I have a message for them that would wait for their
return? Here I managed to deliver half of my message. I told him
that some guys Roberto had messed around with might come by
looking to cause trouble, but that it was unlikely they really
would. I was assured that if anyone was that foolish, Bronco and
the other cowboys on the ranch would set them straight.

I'd at least managed to deliver—or set in motion the delivery of—half the message. Guilt washed over me about the
other half. I couldn't convince myself that it would be better
for them not to see Roberto this way. Even though they'd
known something like this had been coming for a long time.
For years, in fact. But they wouldn't expect that *I* would be
the one to do it to him.

In a week I would call again. Or maybe I would simply
take my brother's body home.

I took a shaky, stuttering breath. My eyes were blurry
when I gazed one last time at the disfigured carcass on the
bed. Then I walked out of the room.

In the hallway Mary Chang lay on a yellow vinyl couch.
That was something else I was ashamed of. I'd come in only
three times over the last forty-eight hours, staying for only a
few minutes each visit—it was all I could bear. But she'd been
here, it seemed, the entire time.

"Protecting our star witness," she'd said.

But I knew different. She had another reason for being there. Guilt—the same as mine, but probably nowhere near as intense. And maybe also a sense of loss.

She was asleep. The nurses had covered her with a thin hospital sheet. In a chair across from her was a U.S. Marshal who looked a couple of decades beyond retirement age. He was Roberto's official protection—Mary was here on her own. The marshal was asleep, too, showing just how seriously the government was taking things.

I stood on the linoleum for a minute and watched her, forcing away the image of her and Roberto making love, all green and blurry in the starlight scope.

Mary opened her eyes, rubbed them, and sat up. I noticed that she was back to dressing in her professional clothes—a severe skirt and blouse. The last time I'd seen her here, she'd still been wearing her khaki shorts and a pullover sweatshirt. Her legs and hair had been dusty with dirt from the mine.

"Hey," she said.

"Hey yourself."

"You look good in a suit. Not so much like a dirtbag rock jock."

"Thanks," I said. "I think."

"How's Roberto looking?"

"Like shit."

She smiled, as if I'd made a joke.

"I always thought he was too handsome. The hair, the eyes, the body. It was too much, you know?"

I didn't say anything but made myself smile back. She didn't sound anything like the uptight Fed I'd met in Salt Lake. *Could that really have been less than two weeks ago?*

"I heard you caused a disturbance at the arraignment this afternoon."

"It wasn't much of a disturbance."

"Tom called and said that you went for Hidalgo. And that

you really freaked everyone out even before that, staring at him the whole time. The lawyer, Horton, has asked the judge to exclude you from the courtroom, unless you're giving testimony. And the marshals have seconded it. Even Davadou, the A.U.S.A., agreed."

"I know."

I sat down where her legs had been on the short couch. I leaned back until my head thumped on the wall and then I closed my eyes.

"Sorry," I said. "Going there was a mistake. Davadou has enough to worry about."

"More than you think, Anton. Everyone's a little worried about this case. A lot—maybe all—of the evidence could be suppressed due to the illegal entry. I've heard the DOJ already has some PR flacks looking into who's going to get the blame. And the State Department's screaming for us to kick him loose. They're afraid if he's convicted, Hidalgo will talk about all the people in Mexico City who are on his regular payroll. People will start to wonder why Congress keeps certifying what's essentially a narcocracy."

"Money," I said dully. "Trade."

"The corporations that make the big campaign contributions rely on Mexico for cheap labor and to buy our products—"

I cut her off.

"I know, Mary. You've told me."

"Okay. But you really shouldn't have gone for Hidalgo. He's already got you in his sights, Anton. Your parents probably, too. That's the way he works. That's why he is so successful. Have you warned them?"

I nodded, banging my aching head on the wall.

"There's a lot of his people still in Mexico and the States other than those we arrested two days ago. He's got soldiers everywhere. There's a chance some of them might remain loyal. I hope you're watching your back, too."

I hadn't been. I hadn't been watching anything at all.

"Do you still have a job?" I asked.

She laughed. It was sad and short.

"For the time being. With Hidalgo in custody, they can't fire us. Not, anyway, until the case is resolved one way or another. The only thing that's certain is that we aren't going to be getting any promotions. No one's saying I'm going to be the youngest Special Agent in Charge in a major city anymore. Right now Tom and I are pariahs. You know what that's like, don't you?"

I felt another sad smile directed my way but I couldn't open my eyes or force my mouth to return it.

Things really couldn't have been worse. Or maybe they could.

It was night already, but when I got off the elevator on her floor I knew that Rebecca wouldn't be home for hours. She often worked late, trying to meet a deadline. Right then, though, I suspected she didn't have a deadline. I was pretty sure she was avoiding me.

Two days earlier, she'd met me at the hospital in the middle of the night. The Flight For Life wouldn't take me on board, so I'd red-lined my shuddering old truck four hundred miles to the south and east. Rebecca got there long before I did, and was the first "family" to see Roberto when he was brought in. It hadn't been a good look, but it had been more than enough.

Rebecca had been sympathetic. She'd said all the right things. She even trembled and cried in my arms when I told her what happened to my brother, whom she'd never liked. But there was a coldness lurking beneath the compassion. A hard anger. I'd done what I'd promised her I would never do again. I'd taken chances and risked costs that were greater than I could pay. Uncharitably, I could almost hear the thoughts that must have been going through her head. *What kind of husband will he make? What kind of father? If he's taken those kinds of chances with himself, with the brother he's always worshiped, what kinds of chances will he take with his child?*

And I didn't cry with her. I don't know why. I tried but I couldn't. Even when she held me and she let her own tears run over my chest. I had the feeling she wasn't just crying for Roberto. She was crying for me. She was crying for us.

Later, the next night, she'd wanted to know why I hadn't cried with her. When I didn't answer, she took my face in her hands. She stared up at me from inches away with brown eyes that up close had all those flecks of color, and said, "I'll be here when you want me, Ant. Whenever you're ready to stop acting like a zombie. Let me know and I'll be here."

Then she'd gone back to work.

Now, as I put my key into the door, I was surprised to get the feeling that someone was on the other side. Not Rebecca. Not just Mungo—who I'd finally figured out I'd left in the loft. Someone else.

It was in the air. I sniffed it, the way Mungo would. What I smelled was a cheap cigar odor invading the hallway. I touched my hip for the butt of my gun, but of course it wasn't there. It was in an evidence locker somewhere. Crouching, I took the spare out of the ankle holster. The little Beretta .22 was ridiculous, but so was what I was doing. I realized it as soon as I palmed the little gun and stood. I knew that smell. I knew those cheap cigars.

Gun still in hand, I turned the key and pushed hard.

It slammed against a bumper on the inside wall. I stopped the rebound with a foot while pointing the little gun in a ready position at the floor.

"QuickDraw!" Ross McGee said from the couch that faced the door. He was wide-eyed, and his cigar was arcing in the air just over his head.

I moved fast, pinching the wet cigar off the hardwood floor just seconds after it bounced, spewing ash and burning embers. I pinched those up, too, and ran for the sink.

"What the hell are you trying to do to me? Make me an old man before my time?"

My fingertips were too calloused to blister, but the same wasn't true for the floor. I scrubbed at it with a sponge while ignoring my boss.

Mungo came out from the bedroom, where she'd been hiding from either the man or the stench. She was peering around the corner of the doorjamb. Her yellow eyes were narrow, her ears laid back, and her lips pulled up in what was something more than her usual nervous smile. Her expression wasn't entirely McGee's fault. I'd been neglecting her lately.

"Rebecca's going to be thrilled that you've been smoking in here," I told my boss.

"I cracked a window. Besides, I'm her godfather."

"You don't need to always be rubbing that in my face."

I tossed the keys on a shelf. Mungo came creeping toward me, hugging the wall and staying as far away from McGee as possible. Right then I'd have liked to do the same. I'd have liked to turn around and run.

"I hope you didn't let him steal anything," I said as I patted the wolf's head.

"Ha. You've already stolen the only thing I ever valued. And now you're trying to steal my job, too."

"What do you mean?"

"The suits, boy. The suits." He meant the administration and the politicians who ran the office. "They're getting some heat from our federal friends. They don't like the fact that I sent the state-patrol SWAT in without seeking approval from higher-ups."

"Tell them to blame me."

"I did, but they won't listen. It was on my order."

I knew he was lying about the first part. McGee always took the heat when his agents, as he colorfully termed it, "screwed the pooch." It was some philosophical leftover from his prior career in the army. He believed that he was responsible for the men under his command, and that they were responsible to him. The suits didn't mind this bizarre philosophy because they were more than happy to blame McGee. That was fun for them. They would have loved to fire him. The only problem was that after twenty years at the Wyoming Attorney General's Office, he had too much dirt on everyone. The drunk-driving arrests; the legislators' kids who'd been caught with mushrooms or X, then had their charges quietly dismissed; the hundred other petty scandals. They couldn't fire him, but they did everything they could to try and get him to quit.

"Is it big trouble?" I asked.

"Nothing I can't handle. Don't worry about it."

That first part, too, was probably a lie, judging from the way he looked away. But I didn't pursue it. I'd never heard him tell me not to worry about something, either. I guessed it was his way of offering his condolences. It made my throat swell a little.

"How'd you get in here, anyway?" I asked.

"As Rebecca's godfather, I take my responsibilities very seriously. I like to stop by unannounced and see what kind of lowlifes she's shacking up with."

"Just me, I hope."

"Only the latest and lowest in a *very* long list."

The evil gleam was back in his eyes. I was glad to see it. For a moment there I could feel myself beginning to thaw.

I got myself a cold glass of water. I held it to my cheek for a minute before draining it. McGee ordered me to crack open a bottle of Glenmorangie that Rebecca kept for him. I gave him the drink and the bottle and then slumped in the chair opposite him.

Leaning forward, he filled my water glass with the Scotch. I drank some and made a face.

"Where you been today, boy?"

"Here and there."

"I heard you riled them up at the courthouse."

It was only three hours earlier, but everyone seemed to know already.

"I just looked at the guy, Ross."

"You went for him. Don't deny it."

His beady, wet eyes were piercing. He did this to me sometimes. Opened up my head and heart and seemed to delve around in there.

"Where did you hear about it?" I asked.

"Sweet Rebecca. She learned about it right after the event. From another reporter who was there, hoping there would be fireworks for tomorrow's paper. Wasn't disappointed, I gather. Rebecca called me then. Thought I should drive down and have a little talk with you."

"There's nothing to talk about. I made a mistake, going there. I won't do it again until I'm called to testify at the prelim."

McGee nodded. "You'd better not. I heard about it from the A.U.S.A. A guy named Davadou. He wants you warned off. Officially."

"Okay. I'm warned. Now, do you mind taking off? Rebecca probably won't be home for a few hours and I want some peace."

McGee chuckled grimly.

"You're warned off unofficially, too, QuickDraw."

He held up a thin white envelope. The upper edge was ragged where it had been opened. I could see my name on the outside, along with Rebecca's address. Who but McGee knew I stayed at Rebecca's address when I was in Denver? There was no stamp. It had been hand-delivered.

He waved the letter in front of me, impatient for me to

take it. I could make out one of the names where the return address was printed. Horton, and a bunch of other lawyer-sounding surnames.

I took it.

"Mr. Burns": it said under the law firm's letterhead. "You are hereby notified that you will desist in any further attempts to contact, in person or by proxy, our client, Jesús Hidalgo-Paez, or any of his personal or business associates. A restraining order is being sought at this time. Any further attempts on your part will result in criminal prosecution."

Bullshit, I was thinking. *I'm a cop. They can't stop me from talking to whoever I want.*

But I knew that they could. And how would it look in court when the defense attorney asked me, *Isn't it true, Agent Burns, that Mr. Hidalgo had a restraining order issued against you?* And when I tried to explain, *Just answer yes or no, Agent Burns.* The jury would see it as a vendetta by a disgruntled cop. By a disgruntled cop with a history that's more than a little tarnished. That was obviously a part of the defense's plan.

I read on:

"Attached to this notice is a brief note our client insisted on you receiving. This communication is intended by our client and this firm to be the FINAL communication between yourself and Mr. Jesús Hidalgo-Paez."

The letter was signed by Jeremy Horton. The cc: list included all the other attorneys on Hidalgo's defense team. I could imagine how they all chuckled when contemplating writing it, how clever and lucky they were. And how pissed Horton must have then been when Hidalgo insisted he attach the note.

There was a paper clip attached to the page. On the other side was a small note that was written in Spanish, in a barely legible hand.

Greetings, Antonio Burns. I was profoundly saddened to hear what happened to your brother. He was a very good friend to me. Climbing is a dangerous hobby, no? He always described it as "feeding the Rat." I can only hope that his Rat is now well-satisfied. Please convey my condolences to your mother, Maria, and your father, Leonard, on their Patagonian ranch, as well as to your fiancée, Rebecca Hersh, who I understand lives at this address here in Denver. Yours truly, Jesús Hidalgo-Paez.

Below it was a tiny, simple picture. It was like the sticker I'd seen on some of the *sicarios*' and bangers' cars, where it had been placed like a little inside joke. It was a simple circle. Two dots for eyes. And, where the smile on the smiley face belonged, a wagging tongue instead.

I thought I'd been scared over the last couple of days. Almost paralyzed by the fear of what would happen to Roberto—the worst being that he would live—and terrified out of my mind that Hidalgo would walk. That justice would fail.

But the letter made a new kind of fear rise up in my stomach. One that felt to me like it does when I take a huge, whipping fall off the rock when everything's out of your hands. The kind of fear that comes with a little bit of thrill. The kind of fear that I'd spent years seeking out. I was no longer cold and willing myself to become an ice cube. I was starting to get hot.

McGee was talking.

"It came by messenger. About twenty minutes ago. Not too smart of Mr. Hidalgo. Horton—that prick—must have had a fit. Davadou can try to get it admitted as evidence. Or there might be an iffy case for witness intimidation."

I shook my head.

"It's too vague. It won't get anywhere."

McGee talked some more, arguing that he was the lawyer, not me, but I didn't really listen. I was too caught up in the strange pleasure of this chilly new me.

Why hadn't I ever considered Rebecca's safety? The thought

had never even crossed my mind. We weren't married yet, we didn't share a surname, we didn't even share a home. Our relationship was more or less a secret. I should have thought about it, but maybe it was just so monstrous a threat that I hadn't allowed it to enter my consciousness. Maybe I'd blocked it out. Another question I asked myself was *How the fuck had Jesús Hidalgo learned about her?* He was powerful, but he couldn't have those kinds of resources. Most of his men couldn't even speak English. But I knew the answer. Horton, the lawyer. He was a celebrity in Denver. He would know people at the *Post*. People who he'd backslap and slip a little juicy gossip. They'd return the favor. Even though Hidalgo had only become his client in the last forty-eight hours, it would have been high on the defense attorney's To Do list to make a few calls about the principal witnesses against his client.

I could almost imagine the conversation he would have had with some editor at the *Post:*

"Do you have anything on a Wyoming cop named Antonio Burns?"

"You don't know who he is?"

"Sounds kind of familiar."

"He's the guy they call QuickDraw. The one who shot those three gangbangers in Cheyenne two years ago?"

Horton, getting excited, would have said, *"You're kidding! This is great. Can you send me everything the* Post *has on him?"*

"I'll even give you something extra. You won't believe it, but he's knocked up one of the reporters here. Pretty girl, named Rebecca Hersh. She did a soft story on him after that bloodbath in Cheyenne. . . ."

"You listening?" McGee demanded, looking at me through narrowed eyes. *"I asked you if there is anything I can do."*

"Yeah. Stay here."

He grinned, showing me his big yellow teeth.

"Never thought I'd hear you say that, QuickDraw."

"Are you armed?"

"What male from the great state of Wyoming's not?"

He flipped open his jacket—scattering ash—and showed me his old service .45.

"Stay here. Take Rebecca to and from her work. Go everywhere with her. She might not let me."

She might not want me.

"Dream come true," he said with a wink, reading my thoughts. "I'll stick to her like glue. Now, is there anything else you want me to do?"

"Just tell me he's not going to get away with it."

The wink and the leer faded.

"He's probably not. But you never know, QuickDraw. Maximum he can get for just cooking the drugs is twenty years. That is, if the Feds manage to convict him."

He left unsaid that the only way it might be more time was if Roberto died. Then Hidalgo could be sentenced to life under the subsection that allows for enhanced penalties where a death occurs.

"But then again, I hate to say it, he may walk on it. There's all sorts of suppression issues relating to the raid."

I let out a little of the chill.

"It's so fucked up, Ross. He's been transporting drugs for years. Everybody knows it. Now he's caught cooking crank in Wyoming. And he had slaves doing the cooking. And he did what he did to my brother and to who knows how many others. He should have the same done to him. Whatever happened to justice?"

"Ah, QuickDraw, QuickDraw. You're my perpetual virgin," McGee said. "You'd think that after working with me for almost a decade, you would have gotten your cherry popped by now."

But I wasn't a naive virgin. Not anymore. That was the problem.

EXTRADITION SOUGHT FOR ALLEGED DRUG LORD ARRESTED IN U.S.

DENVER, Co., August 27—Charges against alleged Mexican drug kingpin Jesús Hidalgo-Paez have been dismissed by federal prosecutors in the U.S. for lack of evidence, but warrants for his arrest have been issued in Mexico. Mr. Hidalgo-Paez continues to be held in American custody pending an extradition hearing today that he is not expected to contest.

During a dramatic raid last week in which four Mexican nationals were killed, officers of the Wyoming State Police and Wyoming Attorney General's Office arrested a total of 23 men on a remote mountain ranch. Seventeen of those arrested were subsequently charged with crimes ranging from conspiracy to distribute narcotics to possession of illegal weapons. One police officer suffered a minor gunshot wound while making the arrests. Another man was critically injured.

Mr. Hidalgo-Paez is said to have strong ties with key officials in Mexico's government and with that country's largest political party. Yet some American authorities believe he also heads one of Mexico's most violent drug-smuggling cartels. Court documents filed in Denver allege that a methamphetamine "superlab" was discovered in an abandoned mine on the Wyoming property where last week's arrests took place.

In a surprising move yesterday, Assistant U.S. Attorney Michael C. Davadou dismissed the charges against Mr. Hidalgo-Paez. "The Mexican courts have far greater charges and far superior evidence," Mr. Davadou told reporters in an afternoon press conference.

He went on to say, "Unfortunately, some Wyoming police officers jumped the gun here. They went onto that property without a proper warrant or any judicial authority. The evidence discovered, I've determined, is likely to be ruled inadmissible as the fruit of the poisonous tree. The government is duty-bound not to pursue charges they don't believe they can prove in court."

In the United States, before police may enter a suspect's property, they must have either the consent of the landowner or a search warrant based upon probable cause. "Fruit of the poisonous tree" refers to evidence that is discovered pursuant to a faulty warrant. Such evidence is generally deemed inadmissible at trial by American courts.

Mr. Davadou had some harsh words for the Wyoming authorities who conducted the raid. "Their intentions were good, but their manner and method were without justification. They jumped the gun, is what they did, and they should have known better. Even more unfortunately, they ruined a federal investigation that was under way. If it had been allowed to proceed, I believe we would have a solid case against Mr. Hidalgo."

An official spokesperson contacted at the Wyoming Attorney General's Office seemed caught off guard by Mr. Davadou's accusations. The spokesperson declined to make a comment other than to say, "He said that? I thought the FBI asked for our assistance."

At a hearing in federal court today, it will be determined whether Mr. Hidalgo-Paez will be transferred to Mexico to face charges there. That country only rarely seeks the extradition of its nationals, and generally refuses to cooperate with U.S. authorities seeking extradition of those captured in Mexico who are charged with narcotics crimes that could carry a life sentence. A source in the U.S. Department of Justice indicated that in this instance it is expected that there will be "full cooperation between the two nations."

THIRTY-ONE

The article in the *Denver Post* four days later hit me like a punch on the chin. I literally saw stars. Nobody had told me it was coming. Not Mary, not Tom, not McGee. Not even Rebecca, who worked at the paper and who had had to know the blow was being thrown.

I read it at a Starbucks around the corner from Rebecca's loft. Mungo and I were sitting on the patio, where Mungo was receiving both tentative pats and dirty looks from the other patrons. I'd had a thermos filled that I intended to take to the hospital. I expected to find Mary still hovering there, and I thought she seemed like the kind of woman who'd appreciate a little Starbucks instead of coffee out of a vending machine.

After I read the article, I just sat and stared. It finally sank in. Not that the Mexican charges were probably bullshit, and not even that it was likely Hidalgo would walk. What sank in was how I'd been used. How Roberto and I had been used.

A blowtorch fired up in my chest. It felt more like a flamethrower. It seemed that simply by looking around the café, I could set everyone and everything aflame.

I tried to cool down when I dropped Mungo off at the loft, which was empty. McGee had taken to spending the mornings at the *Post* building with Rebecca. According to her, he would by turns harass and charm all the women there, from the senior editors to the editorial assistants. The men he ignored, of course.

Be cool, be cool, I told myself as I threw on a suit while feeling a sucker's humiliated fury. I was glad McGee was out. I was too hot for conversation with him. I didn't want him trying to talk me out of doing anything dumb, or saying anything stupid. I was smart enough, though, to leave the little Beretta in a drawer.

I half walked and half ran to the courthouse.

The security there didn't like something about the way I looked—maybe it was something in my eyes, or something in the set of my face. More likely it was the heat I could feel radiating off me. I strained for composure—I didn't want them asking then checking my name. I was afraid that maybe my name and picture were posted somewhere near the screen on their X-ray machine. *Antonio Burns, No. 1 Most Wanted for Stupidity. Believed Armed and Dangerous,* I imagined it saying. I wasn't armed, but I sure as hell felt dangerous. As dangerous as they'd once believed I was.

The security guards let me through after some suspicious looks and a pat-down with an electric wand.

The daily docket posted by the elevator showed an extradition hearing for Jesús Hidalgo-Paez, *mi amigo,* El Doctor, in Courtroom 6B. A different judge—this one an immigration magistrate—was presiding. The hearing was scheduled for 10:00 A.M., which was a half hour earlier. That didn't worry me. I knew that these sorts of hearings ran late, especially when they required the attendance of Hidalgo's half-dozen lawyers, not to mention the press.

I thought I'd made it until I got off the elevator and stepped into the glass, marble, and steel corridor. Two marshals were standing outside Courtroom 6B, looking my way.

When they saw me they started coming down the hallway toward me.

I stood smoldering by the bank of elevators. I didn't know whether to run or fight. The impulse was to fight. To what purpose, I couldn't say.

One of the elevators behind me chimed. The marshals were twenty or thirty feet away and walking slowly, cautiously, as if I were Mungo, a wolf loose in the corridors of the Alfred A. Arraj Federal Courthouse.

"Anton?"

I looked over my shoulder.

Mary and Tom were getting off the elevator. *They* were the people I'd come to see. Not Davadou, the flunky A.U.S.A. bullshitter. Not even Hidalgo.

"What are you doing here?" Tom demanded. "You're prohibited from entering the courthouse without a subpoena, Burns."

Tom was in a crisp blue suit, his reddish hair moussed and blow-dried. Mary had cleaned up, too. She wore a skirt, blouse, and jacket, all in different shades of tan. Both of them looked as purposeful and serious as any archetypal federal agent.

But Mary's uncertain smile betrayed her as something else. Something more human, but less scrupulous.

"You set me up," I said.

Then someone grabbed my arm and turned me around. It was one of the two marshals who'd been coming down the hall. Both of them were bland-faced and mustached. And they were very careful. One was holding my arm while the other stood two steps back, his hand on the butt of his holstered weapon.

"Sir, are you Antonio Burns?" the one holding my arm asked.

The urge to fight was almost overwhelming. *But to what purpose?*

I jerked my arm out of his grasp. He jumped back a step, alarmed. Then I stopped, stood very still, and nodded.

"Sir, there's a court order in effect that restricts you from entering this building."

Mary said, "It's okay. We'll see him out."

"No, ma'am. I'm afraid we'll need to take him into custody until we can go and see the judge."

"The order only prevents him from entering the same courtroom as Mr. Hidalgo. He hasn't done that, has he?"

The guard frowned. He probably thought she was a lawyer, and he probably felt the same way about lawyers that I did.

"Who are you, ma'am?"

Mary took a badge wallet out of her small white purse and showed him her credentials. To a marshal, the same as to a state cop, being an FBI agent wasn't much better than being a lawyer. Mary was both. The whole time one marshal studied them, the other's eyes didn't leave my hands. He was probably wondering if I'd somehow slipped a weapon past security. I was tempted to slap my thigh and shout "Boo!"

Mary got her credentials back. Without another word, the marshals reluctantly withdrew down the hallway—looking over their shoulders every two steps—and took up positions outside Courtroom 6B.

"You set me up," I said again, facing Mary and Tom.

Mary frowned at me. Tom smirked.

"What are you talking about?" he demanded.

"You set *us* up," I said. "Me and Roberto. You knew this would happen all along."

Mary's narrow eyes slid off my face. She glanced at Tom, looked at me again, and her gaze dropped to my shoes.

"This isn't the time or the place, Anton," she said.

"I don't know what the hell you're talking about," Tom said. But he obviously did.

"We didn't know this would happen, Anton," Mary added quietly, looking up then down again.

"You knew it was a possibility."

"Yes," Mary admitted. "Not what happened to Roberto, but we knew that extradition was a possibility."

A trigger was pulled. A steady stream of fire came pouring out of me. I felt myself smiling, the way I did when I was really mad.

"No. You did more than that. You planned it all. Everything. Possibilities and likelihoods and everything. You mapped it all out. You made your calculations."

Both of them were silent. I kept spewing flame.

"You got your friend—that junior agent, Damon Walker—you got him killed when you pushed him too deep too fast. And that made you guilty and mad. You already knew about Roberto. Even in San Diego you would have been in on that, trying to arrest the Colorado fugitive last fall before he took a plane out of LAX. And you would have known that he'd once been involved with Hidalgo. So after Walker was killed, you remembered Roberto again, and found out that he was in South America. And you got an idea."

"So what?" Tom said.

Mary's eyes remained on the floor.

"You read those files. About him, first, then about me. You knew Roberto was a killer. You thought I was a killer, too. And you knew we were close."

"We were desperate," Mary said in a very soft voice. "They were shutting us down. No one was doing anything—"

I rode over her.

"You believed everything you read, didn't you? *Quick-Draw,* and all that. Then you set this up. You didn't think you could lose. Hopefully Roberto would just kill Hidalgo. Execute him. You did your best to brainwash him with all the bad things Hidalgo had done over the years. Or maybe Hidalgo would whack Roberto. It didn't really matter, because if that happened, you thought from reading about me, then I'd be sure to go in and kill Hidalgo. *QuickDraw,* you thought. *He's done it before, he'll do it again. Especially for family.* Tom even pushed me to do it—that night we went in to leave the note for Roberto. If none of those things happened, you figured we'd at least get enough evidence on Hidalgo to arrest him, and then either the Department of Justice would roll the dice on a trial and make you guys heroes, or they'd send him back to Mexico. If he went back to Mexico, the court documents would show that there'd been an informant, and it wouldn't be hard for Hidalgo to figure out who that was. Then Roberto or I would still have to kill him or else he'd be coming after us and our family. *La corbata,* remember? We'd take all the risks. And one way or another, you'd get what you wanted: Hidalgo preferably dead, or at least in prison."

"We were risking everything, too," Mary said very, very quietly.

"Like hell you were. You were risking nothing. Maybe your careers, but you both can go get jobs with a security firm that will pay twice what you're making now. Spend your days hanging out with CEOs and foreign dignitaries."

"We didn't know it would turn out like this. . . . After what happened to Damon—"

"You hoped it would, Mary. You hoped it would."

"No. I didn't know Roberto would . . ." But she didn't say anything more.

Mary Chang, former rising star within the Bureau's ranks, was starting to cry. Not snuffling and sobbing, the way I'd been doing occasionally over the last few days, but grimly. Tears rolling down over her cheekbones.

"What I don't understand is, if you wanted him dead this

bad, why didn't you just do it yourselves? Tom could've gotten up into the notch with a sniper rifle and taken him out by the pool."

Neither one of them answered my question. But the answer was plain to me. They were too chickenshit. They wanted somebody to do it for them. They thought they had the perfect guys for the job.

"You're all worked up, man," Tom said, mock-soothingly. "You need to take a vacation or something. Do what you Wyoming guys do on vacations. Go hunting, right? I hear there's some good hunting down south."

THIRTY-TWO

That night Rebecca worked late. Not at the *Post,* but in the small second bedroom, which she'd made into an office. Her topic—the toxic chemicals the Shattuck Chemical Company had left behind when they shut down their Denver operations—was one she was worked up about. She'd talked about nothing else through dinner. I suspected, though, that her sudden chattiness had been at least partially intentional.

In the next room McGee snored on the ash-strewn couch. There are few things less pleasant than sharing a house with your obese, drunken, emphysemic, and taciturn boss. But this night I could name one of them: burning yourself up at a rate you know you can't possibly sustain. But you know you have to.

"How was Roberto?" Rebecca whispered when she came into the bedroom.

I was lying in bed and staring out the window at the lights of Denver. It was after ten. I'd been there alone in the dark for an hour. Even with the balcony window all the way open, the downtown traffic noise and the drunken college boys' shouts were doing little to smother the sound of McGee in the other room.

"Same," I said. "They don't really expect any change."

I'd gone straight to bed without interrupting her when I got home from the hospital. What I'd said about no change being expected wasn't entirely true—the doctors were contemplating trying to remove the debris of some of the exploding disks in his spine. I just couldn't bring myself to talk about it.

"Well, that's better than worse, Ant."

What she meant by *worse* could only mean dead. I would have considered it a great improvement. But when I'd seen Roberto, he was still hanging by that same proverbial thread. And I still didn't have the balls to cut it.

Her sandals clacked on the floor as she kicked them off. I heard the hiss of silk as she slid out of her skirt. Then silence as she worked the buttons on her blouse. I turned over so I could watch her. She was down to a bra and panties.

"What do you think you're looking at?"

Her whisper was suddenly a little more throaty.

I didn't answer. Instead I wondered about the question. I wondered why she turned me on so much. It wasn't just how she looked and talked or how smart she was. Or even how she made love—taking as much pleasure from giving it as from receiving. And it wasn't that she, the city girl, was so different from all the other girls I'd known. All those climbers and kayakers and mountain bikers and trail runners and skiers and backpackers and windsurfers, all the tan, lanky, outdoorsy girls with their skinned shins and elbows. I'd lost interest in them sooner or later because they shared all the same thrills with me. But Rebecca was exotic. She kept me off balance. One minute she wants to marry me, the next she decides I'm inappropriate material for a husband/father. And the minute after that she wants to jump my bones.

"Well, what are you looking at?" she asked again.

The throatiness was still in her voice. It was a tone I'd always liked, but it didn't sound genuine right now.

She was taking a clip out of her long hair, then shaking her hair out with her fingers. Looking deliberately seductive.

Again I didn't answer. Instead I lunged for her. And in the process I pulled the sheets and the mattress cover half onto the floor.

She was quick, but I was quicker. *QuickDraw*. I got ahold of her wrist just as she tried to jump away. I dragged her back into the bed. She didn't fight. Not much, anyway. I caught the knee that was aimed—with only a little bit of malice—between my thighs at the last moment. There were a few minutes of grunts and grips and bites and kisses before I got her out of the bra and underwear. She didn't stop fighting entirely until she was mounted over me, her hair forming a screen around my head, and tipping one pointed nipple and then the other into my mouth.

Everything was so right for a little while. But I couldn't completely forget that everything was so *fucking wrong*.

It wasn't until later, when she was breathing hard like a rider who'd just taken a horse over the hurdles, and I was blowing like the horse, that we spoke again.

"You're coming back to me," she said.

"We'll know in a few minutes."

She tapped my forehead with hers.

"You know what I mean."

"It's going to be all right," I said. I didn't believe it, but it was easy to say.

"I'm glad. Let me know what I can do to help."

"What you just did. In about ten more minutes. Then every night for the next fifty years."

She laughed. Like the seductive voice she'd put on earlier, it sounded artificial to me. And I think she knew it. The passion fled and I felt the sadness coming back over me. We didn't say anything for a while. We just continued to inhale each other's breath. It had been a long time since we'd last discussed getting married and taking the step of setting a date. I knew that now was not the time to bring it up. She may have just jumped my bones, but I sensed that she was less sure than ever that she should marry me. And I couldn't blame her.

"Did anything happen today?" she asked obliquely.

She never mentioned Hidalgo's name. I knew, though, that she'd looked him up in the paper's archives. And I knew that he scared her or else she wouldn't be putting up with McGee and me infringing on her freedom.

"You mean besides your coming in here to seduce me so I'd feel better? Yeah. Hidalgo got himself extradited. He's going back to Mexico."

"Good. I imagine he belongs in a Mexican jail."

I didn't say where I thought he belonged.

Instead I said, "Do you know what Mexican jails are like? It's only uncomfortable for the poor. If you've got money, they're like fine hotels. You can have whatever you want. A DVD, a personal chef, a water bed, telephones, a computer, AC, whatever. With money, you can even be 'paroled' to go to soccer games or discos. They even have conjugal rights as often as you like. Or at least as often as you can pay for them."

"If you ever go to jail then, Anton, make sure it's in Mexico." She failed to add that it was so she could come see me.

I chuckled at her stunted joke. But what I was thinking was that such a thing might not be all that unlikely.

"Not that Hidalgo will ever see the inside of a jail," I went on. "According to those FBI agents I was working with, he'll be bailed out the moment he steps off the plane, or he'll be granted house arrest on his *estancia* in Baja."

Mary and Tom had also told me that the Mexican charges would likely remain pending against him, but his friends on the Mexican courts would see to it that the case never went to trial. They'd leave the charges hanging out there just to keep the United States government from looking foolish.

"With him out of the country, does McGee still need to stay here?" Rebecca asked. McGee wasn't snoring anymore from the other room. I wondered if we'd woken him up. "He's a sweet old guy, and I love him, but he's making me crazy. Following me around everywhere with his gun, showing it off, and behaving like the dirty old man he is with every woman in the office."

"For a little while," I said. "Please."

We were quiet again. Our breathing slowed. She remained crouched over me and I had a mouthful of her hair. Down on the street someone was yelling about the Rockies. I assumed they meant the baseball team, not the mountains.

"You know I'd do anything for you, Ant."

I waited for the *but*. It came, but gentler than I expected.

"But I can't go on for very long like this. You're so morose—and that's okay—but if you want to try to make this work, you've got to share with me. Tell me what you're thinking and feeling."

What I was feeling, even with her lithe weight on top of me, and with me still inside her, was grief and fear and hate and rage. I wasn't going to share that. Not only to protect her from it, but because it was mine.

"Give me a few days. Maybe I should get out of here for a little while. Get my head back on straight."

"I think that's a good idea."

I had the feeling that she was telling off the father of her child in the gentlest way she could. We'd hit a brick wall.

Rebecca was a sound sleeper. With all the noise in downtown Denver, to live where she did you've got to be. When I was sure she was deep into her dreams—whether or not they included me—I got up out of the bed and put on my clothes.

"You're really a sick bastard, Burns," McGee growled from the couch. "To do that to a man's goddaughter while he's in the other room."

"I'm a lot sicker than you think, Ross."

"I doubt it. Where do you think you're going?"

"Out for a little bit, Mom. I'll be back."

I hadn't told either one of them about how the Feds had used Roberto and me. How they were still using us. McGee had had some lurking doubts about me since that night in Cheyenne two and a half years ago. Even though he'd protected me afterward, he'd never been entirely convinced what I'd done was kosher. Why reinforce those doubts? Why give him the chance to stop me?

Mungo got up out of her giant beanbag bed and tried to come with me. I didn't blame her. Sleeping in the same apartment as McGee was bad enough—being in the same room must have been excruciating for her. She stood in front of the door to the hallway, blocking it. I pushed her away but she just squirmed right back.

"Stay, damn it. I'll be back, Mungo. I'll be back."

When I opened the door a crack she rammed her nose into the space. I let her worm out into the hall. Then, feeling like a treacherous jerk, I grabbed her tail then her collar and shoved her back inside. I tried to ignore the devastated grin she gave me as I shut the door.

Down in the garage, I intended to switch Rebecca's plates with the Pig's. I thought Wyoming plates would be automatically suspicious where I was going. Besides, her little two-seater Porsche would look better with Wyoming plates. Kind of like a toy poodle with a spiked collar. But once in the garage, I had a better idea.

There was a Hummer parked diagonally across three

spaces in a garage where even a single slot was in high demand. The Hummer had three strikes against it. One was simply that it was an obnoxious car. Two was that it was taking up too much space. And three was that it carried California plates, and there were already far too many Californians coming to the mountain states.

I took off the license plates with a screwdriver. While I was unscrewing them, I noticed that the bumper was entirely free of scratches. The car had never been driven off-road, and probably never would be. I also noticed the green bumper sticker that said, "Doing My Part to Change the Environment . . . Ask Me How!" After getting giddy on too much wine one night, Rebecca had ordered a hundred of them over the Internet. I had to laugh. She must have been putting them to good use. The one she'd put on the Pig had taken me a half hour to scrape off.

Then, all alone, I started driving south.

4

Fate has written a tragedy; its name is
"The Human Heart."
The theatre is the House of Life, Woman the
mummer's part:
The Devil enters the prompter's box and the
play is ready to start.

—*"The Harpy"*
Robert Service

THIRTY-THREE

I crossed the border at Mexicali after putting on my stolen California plates. The drive over the mountains and then across the desert had taken all night and half the next day. A little more, actually, because I had to make a pit stop in Arizona to buy a shotgun.

The one I chose was a new Mossberg Compact. It was solid black, with only a foot and a half of barrel. A fraction of an inch longer, I was told by the salesclerk, than the legal limit for shotguns. Anything shorter and it would have fallen into the illegal sawed-off category. The gun had a pistol grip instead of a standard shoulder stock. It held eight rounds. According to the instruction manual, it was for "home-protection purposes." That description suited me.

I bought a box of 12-gauge birdshot shells at the same sporting-goods store where I bought the gun. An hour later I fired them all off on some BLM land that was already littered with brass and bullet-scarred beer cans. The gun worked well. The cans simply disappeared when I pointed the gun at them from a few feet away. It was like they had never existed. The explosions that occurred each time I pulled the trigger seemed to tear jagged holes out of the world that I thought I knew.

In the next town I parked to the side of a gas station that advertised "Ammo." I put on my crumpled cowboy hat and paid cash for a different brand and a different type of shell. This time I bought buckshot—shells filled with chunks of lead that are capable of knocking down large mammals.

Unlike rifles or pistols, shotguns don't leave much in the way of forensic evidence for later identification. There is no way to "fingerprint" what comes out of the barrel. But the pellets, if recovered and matched to a manufacturer and then the buyer, can make for a sort of loose, circumstantial link to the person who might have done the shooting. That was the reason for my caution.

It was also the reason I'd left my little Beretta in Rebecca's loft. It was too small to do the kind of damage I was planning to do, and its rifling marks were registered—as are all its employee's guns—with Wyoming's Division of Criminal Investigation.

If anyone actually bothered to investigate the crime I was thinking of committing, I wanted as little connection from the act to me as possible.

The other side of the border was like the other side of the earth.

I crossed over in midafternoon. There wasn't a queue going south, and the sole Mexican border guard just waved me through without getting out of his chair in the air-conditioned booth.

Things looked to be very different for the people who were heading north. A long line of cars and trucks steamed in the blazing heat. Horns occasionally blared, and curses were shouted from open windows as fists pounded on steering wheels. The American customs agents in their sweat-soaked uniforms questioned the occupants of each car. Every now and then they waved a car over for closer scrutiny, maybe with a dog. I didn't envy their jobs. They were paid even less than Wyoming DCI agents, which, believe me, isn't much.

It was easy to see why Hidalgo was able to turn so many of them. Twenty thousand dollars for simply waving through a specific car would be hard to resist.

I didn't hit traffic until I entered the town of Mexicali, where even going south things slowed to a crawl. The cars around me that had American plates were besieged by hucksters, panhandlers, and either pleading or snarling kids. Windows were rapped with dirty knuckles and windshields were smeared with dirty rags. I was pretty much left alone despite the California tags. The Pig, with its mismatched paint, rust, and badly tinted windows, seemed an unlikely candidate from which anyone could expect a handout.

I kept the windows rolled up and the doors locked anyway. The air conditioner cranked, too, although it wasn't doing much good because the heat outside was so intense. I switched CDs, taking out Roberto's José Cura and slipping in the Grateful Dead. I skipped to "Mexicali Blues" and turned it up.

When Roberto and I had come through here ten years earlier, the truck was almost new and we were relatively innocent. I remembered how a nearsighted street kid mistook us for yuppie stoners or maybe college boys on spring break. He tried to lift a backpack out of the rear seat when we stopped for a light. Roberto snatched him up by the throat and curled him like a dumbbell. For several blocks he held him this way, outside the car, speaking soft Spanish and both reprimanding and teasing the terrified teenager before giving him a buck and letting him go.

The population had visibly grown since then, probably because of NAFTA and all the new *maquiladoras* that assembled electronics and industrial parts. The poverty had grown, too. There were even more people packing the narrow streets. Vendors, gangbangers, pickpockets, and a few tourists whose guidebooks must have predated the Mexican Drug Age. There were even some—but not many—regular people.

The Pig rattled over urban roads that were paved with cobblestones, gravel, or potholed blacktop. Or, occasionally, a mix of all three. The other cars with me in the melee of Mexicali's streets were a mix, too. The majority were American beaters, mostly pickups and four-door sedans. But there were a few armored Mercedes and BMWs that carried managers from their homes in Imperial Valley across the border to the *maquiladoras* outside town. And there were a few of the big four-wheel-drive SUVs favored by Hidalgo's *sicarios* and *gatilleros*. Probably they belonged to the Mexicali Mafia, but I couldn't be sure. None I saw had the small yellow tongue-wagging sticker pasted to their back windows or bumpers.

I drove down a street of cinder-block garages covered with graffiti and cracked parking lots where older men sweated and worked in the unbelievable heat. I saw some of them refitting a truck with solid rubber tires and a huge steel grille. They were obviously getting ready for a high-speed, wrong-way run through the border crossing. It is a technique that has become increasingly popular despite the number of innocents who die in the spectacular crashes that sometimes result.

I passed some vacant lots where soon-to-be illegal immigrants camped in the shade of cardboard boxes. At nightfall they'd be making their move through holes cut in a flimsy chain-link fence. I saw more than a few of them organized into groups by either coyotes or drug smugglers.

The ones who would work for the smugglers—the *burros,* or mules—were easy to spot. Their clothes and fifty-pound packs were in the process of being spray-painted black, just as Roberto had described. Carpet was wrapped around their shoes to conceal their heavily weighted tracks. Even so, these boys in their late teens looked woefully unprepared for the desert in August. *Without someone like my brother to guide them,* I thought, *a lot of these kids are going to die.*

Like the sense of imminent death and the crime and the trash and blowing dirt, the air pollution was also highly visible. It hung over the city in a brown cloud so dense even the wind couldn't lift it.

I was enormously relieved to find my way out of the maze of city streets and onto the highway. Night had already fallen when I shook free. I popped open a can of Tecate to celebrate and put the Pig into fifth gear. The highway could take me all the way west toward Tijuana, but I intended to go only halfway there. My entire trip would be in the Border Corridor, the strip of land within a hundred or so miles of the U.S. border.

No tourist visas or passports are needed here. It is a "free-enterprise zone" in every sense of the term, where roughly one-third of all the narcotics entering the U.S. are stashed, processed, and packaged. Coca from Colombia, black-tar heroin from Sinaloa, pot from all over Mexico, and methamphetamine manufactured from scratch.

This was the place, I remembered from the documents Mary and Tom had shown me, where Hidalgo had fought his bloody war with the Arellano-Felix brothers of Tijuana on one side and the Carrillo-Fuentes syndicate of Juárez on the other. The Border Corridor is where even Mexican government officials admit that eighty to ninety percent of cops, prosecutors, and judges work for the cartels. Two months ago on this very highway, a car with three *federales* in it was stopped by narcos. The Mexican federal agents were tortured, shot, run over, and finally thrown off a cliff. It was here that a chief of police was shot to death last year with sixty rounds from an AK-47 while driving himself to work in a stolen car. The previous chief had died a similar death. So had a leading presidential candidate campaigning in the state, two governors, a score of prosecutors and judges (who either chose the wrong metal when offered *Plato o plomo,* or chose the wrong cartel to work for), fifteen state-police officers in the last year alone, along with six agents from the Mexican Attorney General's Office, hundreds of cartel soldiers, and countless civilians.

This thin strip of Baja averaged more than a thousand drug-related murders a year. No perpetrators ever seemed to get caught. Even the few honest cops turned their backs when the corpse had a slit throat with the tongue pulled out. Signatures of the other cartels—bound hands and feet, masks, particular burns, missing limbs, etc.—were similarly ignored. Sometimes corpses were transported from the U.S. across the border and into the corridor because it was only there that no one would look into how the corpses became corpses.

But straight and well-paved, the east–west highway really wasn't all that bad. Not, at least, if you ignored all the burnt, smashed, or otherwise abandoned cars on the sides of the road. There were lots of pretty shrines—white crosses, laminated photos nailed to them, and dried-up flowers marking the places where bodies had been discovered.

I probably drove faster than I really needed to. This place had a bad vibe.

Past a town called La Rumerosa, I pulled off the highway and onto a dirt road. I recalled that it would be all dirt from here on out. Other than that recollection, I had only vague memories of how to find my way, as Roberto had served as the navigator on that trip. But I knew the name of the last village before the deep canyon that led up into the mountains— Colonia de la Tajo. A topo map I'd bought listed the dirt road dead-ending at the village as "16."

The road turned out to be fairly well-marked for Mexico. Every few miles there would be a bullet-ridden sign with the number 16 on it nailed high up on a cactus. If more than a couple of miles went by without my seeing a 16, or what I could make out as a 1 or a 6, or at least the stars shining through a vicious wound in a cactus, I would turn around and drive back until I found a fork I'd somehow missed in the dark.

For the next three hours I was lucky to hit third gear. The headlights lit up more broken cars, abandoned appliances, and makeshift shrines, as well as thorny ocotillo bushes, elephant trees, and giant cardon and cirio cacti that stood up to fifty feet tall. I remembered a lot more of it as the miles passed. Even some of the wrecks looked familiar. For a while it felt like Roberto was riding next to me, smoking a joint and telling me about how we were going to climb in a region he called Poor-Man's Patagonia. Thinking of him this way was a lot better than picturing him in that hospital bed.

Then I finally hit Colonia de la Tajo. And it looked nothing like what I remembered.

Ten years ago it had been a sleepy town consisting of a few mud-brick shacks with tar-paper roofs. We'd bought beer from an old lady who kept the bottles on the end of a rope in a well, and then sat with her in the shade of a mesquite until the afternoon's heat wore off.

But now there was a real bar, complete with neon signs and a half-dozen trucks around it. There was also a baseball field across the road that would have been the envy of any American Little Leaguer. The grass was well-tended and it had stadium-type lights illuminating it. Although it was eleven at night, there was a game going on. Kids dressed in neat, bright uniforms were playing. Their parents watched from steel bleachers while nervously eyeing the *sicarios* who'd stumbled across the street to cheer.

Just past the bar and the ballpark was an open Jeep with red and blue lights mounted on the roll bar. Two police officers in braided uniforms sat inside, keeping watch on the *sicarios* and apparently keeping them in check.

The village appeared clean and orderly. I noticed a schoolhouse and a *clínica* farther on. The single dirt road leading through it was even bordered with stones that had been painted white. It was obvious Hidalgo gave something back to the community that protected him. But it didn't make me like him any better.

I drove through it fast, but not fast enough, I hoped, to draw too much attention from the policemen. Caught by the stadium lights, I nodded at them and grinned, doing my best to look like just another dirtbag rock climber who came this way for the remote granite walls. They may or may not have been able to see me through the cracked tint on my windows.

As I hurried past, I couldn't help noticing that several of the pickups in front of the bar had small yellow stickers on their back windows.

Beyond the village, the road deteriorated as the earth became stonier and the relief increased. I was headed up a deep, wide canyon that I thought had to be Cañón Tajo, but there was no way to be sure. There were no more signs and, in some places, apparently no road. But at least there were no headlights in my rearview mirror. Every few minutes I would turn off my own headlights and scan behind me. Then I would study the sky, looking among the stars for the pale tombstone that would be El Gran Trono Blanco, the largest wall in Poor-Man's Patagonia.

Sixteen hundred feet high, Trono Blanco is supposed to be a little higher than the unnamed wall nearby that Roberto and I had climbed on Hidalgo's land. From Trono Blanco's summit I was pretty sure I'd be able to get a view of the Hidalgo hacienda. Besides, I'd always wanted to climb the higher wall. Roberto and I would have done it that trip if we hadn't been chased off the other wall by rifle fire.

The tall cacti disappeared, to be replaced by prickly pear, mesquite, and even some ponderosa pines as I drove higher. The air got a little cooler, too, and I rolled down the windows so that I could lean out and look for faint tracks marking the road. It smelled better up here. Wilder. Supposedly there were still grizzly bears in the Sierra Juárez. At least that was what Roberto had said a decade ago.

I drove on, permanently in four-wheel low now.

An hour later I admitted to myself that I was totally lost. I was no longer even sure if I was on the road, or any road. For over a mile there had not been a single tire mark. There hadn't even been any trash. I needed to camp and wait for daylight.

I bounded up one last hill, banging over sharp-edged rocks that were large enough that I worried about tipping or ripping out an axle. I took it fast, though, because the hill itself was steep enough that if I slid back down it I would probably end up sitting on my tailgate. If any of these things happened, it would be a long walk out. And it might be a little uncomfortable, too, having to flag down a ride from a pickup with a little yellow sticker in the back window.

Roaring over the crest, nearly airborne, I almost slammed into the back of another car.

I skidded to a stop only a few feet from it. The car was a Ford Econoline van that looked as battered as the Pig. It was mounted high up on enormous off-road tires. The back windows were plastered with stickers for climbing gear, the Access Fund, and one that said, "Bad Cop—No Donut." Close by were the orange flames of a campfire. My headlights lit up four people with huge eyes and open mouths. All were young, three of them blond, and they looked like they were just barely climbing back into their skins.

I killed the engine and got out. Music was playing from a boom box.

"Sorry about that. I didn't know anyone was up here."

I spoke English because they obviously weren't Mexican. It wasn't the color of their skin or their hair—Mexicans, like Argentines, can be blond—but their clothes and postures.

"Holy shit!" one of the girls said, laughing a little wildly. "Where'd you come from, dude?"

"I'm not really sure. I thought it was the road."

"The road's that way." She pointed off somewhere into the night, still laughing. "Who the hell are you?"

"My name's Robert," I said.

It wasn't the smoothest pseudonym, and I was embarrassed that it was the best I could do in a split second and still make it sound natural. I'd been an undercover investigator for eight years, after all. But I knew it shouldn't matter. I could have even used my real name. I'd be out of here in a day or two, and these people wouldn't likely be talking to anyone out here but themselves.

They introduced themselves. Tony, Kevin, Barb, and Lydia. It had been Lydia who had spoken first, but it was hard to tell the two girls apart. Both were small and wiry and both had dreadlocked blond hair. Both were either high or unnaturally peppy. Kevin was also short, with a thick body and black-Irish features. Tony was about my height and was even thinner than either of the girls. His blond hair was as long as Rebecca's.

I saw right away that they were climbers, too, even though the bumper stickers had already suggested it. They had the sunburned faces and arms, along with the scrapes and scabs, of seasoned desert wall rats.

"You know how far I am from Trono Blanco?"

Kevin answered, "Yeah, man. That's where we're headed

tomorrow. You can't see it from here, not even in the daylight, but it's about a three-mile hike. You going to climb it?"

"Maybe. I thought I'd check it out."

"Solo, huh?" Lydia asked.

"Rope solo. I'm not crazy." *Not like Roberto. Not quite yet. But just by being here I'm well on the way.*

Tony said, "You can hang with us if you want. There's supposed to be safety in numbers down here. Word is, a lot of people have been getting ripped off. Chicks hassled, too." He glanced significantly at Barb and Lydia.

They laughed at him.

"You're the only one that's hassling me, Tony," the one called Barb said.

Lydia added, "Dude, no one comes here in the summer. Too freaking hot. No one's that dumb but us. And Robert here."

I was invited to sit around the fire. The wood was mesquite and it smelled good. Lydia handed me a cold can of Tecate, then returned a minute later with a slice of lime that she shoved through the hole.

"Want to get baked?" Tony asked.

"Too tired, thanks. A beer's about right."

They passed a bong while I sipped the beer. There was a full moon overhead and just as many stars as in Wyoming. While they talked about places they'd been climbing, and asked only a few questions about me, I remembered sitting at a similar fire with Roberto. I'd drunk the same kind of beer, too, while he smoked the same sweet pot they were smoking.

I could feel myself starting to let go of things. God knows there was a lot to let go of. I didn't feel the same panic when I thought of Roberto and his ruined body. And I didn't feel like much of a cop anymore. These people had accepted me as one of them, a wandering climber, just looking for the next rush of adrenaline. And that's how I felt.

I asked how long they'd been here and what they'd found to climb. They'd been camping for three days, mostly bouldering and getting warmed up for El Gran Trono Blanco, and were all but out of batteries and ice.

"Trono Blanco's why we came," Kevin said. "It's the real deal, man. You'll see it tomorrow. Climb with us if you want. We're going to try to do it in a day—the Giraffe Route, you know? Rock's supposed to be as good as anything in the Valley."

The Valley was Yosemite, home of perfect granite and huge walls.

The music stopped. Tony got up and changed the CD. He put on an old one, Van Morrison's *Moondance*. It had to have been recorded years and years before any of them were born, but the girls were immediately on their feet. They started dancing together while Tony bobbed his head and Kevin grinned at me.

"These chicks like to dance," he said.

I was beginning to be able to tell them apart. Barb was just a little bit heavier and wore silver bracelets that flashed in the firelight as well as a tank top. Lydia wore only an athletic bra and a pair of shorts. She had a pierced belly button, too, with a ring in it, and I bet Barb had something similar. Both also had a couple of tattoos and some other pierced parts. They danced with their eyes closed, swaying and lifting their arms like it was reggae that was playing.

Only when the CD's volume began to fade as the batteries wore down did they stop dancing. Then both of them plopped down next to the fire, breathing a little hard. Their bare skin was shiny in the firelight. I could smell the sweat and the sunburn and the dust coming off their skin. I felt like I was getting high, just inhaling them.

I decided it was time to get some sleep.

There were two tents standing nearby that were identical

in all but color. Both were stained and patched with duct tape. They were pitched thirty feet apart, on what were probably the only relatively flat bits of ground. I stomped around in the brush with a flashlight, looking for a place I could throw my bag. I didn't find one, but I did find a tarantula with glittering black eyes. He scurried away when I held the light on him.

"Hey, Robert," one of the girls—I think it was Lydia—called to me. "You can crash with us, if you want. We're smaller than the boys, so there's a little more room."

"No, thanks. I'm going to sleep in the truck."

But the offer touched me. Not just because they accepted me enough to make such an offer, but because of its total innocence—whether or not there was anything sexual behind it. Who but these people would take in a stranger like me? These had once been my people. Why had I left them behind when I became a cop?

And I didn't feel quite so good anymore. I didn't deserve the offer, the trust. I was like the tarantula—out hunting in the night. *I've come here to kill, you know.*

THIRTY-FOUR

.

I woke up to very bright light. It was far too bright to be day-light. The light was flooding into the open back end of the Pig from down the ridge crest. Squinting into it, I could make out that three lights were bouncing rapidly toward me. Two of them were headlights. The third—and the brightest—appeared to be mounted higher up, like on a roll bar.

The cops, I thought. Which isn't comforting when you're in Mexico. As if in response to what I was thinking, flashing blue-and-red strobes came on to either side of the bouncy spotlight.

"What the hell?" Kevin called from his tent.

The blue nylon was completely lit up. Both Kevin's and Tony's silhouettes were distinct and moving inside it. The flat spot where they'd staked the tent, I now realized, was on the road itself. And the vehicle wasn't slowing as it slammed over rocks and bushes toward them. Barb and Lydia's tent was a lit-tle farther down the hillside.

My first move was to reach under the driver's seat, where I'd hidden the shotgun before crossing the border. My hand closed on powder puffs of Mungo's hair before finding the beveled surface of the shotgun's pistol grip. Then I let it go.

These are cops, I reminded myself. *They're probably here to rob us, not kill us.* And it was highly unlikely that either I or my truck with its false plates had been recognized when going through the village.

I shielded my eyes and held up my watch so that it caught the light. It was three-thirty in the morning. I kicked off my sleeping bag just as the approaching Jeep skidded to a halt in front of Kevin and Tony's tent.

The lights remained on, but the engine was turned off.

"You do not have permission to camp here," a voice called from beyond the lights.

Kevin staggered out of the tent, followed by Tony.

Kevin said, "Hey, man, we didn't know that. We heard you could camp anywhere you want down here."

"You do not have permission to camp here," the voice repeated in accented English.

The officers had both gotten out of the Jeep and were walking toward us. Two silhouettes coming out through the blinding light. One was short and fat, the other more regular-sized. They were close together and holding only truncheons—in violation of what was standard practice north of the border. They were arrogant and sloppy. I could have taken them both out with a single blast of buckshot. But these men knew that they had very little to fear from what they considered crazy but harmless rock climbers. There were far greater dangers out there, although you could alleviate them somewhat by working for the right cartel.

"These mountains are federal land," I protested, speaking Spanish. "They do not belong to you. You have no right to tell us we can't camp here."

Both of them seemed surprised that I spoke Spanish. And spoke it forcefully, too. I could see them clearer now. The short one was older, maybe in his forties or fifties. He didn't

look particularly mean. The other one was so young that his
mustache was just a wisp of hair.

They looked at each other. Then the older one spoke.

"Nevertheless, you must have a permit. And you have no
permit."

"Where do we get a permit?"

He grinned and thumped his chest. "From me!"

"This is bullshit!" Kevin said. "What's he saying?"

Lydia and Barb had gotten out of their tent, too. Lydia
was still in her bra and shorts, Barb in her tank top and apparently nothing else. The older cop leered at them. The younger
one's eyes grew large while his face became tight.

The younger one said in English, "We search you for
drugs. Lots of hippies come here. Smoke bad drugs. Be in
much trouble."

Then he stroked his truncheon meaningfully.

It was inevitable that they would find at least the bong,
which I didn't think the climbers would have bothered to
have hidden. The shotgun would be easy to find, too, and even
harder to explain. And then I knew what would happen next.
A *mordida,* a fine, payable either in cash or sex, would be demanded.

I decided to short-circuit things.

"If we're camping illegally, can't we just buy a permit and
be done with it?"

This perked up the older officer. He was no doubt tired at
half past three in the morning, and seemed to appreciate my
coming to the point. He scratched his head as if wondering
why he hadn't thought of it first.

"Yes, señor. But the permit for camping here is very expensive. Twenty-five dollars per person."

It was simply an opening offer. I wanted to argue, to hag-
gle the way my mother had taught me. I knew I could turn the
twenty-five dollars into just a couple of bucks—neither the

climbers nor I looked like we had anywhere near twenty-five dollars. But I also wanted to get the cops out of here. And I wanted them to leave happy. I didn't like the way the younger one was looking at Barb and Lydia now. I could see that he would be happy to take payment in flesh, whether or not cash was offered.

"Twenty, and go," I said. "I want to go back to sleep, so I will give you everything I have."

Barb must have spoken a little Spanish, because she stepped toward us and started to protest.

"Hey. We don't have that kind of scratch—"

As she stepped toward us, the younger cop stepped toward her. The thin tank top she wore was made transparent by the beams of three bright lights. His eyes were all over her. He whistled appreciatively.

"Don't worry about it," I told her. "Go get back in your tent."

"Don't tell me—"

"Just do it. Now!"

She made a face but turned and marched back toward the tent.

"Twenty and you will leave us," I said firmly, getting the cops' attention back on me.

The younger one didn't look pleased. He clearly wanted something else, something more.

"That's all you will get. Otherwise I will make a lot of trouble for you two."

I gave them my hardest look. Like Roberto's, but without the crazy grin.

The older cop nodded. "Twenty each. That's one hundred American dollars."

Instead of taking out my wallet, I waved the officers over to the side of the Pig. I opened the door and had the old, fat cop shine his flashlight into the side pocket, where I kept five emergency twenties. I made sure that he saw that there wasn't any more money there other than a roll of quarters. I gave him the five bills.

He grinned at me.

"You buy permit, so now you will have no more trouble. Not from *policía,* not from the *bandidos* who are all over these mountains. I will see to it myself."

"I know you will. Thank you."

He winked.

"Sleep well, señor."

They got back in the Jeep, turned around, and bounced off into the night. In a couple of minutes their taillights disappeared.

Lydia came up and touched my arm.

"Thanks, Robert. You didn't have to do that, though. Those guys had no right to demand money from us. Without people like us coming down here, spending our dollars, they wouldn't have a pot to piss in."

I shrugged and didn't laugh. I doubted she and her friends were spending very many American dollars on the local economy. Besides, it was drugs that fueled things down here. A one-hundred-billion-dollar business, although it was hard to tell by the look of things.

"They live here," I told her. "They've got the guns and the badges. What are you going to do?"

THIRTY-FIVE

The rock looked like whitewashed granite. There was close to two thousand feet of it rearing up out of a maze of piñon and juniper canyons. The entire east-facing wall blazed in the early-morning light. It reflected the sunlight like a mirror.

"Look at that fucker," Tony said with awe in his voice.

"Man, that thing's a monster," Barb agreed.

We stood atop a canyon rim that was nearly as high as the shining summit but a couple of miles off. I could see that it was going to take a lot of bushwhacking and scrambling—maybe even some rappelling—just to get to El Trono's base. Three hours of it, possibly a lot more. Then there would be sixteen hundred feet of difficult, vertical-to-overhanging rock to climb. Not to mention the hike back out. And it was already getting hot. All I had in my backpack other than climbing gear and binoculars were two quart bottles of water and a handful of PowerBars.

There'd been a time when I would have gone for it anyway. And I would have suffered, but loved every minute of it. But that time had passed. It wasn't what I'd come here for anyway.

"I'm going to have to bag out on the Giraffe," I said,

naming the hard route they were headed for. "It's too big for me to do in a day. And the approach looks heinous. I'm going to try to do something a little shorter on the south face instead."

The south face of El Trono was a smaller wall, only eight or nine hundred feet high. But it still led all the way up to the summit, where I hoped to get a good look at Hidalgo's hacienda and then make my plans.

The four desert rats looked at me. Their packs weren't any bigger than mine. They couldn't have much more water or food.

Tony said, "You sure, man? You're going to miss out on an epic."

That's what I was afraid of. An "epic climb" is one where everything goes to shit and you come out alive by only a hairbreadth.

One of Roberto's expressions came to mind. I shrugged and said in his soft voice, "You eat what you can kill."

All four of them looked at me a little strangely. Kevin grinned and nodded, though. He liked that. So did the others.

"I already know that thing's going to eat *me*," Lydia said. "So I'm going to do the south face with Robert."

No one argued with her. In the climbing world, it's considered bad manners to try too hard to talk someone into doing something that might get them killed.

We headed down into the canyons as a group. Much of the descent was torture. There was a lot of getting speared in the calves by yucca, a lot of precarious boulder-hopping on house-sized rocks, a lot of dusty scrambling down hot, gravelly stone, and a lot of bushwhacking through canyon floors thick with manzanita. It was so hot that we took off our shirts despite the stinging slaps of thorny branches. The men would have taken off their shorts, too, and the women their sports bras and shorts, if there hadn't been a great likelihood of getting poked or swatted on some particularly sensitive body parts. All of us were pouring sweat that, like our cursing, was turning from fragrant to stinking.

The torture came to an end not far from where we would need to split into two groups: Lydia and I for the bottom of the south face, and Kevin, Tony, and Barb even farther down-canyon to the base of the bigger east-facing wall.

Here, in a little side canyon that dead-ended in a cliff, we stumbled onto a copper-colored pool of water. It was shaded by Washington palms and it looked a little like a desert oasis. We all plowed straight into it, taking only time to dump our packs of ropes and gear on the rocky bank.

The water felt so good it was like chilled silk on my skin. I closed my eyes and ducked my head, letting the water embrace me completely. Letting it suspend me in its gentle, cool grasp. I almost didn't want to come up for air.

A little while later we wrung out our clothes and laid them on rocks in the sun to dry. We dried ourselves in the shade. It was interesting to be back in a world where naked-ness was accepted. More than that, where it was preferred. No one took it too seriously. The girls teased the boys and the boys teased them back. The only thing that mattered to any of us was that we were soon going to be on the rock with a lot of air beneath our heels.

The anticipation was building. Despite all the things I should have been worrying about—like: Was I, a sworn peace officer, really going to kill a man in cold blood?—what I really wanted to do was feed the Rat.

The chalky cliff of the south face loomed over Lydia and me as we booted up and flaked out a rope at the base. The rock looked manky—crumbly and weak—but it was surprisingly solid to the touch. I remembered thinking exactly the same thing ten years earlier when Roberto and I had first touched similar rock only a couple of miles away.

With the others down toward the base of the east face, Lydia had suddenly become chatty. She started asking me all these questions about myself that I didn't really want to answer. So I turned it around and started asking about her—where she came from, where she was going, and all that. A long time ago I learned that people like talking about themselves far better than asking questions. It's a useful thing to know when you work undercover.

"Are you dating one of those guys?" I'd asked at one point. I meant Kevin or Tony, but I could have been referring to Barb, too.

She chuckled. "Ha. It's a little complex. See, I used to hang with Kevin, but we've pretty much stopped that. Dude was getting a little serious. Barb's hooked up with him a couple of times since then, but not so much lately. She's slept with Tony, too, the slut. Now he follows her around everywhere like a puppy dog. I guess I should admit that I hooked up with him once, too."

It was funny, how it all came back to me. How I knew Lydia and her friends so well and I'd only met them. I knew how it worked. I remembered it, and I missed the complete innocence of it. You start traveling together, everything casual, everything about the climbing. Then there are starry nights around campfires when it's too dark to climb anymore and the hormones swirl around in your blood because the adrenaline can't. While music plays on some tinny boom box held together with duct tape, wine and marijuana are passed around, and so, later, are the partners. Everyone so determined to remain a free spirit, yet still occasionally falling into brooding, desperate adult attachments.

"Anyway," she said, her blue eyes bright, "if that sick little history didn't freak you out too much, then you should know I'm available. And interested."

I smiled but didn't respond. I was too caught up in the memories to decide whether to flirt back or to gently put her off. Too caught up with thinking about how I'd outgrown all that—with a pregnant woman in Denver who was doing her best to let me down gently. I was too caught up to even think of further questions to ask.

"I guess I should tell you that Barb is, too—the slut. But it's only fair, so you know."

I still didn't answer.

"Well?" she pressed.

I brought myself back to earth. "Hey, I'm really flattered. Or at least I would be if I weren't the only man within a hundred miles that you haven't slept with."

"Hey! I didn't sleep with either one of those creepy Mexican cops last night!"

"That's true. Okay. I really am flattered. But I'm too old for you. What are you, nineteen?"

"Twenty. And a Scorpio. You know what that means, don't you?" She gave me a wink.

I didn't, or at least I couldn't remember the lessons about astrology and auras that some old girlfriend had tried to teach me, but I nodded anyway.

"Anyway, you can't be much more than thirty, Robert. And it's not how many years you've lived, but how many lives. And I bet I've lived as many as you, if not more."

"I bet you have," I agreed. To be this free you had to be either really naive or really wise. Either way, I was envious. "I told you. I'm flattered."

"But?"

"But what? I like you. And Barb. And Kevin and Tony. We'll see, okay?"

She shook her head and laughed. "Oh, man. You're cool, you know that? You're going to be trouble."

I was less cool—and more conflicted—than she knew. But she was right about the trouble part.

In graduate school at Colorado I took a class called Theories of Justice. We were forced to read a book by Leo Tolstoy, which I found I liked in the end. It was called *The Kingdom of God Is Within You,* and the book was supposed to be the basis for the philosophies of people like Gandhi and Dr. Martin Luther King—people I'd always admired. The book made a case for pacifism. The professor argued that it proved that tyrants, from Hitler to Saddam Hussein, would have simply withered away without wars and the resulting loss of lives.

This came into my head when I was about six hundred feet off the deck. I was sitting on a shallow ledge atop a buttress. The ledge was two feet wide, two feet deep, and exposed on three sides to nothing but space. My legs swung free. I was belaying Lydia up to me as she worked on a difficult fingertips-only corner on one side of the buttress.

At first I thought these thoughts and memories might be hallucinations caused by the onset of heat exhaustion. But it wasn't that hot anymore. Clouds had been forming over the last hour, and the wind had been rising. My sweat was drying on my skin.

I could remember some of what Tolstoy had written. He had talked about a "ruffian" who was pursuing a young girl, intending to rape or kill her. "I kill the ruffian and save the girl. But the death or the wounding of the ruffian has positively taken place, while what would have happened if this had not been I cannot know. And what an immense mass of evil must result, and indeed does result, from allowing men to assume the right of anticipating what may happen. Ninety-nine percent of the evil of the world is founded on this reasoning—from the Inquisition to dynamite bombs."

I wanted to believe in this as I had back in school. It would be so easy. Finish the climb and walk away. Get back in the Pig, drive back to Colorado. Wait and see what happens. Maybe Hidalgo will decide it's too dangerous to bother with my parents, Rebecca, and me. Maybe he'll let it go.

But Jesús Hidalgo is not just idly pursuing me and my family. He has already taken a significant step toward harming us. More than that—he's all but killed Roberto.

I realized I wasn't going after him just to preemptively eliminate a threat. I was going for a little payback, too. A little justice. The fury was still in me, not as hot as it had been in the potash mine, but somehow even more powerful. Radioactive. It was ironic, but the emotion that had made me want to be a cop in the first place all those years ago came back, right as I was contemplating doing something totally lawless, in violation of sworn oaths and Tolstoy's virtuous theory.

Did he think he could terrorize all these people for all these years and not pay a price? Did he really think he could get away with it? Was he so fucking cocky that he thought he could do what he did to my brother with impunity? He was, and he did. And he needed to be taught otherwise. Better than that, he needed to disappear from the earth like those beer cans I'd blasted in the desert.

I was becoming more and more like Roberto. Not the Roberto who was lying lifeless and broken on a hospital bed. And not like he'd been shortly before—the wolf peering out from the trees and watching the children play. But the Roberto I'd always worshiped and feared. The one who was *destraillado,* as Mom said. Unleashed. *Do what needs to be done and don't worry about the consequences.*

Lydia's taped palm smacked the ledge just as the first raindrops started to fall. She pulled herself halfway up, looked at the tiny ledge, then squirmed her sweaty body onto the only space available—my lap. She pulled off her slippers while I reached behind me and tied her into the anchor I'd built. At first the rain was soft and warm. As warm as Lydia's skin. I thought it would only last a minute, then evaporate off the hot wall ten minutes later.

But I was wrong. The rain picked up. The wind, too. Soon it became a torrent. It spilled over the top of the wall above us like a waterfall, washing over us.

"What the hell is this?" Lydia yelled, laughing, pleased to be so suddenly cold. She was holding out her cupped palms to catch and drink as much of it as she could.

"It think it's called a *chubasco*. It's like a short, sudden squall. I've heard they get them a lot in Baja."

It was exactly what had happened to Roberto and me ten years earlier. In almost exactly the same place, at very close to the same time in the afternoon. I thought I could even see where we'd been—a white dome of rock a couple of miles away that some ancient glacier had sheared in half. We'd been three-quarters of the way up, just like Lydia and I were now, when the storm hit. We'd bivied on a ledge not much bigger than this one, shivering and talking and laughing all night. Then we'd been woken up by the gunshots of Hidalgo's men. My introduction to them.

"Great timing," Lydia said. "I was ready for another bath. I've been sweating like a pig on this mother."

"It would have been better if we'd made it to the top before it hit."

"No way. This is more fun. I just hope the other guys are all right."

With her squirming in my lap, her damp dreads batting my face every time she turned her head, and the skin of her all-but-bare back and legs sticky against my chest and thighs, I had a hard time not letting my newfound *destraillado* side take over. She didn't make it any easier.

"This harness has a cool feature. I can take off my shorts without untying from the rope. Want to see?"

"That's okay," I told her. "I believe you."

"Come on. You ever done it up this high? Man, it's a rush."

"Actually, yeah, I have." A lifetime ago there'd been a woman—a client—whom I'd found myself bivying next to on the Thank God ledge of El Cap.

She turned around to face me. To straddle me, too, six hundred feet in the air. There was no other way to look at each other on the little ledge, but I'm not sure looking at each other was strictly necessary. It wasn't necessary, either, for her to press her chest against mine or to say, with her mouth and eyes just two inches away while the rainwater streamed down our faces, "Are you going to kiss me or what?"

I didn't, though. Not at first, anyway. I bit her neck instead. Right where the trapezius meets the throat. And I tasted the sun on her skin even though the sun was buried somewhere beyond the dripping clouds.

She purred like a lynx. She wrapped her arms behind my back and pulled me to her, crushing me with her thin, sunburned arms. She bit my neck, too, before she pushed her face into mine. Then her tongue was in my mouth, and the tiny dumbbell that pierced it was clicking against my teeth.

"Let me show you that trick with my shorts," she murmured, biting my neck again.

"No. This is fine right now."

"For you, maybe."

She started kissing me again. Meanwhile, both the rain and the wind fell off. At about the same time she finally stopped grinding her hips down on mine and seemed content just to touch and kiss.

It may not excuse things, but I didn't feel like I was being unfaithful to Rebecca by snogging with this girl who was as free as a wild animal. And it wasn't just that we'd hit that brick wall. Rebecca lived in another world. And right then I needed the contact and the reassurance. I needed to feel like a human being, not a killer. I needed to feel like my old self, long before I started carrying a badge or earned the epithet QuickDraw. I needed to be free, like I'd been in my guiding days. Being Roberto was a little scary.

"Hey. This is nice," Lydia said. "I knew there was something to you older guys besides not being able to get it up all the time."

We topped out in the late afternoon, an hour or two before dusk. The summit was empty. Just bare rock and a few twisted junipers. The sun had returned when the rain had stopped, and now it was drifting down toward the Pacific Ocean. The *chubasco* had swept the sky clear of all the atmospheric dust and pollution from Tijuana and Mexicali. I thought I could see the blue water on the horizon. On both horizons, actually. The peninsula is only a hundred miles wide, with the Pacific to the west and the Sea of Cortés to the east. We were standing on its highest point.

While Lydia crawled to the edge of the east wall to look down its sixteen-hundred-foot face and see if she could spot her friends, I scanned the other direction with the binoculars I'd brought in my pack.

"You see them?" I asked.

"No. I hope that the—what did you call it? A chubby Tabasco?—didn't wash those guys off."

"They probably just rapped. It looked like hard climbing. They probably only got up a couple of pitches before the rain started. Maybe they'll try again tomorrow."

"I don't know," she said. "Kevin was pretty determined to nail it today."

She stayed at the edge, brown legs splayed on the rock and dreadlocked head hanging in space.

I found the hacienda easily enough. Surprisingly close, too. It was perched on a hill above some other buildings—barns, storage sheds, and a sort of crumbling dormitory for Hidalgo's *sicarios*. There were cars down there, too, some that I recognized from Wyoming, and a sort of palm-frond–covered cabana where a bunch of the gunmen appeared to be drinking beer and getting stoned. I counted at least twenty men. I was sure Zafado was around somewhere, either drinking with the men or up at the fine house on the hill.

The house itself was a single-story structure with white walls and a red tile roof. It sprawled on the hilltop amid green lawns and, just like in Wyoming, a turquoise swimming pool. I could see only a corner of the pool, so I couldn't tell if Hidalgo was sitting by it the way he liked to do in Wyoming. But I did see maids moving around in their starched black uniforms. They wouldn't be wearing them if the *jefe* wasn't home. I tried to see in the windows but couldn't see much because of the gauzy white curtains that swayed in the breeze. But I could see that many of the windows were open, and that none of the windows had bars.

El Doctor was definitely home, I decided, and it wouldn't be hard for me to invite myself inside.

"What are you looking at?"

Lydia had wrapped her arms around me from behind. She was pressing herself to me again.

"That house down there."

"Nice place. Who lives there? Some Mexican movie star?"

"No one."

"Hmm?" she asked, purring again, her cheek against my shoulder blade.

"I don't know."

The only road leading to the house came from the other side of the mountain range. That was good, although it meant that it would be a tough day's hike from the campsite and the Pig. Tough because of all the canyons and manzanita. It would be deep into the night before I got there. But the night and the canyons and the dense vegetation would make me all but impossible to find after a shotgun blast woke everyone up.

I would spend the night with Lydia and the desert rats then leave early in the morning.

THIRTY-SIX

That night, sitting around the campfire, there was no more cold beer. The ice was all gone. But there was warm wine. And there was pot.

Marijuana was something I'd never thought of as being any worse than lite beer. I'd never bought into those claims from the federal government that it was a "gateway" drug. I'd never seen a marijuana overdose. And I'd never seen anyone do anything really vicious while on it, unlike whiskey and crack and meth and all the rest. Stupid? Sure. Violent? No.

I drank my share from the fat green jug, and was even tempted to take a couple of hits off the bong. But eight years as primarily a narcotics agent, plus my recent insight into the illegal-drug industry beyond Wyoming's borders, helped me overcome the urge. Besides, I knew I needed a relatively clear head for what was going to come. And I was feeling so different from my usual self that it was like I was kind of stoned already.

Kevin, Tony, and Barb had beat us back to the campsite. As I'd predicted, they made it only four pitches up the Giraffe before the *chubasco*—or "chubby Tabasco," as Lydia said—forced them to rappel off the wall. According to them, the torrent of water washing down the east face had been so bad that they worried about drowning while still five hundred feet off the ground. They weren't too dejected, though. They'd had fun. And they were happy that Lydia and I made it to the summit. They'd left their ropes behind on the east face, intending to head back early the next day. They planned to jumar up to their high point and finish off the route.

Lydia teased them, using variations of Roberto's favorite climbing maxim, which I'd told them earlier: "You eat what you can kill."

"You choked on what you couldn't swallow," she said.

"We bit off more than we could chew," Barb agreed.

"We drank more than we could swim," Tony ventured.

"We rapped what we couldn't climb," Kevin said.

It became a game as they passed the gallon bottle of bad wine and the bong. It continued, getting rowdier, through a dinner of rice and beans and tofu hot dogs. The meal may not sound like much, but it was the best I'd had in years. I tasted every exotic spice that the girls mixed in with the beans. I drooled over the charcoal-crunchy skin of the well-done dogs. I drank the wine like it was some spectacular California vintage instead of buck-and-a-half Gallo.

Lydia finished the game by shouting into the night, "The Giraffe killed and ate *you*. And the giraffe's a friggin' vegetarian, you wimps!"

My new friends were having a good time. It was a party even though the batteries for the boom box were dead and there was no dancing. One of those times where you feel so connected to each and every person present that they might as well be your brothers and sisters instead of pretty much total strangers.

So they thought I was out of my gourd when I told them they should pack up and head north at first light.

"No way, man. We aren't going anywhere. We've got to

eat that Giraffe. We can't get our asses kicked by a vegetarian route," Kevin said.

Tony added, "We've got four ropes plus gear still on it."

"I'm staying here forever," Lydia said, slouching low in a camp chair next to me, the bong held between her knees. "Gonna start a climbing camp like that one at Potrero Chico. Up by that coppery pool. Gonna call it Campo Robert. After my new guru here. The guy who's gonna be my lover whether he wants to be or not. And our motto's going to be 'Eat What You Can Kill. *No Mas.*' Right, Robert?"

"Listen to me for a minute. I'm serious. You need to pack up and split."

Tony was the only one sober enough to suspect that I wasn't kidding.

"Why?"

"Because there's going to be serious heavy shit going on around here by tomorrow night."

"What are you talking about?"

"You ever hear of the Mexicali Mafia?"

"That's like a prison gang or something, right?"

I shook my head. I had all of their attention now.

"No, that's La Eme, or the Mexican Mafia. The Mexicali Mafia is associated, but they work out of Baja. Right near here. And they're some really bad people. Worse than La Eme, even, and that's the major leagues as far as gangs go in the U.S."

"What are you talking about?" Barb demanded. She wasn't laughing anymore.

"Just listen. These guys, the Mexicali Mafia, they have their headquarters in a house on the other side of Trono Blanco. You can see it from up on top. It's the only place around. White with a red tile roof."

"That's what you were looking at?" Lydia asked. "With your binoculars?"

"Yeah, we'll see it if we ever make it up the Giraffe," Kevin lamented.

"Listen to me. These guys—the Mexicali Mafia—they kill people. They have a signature way of doing it, too. They cut their throats and pull their tongues out through the wound, then they let the victims drown on their own blood. They've done it hundreds of times down here to people they don't like, or to people who get in their way. And when they do it to someone, they don't just stop there. They do it to every family member, from little kids to grandparents. In Ensenada a couple of years ago—just sixty or so miles from here—they slaughtered eighteen women and children in a single night."

"Jesus," Lydia said, now unsure whether or not I was kidding.

No, Jesús, I wanted to correct her. Instead I said, "There's a good chance that tomorrow night they'll be running around in these mountains. There's also a good chance they'll be really pissed off."

"Why?" Tony asked.

"You know what happens when you poke a stick in a wasp's nest? I'm going to do something like that tomorrow night. You don't want to be around here after that. You don't want to be in Baja at all."

There was a long silence except for the snap and crackle of the fire. A mesquite branch exploded, showering sparks, and they all nearly leapt out of their skins. Then Lydia leaned over and took the bottle from me.

She said, "No more wine for Señor Robert. And it's a good thing you passed on the dope, dude."

"Was that, like, a ghost story?" Barb asked.

Kevin, laughing, put a forearm across Barb's throat and flapped his other hand beneath it. Like a wagging tongue. She beat at him with her elbows.

"I'm serious," I said.

"You're putting us on," Tony insisted. But he didn't look so sure.

"Stop it, man," Lydia said, grinning and putting her hand on my knee.

"How do you know about these guys?" Barb demanded. She sounded sober now. And like she might get a little hysterical. "How would you know something like that?"

I smiled. It was Roberto's smile. I could see it in their faces as they watched me.

"I used to work for these guys. They fucked me over. Now it's their turn to get fucked."

Nobody restoked the fire as I told them a story. By silent consent everyone was content to let the flames die rather than have them serve as a bright beacon marking our camp to whatever bugaboos were out in the night. The story I told them was low on details, middling on truth, but high on motivating them to get the hell out of this place before the next night.

I said that I used to work for this guy named Jesús Hidalgo, head of the Mexicali Mafia. That, when I wasn't off climbing somewhere, I paid for the next trip by guiding men carrying packs of cocaine and heroin through the Sonora Desert. That I kept them alive when they otherwise would have died from heat or thirst or by being shot to death by Border Patrol or *bandidos*. That I had a brother who was a cop, and that this Hidalgo had really messed him up. Wasted him, actually. And finally, that I was going to do the same to Hidalgo. I punctuated it by getting up and fetching from the truck the ugly, short shotgun with its pistol grip.

Roberto was in my voice as I spoke. He was in my permanent grin and every gesture. He was in me so deeply that it felt like I might need to get an exorcism when the job was done.

They didn't want to believe me, but I knew the story of the Mexicali Mafia and the things they did to people sounded so horrible that it had to be true. But more than not wanting to believe me, the desert rats didn't want to believe that people could actually behave this way. My new friends were so innocent in spirit that they were like another species of *Homo sapiens*. A very different species from what I'd been living with for the last eight years.

They were true believers. Just like so many people I've admired and, at the same time, scoffed at over the years. The public defenders who were convinced I was railroading their clients with planted evidence. The climbing partner who believed that God would only take him when it was time, so he felt free to take huge risks. Mary Chang, who, before her agent was murdered, had believed absolutely in law and government.

I couldn't help but be a little awed by the desert rats' faith. They kept it in the face of all that was around them. Tony, with his skinny muscles and long, thin hair, surely had gotten the shit kicked out of him frequently as a teenager. In both Barb and Lydia I could detect a little of the victim—a sense I'd developed in eight years as a cop. As kids or juveniles I thought it probable that they'd both either been abused or molested by someone they trusted. Even sturdy Kevin—I could imagine a domineering father outraged that his son wanted to *climb rocks* instead of play football. Looking at him, I could hear the echoes of shouts, shoves, and then punches.

But they kept their faith. I envied it. They took their joy where they could find it, and they pursued it every minute of the day. Like Roberto said, they ate what they killed.

And here I was, one of them, and I was going to do something terrible. Something that should have been impossible for any human being to do, something that was forbidden by the concept of civilization, something that the rule of law outlawed. But empathy, civilization, and law had all failed to deal with a man like Jesús Hidalgo.

What I was doing to the desert rats made me feel a little sick. Like I was shaking them awake when they desperately needed their sleep.

"I'm too stoned to tell whether you're messing with us or not. Let's talk about it in the morning," Kevin said. "We'll decide if we're going then. But, man, whether you're messing or not, I don't think I want to hang with you after this."

Barb was crying quietly. Tony just looked into the dying embers, stunned. Lydia sat beside me with her dreadlocked head bowed low. I wasn't one of them anymore.

Barb followed Kevin into the tent he shared with Tony. Tony stood outside it for a minute, watching them disappear inside then pull the zipper. He turned and headed down the slope to Lydia and Barb's tent. I was surprised later when Lydia crawled into the back of the Pig with me.

"Man, you are a *trip*," she whispered.

"Then how come you're crawling into the back of my truck with me?"

She grinned. Then, on all fours, she bounced up and down on my sleeping bag. The shocks squealed in protest.

"This thing's a piece of shit."

I had to laugh. That's what Mary Chang had said about the Pig the first time I met her. It was only a little over two weeks ago, but it felt like years. Lifetimes.

"Everyone would hear if we got up to something in here. You should go sleep in your tent."

"I've seen you before," she whispered. "I know who you are."

"Oh, yeah? Who?"

"In the climbing magazines. You're not 'Robert' but Roberto Burns, right? You've cut your hair, but I recognize you. You're the guy who used to do all those insane solos."

"I used to. Not anymore."

"Yeah, I haven't read about you doing much lately. I just wanted *you* to know that *I* know who you are."

"Okay. You should go to your tent and sleep."

"Nah," she said, sitting down cross-legged on my sleeping bag, rubbing her eyes, then looking down at me. "I'm going to stay with you tonight. You don't know it, Roberto, but you need me."

Some coyotes began howling off in the night. I thought that maybe they were calling for me. Only it would turn out that they were coming for me.

THIRTY-SEVEN

Someone was tapping on the side of the Pig.

When I opened my eyes I saw nothing but blinding white light. Once again—for the second night in a row—I woke up to something that was far too bright for dawn. For a moment I thought maybe it was Kevin or Tony, screwing around to get even with me for scaring the hell out of them around the fire. But no, they wouldn't do something like that. They didn't have that kind of mischief in them.

It had to be the Mexican cops coming back to shake us down again. *Bastards.* Or maybe they'd told some of their cop buddies where to find us, told them that the pickings were easy and the girls were pretty in the hippie climbers' camp. They would be armed, but they wouldn't be drawing down. I'd already seen that Mexican cops in the Border Corridor were arrogant, sloppy, and dirty. They wouldn't be expecting a hippie climber to pull a sawed-off shotgun and jam it in their faces.

I was operating on autopilot. And it was Roberto who'd done the programming.

Mouth open, eyes squinted against the light, I raised my head and felt Lydia's dreadlocks slide off my neck. The light was a flashlight. Someone was holding it right in my face, his arm inside the open side window of the Pig. Lydia twitched in her sleep. She was half on top of me. As gently as possible, I nudged her off and to one side in the narrow confines of the Pig's cargo area. She murmured something but didn't jerk awake.

The light stayed in my face, blinding me. I shook my head and made a sleepy, confused noise. Then I snatched for it with my left hand while twisting around to reach under the driver's seat with my right. I caught the flashlight a second before I found the pistol grip of the shotgun. I shoved the light away, banging the arm that was holding it against the side of the window so that whoever was holding it would have to let go. The shotgun snagged under the seat as I tried to wrench it up.

"Eh eh eh," a voice said, too calmly. "Don't do it, my friend."

Something cold and metallic was pressed into the hollow of my throat. Smelling oil and cordite, I recognized the object. I also recognized the voice.

Oh shit.

A rush of fear shot through my veins and into each and every capillary.

"How are you, my friend? Last time I saw you, we were under the earth. You were supposed to stay there," Zafado said in Spanish.

The flashlight was withdrawn through the window when I let go of it, but its beam was still directed in my face. The cold muzzle of the gun remained pressed into my neck. Lydia was moving now, waking up.

"Hey," she said irritably. "Hey, man. What's with the light?" She made as if to snuggle up to me again, grasping at me with her legs and arms.

Before I could say anything, she was ripped off me. The sleeping bag that had covered us was torn off, too. Someone near the open tailgate had grabbed her by the ankles and jerked her right out of the truck. Her fingers grabbed without purchase at my legs as she went. I heard her hit the stony ground with a thump and a curse.

So there was someone else. At least one other person. I couldn't risk an attempt to grab the gun at my neck before it fired. I couldn't risk a fight like this, confined in the cramped cargo space of the Pig, against multiple assailants and with innocents around.

I let go of the shotgun. It was still trapped under the seat. *I should have slept with it against my thigh. Stupid.* The fear was oozing out of me in the form of a chilling sweat. I held both hands in front of my face to shield it from the light.

"That's good. Now come out, come out, my friend. Real slow, or your girlfriend might get hurt."

I scooted out of the open back end of the truck. The air outside raised goose bumps on my naked flesh, every tiny hair standing on end.

Three men stood in the moonlight. Zafado, holding the flashlight in one hand and his too-familiar chrome automatic in the other, was grinning through his large, crooked teeth. A big man whose name I didn't know was there, too. A gang-banger, shaved head and all, but older than the others, with an obvious pedigree of prison bulk. Bruto's replacement, I guessed. He was dragging Lydia to her feet with an arm around her neck.

Standing to one side and looking amused was El Doctor, Jesús Hidalgo.

"*Buenas noches,* Officer Burns," he crowed in a singsong voice. "My lawyer informed you not to try and contact me, did he not? And yet here you are, just a few miles from my home. Shame on you. I was most surprised to learn from my police friends that a man who looked like you was in the neighborhood."

He had a machete that he held comfortably at his side. He looked very composed and comfortable. Very pleased with himself. His wavy hair was combed, his mustache well-brushed. He was wearing a black polo shirt and khaki pants, looking quite preppy for a night in the mountains. I remembered how Roberto had described finding him at over twenty thousand feet on Aconcagua—in a Ralph Lauren down jacket and untreated leather boots.

"So my *capitáns* and I had a talk," he continued. "We thought maybe we should take an evening drive over the hills and see who this fellow was, this man who when described seemed a lot like someone who wasn't supposed to come near me. I would have liked to have brought Bruto, but of course you killed him. That was a shame. He was a loyal friend. Shorty I wasn't so sad about. He was a perverted little monster. Useful, though. But Bruto, now he was a good man."

"A good man," Zafado echoed. "He was my friend too."

I said nothing. The gangbanger had gotten Lydia to her feet. One bulging bicep was cinched against her throat. With his other hand he was groping up under her oversized T-shirt, the only thing she had on. The fear and rage and helplessness made me feel faint.

But Hidalgo's words kept me on my feet.

"So how is your brother? I understand he is still in the hospital, where he is being protected by an aged U.S. Marshal and a young Chinese woman. It doesn't seem that the Americans are taking his security very seriously. Is his condition as grave as I fear?"

I still said nothing. But I looked to Lydia, and saw that her mouth was open in a silent scream as the banger's free hand moved over her breasts, kneading them roughly. He was murmuring to her with his mouth pressed against her ear.

Hidalgo followed my gaze.

"Tell me, who is your young friend? This almost nude

young lady, and you here, entirely nude yourself. Shame on you, Officer Burns. This is not that reporter who lives in Denver. I've had someone watching her. Just last night she was in Denver, being watched by a man who looks like an overweight bulldog."

Zafado glanced at Lydia, too, and snorted at what his fellow *capitán* was doing. Turning back to me, he said, "Hippies. You lie with dogs, my friend, you will get fleas." He held the light on the mark Lydia had left on my throat. "Or maybe rabies. Then we have to put you down. Like a dog, no?"

I couldn't believe I'd put Lydia and her friends in this position. Just as I had allowed Roberto to be sacrificed. What I felt was horror, and, as Hidalgo had said, shame. No one had hurt me yet, but what I felt was something like a brutal blow to the gut. I finally managed to speak.

"Let her go. She doesn't know anything."

Hidalgo chuckled. Zafado joined in. The big banger was too busy cooing in Lydia's ear. He'd pulled her shirt up almost all the way to her neck.

A zipper tore open a little distance away. Kevin and Barb crawled out of the tent that was next to the van. Tony was walking up the hill from the other tent. All three of the desert rats were bleary-eyed and stumbling, not understanding what was taking place by the back of my truck.

"What's going on?" Kevin called, coming closer. "Who are these guys?"

Hidalgo answered him in English. "Stay right there, young man. The three of you will stay where you are, please."

They did, standing as still as statues on the dirt road as they took in what was happening. Me naked, with the strangers and Lydia—also naked—standing by the back of the van. Zafado's gun was pointed at my face; next to him stood the urbane-looking man with a machete who had turned to talk to them, and the big, ugly banger with his arms wrapped around and still moving over Lydia's bare skin.

"Let them go," I insisted, to more chuckles. "All of them."

Hidalgo turned back to me to explain what was so funny.

"You think I'm going to harm a bunch of dirty children who are no threat to me?" he said in Spanish.

Yeah, actually I did. That was his signature.

"What kind of man do you think I am?" he asked with mock indignation. He turned again to Kevin, Tony, and Barb while Zafado remained facing me with the gun pointed at my face.

"Do you know this man's name?" Hidalgo asked them in English.

"Robert," Tony mumbled.

"What did you say?"

"Robert!" Barb half shouted. She was trembling, holding on to Kevin's arm with both of her hands. She looked like she might fall down without it. I knew how she felt. But I had nothing to hold on to.

Hidalgo laughed. Once again, Zafado joined in. The banger was too busy.

Hidalgo said, "No? Really? Robert. That is an interesting name. In Spanish we say Roberto. I once knew a man by that name. Where is your friend Robert from?"

"Never told us," Tony mumbled. "And he's not our friend."

"We just met him here the other night," Kevin said. "Never seen him before until then."

"Very good," Hidalgo said. "Then all you must know about him is that he is a very bad man. Forget you ever met him. Now you go. All of you. Bye-bye."

"Keep the girls," the banger protested suddenly, his hand now between Lydia's legs. "We can have some fun with them."

Hidalgo shook his head, a little reluctantly. In Spanish he

said, "We will have our fun with this man here, Roberto, as he now calls himself. We can pretend we once again have our hands on the real Roberto. Now let go of that young lady. She has nothing to do with our business."

The banger hesitated then let go, scowling. Lydia broke away from him and staggered toward her friends. I saw that her eyes were very wide before her back was to me. Opened in a way and to a degree that she might not be able to ever properly close them again. She'd seen and felt things that weren't so innocent. But then I suspected she'd known them before, and had overcome it. This time, though, maybe not.

Kevin grabbed her as she half fell into him. He yanked her shirt down over her buttocks.

"Bye-bye," Hidalgo said again to the desert rats.

When they didn't move, he flapped his hands at them, motioning them into the van. While a little feminine, it was a particularly effective gesture because of the machete. The blade flashed in the moonlight. And this just hours after I'd told them about *la corbata*.

Then they moved as one, in a sudden leap toward the jacked-up van. There was a brief Three Stooges rush into it. When they finally got themselves sorted out, Lydia was in the driver's seat. I hoped she could drive it—the van was so big and she was so small. They needed to get out of here before Hidalgo changed his mind. Before the banger discovered he had some free time on his hands and that the night was still young. That maybe catching up to them before they reached the highway would be a good idea.

I almost hoped they'd take their time with me.

The engine cranked to life and the rear lights burned red as Lydia managed to flip on the headlights. I felt myself painted crimson by their glow. The van was already facing away from us, and she would have a clear shot down the road.

There was a click as the van was put into gear. The engine revved and the tires crackled forward.

Hidalgo turned back to me.

"Now it is just us. Old friends, yes? Connected through your brother. Too bad he's going to die, by the way. I was sorry to have to cut his throat after he took that great fall. You see, I'm only a simple businessman. For the sake of business, I sometimes have to do things that I'm not always happy about."

But his grin gave the lie to his words. He was mocking me. For fun. The red taillights made him and his *capitáns* look like devils. They glowed brighter when the van bucked twice and died.

Slightly irritated, Hidalgo turned around. The banger turned, too, looking hopeful. Zafado kept his eyes and his gun trained on me.

The engine cranked and caught again. The red glow dimmed as what had to be a shaking foot was taken off the brake. Hidalgo turned back to me.

He gestured again with the machete, this time tapping the flat of the blade against the upper part of his chest.

"Okay, now, Antonio or Roberto or whoever you want to be. Do you know how to tie your own necktie? Many men do not, I'm afraid. I will have to show you." Then to Zafado, whose gun was still pointed at my face, "Shoot him in the groin. That way he won't struggle too much."

The van clicked into gear again. *Go, go.* Then white lights—the reverse lights—came on. *Shit,* I thought. *She can't drive it. She doesn't even know how to put it in gear. They aren't going to get out of here.*

The van lunged backward. It was so sudden, so surprising, and so fast that I didn't even leap out of the way. I just stood there, frozen, as the engine roared and the big rear end that was plastered with stickers slammed toward me.

As if in slow motion, Hidalgo's head snapped back when

the bumper hit the back of his legs. His head smacked into the window, spiderwebbing the glass. Zafado took it on the shoulder. The banger, who was still turned hopefully toward the van, took the impact in the face and chest. Then Hidalgo flew into me and we both sprawled into the back of the Pig.

In the glow of the reverse lights, still advancing, I saw Zafado and the banger fly by, one on each side. The lights blazed red as the brakes were stomped. Tires skidded on dirt and rock. The bumper was on my shins, but just touching, not breaking.

For a moment I was too shocked to comprehend what had just happened. How the tables had suddenly been turned. Jesús Hidalgo was groaning in my arms, where Lydia had been ten minutes earlier. But his were definitely not groans of pleasure. The tailpipe was cutting into my ankle, the pain lighting me up with something like exhilaration.

I was tempted to laugh. Lydia—damn, she was pretty tough for an innocent little elf.

As I regained a sense of time and place, the white lights went out as the transmission clicked again. The van slowly began pulling forward. Its red taillights began to dance as the van bounced over ruts and rocks, accelerating. In my arms, Jesús Hidalgo—El Doctor, killer of maybe thousands, the great, untouchable drug lord himself—was limp and groaning louder. The van geared down expertly to drop off the ridge. Then it was gone, lurching into the darkness. I never saw it, or any of the desert rats, again.

I pushed Hidalgo off me. He collapsed onto the ground at the rear of the Pig. I retrieved the pump-action shotgun with the pistol grip from under the seat and stepped completely into the night.

The world tore open three times. Three souls disappeared. Maybe four, if you counted my own.

THIRTY-EIGHT

L ike that night in Cheyenne almost three years before, it wasn't exactly self-defense. It was close, within a minute or so, but not as close as that night when a blizzard was tearing down out of the Medicine Bow and I pushed through a ranch house's ramshackle door.

Maybe an argument could be made that would have allowed me to feel somewhat okay about it. After all, it wasn't done in cold blood. Not entirely. At least it wasn't the straight-out assassination I'd intended to commit in Hidalgo's home. And there wasn't any doubt what they were going to do to me. What Hidalgo was going to do, personally, with that machete, after Zafado incapacitated me with a bullet through the groin. *La corbata.* Their imminent intentions should have provided some philosophical relief.

But they didn't. I'd clearly stepped over the line.

Murder in the first degree—the most repugnant of all crimes—is the *deliberate and premeditated killing of a human being*. I examined the evidence and built a case against myself. The initial drive to Mexico. The purchase of the vicious little shotgun. The clandestine buying of shells manufactured to knock down large mammals. The reconnaissance of the hacienda from atop Trono Blanco. And finally, the three point-blank blasts of buckshot to already wounded men who were no longer an immediate threat to my well-being.

Self-defense, as defined by the law, didn't apply. And Leo Tolstoy, who was smarter than me, was probably right about preemptive violence.

I was guilty not just once but three times over.

At first I felt very little. Numb, and that was all. Neither horrified nor triumphant nor vindicated. I collapsed the tents and straightened up the camp. I threw everything but the bodies in the back of the Pig. Then I washed off my blood-encrusted legs and dressed. As light began to gather out over the Sea of Cortés, and the flies began to gather around the campsite, I looked around one last time then fired up the old truck.

The road wasn't much easier to navigate in the dawn than it had been in the night. I was helped a little by the tracks from the van's oversized tires. I came to a fancy jacked-up pickup about a half-mile from the camp. It was where the narcos had left it before making their final approach on foot. On the back window of the pickup was one of those little yellow stickers. A happy face with a protruding tongue instead of a curving line for a smile. I stopped, got out, and scraped it off. I put the shredded sticker in my wallet. Next to where my badge should have been.

I wondered what Zafado had done with the gold-and-silver shield. He'd taken it from me in the mine and it had never reappeared. That was all right. I'd given it away in the mine as much as he'd taken it, and I'd given it away again in Mexico.

The outwardly pleasant village of Colonia de la Tajo was empty except for some roosters on the road and a goat on the baseball field. The town would get a new *patrón* soon. Some-one—less or perhaps more brutal—would step in to fill

Hidalgo's shoes. As even Tom Cochran had admitted, the monster always grows a new head. He'd also said that there is more than a little pleasure to be taken in lopping the old one off.

At midmorning I crossed the border back into the United States, the place where the law was supposed to mean something.

The sweating INS agent asked me the purpose of my visit to Mexico.

"Pleasure," I answered.

I hadn't found it, though. Not even after having lopped off *the* head and those of the three main *capitáns*.

I saw Mary Chang before she saw me.

She was on the yellow couch in the hospital corridor, reading this time instead of sleeping. Like when I'd confronted her by the elevators in the courthouse—or when, more accurately, she and Tom had confronted me with the ultimate goal of their plan—she was dressed in an expensive-looking suit. The thing she was reading was a slick brochure. As I came closer, I saw it was for a high-priced security firm called Krull and Associates.

I guessed she'd lost her job, or was about to lose it. I didn't feel too bad. She deserved it, just as I now did. She'd been the one who'd started this whole thing when her friend and colleague was murdered by Jesús Hidalgo. Besides, Krull would be happy to pay an attractive female minority agent with both FBI experience and a law degree double or triple her government salary. I knew that Krull even had offices in Denver, if that was where she wanted to be.

Maybe what she felt for Roberto was true, or maybe it was just plain guilt. Or maybe it was simply the need to protect him—something she no longer needed to do. I didn't ask her motivation and she didn't tell me. In fact, I refused to speak to her at all.

"Anton! Where have you been?" she asked, slapping down the brochure and jumping to her feet. She knew the answer because where I'd been was where she'd intended for me to go all along. It had been the plan before she'd even met me.

When I didn't answer, or even acknowledge her presence, she asked with less pretense, "Are you okay? What happened? Did you get him?"

I walked past her into the ICU. I closed the glass door firmly behind me.

Roberto's position in the bed—still in the Intensive Care Unit—was unchanged, although he had somehow managed to get a new wound on his throat. It was a jagged, scabrous tear sewn shut with wiry black stitches. It ran vertically from just below his chin to the V where his collarbones connected. It crossed the old wound, making an X.

When I first saw it, I thought they had somehow gotten to him. That Hidalgo's men were still out there, still hunting, and that my crimes had been for nothing. Or that Hidalgo was so evil he had the power to reach out from the grave.

But Roberto's tongue was still in his mouth, as far as I could tell. And the new wound was vertical, rather than horizontal. Almost choking, I demanded an explanation from the attending nurse. It seemed that there had been some changes in his condition after all. And that they'd been for the worse.

My brother might actually live.

A day earlier he'd begun to breathe on his own. The tube down his throat had been removed. There had also been an indication of electrical activity in his brain. Based on these findings, which the doctors considered positive, they'd performed another surgery. I nearly vomited when a nurse told me the details.

The four-inch incision was made in his throat. His trachea

and esophagus were pushed to the side. The root of his tongue, presumably, as well. The fragments of two exploded disks were removed from between three of his vertebrae. The hope was that the vertebrae in his neck would fuse together. Then they'd stitched up the wound, twisted some new screws into his skull, and attached a steel frame that went down to his shoulders. All this so that, if he did ever wake up, he might only be paralyzed from the waist down, below where his spinal cord had been completely severed, instead of from the neck down.

His eyes were half-open but unseeing. I gently touched my forehead to his and looked into them. The famous blue irises were pale and watery. The whites around them were crimson—stained from burst blood vessels in his head.

"It's up to you, bro. Live or die. Live, and I'll find a way for us to climb again. I promise. Die, and I'll think of you every time I'm feeding the Rat."

I wiped my face on my sleeve then dug out my wallet. For a minute I stared at the empty space where my badge had been Velcroed. I remembered when I'd received it after taking an oath following my academy training in Rock Springs. Roberto had shown up for the ceremony. How he heard about it I never knew. He was traveling constantly at the time, doing his solos in Yosemite and the Black Canyon and down in Patagonia, doing his speedballs, too, and almost always attended by a photographer from one of the climbing magazines.

I'd been so affected by his quiet, amused presence at the ceremony that I couldn't refuse to follow him to Laramie and a party he knew about. It was all climbers—playing music, demonstrating moves in the air, and smoking pot. I pretended not to see or smell the pot. Then I felt my wallet slide out of my pocket. Roberto ran up to a group passing a pipe, the badge in his palm, screaming, "POLICE! GET DOWN!" He ripped the pipe out of a stunned girl's hands, sucked it off, and ran off laughing.

From the pocket behind where the badge should have been, I took out the shredded yellow sticker. I pushed it into his palm and closed his fingers around it. Unlike myself, my brother wouldn't have any qualms about the trophy.

Holding my brother's fingers closed around the sticker, I thought that maybe Mary would find it there. Then she would know for sure what had happened. And then I would see if she stopped hanging around in the hallway. Or maybe a nurse would notice it first and throw it away. Maybe Roberto would wake up, see it, and grin his mischievous grin.

What I did know was that the murders of Jesús Hidalgo and his two *capitáns* would never be reported or confirmed. The bodies would disappear from the campsite. They were probably already gone. Someone other than the coyotes would clean up what was splashed on the stony ground. The Mexican cartels had a history of covering up the deaths of their leaders. Just like Ramon Arellano-Felix and his rival, Amado Carrillo-Fuentes. They didn't want to admit that another cartel had succeeded in taking out their leadership. Instead they wanted the uncertainty and legends to grow.

Rumor has it that both narcos are still around, still running things. Jesús Hidalgo, too. That's what the *narcocorridos* are singing about, anyway. The disciples of Saint Malverde are still out there. In vengeful spirit if not in fact.

"Where the hell have you been, QuickDraw?" McGee growled when I opened the door to Rebecca's loft.

Then Mungo hit me like a freight train, bowling me backward into the hallway.

It seemed that with the wolf, at least, all would be forgiven. She planted her paws on my chest and half licked and half gnawed at my throat. Somebody still liked me. I didn't think there were too many others.

Once I got out from under a hundred pounds of hair and bone and slobber, McGee barked his question a second time.

He was slumped on the couch that lately had been serving as his bed. As usual, there was ash and food in his beard and a suspicious glare in his bloodshot eyes. His old .45 automatic lay on the table in front of him.

I made my voice cheery.

"Looking for my head, boss. Trying to get it on straight. Where's Rebecca?"

He waited a beat.

"Where do you think?"

I didn't answer. He knew that I knew she'd be at work. And he knew that was why I'd come here instead of going there. I gave up on the false good humor.

"You can put that away," I said, pointing to the gun. "Rebecca's safe now. Thanks for keeping an eye on her."

It was his turn not to say anything. He didn't speak for a long, long time. But his silence spoke volumes. As did his eyes. He picked up the big, blunt gun and dropped it into his brief-case without looking away from me. Closed the lid, spun the combination locks. When he finally spoke, it was as if he hadn't heard what I'd said.

"Christ, Burns. You've been gone three days without telling anyone where the hell you were going. The office is go-ing out of their minds. The AG wants an interstate BOLO put out on you." A BOLO—Be-On-the-Look-Out—is what used to be known as an APB, an All Points Bulletin. "An investiga-tive team's been formed to decide whether or not to press charges or take disciplinary action for you going into that mine without a warrant."

"What's going to happen with that?"

As head of the Division of Criminal Investigation, McGee

would oversee the investigation. And, after consulting with the governor and the Attorney General, determine the outcome.

"Disciplinary, you undeserving bastard. A mere lowering of grade and pay. The Feds want the whole thing kept quiet. They threatened to cut the Department of Justice grant money if the Attorney General doesn't do what they want. So there's going to be no charges, no trial."

I smirked. Of course they wanted it kept quiet. They didn't want their rogue agents' actions becoming public. They wanted it to look like some big screwup by the hick Wyoming police. *Those cowboys were too dumb to know they needed a warrant*. And my pay couldn't get much lower, anyway. But whatever it was would be enough. It's not hard to get by when you're happiest sleeping on the ground. And that was where I intended to do my sleeping for the foreseeable future.

"And a special assignment," he added, showing me an evil grin. "Seems the governor is all worked up about some supposed gay-sex ring going on late at night in one of the Cheyenne city parks. Wants it cleaned up, pronto. So we're going to put you in leather pants and run a little sting. You have no idea, QuickDraw, just how far you've got to go before there's enough evidence to arrest. I hope you can still touch your toes when it's all over, and that you can pucker your lips without ChapStick. I'm going to want a dozen arrests before you get another assignment."

I had no doubt he would make me go through with it. Just as I had no doubt that any charges I reluctantly filed would be pled out. A similar sting had been run two years earlier at the governor's insistence, and conducted by another DCI agent deep in the doghouse. McGee, who lacked the governor's homophobia, had reduced all Public Indecency charges down to Following Too Close—a two-point traffic infraction and a twenty-dollar fine.

I'd take my punishment. It was probably a lot less severe than I deserved.

"I want you in Cheyenne tonight. You're to report to the office, and to the investigative team. You are not to go anywhere or do anything until their investigation's complete. You understand me, boy?"

"Tonight?"

"Tonight."

I nodded. Then I asked, "How about Rebecca? How is she?"

The evil grin he'd worn when describing my next assignment completely disappeared. It was replaced by a frown and a glare that were even harsher than when I'd first come in the door. He might be able to forgive—or at least justify to some degree—my forays into the dark side of the law. But this was clearly something that was inexcusable.

"If you leave this town without speaking to her, I'm going to take you apart with my own hands."

He flexed his fat, powerful fingers for emphasis.

So my last stop before leaving town was at the *Denver Post* building. I showered and shaved before I went, and even put on my navy going-to-court suit. I was clean on the outside, at least. After security probed at me with an electric wand, I rode the elevator up to Rebecca's floor. She was in. The receptionist listened to me say my name and nervously told me to go on back.

As I walked passed the cubicles with clicking keyboards and ringing phones, the whole room seemed to pause and stare at me. I didn't feel so clean now. *That's the guy,* I imagined each face thinking. *The one they call QuickDraw. He did that terrible thing in Cheyenne a couple of years ago. Killed three young men and planted weapons on them—at least that's what they say. God only knows what else he's done.*

If God were here to tell them, they could add another three black marks to my name. And this time it happened to be true.

Suddenly I was the guy they'd always suspected I was. The killer Mary Chang and Tom Cochran had set up to commit a righteous murder.

Rebecca had written an article about me after the civil suit that followed what had happened in Cheyenne was finally settled. It had been a fair piece, describing the facts of the shooting as well as the suppositions of the dead men's families and the accusations of their lawyer. The *Denver Post* staff knew when we'd started dating. Rebecca had told me it was the gossip event of the year. *Our own enfante gâté, our jewel, running around with a very bad boy.* And I assumed they all knew by now that she was pregnant. Even if she hadn't told them, she was starting to show.

Their stares made me feel like a freak. Reporters are naturally suspicious of police, and my background certainly didn't do anything to lessen that suspicion. On the plus side, though, at least I didn't have to worry about any of her colleagues hitting on her in my presence.

"Hi," Rebecca said, looking up from her cubicle in the crowded, noisy room.

She was dressed in a sand-colored pair of loose linen pants and a white sleeveless shirt. The shirt was untucked. Her hair was pulled back severely, which always made her look very young and vulnerable. Despite the clamor of the room, Rebecca looked calm.

She didn't stand to embrace me. The brightness in her voice had nothing to do with what I saw in her eyes.

"Anton. You're back."

"Hi."

"I've been worried about you. Are you all right?"

"Yeah. I'm fine."

"Where have you been?"

I tried the line that had silenced McGee.

"Looking for my head."

She stared at me for too long without speaking. Then, in a very quiet voice, she asked, "Did you find it?"

I nodded. "You don't have to worry about Jesús Hidalgo or the Mexicali Mafia anymore."

She pretended not to have heard, just as McGee had pretended.

"What are you going to do now?"

"I've got Mungo in the truck. Ross says we're supposed to be in Wyoming to meet with an investigative team tonight."

"Are you going to be there for a while?"

"Yeah. I think so."

Now she nodded. "Okay. I think that's probably for the best."

THIRTY-NINE

Two hours later Mungo was literally leaping up and down in the backseat, bouncing around the inside of the truck like a furry rubber ball. We'd crossed the Wyoming state line, gotten onto I-80 west instead of going straight into Cheyenne, and were coming to the turnoff for Vedauwoo. I'd decided that the misconduct investigation and the deposition I was required to give could wait a couple of hours. The Pig wheeled onto the turnoff, vibrated over the cattle guards, and we were soon on a rutted dirt road among granite towers and beaver ponds.

This was the place where Roberto and I first became addicted to getting high. I was maybe seven, and Roberto a couple of years older, when Mom and Dad brought us here. At the time the family was stationed at the nearby Air Force base in Cheyenne. Dad had finally convinced Mom that his boys were old enough to climb.

I parked in an aspen grove that was near a small stream. Mungo didn't wait for me to open the door for her—she squirmed out the window and fell to the ground. Finding her feet, she sprinted into the trees.

I followed her to the base of a two-hundred-foot rock that

was split by a hand-sized crack. The route was called Friday
the Thirteenth; Roberto and I had been so proud to follow
Dad up. We were proud to have Mom nervously watching
from below, fretting the same way she fretted whenever Dad
went off to conquer some Himalayan monster. I felt like a little kid again as I booted up, remembering the oversized
climbing boots my brother and I shared back then. I could
hear Roberto laughing, nearly levitating in his excitement to
get off the ground.

The rock seemed to touch me back when I stroked it. It
held my hands with a firm grip when I shoved them into a vertical crack. Nothing had changed. Everything was so familiar.
I pulled up and started climbing. There was a long way to go.

I tried not to ask myself if I had changed, or if I'd always
been this way. Some questions are better left unanswered.
Anyway, I supposed time would tell.

ABOUT THE AUTHOR

CLINTON McKINZIE is the acclaimed author of *The Edge of Justice, Point of Law, Trial by Ice and Fire,* and *Crossing the Line.* He was raised in Santa Monica, California, and he now lives in Colorado with his wife and two sons. Prior to becoming a writer, he worked as a peace officer and deputy district attorney in Denver. His passion is climbing alpine walls.

Don't miss the next exciting
Antonio Burns novel

BADWATER

by

CLINTON McKINZIE

Available May 2005
from Delacorte Press

Please read on for a preview

CLINTON McKINZIE

BESTSELLING AUTHOR OF *CROSSING THE LINE*

BADWATER

A NOVEL OF SUSPENSE

BADWATER
on sale April 26, 2005

The day it all began, I was doing the same thing I'd been doing nearly every day for the past year: beating the bushes in the state's vast forests and trying like hell to stay out of trouble. I was intent on lying low, minding my own business, and bothering no one but the shitheads who were cooking meth in the woods. This had been my sole occupation ever since an agency already inclind to be suspicious of me had become positively paranoid about my methods of investigation.

Now I was determined to give them nothing to suspect. As far as I—and my office—was concerned, I was out of the investigation business entirely. I'd been essentially demoted from a top-rated undercover agent to the role of a mere scout.

Under this new unofficial job description I would drive each day along remote logging and mining roads in the wilder portions of the Lower 48's least populated state. The rusty Land Cruiser I called the Pig prowled the backcountry in low gear, my wolf-dog Mungo drooling out one of the backseat windows. Both beast and driver scanned the roadsides for items such as "death bags," strewn kitty litter, cold medicine wrappers, lithium batteries, and glass jars filled with murky liquids. All of these were signs that somewhere nearby we would surely find a clandestine methamphetamine lab.

Meth—also called crank, speed, ice, glass, crunch, and crystal—had become the number-one societal problem in Wyoming, surpassing even the red-faced shouting war between the extraction industries and the enviorontmentalists. Ninety percent of crime in the state could be traced back to meth. Something like forty percent of kids admitted to having tried it, and a lot of them swallowed the hook. They traded normal lives and desires for multi-day psychotic binges, permanent brain damage, oozing sores, nowhere futures, and an overwhelming need for more.

I had seen it a thousand times in the course of my eight-year career in law enforcement. I'd come to consider giving a little tinfoil-wrapped packet of yellow crystals to a kid a crime far worse than handing one a loaded gun. The stuff is so addictive and mind-warping that it makes whiskey and pot seem as harmless as Gummy Bears. Bikers started cooking this scary shit in the late eighties and early nineties, but in the new century it's being produced by grade-school lab nerds, trailer-park yokels with Internet access, and some very well-organized Latino gangs.

It was the gangs and their so-called "super-labs" that were my primary prey. Or had been, anyway. A year ago I'd broken up the biggest one in the history of the West. But it was that very same bust that, for the second time in my career, had gotten me reprimanded and very nearly arrested. It had also utterly devastated my personal life, costing me just about everything but the dog and the truck. My job was still to hunt the drug and its dealers, but the subsequent investigations and arrests were handed to federal agents or local police who had less "colorful" backgrounds than Special Agent Antonio Burns; officers who could testify in court without a famously disputed shooting and a drug kingpin's odd disappearance following them around to cast doubt upon their credibility.

Although I hated to admit it even to myself, and despite the badge I still carried in my wallet, I'd become little more than an informant—the lowest of the low in the law-enforcement pecking order. A rat. I'd long since stopped blaming bad luck or bad judgment for my predicament. Instead I'd come to believe it was an arbitrary result of a flawed and often corrupt system. And I wasn't sure how much longer I could remain a participant in a system that had first disappointed, then betrayed me. Or maybe, just maybe, I'd disappointed and betrayed it.

The afternoon of June 14 began with Mungo and me spotting three black trash bags in a roadside ditch. This had become an almost everyday discovery. Either there was more cooking going on or I was becoming very good at guessing where we would find the clan labs. Mungo wrinkled her snout at the plastic sacks and gave her signal; she coughed in a very unladylike manner, as if she had a hairball lodged in her throat. The ammonia scent was so strong that I could smell it myself. My eyes watered as I got out of the truck and pulled on a pair of rubber gloves.

All three bags were partially inflated. Full, I knew, of nasty gases and liquids. Phosphine. Anhydrous ammonia. Crystal iodine. Hydrochloric acid. Stuff that even the dumbest cranker is smart enough to keep the hell away from themselves and their lab. So what the motherfuckers do is dump them in a place like this, where maybe a little kid can find them and wonder what's inside.

I gently lifted the sacks by their tied-off necks and carried them deeper into the woods. There I concealed them as best as I could. It pissed me off that I didn't have the equipment and protective gear to deal with them properly. In the unlikely event the state or federal government would somehow scratch up the funds to do proper sanitation, I recorded the location on my handheld Global Positioning System.

A little way further down the road we came across a fresh doubletrack leading into the trees. The path had obviously been made by an all-terrain vehicle—it was too narrow for the Pig, and the torn earth had obviously been the victim of some very knobby tires. This in a place where no one—not even poachers or asshole off-roaders intent on tearing up a meadow somewhere—would have a legitimate interest in going.

I stopped and listened carefully. When I didn't hear the banshee wail of a two-stroke engine, I let the Pig creep on down the road for another quarter-mile, then parked in a turnout. Mungo leapt out and sniffed around while I laced up my running shoes and slung on a small pack. Consistent with my mantra of avoiding trouble, I left my duty weapon under the Pig's front seat. Trouble was all the .40 Heckler & Koch had brought me.

I looked, and wanted to look, like a grad student on summer break. *Just hanging out, dude, doing a little tramping through the woods.* If I looked anything like a cop, I knew there was a pretty good chance I'd be shot on sight. So my hair was a little long, my face unshaven, and my shorts and T-shirt appropriately baggy and torn. Mungo was disguised, too, with a bright red bandana around her neck. But she looked away disdainfully when I offered for the hundredth time to enhance her costume by letting her carry a floppy fabric Frisbee. She had her pride.

The disguises were good, though, even without the Frisbee. It was only with a very close look that someone would notice the creases around my eyes suggesting I might be a little old for a grad student, or that Mungo was no oversized Shepherd/Malamute mix but actually a half-wolf.

"Vamonos," I called to her.

On foot, we headed back down the road and then turned onto the doubletrack.

Within a few minutes we were hoofing it through a forest of lodgepole pines, with Mungo bumping her bony shoulder against my thigh. The sun cut through the needle canopy overhead in dusty rays and the trail wound around trees, drop-offs, and boulders. Mungo stayed at my side even when a squirrel taunted us from a high branch. We moved easily together—at least one of us was well-trained. Her light-footed tread was something I tried to emulate, and I swung my head as often as she did, smelling, looking, listening.

Mungo's vigilance was due to a genetic instinct that had her always searching for something she could kill. My awareness, however, was defensive. It came from too much experience with booby traps.

These came in many forms—fishing line connected to detonators or mounted shotguns on the trailside, punji stakes in concealed pits, bear traps, poisoned hypodermic needles hidden in brush, fishhooks dangling from branches at eye level, and once, quite memorably, a half-starved mountain lion chained to a tree. Then there were the crankers themselves to worry about, as they are almost always armed a hell of a lot better than I would ever be, even with my duty weapon. The labs they protected could be anything from fancy trailers to canvas tents with crates of cold medicine and lithium batteries stacked under tarps. Dead or dying trees were always nearby, though— killed by the byproducts that then sank down into the groundwater. The cooking process produced six pounds of highly toxic waste for every pound of meth. Poured in a trout stream, it would kill every fish for miles downstream. A lot of it seemed to get sucked up into the brains of the crankers, making them meaner and more prone to violence than a sack full of rattlesnakes.

Once I found the lab, if it was unguarded, I intended to snap a few pictures with the digital camera in my backpack, record the longitude and latitude on the handheld GPS, and later e-mail both files back to the main office in Cheyenne. Maybe they would send out a SWAT team with a HAZMAT disposal crew. Or maybe not.

Not was most likely, I had learned. There simply weren't the resources to bust up and then clean up every lab I'd found in the last year. Each site, it was explained to me the first few times I'd complained (later they just ignored me), could cost from $5,000 to $150,000—an amount of money sorely lacking in this economy, especially in a state with no income tax. I understood this, but it still pissed me off. This shit was killing people, after all. I even knew about it firsthand—and not just through my undercover observations. My one and only brother was among the hundreds I'd seen wrecked by drugs.

So far, though, I had managed to keep from firing the extremely flammable labs I'd found with flashbang grenades, managed to keep from arresting the cooks after encouraging them to "resist," and even managed to keep from screaming and pushing the office suits into walls, although sometimes it had taken deep breathing and seated meditation to cool the impulses. *I will be nothing but a good scout,* I constantly reminded myself. No trouble. *Just do your damn job—nothing more!,* as my boss commanded me each time I reported in. Find the labs, turn them in, and do nothing.

Then wait and watch as nothing was being done.

I tried to be philosophical about it—*Hey, Ant, you get to spend your days wandering around in the woods with Mungo. You even find and get to rope up on cliffs no one's ever been on before. C'mon, man, a lot of people would kill for this job*—but the frustration had me grinding my teeth day after day. Pumping some chemical through my veins that was even meaner than meth. It had polluted me. It kept me from driving down to Denver and trying to win back the woman I loved, not to mention the daughter she'd given birth to six months before.

It wasn't just that the shitheads were getting away with it, it was that they *knew* they were getting away with it. And that other people knew—my own office, for God's sake, the state's chief law enforcement agency—*knew* that they *knew,* and let them go on laughing at the law. That was what really pissed me off—it actually enraged me.

But—*deep breath, center yourself, Ant*—I was being a good boy. I was becoming adept at avoiding trouble. Until this day, when trouble came looking for me and demanded yet another confrontation.

It was Mungo, of course, who first sensed its presence.

We were moving down the double-track at an easy pace, our noses, eyes, and ears taking in everything that our vastly unequal senses were capable of, when Mungo suddenly whipped her hatchet-shaped head to the left. Ears pricked in that same direction, she lifted her nose high and snuffed the air. I watched her eyes—in them I was pretty sure I could read whatever she was smelling, whether it be a moose, an elk, a bear, a stranger, or a booby-trapped clan lab.

The yellow eyes narrowed. Like she was frowning; no, confused. She confirmed this interpretation by glancing up at me, cocking her head, then going back to testing the air with quivering nostrils. Her big, pointed ears working, too, like some sophisticated radar system, her head moving this way and that. I waited for her to lock on.

"Qué pasa?" I asked when she did.

Mungo kept staring into the trees, straining her neck forward a little. She let out a soft whine. What the hell? I still didn't know what she'd locked onto. What was weird was that I didn't think she knew, either. All I could hear was the touch of a breeze in the treetops and the faraway rumble of a lot of water moving fast over stone. All I could smell was pine needles. I finally got impatient.

"Okay, Mungo. Whatever it is, let's check it out. *Vamonos.*"

I lifted my hand and flicked my fingers in the direction she'd focused on.

Mungo took a few hesitant steps off the double-track and into the trees—head still high, examining the air, not the ground—and then she shifted up into a higher gear. Within twenty feet she was moving at a fast trot.

Even just loping along, she traveled at a speed that I could only keep up with in an almost-sprint, something I wasn't willing to do when chasing the unknown. Mungo was aware of her master's shortcomings, however, and paused every hundred yards or so to wait for me. Her tail waved me on like a beacon. The forest's undergrowth wasn't particularly heavy, as the high canopy above only allowed light to enter in dusty beams. I was able to move pretty fast through it, not worrying too much about breaking an ankle but still imagining hanging fish-hooks and punji pits.

I'd only been running for four or five minutes when I heard the first faint strains of what had been undoubtedly a cacophony in Mungo's ears. It sounded like yelling. Coming from not one person, I guessed, but several.

I slowed, holding my breath so I could listen. The forest had gone silent but for the rush of blood in my ears. The usual birds were quiet, the squirrels not chattering at all. Only the river was still rumbling away as a bass background from the distant screams. Then I picked up the pace until I was actually sprinting. As I ran, vec-toring in on the sounds myself now, I mentally unfolded a map in my head.

The way the sunbeams slashed across the forest told me that I was heading west. Toward the Badwater River, which couldn't be more than a quarter-mile away now. Just beyond the river—on the other side—ran a state highway. Maybe a car had plunged through a guardrail and gone into the river. Or maybe a raft had flipped on the rapids and the survivors were screaming for missing raftmates. But, no, some of these screams, growing in volume as I neared, sounded angry. Others were pleading.

"I'm going to kill you!"

"You killed him! You killed him!"

"Do you see him?"

"Oh God, can you see him? Where did he go?"

"You're dead, you fucking fag! You're dead!"

What the hell? I asked myself again. Then I could hear a siren. Good. Somebody else's problem now, whatever it is. But I didn't—couldn't—slow.

Mungo was out of sight. When I'd begun sprinting, she'd blasted on ahead. Following the shouts, the siren, and the rumble of the river, I came to the edge of the forest. It ended so abruptly that I had to hook the trunk of a tree with one arm to avoid running right off a ten-foot bank and falling into the water. Mungo wolfishly grinned at me—*ha ha*—from a few feet to one side, where she had stopped under the cover of some willows.

Despite the constant boom of whitewater both up- and downstream, the water below was slow and peaceful. Directly across the river, though, there was anything but peace.

Two highway patrol cars, lights still flashing but sirens now silent, were parked on top of a hill a little ways back from the river. That hill met the river with a rounded cliff that was twice the size of the opposite one I stood panting on. The cliff was actually an enormous boulder. To the south—left—side of the cliff was a beach composed of round stones, and on it raged two screaming boys. Both were being physically restrained by a beefy state patrolman. The other trooper—a tall, thin guy—was thigh-deep in the river, his head pivoting rapidly as he stared into the gold and green water in front of him. There was a pale young man in an orange lifejacket in the river, too. He was charging around in the water like a maniac. Downstream floated a raft that was fighting the current—a man onboard rowing hard, and a passenger, a woman with black hair, sobbing.

"What happened?" I yelled over the shouts of various people.

The tall trooper in the river jerked up his head.

"Who the heck are you?"

"Antonio Burns. DCI." DCI is my employer, Wyoming's statewide Division of Criminal Investigation.

The trooper, who'd immediately gone back to scanning the water after asking his question, popped his head up again. He looked at me with surprised eyes and an open mouth. Then the eyes narrowed suspiciously. I knew it was my name, not the name of the agency I worked for, that caused the reaction.

"They call you QuickDraw, right?"

I stared hard at him, not answering, as a bloom of heat spread outwards from my chest. He quickly looked back down the water, muttering, "Oh. Sorry."

"What happened?" I asked again in what I hoped was an even voice.

"Kids say that guy in the lifejacket pushed their cousin—a ten-year-old boy—off that cliff over there."

The maniac in the lifejacket stopped splashing around. Now he looked up, and I saw the silver flash of a pierced eyebrow, gelled spikes of blond-tipped hair, and the tattoos on the man's neck and arms.

"It was an accident! I told you! He went in right there!" He pointed a thin arm at what looked like deep water beneath the stone cliff. "Yell if you can see anything from that angle, okay?" Then he went back to splashing and peering through the golden shallows that rimmed the darker water beneath the cliff.

I didn't try to make sense of it. The most basic fact was obvious.

"How long's he been under?" I yelled as I shrugged off my pack and kicked off my shoes.

"Don't know," the tall trooper said. "Ten minutes, maybe. Might be fifteen."

"Oh my God!" the other man cried.

I turned around and began to lower myself down the bank, holding on to loose rocks and roots. I paused to hiss *"Paranda que!"* to Mungo where she was still concealed by the willows. I didn't want her jumping down after me, or getting shot by the cop, who might be surprised to notice a wolf on the bank. The water below looked fairly deep, but I knew better than to dive. Looks can be deceiving, and I was trying to be very careful about my neck these days. Both figuratively and literally.

"We got a 911 call maybe five minutes ago from the lady in the raft," the cop was saying. "She saw the whole thing and has a cell. We were running a trap on the highway just a mile away—"

I didn't hear the rest. Halfway down the

bank, a stone I was gripping with one hand ripped out of the dirt at the same time a slippery root did in the other. I fell five or six feet, landing first on my bare feet and then my ass as I rolled all the way onto my back in ankle-deep water, banging both elbows hard on submerged stones. Embarrassing for a climber, but it was a good thing I hadn't jumped. The depth certainly was deceptive. And the water was outrageously cold—pure glacial meltwater running out of the Winds, its temperature only a degree or two above freezing.

But that's good, I told myself as I struggled to reclaim my breath and scramble to my feet on the slippery rocks. Ten minutes, maybe fifteen. I thrashed forward into deeper water near the river's center, thinking that the frigid water would slow oxygen-starved blood, and remembering a case where a young girl had been under the ice for forty-five minutes before being hauled out and resuscitated. Hypothermia when drowning can be a blessing. Lessens the amount of potential brain damage caused by prolonged submersion. There was a chance, anyway. Thigh-deep now and pushing a wake that splashed all the way up to my chest, I could see before me the dark green water in the pool beneath the big boulder.

I could also see a thin branch floating *upstream,* beginning to turn a slow arc back in the direction it should be floating.

Whirlpool! I thought too late, just as I jumped up, then porpoised headfirst into the deep water.